Pearl

DEIRDRE
PURCELL

Pearl

headline
review

First published in 2010 by
HEADLINE PUBLISHING GROUP

1

Cataloguing in Publication Data is
available from the British Library

ISBN 978 0 7553 3225 0 (Hardback)
ISBN 978 0 7553 3226 7 (Trade paperback)

Typeset in Bembo by Palimpsest Book Production Limited,
Falkirk, Stirlingshire
Printed and bound in Great Britain by
Clays Ltd, St Ives plc

Headline's policy is to use papers that are natural, renewable and
recyclable products and made from wood grown in sustainable
forests. The logging and manufacturing processes are expected
to conform to the environmental regulations of the country of origin.

HEADLINE PUBLISHING GROUP
An Hachette UK Company
338 Euston Road
London NW1 3BH

www.headline.co.uk
www.hachette.co.uk

For my truly brilliant friend, Frances Fox.

ACKNOWLEDGEMENTS

This novel has had a long gestation. I wish to thank everyone at Hachette Books Ireland and at Headline, who stuck with me right up to the day the first copies came from the printers. So very sincere gratitude to Breda Purdue, M.D. for Ireland and Ciara Considine, my editor. Thanks too to the rest of the Dublin team: Jim Binchy, Ruth Shern, Margaret Daly, Ciara Doorley and Peter McNulty, all of whom deserve their places in Book Heaven, as does my London editor, Charlotte Mendelson.

My agent, Clare Alexander of Aitken Alexander, has been more than patient – thank you.

Profound thanks to my copy-editor extraordinaire, Hazel Orme, who has been with me for every volume, fiction and non-fiction, since my first tentative steps into the world of publishing, and whose meticulous grasp of detail never ceases to astonish me.

I love the cover of this novel; thanks to Karen Carty of Anú Design who has excelled herself.

To my husband, Kevin, thank you for all the dinners and the cups of coffee, for a push when I needed it, but most of all for your love.

Adrian and Simon, my two dear sons, thank you too for hanging in there – and thanks, Catherine O'Mahony (hi Eve!) for your interest and sterling personal advice.

Thanks from the bottom of my heart to a cohort of staunch and loving friends and colleagues from different fields, all of whom have been acknowledged many times in previous books and who continue to travel with me, step by step.

Finally, thanks to Frances Fox, to whom this book is dedicated. Frances, you will never know how much you helped . . .

THE SONG OF WANDERING AENGUS

I went out to the hazel wood,
Because a fire was in my head,
And cut and peeled a hazel wand,
And hooked a berry to a thread:
And when white moths were on the wing,
And moth-like stars were flickering out,
I dropped the berry in a stream
And caught a little silver trout.

When I had laid it on the floor
I went to blow the fire aflame,
But something rustled on the floor,
And someone called me by my name:
It had become a glimmering girl
With apple blossom in her hair
Who called me by my name and ran
And faded through the brightening air.

Though I am old with wandering
Through hollow lands and hilly lands,
I will find out where she has gone,
And kiss her lips and take her hands;
And walk among long dappled grass,
And pluck till time and times are done
The silver apples of the moon,
The golden apples of the sun.

W. B. Yeats

PROLOGUE

I went back to Drynan Wood only once.

I went on an impulse, the strength of which astonished me, but the image of what was to happen to those ancient trees, the talismans, even sentries of my childhood, haunted me. The thought of them being bitten by saws and axes until at last they fell, to be dragged away in chains, upset me to a degree I cannot really explain without sounding unhinged.

During the four decades since I had left Kilnashone for Dublin, the wood, which had covered 270 acres and had been one of the last remaining virgin broadleaf forests in the country, had been decimated piecemeal for its valuable timber, but the final tranche was now to be sold off to pay the estate taxes of our former English landlords. This was information I had discovered in a newspaper article: its focus was semi-humorous, based around a fairy tree, a hawthorn, growing deep inside the forest and overhanging the Drynan river from its roots on the bank. The journalist concerned had interviewed some of the locals in the village to ascertain what their attitude was to its being felled with the rest. She had secured the story she sought: predictions of dreadful events, an account of the curse to be visited on those who dared to attack it.

She had also come away with the view that most of the people in Kilnashone considered neither the Castle, which was still in ruins, nor its demesne, to be any business of theirs. One man, who had not wanted to be named, was quoted: 'They left us in the lurch when they ran away from this country forty years ago, bad cess to them, and the word is that they'll be bringing in their own contractors from England to do the clearing. Why should we care what happens to their bloody trees?'

I cared deeply. I revisit those trees almost nightly in my imagination. I am a writer by profession and, under varying guises, have

1

included them in my stories, sometimes singly, sometimes merely as locations and sometimes, fancifully, as symbols of hope and endurance. At some level I believed that as long as Drynan Wood stood so would the possibility that my own hopes might be realised.

How did I become so old? Almost fifty years of age, which sounds sere and settled.

To me I am still fifteen, the age I was when my living was arrested. Yes: I wake, I dress appropriately, I participate in the minutiae of life, I write, eat, smile at visitors, go to concerts and the theatre; I participate in social conversations to the extent that I do not think I am seen as an oddity.

On the rare occasions I am interviewed in connection with my books, I am reflective but positive about the wider world – and the resulting pieces are consistently flattering.

But I am still fifteen, and for me, as long as those trees stood, majestic in their survival through storms and drought and even floods, there was hope. Reason would dictate, and does, that to maintain faith against all empirical evidence is insane, but reason is not my territory.

And so, with a mixture of excitement at revisiting my childhood and dread at what I might find, I took the early-morning bus for Cork, which I knew would stop in Kilnashone, along with many other villages in the midlands.

The lives of our family had revolved almost entirely around Kilnashone Castle, but in one way or another, during our time there, the livelihoods of almost everyone in the district depended on the estate. With the demesne wall as one boundary, our village had been laid out around a wide green almost two hundred years before I was born. Strictly speaking, the Castle was not a real castle: in size and importance it was minor in comparison with some of the other great Irish houses, but with its elevated position commanding a 360-degree view of the rolling countryside, crenellated walls, stable yards and broad entrance avenue sweeping uphill between two rows of chestnut trees, it was grand enough to impress us, who lived in the two-storey gate lodge adjoining the massive gates.

When my bus pulled into the village, it seemed initially that very little had changed in the decades since the terrible events of April 1923. Some of the shopfronts had been painted different colours from those I had remembered, with different proprietors' names over their doors, but the Castle's gate posts and high boundary walls were intact and as imposing as ever. However, the huge iron gates, which were open, had rusted and, entwined with ivy, grasses and brambles, were probably now immovable.

As I passed through them, I saw that the trees on either side of the avenue had grown so big and unruly that they had created a roof across the broad expanse of the avenue, now rutted so deeply that, although it had not rained for days, some of its potholes hosted small ponds. Even at close quarters, the mullioned oriel window of the gate lodge, where my brother, sisters and I had been born, seemed in good order, but the gingerbread on the canopy over the padlocked front door was gapped and filthy. I peered into the interior through the webbed, grimy window of the kitchen. The range, built into the fireplace, was still there, but the only other thing I could see in the gloom was an upended wooden chair, with one broken leg.

Rather than enter the forbidding tunnel over the avenue, I went around the side of the house to head directly to the forest, via what had been our kitchen garden, now a waist-high wilderness of weeds, wildflowers, more brambles, and plants I could not identify. It, at least, was busy and alive as bees foraged in its depths while butterflies flitted between it and the buddleia crowding the pathway from the house. Had she seen the state of it, Mama would have been horror-stricken. She had not tolerated even a seedling weed.

Crossing the hay meadow at the back of the lodge, I looked to the right and could see the back of the roofless castle, its many chimney stacks still proudly etched against the sky, useless now. Around one at the near corner was a piece of ragged scaffolding as though at some stage someone had thought to effect repairs but had thought better of it.

The wall of the stable yard looked untouched, although I knew only too well what devastation lay within. Although it was a warm day, I shuddered.

My heart started to thump as I passed under the lich-gate and into the old, unused cemetery: during that April of 1923, it had figured largely in what had happened, almost as largely as the forest itself, visible now at the far side of the field beyond the graveyard's back wall. I had expected immediate visual devastation, but as far

3

as I could see, the vanguard of the trees – on this side – had remained untouched. Against the sky the long high line of Drynan Wood seemed intact.

Once inside, I instantly recognised the trail my sisters, Willie and I had often trodden as we made our way to 'our' glade on the banks of the river. Of course the forest had changed in the intervening years: it was now so dense that the sunlight which, in my memory, had always filtered through the leaf canopy to dapple the ground was unable to do so. As a result, thankfully, the growth was not as impenetrable as I had imagined it would be and I pressed ahead.

Nevertheless, only fifty yards in I stopped. For some reason, although I was where I had intended to be, I was afraid to proceed. The silence, on this still, humid July day, was eerie. Although I could hear rustlings in the undergrowth nearby as the woodland creatures went about their business, the birds were either asleep or absent about theirs and I stood there, heart racing, trying to decide whether or not to turn back. I had not told anyone I was coming here in case one of my sisters, Opal or Ruby, insisted on coming with me: I had felt the need to do this alone. Now I thought this had indeed been the mission of a sentimental fool. While I stood there, hesitating, something, a butterfly or a moth, fluttered from plant to plant near my feet and, afraid I might step on it, I jumped backwards.

My indecision now had little to do with eeriness or silence. This had been the playground and forge of my childhood. I knew almost all its pathways and open spaces and was not afraid of anything in it. I did fear, though, that somehow our glade had already been obliterated by the chainsaws, and I could not have borne that.

I looked at my little wristwatch, the one I had worn for decades: I had only two hours before I had to catch the return bus to Dublin. For goodness' sake, I scolded myself, either go and see what you came to see or leave now.

I went deeper for several hundred yards, until I came to our open glade, the place where, as children, we had dreamed and planned, argued and made up, cut our lips on grass whistles and played jacks. The clearing, about ninety feet long and seventy wide, was no longer a clearing but recognisable because the tree canopy was absent – if not, perhaps, for much longer. The ground was already overgrown with brush and saplings, some quite large, pushing through the moss and grass, and I had to be careful that my linen skirt did not snag.

The river was exactly as it had been and, yes, the journalist's fairy tree still leaned into it. Its crown – almost circular over trunk and limbs – was thicker than I remembered, but otherwise, even in height, it had barely changed at all.

Our willow tree, on the other hand, had grown monstrous, its riverside fronds trailing in the water and creating little waves of resistance to the current. At one point in its long life it had had a double trunk, but long ago someone had cut down one, leaving a wide, comfortable stump that could fit two children. This had served, variously, as throne, seat, podium and, in my case, silent witness to the hopes and dreams I had maintained for decades, beyond all reason, and which had brought me here today. It was cracked and almost black but seemed as sturdy as always and now, heedless of damage to my skirt, I sat on it.

Immediately the memories flooded in – of our brother Willie's doomed efforts to construct a swing from the branches of this willow, of hide-and-seek, of the thrilling attempts we girls made at foretelling our future with dandelion clocks. You held one in your hand by the stem, inhaled deeply and blew hard. If you successfully blew all the seeds off with one breath, you were the object of passionate love. If some remained, the lover had doubts. If most of the seeds were still adhering, there was no lover at all.

Probably because I was the eldest and therefore had the most developed lungs, I had succeeded, more often than not, in denuding the stem, while the best poor little Ruby could achieve, at eight years younger, was about half.

Our Willie scorned such girlish conceits, but if he found a dandelion clock, he would do the next best thing. He would make a secret wish and blow. If all the seeds flew away, it would come true. For Willie, no amount of teasing or tickling would ever get him to admit what his wish was . . .

He loved to tickle trout, beautiful speckled creatures, usually around ten inches long. On sunny days, they seemed to loll about, taking their ease among the pebbles and stones in the shallows. They were so wonderfully camouflaged that you could see them only if they moved. But while Papa had taught him how to do it,

5

he had emphasised that under no circumstances was our brother to take the fish out of the water. 'I'm teaching you, Willie,' Papa said, 'for later when you're grown-up and you have permission to take a fish. That trout doesn't belong to us. It belongs to Lord A.' Above all, Papa was loyal to his employer and had little sympathy for anyone who abused the Aretons' generosity in allowing access to their demesne.

Something moved now at my feet and, opening my eyes, I saw it was a wren, little tail upright, looking straight at me. In child-hood, encounters with sparrows had been commonplace but I had never been so close to a wren before. I held my breath but I must have made some movement because it flashed off with a whirr of its little brown wings and came to rest on a bush at the far side of the river. There, it cocked its head and continued to look at me. I felt absurdly privileged that it was still interested.

I shook myself out of such absurd thinking, stood up and pushed on through the foliage at the far side of the clearing, travelling through the trees with some difficulty, emotional as well as physical, until, quite suddenly, the light improved. Then I emerged into full sunlight and was shocked into immobility.

My path to this place had been burned into both my dreams and nightmares so I knew I had not gone astray. I had walked in the right direction and for the right distance but now I was confronted not with the lushest and oldest part of the forest, as I had expected, but with what seemed a vacated battlefield, a carpet of dead and brittle branches out of which rose the remains of trees that had once been as regal as barques. Reduced to jagged stubs, like rotting teeth, their nakedness was already half covered with ivy and other audacious greenery.

When I could move again, I backed off. I could not bear to see this. I had thought that to visit here would somehow be cathartic and, had it been as I'd expected, it might have been. Now, all I could think was that, as kings and queens of the forest, the trees had witnessed my glory, but as ugly stubs, they were testament to my shame.

As fast as I could, I went back to the clearing. From the bag I carried, I took out a shoebox, opened it and quickly removed a set of six school jotters. At the last minute I set aside one, I tore off the last few pages from another, and stuffed them back into my bag. Then I knelt on the riverbank and placed one of the remaining notebooks in the running water, watching while the ink ran so that the writing became indecipherable. I did the same with the second, then the third, the fourth and the fifth and when, swirling like untidy little rafts, they had been carried downstream and out of my sight, I stood up and went to sit on the stump.

If I had thought that this would be helpful in obliterating what I had not been able to forget, I was wrong again. As a writer, it is probable that I suffer from a somewhat overblown sense of drama – although my sisters, who think me bland and reserved, would probably not agree. (I am reserved, but not so that I am unemotional.) Now, instead of catharsis, I felt only emptiness.

I had drowned the record of what, if I were to be truthful, I still hoped for. And while letting go of the past had seemed a good idea when I conceived it, now it felt like a showy gesture, stupid and pointless. The river chuckled and mocked me for it, the willow leaves rustled their derision. I felt more alone and solitary than ever. I was close to tears but would not cry. Pearl Somers does not cry: she endures.

I took one last look around, although I had no desire to super-impose the image of this overgrown place on the mind-picture I had preserved from when I had been young and happy – until that April of 1923.

I had done what I had come to do, and it was time to go back to the bus.

While I skirted a clump of vegetation growing vigorously on the most open part of the ground, something round and greyish white caught my eye. A full, ripe dandelion clock, ready to release its feather-light cargo.

To capture it at this time and in this place suddenly became the most important task of my life.

Thanking goodness that there was no human being around to see what I was doing, I bent and carefully detached the puffball from its stem. Then I, Pearl Somers, almost fifty years of age, moder-ately successful author with a growing reputation, took a deep breath, blew as hard as I could and was delighted when all of the seeds floated away.

1

PEARL

As I embark on a new life of work and living in a place unknown to me, I remind myself that once upon a time, I, Pearl Somers, aged fifteen, really did live with my family at the gate lodge of Kilnashone Castle in a village in the middle of Ireland, and that it is also true that we were happy there until our Willie was killed.

What happened afterwards with a Certain Person is locked for ever in my heart. I shall carry that love with me to my grave. I know now, however, the truth of the saying that a heart can break. Mine certainly has. The pain may diminish over time but the fracture will never heal, yet on this date I 'put away childish things', as Scripture advises. In the matter of chronicling our family as I have done for many years, I have today attempted to hand on the baton to Opal, a useless conceit, I am sure, because she will probably write enthusiastically for two days and then abandon the enterprise. So be it. Perhaps Ruby will be interested. I shall encourage her when she is older.

Before I finish, however, I would like to record once and for all that I was not happy to have Master Browne as my teacher. He treated me unfairly, although I did not protest: Mama has warned that, because of our special station in Kilnashone, we should never leave down our family in public by being impolite or disrespectful to persons of note such as the Canon, the Sergeant and Master Browne.

Within the privacy of these pages, however, I hereby admit

that I found it hard to respect Master Browne every time he read out other pupils' essays and ignored mine, or when he said my prose was too flowery, or when he mocked me and my family for being in thrall to the British Empire. He said many times, too, that I would not go far. We shall see, Master Browne!

And finally, goodbye, my love, from your broken-hearted Pearl! Wherever you are, as I write these last words tonight, I hope the world is kind to you. Here, our village sleeps under its blanket of deep blue. The fox is silent, the fields rest, the rock roses have closed their petals in expectation of a new dawn.

Such drama! I have to smile when, nearly five decades later, I come across what I have left of these youthful effulgences, written as journals. From the age of ten or so, I faithfully kept these journals until I left home in 1923. I was fifteen then, I am sixty-two now, but I have only to glance at those opening sentences and I am back in Kilnashone.

I made a grand, dramatic gesture and disposed of most of these scribblings many years ago, keeping only one jotter and a few pages from another. The piece above, which I have just reread, was written on the night before I left home for my first job in Dublin and I preserved it because of that. As for the full jotter, I kept it because it was to be my 'writer's notebook', containing extravagant descriptions of Drynan Wood, a place that was very important to me in my childhood, plus colourful, descriptive notes about my brother, sisters, other relatives, our house and my parents, meant to jog my memory of childhood, since that, it is said, is the source of all stories for all writers.

I have kept other small things – some of Mama's recipes, her Butterick dress patterns, even a birthday card I got from Lady Areton, the wife of Papa's employer, and some time in the future I may pass the lot on to Catherine, perhaps when she comes back from her summer in America. Although she is only nineteen, she may be interested in her family history, particularly as I have written a page or two about her granny, our unfortunate cousin, Iris.

What a privileged life young people, especially students, lead these days – summer jobs in America, no less! However, Catherine, poor child, deserves every piece of good fortune that comes her way because she is a dear – and although we are generations apart, I do feel close to her. In some ways, although we have had completely different upbringings, she reminds me a little of myself at her age. This may be because of her tendency towards impetuosity – although living as quietly as I do nowadays, I doubt that even by the wildest stretch of anyone's imagination I could be considered to exhibit such a trait now, at least on the surface. I have probably sublimated my early unruliness into my writing.

From the time I learned to read, I wanted to be a writer and I have achieved some modest success in that field. Now that I have, one would think that the scribblings of those early years would be of use to me, especially when, inevitably, recollection is frayed. Yet while I poured out torrents of disjointed and highly emotional sentences in response to the events and aftermath of that terrible, haunting night in April 1923, I have never had recourse to them. I am not sure why, since authors are reputed to be ruthless with their own and others' lives.

I fear I am not ruthless, and even if I were, there is a question of credibility. I doubt a modern reader would believe that a fifteen-year old, as I was then, could feel so deeply and suffer so much. 'Such a to-do about puppy love!' I can hear the cry. I beg to differ. My heartbreak was real and, although it is contained now, remains so.

In any event, my recollection of every detail of that night, of the entire year afterwards, is so vivid that I have no need of prompting to bring it back into being. It is astonishing to me that I survived such a year to live what is, on the surface at least, a relatively normal life.

I was the eldest of the children in our family. My sister, Opal was next, then my brother, Willie, and Ruby was the youngest. In March and April 1923, Opal was twelve, Willie was eleven and then there was quite a gap to Ruby, who was only seven; in her lighter moments, Mama referred to us three girls as the Three Jewels. The name stuck and in school was used sarcastically against us – 'Too precious for Kilnashone' or similar barbs.

There had been other babies born or miscarried between my arrival and Ruby's. I recall being told of a midnight crisis in our house when, with the midwife in attendance, Mama was rushed off in an ambulance – but no child came home with her the following day. Such occurrences were not rare in our village and phantom siblings were locked into families where their names survived only as private memories. Their burial plots, if they had them, were unmarked because, unbaptised and stained by Original Sin, they lived now and for ever in Limbo, neither here nor there, destined to spend eternity between the living and the spirit world.

When I was young I pictured Limbo as a huge dark room, into whose padded walls were tucked columns of tiny souls, so many flickering millions that the room was illuminated by their glow. Those little souls, having neither heads nor limbs, were unable to move, to see, to hear, to speak or to touch each other, and although we were assured that the little children in Limbo did not suffer, we were also told that they longed to see the face of God. A permanent state of longing. Without being sentimental, this perfectly reflects the way I have spent my life. I am sure that Mama thought a great deal about her own lost babies in Limbo but she never mentioned them, and for us children they existed only as echoes.

One sultry August day our cousin Iris, a solemn little girl, was with us. She and her parents, our aunt Margaret and uncle Bobby (who were my godparents, as it happened) had come to stay with us, and I think I remember that day in particular because, as it turned out, this was the last day we were all together in that manner before the events of just eight months later sundered our lives. The day was memorable for other reasons too: as a gift, Uncle Bobby had brought along a frightened little Pomeranian dog of about three years old. I'm not sure Mama was best pleased – we had never had a dog before – but Uncle Bobby ignored her frowns. 'From one of my elderly female patients who's going into a home,' he boomed, handing it to Ruby, because she was the youngest. 'Dogs aren't allowed in homes. So you take care of him now, Ruby. He's a good dog and he's housetrained so you won't have any trouble with him. His name is Roddy.'

Ruby bobbed a polite little curtsy. 'Thank you,' she said, as she took the shivering bundle of golden fur. From then on, she and that little dog were inseparable and Mama had no option but to accept the situation.

Iris, who was the same age as Opal but smaller and slighter, was an only child with pale, stringy hair and a weak chest, an affliction

12

I found rather odd in a doctor's daughter, until I was told she was actually lucky to be alive: Uncle Bobby's dedication and professional skills had pulled her through all kinds of early health crises. We pitied her for her afflictions and tried to be kind to her. Ruby said that she could be her extra sister while she was staying with us and immediately offered Iris a turn with her dolly, her pride and joy, brought home from the Castle by Papa quite recently – Miss Isabella had outgrown her.

We benefited greatly from Castle cast-offs, and whatever about clothes and toys, my delight was to see Papa arrive with a basket of books. Their bindings were usually pristine and had never been cracked. Opal was the only one of us who was never impressed, although she always watched the rest of us to make sure we did not get something better than she did.

Anyhow, having no idea that this was to be our last communal outing of this nature, we were lazing under a huge willow tree growing on the bank of the river in a glade we frequented so often that we had begun to think of it as our own. The tree had been a double, with a bifurcated trunk, but someone long ago had cut down one, leaving a wide, comfortable stump that could fit two children.

With all the petting and loving he had received in the hours since his arrival, our new dog, Roddy, had found his bearings and was nosing around in the undergrowth. It was a beautiful, very still day and even the willow was quiet; the light was greenish where we sat and, except for the buzz of bees and other insects, all we could hear was the chuckle of the water and the odd chirp. And Willie, of course. Willie, precariously perched on a rock that was perhaps too small and jagged for sitting, was pegging pebbles into the water, making big splashes, and in danger of overbalancing with every throw.

Ignoring him, we girls were teaching Iris how to make grass whistles, showing her how to clasp her hands, to put a single blade tightly between the raised thumbs, place her lips on it and blow hard. It's quite easy and you can make quite a loud sound, but you have to be careful not to cut your lips: the grass blade can be sharp. Iris, who seemed quite clever, was able to perform within minutes.

As the eldest, I then decreed that the four of us girls should lie on our backs to talk about our futures. I made rules. No plan was

13

too silly or impossible to be ruled out. 'Whatever you want,' I said, 'you can say. This is the magic hour and everything we think about could really happen.'

'I'm going to be a racing driver!' Willie said immediately, continuing to peg his stones. 'And it won't be in an oul' Ford either!' The passage of the Gordon Bennett road race through Kilnashone twenty years previously was legendary in our district. The village still benefited from the good road that had been steamrolled specifically for the great occasion.

'Oh, don't be daft!' Opal sat up, spoiling the atmosphere of enchantment I was trying to create. 'How could you be a racing driver? Where would you get the money?' She and Willie, close in age, were constantly squabbling.

'Hush, Opal.' I pulled her back into position. 'I'm in charge. And I did say that no idea was going to be too silly. Let Willie speak.'

'Not fair!' Opal sulked. 'You're always on his side. He's your pet.' But she did lie back.

'Go ahead, Willie.' I lay back too.

'Well . . .' Willie came and sat near us, but not near enough to be thought of as a cissy girl. 'We're only at the beginning,' he said. His voice was low and important, like Papa's when he had something he wanted us all to listen to. 'In the future, motor-cars will travel so fast that they'll make a racehorse look as slow as . . . as slow as . . .' He was foxed.

'As a tortoise?' Ruby pronounced it 'tortoith'. She had a lisp.

'Exactly. As slow as a tortoise. Good girl, Ruby!' He reached over to pat her head and she smiled up at him.

'You still can't tell us where the money's going to come from.' Opal scowled.

'From my winnings!' Willie glared.

'Shush. Both of you.' I did think Willie was on a flight of fancy. Papa was a chauffeur, and although Lord A supplied him with a Ford, it still took him hours and hours to get to Dublin. 'You next, Ruby.'

'I'm going to marry a printh and be a printheth,' Ruby stated, with the same certainty as Opal, who spoke next and, typically, told us what she did not want: 'When I grow up I am never ever going to get my hands dirty. I'll work in Clery's in Dublin and wear the height of fashion.'

She went on then, to tell us that, one Christmas Eve, a young man would approach her to help him select a suitable gown as a gift for his rich mother. He would be instantly smitten by her beauty. 'After we get married we'll live in a huge big house in Dublin and instead of working in Clery's I'll have an account there. And I'll never ever have to scour the pots or vessels or make the beds because we'll have tweenies and skivvies and – and—'

'Oh, pooh!' Willie forgot about keeping his distance and shoved his scornful face right up close to hers. 'You're a big lazy lump, Opal Somers!'

'I am not! You're the lazy lump, Willie Somers.'

I had to pull them apart. But even while I chided him I had to agree with Willie. Opal, Mama had said more than once, had ideas above her station.

Our cousin Iris did not know what she foresaw for herself. 'I think I'll just get married,' she decided. 'And I want lots of children to look after me in my old age. I think I'll have seven.' Then: 'What about you, Pearl? Will you get married?'

'I suppose so.' I had thought about it, of course. It was what every girl thought about, but even as I said it, I wondered. Many of Miss Austen's most interesting heroines had no suitors, or suitors so singular as to be very special indeed and therefore rare.

2
PEARL

Our lodge at the gates of the Castle ran to just four rooms. The most important and least used was the tiny parlour, smelling always of the lavender polish deployed on the table, chairs and china cabinet by my two sisters and me every Saturday afternoon. There were two bedrooms above the kitchen from which we could actually see the big house at the top of the avenue; upstairs and downstairs were joined by a steep, ladder-like staircase hidden behind a latched door and entombed between walls darkened by age and smoke.

Our home, with its additions of a lean-to scullery and an outside privy, was no palace, but it was snug, with thick stone walls, tiny leaded windows with deep ledges, and an inglenook fireplace that, to my eyes, was as grand as the one in my childhood picture book of Cinderella raking the ashes from her stepmother's. That fireplace, housing the range, was festooned with all kinds of ironware, and hooks for tools, brooms, pots, pans and flatirons, flitches of bacon, harsh-smelling salted ling, and makeshift clothes lines to dry socks and linens when the weather was inclement.

Neither Willie's nor Mama's attitude to that fireplace was quite so romantic; her dream, I remember, was to have a modern range, a smaller version of Cook's belching monster up at the castle. As for Willie, his loathing of ours stemmed from his chore: every Saturday he had to chop enough wood to feed it over the coming week.

I remember few visitors when we lived at Kilnashone, save those I have already mentioned, our aunt Margaret, our uncle, Dr Bobby Madden and, of course, Iris. They were our only proper guests, certainly the only ones who seemed to like us enough to come to stay.

Our uncle's cheeks and nose were red from the scourge of drink and this was a family secret, but he was jolly and we children liked him. I was not sure how Mama felt about him – she certainly disapproved of his habit of giving us handfuls of farthings and halfpennies from his jingling pockets: 'That's enough now, Bobby. Don't spoil them, please.' Willie, a nosy-parker who could repeat most conversations in our house, reckoned her displeasure resulted from the source of the small change he always seemed to have: 'He plays cards in public houses, you know. And rings. And darts.'

While Iris usually came by herself for a week during the Easter holidays, the annual August visit of her whole family caused huge but pleasant domestic upheaval: all the sleeping arrangements had to be changed, with everyone shifting to a lesser space. Naturally, as visitors, our relatives had to be given the main bedroom; Mama and Papa came into the small one we three girls shared and we were demoted to the settle bed in the kitchen, with Iris who slept on a mattress on the floor. That meant Willie, who had slept on the settle since we girls got too big to be sharing a bed with him, had to sleep on a sack of straw in the parlour. 'But this is terrible,' Aunt Margaret always protested in her high, fluting voice. 'The poor boy won't get a wink of sleep! We don't like putting you out.'

'Nonsense!' Mama and Papa always fell over themselves with assurances that everyone would be perfectly comfortable and that there was not another word to be said about it.

Whatever she thought of Uncle Bobby, Mama liked Aunt Margaret, and I don't think it was just because they were sisters. They were friends too; my abiding image is of them sitting close together at one end of our kitchen table, Mama's sewing box open, smoke from Aunt Margaret's cigarette curling up to the ceiling, the two of them talking to each other in such low voices that even Willie could not hear what they were saying. They might as well have put up a big sign: No Interruptions.

Our mother and Aunt Margaret came from a very large family and we occasionally received stiffly worded picture postcards from one or other of their siblings when they went on holiday to Tramore or Ballybunion:

The weather is fine today although we had rain yesterday. The hotel is quite nice and the food is hearty. Did you know that our Cousin, John Daly, died early this year? He was married to that girl from Cavan. The funeral was huge. It must have cost a fortune. Very best wishes . . .

Yet none of them ever came near us.

We knew their chilly distance made Mama unhappy, but she would never answer questions as to why we were the black sheep of her family: 'It's unfortunate, Pearl,' she would say, 'but it's nobody else's affair and, anyhow, it's of little consequence.' But she always looked away as she said these things, and I could feel sadness, like mist, drift towards me from her. So despite what she said it was not true that our mother's estrangement from her family was of little consequence. Her parents were now dead, the farm in Kilkenny split between her five brothers. That land was less than thirty miles from Kilnashone and it would have been nice to visit, not to intrude in any way, just to know where my ancestors had come from. But any time I had suggested this, I had been told it was not possible.

I so badly wanted ancestors. According to Papa, the walls of the Castle were strewn with portraits. I wanted portraits too but knew there was little chance of that wish being fulfilled. While Aunt Margaret, Uncle Bobby and Cousin Iris were the only living relatives on Mama's side with whom I was actually acquainted, I had no idea where my ancestors on Papa's side had come from. He had no relatives at all – he was a foundling and had been named 'James Somers' by the nuns who reared him because he had been discovered, well swaddled, in the baptismal font of a chapel on a summer's day.

So, when our classmates shared stories about big family gatherings for Christmas, birthdays and christenings, replete with disgraceful behaviour, quarrels and walk-outs, I, for one, felt deprived. Compared with ours, everyone else's family life sounded turbulent and fearfully exciting.

All we could have offered in return was gossip about our uncle Bobby's drinking and playing cards in the taverns of the big city and our aunt Margaret's hush-hush conversations with our mother about it. Except we couldn't, because of it being the family secret. Our parents would have been very angry if we had let it slip.

Mama's big concern always was that we should be seen as respectable people because of Papa's status as a trusted employee at the Castle. As such, our family occupied a peculiar half-way rank, neither elevated above the village nor of it.

We were not specifically discouraged from associating with our school companions outside school hours, but it was not encouraged either, and each time one of us suggested bringing home a friend for tea, it was never convenient: there was some chore to be done, or a fitting needed so Mama could adjust some garment she was sewing for us.

Our behaviour, you see, had to be beyond reproach. We could not let Lord and Lady A down in any way, and that included indulging in 'loose talk'. 'Loose talk' could cost Papa his job – 'And then where would we all be? We'd be out on the side of the road, that's where.' He would put on his stern face. 'And you children would lose your wonderful privileges. It's not every child in Kilnashone that can live free in the Castle grounds and receive so much bounty.'

I have already alluded to the 'bounty' – for me, the books. 'Another load they won't read, apparently.' He always smiled indulgently when dealing with anything that concerned the Areton children. 'Lady A says we're not to bother returning them. And she has put in a few of her own. She says this one is hot off the boat, Pearl. Straight from London.' He handed me *The Black Moth* by Georgette Heyer, a writer I had not heard of up to that point but whose work I came to adore, so much so that my devotion to it threatened to eclipse even my commitment to my true heroine, Jane Austen.

Although I did read these books, I must admit that I did not much care for Lady A's taste. With some exceptions, the heroines in the romance novels she favoured were lifeless, interested only in hunting parties and balls and European Grand Tours, with few thoughts of their own and certainly no ambitions.

We could not claim to be acquainted with either of the Castle children. For much of the year they were away at school in England, and even during holiday time, they were frequently absent from Kilnashone, visiting cousins or friends in other big houses, to which Papa had to drive them. It was from his rare unguarded comments about them that we formed any views we had.

19

It was not our place to know them, but we were aware that, when he was at home, the main pursuit of the heir to Kilnashone Castle seemed to consist of riding his bay pony around the countryside. He had his mother's fair hair and was big for his age (I sometimes pitied the poor pony) and, according to Papa, was not the world's greatest scholar. 'He's clever, I'll grant you, cleverer than most and with words at will, but even with the fancy schooling and all the rest of it, give him a choice between his horse and his books and there's no competition.' Then, quietly, 'I don't know what's to become of him.' This was a very strange pronouncement from Papa, whose lips were as tight as a purse where the Aretons were concerned.

On the other hand, he always held the girl, Isabella, to be 'as sharp as a tack'. Two years younger than her brother, she was quite plain, no matter how much finery her mother bought for her in the grand shops of Dublin or London. I do confess, however, that we Somers girls did enjoy the feel of the silk and satin fabrics she and her mother favoured and were happy to wear them when Mama had worked her wonders on them so they would fit us.

Willie despised hand-me-downs, a conceit that got short shrift from our mother: 'You'll take these and be grateful. Lady A will be asking how you got on with them and I want to be able to say we got great wear out of them. I won't lie. Anyhow, beggars can't be choosers.'

'We're not beggars.' As the only boy in the family, Willie fancied himself manly and hated this line of talk, but despite all his posturing and grumbling, he had to climb on to the kitchen table like the rest of us so Mama could chalk and pin the cast-off trousers or shirts. In our house, Mama always got her way.

She regarded it as a huge blessing that Papa was so great with Lady A. I gleaned from overheard conversations that this was because the mistress of Kilnashone, small-waisted and tall, with graceful hands and luxuriant, oat-coloured hair that fell over her shoulders, always made sure that the wages were paid to the staff on time. She occasionally sent little treats to us too: a flan surplus to the requirements of their dinner table, or a plateful of fairy cakes, a left over from afternoon tea.

We rarely saw her in person, save as a slice of face and a waving glove through the back window of the car as Papa drove her past our house at the entrance to the demesne or, on a fine day, as a blur of feathers and veil if he had the hood down. We three girls always waved back. We would have done so even if it had not been our duty. Certainly I would because one year, on learning from Papa that I was coming up to my tenth birthday, Lady A sent a boxful of toffee apples made with fruit from their orchard, along with a little card that pictured a kitten sitting on a pink cushion made of real satin. Inside, it said, 'Wishing Pearl a happy birthday from all at Kilnashone Castle'.

I admired our mistress's elegance and, although I did wish to have a writing career, like Opal, I secretly hoped that when I grew up, I, too, could be as modish as she. Of course I knew that was fanciful and I should probably be happy enough with a nice husband to care for me as well as our Papa cared for Mama.

3

PEARL

Lady A required Papa's services mostly when she visited her friends, scattered in other big houses throughout the county, or when she wanted to go to Kilkenny city, where the shops would order whatever she wanted if they didn't have it in stock.

Sometimes, though, he had to drive her all the way up to Dublin where they stayed overnight, she in the Gresham Hotel, he with a friend from our village. Joe McCurg had trained as a tailor locally, then got a job in the alterations department of Clery's department store in Dublin and had graduated from there to be a salesman in Men's Suits on the shop floor. I'm sure tales of his work there, brought home by Papa, influenced Opal in her choice of future career.

The present Lord A, fair-haired, high-coloured and corpulent, was somewhat ugly. He was a much more distant figure and I could count on the fingers of my two hands how often I had laid eyes on him.

I heard from Papa that in other parts of the country the general view of landlords was still unfavourable, but while Lord A's grandfather had been detested, his father had been less so. In the matter of rent, he had tried hard to be fair to his tenants and had, Papa always said, done his best to help some to buy their holdings. Our man – who, at the time of which I speak, had been running the estate for sixteen years – had continued this. Also, on Pattern Day each August, he continued to allow people from the district to trek through his lands to a natural spring, venerated as an ancient holy well. Twice, when in residence at the time of the event, he had even supplied refreshments, apple cider and biscuits, from a cart he had had hauled to the well.

I knew from Papa that, although the Aretons worshipped in their own little chapel tucked away in a corner of the demesne, they were not found wanting when the Catholics needed repairs to their church roof. It was also acknowledged, although grudgingly by some, who referred sarcastically to the Castle owners as 'Lord and Lady Bountiful', that the Aretons had always been the first to buy tickets when a raffle was held for a sick child or a destitute widow in the village.

Whatever about this public benevolence, Papa's unswerving allegiance to his master was at variance with some of the stories about Lord A's behaviour in private. In school, I had heard that, within his household, he was choleric, quite the martinet, and that, especially if he had a few drinks taken, a person would be well advised to stay out of his way. I had never witnessed this side of his nature, naturally, but more than once I had heard of damage done to glassware and furniture, even of a horsewhip used on his son for some misdemeanour. Papa had never raised a hand to any of us and I could barely imagine how it would feel to be threatened with a horsewhip.

It was also rumoured in the village (our school companions repeated everything they heard at home) that Lord A detested his poor son. Nobody knew why, of course, but there were persistent stories that Thomas was not Lord A's son at all, a rumour lent credence by the marked physical difference between him and his sister. Whereas she was squat, like her father, he was tall for his age, with a body shape that matched neither of his parents'. Although he was fair-haired, like them and his sister, his eye colour was another point of controversy: Lord, Lady and Isabella Areton were brown-eyed while Thomas's eyes were blue or light grey – nobody had been near enough to him to be sure which. But it was said that for definite they were not brown.

Although Papa was employed as Lord A's chauffeur and not his wife's, it did not seem so to me because, as far as I could see, he was rarely called upon to drive his master. Certainly in latter years, Lord A had spent more and more time in London on family and Parliament business, and in Scotland, where the family had a shooting lodge with a full staff. During those periods, some quite lengthy, Papa was not required as a chauffeur but as a mechanic: his duties included maintenance of the machinery involved in the working of the home farm, the demesne and the Big House. He always kept the motor-car, his pride and joy, in showroom condition.

Even when I was young, I thought this was a strange way of life for the Areton family, wife intermittently in one country – with her friends sometimes, with children during school holidays – husband in another for most of the time, with the Castle run solely by staff for most of the year. The ways of the gentry were not ours, however, and within our family we never questioned them or participated in the public gossip – although, if I am honest, I secretly enjoyed it and I admit I have used it, heavily disguised, of course, in my stories. As I said, none of us children, even Opal, dared mention such tittle tattle in front of Papa, who would have died rather than listen to a bad word about any of the Aretons.

On one occasion we were in the kitchen, just he and I. I was ironing and he was re-hanging a wall shelf that had threatened to come loose from its bracket. The atmosphere was relaxed, even tranquil.

'Papa?'

'Yes?'

'Don't you think it is strange that Lord and Lady A live such separate lives – in two different countries, even?' I was folding a sheet and had to raise my voice above the tap-tap-tap of the hammer. 'I can't imagine you and Mama—'

The hammering stopped. When he turned, his face, usually so benign, was creased like a gargoyle's. 'We are very lucky to be associated with Kilnashone Castle.' His tone was icy as he looked at me from under his thick eyebrows. 'It is certainly none of our business how Lord and Lady A manage their affairs. I hope, Pearl, that you can accept your good fortune and that this can be an end to your impertinence.' He turned back to his task, gave a nail a final, heavy thump with the hammer and then, not looking at me, sat at the kitchen table, took up his newspaper and spread it out, bending his head over it to signal the end of conversation between us.

'Yes, Papa.' I was contrite as I went back to my task. I should have known better. I was young, and I was to discover not too many years later that my father's loyalty to the masters of Kilnashone was so preternaturally deep it would destroy him.

He still did not look up from his newspaper as I put the ironing cloth and iron away, so I retreated outside to the privy where, insulated from the squabbling of Opal and Willie and the general hubbub of family life, I frequently took refuge with my book. There for a time, enthroned in the twilight under the corrugated-iron roof, the door latched from the inside, I usually had a good chance of not being disturbed except by the more adventurous of the hens, which, in search of insects in the sawdust, sometimes squeezed under the frayed wooden door to peck around my feet. (For ever I will associate the reek of Jeyes Fluid with *Wuthering Heights* and *What Katy Did,* and with the comfortable murmur of contented birds.)

I adored my papa and was always heartbroken at his displeasure. As I lost myself in a scene from one of Lady A's romances, however, the sights and smells of a little Italian piazza, the glare of its white walls, of red and pink bougainvillaea cascading from iron balconies, the musicality of the voluble Italian characters and the aromas of their cooking restored my equilibrium. From the clock tower, a bell lazily counted out the twelve chimes of noon – I could hear every silvery note – *while Lucia, milky bosom quivering under the delicate white cambric of her bodice, felt she might drown in the deep blue eyes of Renato—*

A sudden startling fusillade of hailstones drummed on the roof and brought me back to reality. But in the semi-darkness of the four cement walls I felt secure, my little life at Kilnashone seeming as permanent and rooted as one of the oaks in the forest behind the Castle. Papa had been right. Ours not to question our betters. Ours to be grateful for a nice home and a good living.

I was not to know that, within quite a short time, all of it would be turned on its head.

4

OPAL

Opal Somers.
Kilnashone
Leix
Ireland
Europe
The Wourld

Pearl wants me to write things about my life and my familys life in a diry. I cant think of much to write. She says just to write what I see and hear and feel. She said I have to do it now becos she wont have time.

Well my life is I hate my life. Pearl is above in Dublin now and making her way in the Big Wourld. Funny enough I miss her and I sertainly hate Kilnashone. I wish I was Pearl and living in Dublin. When I am fifteen too I'll get my heels out of here quick. And soon I'll be rich. But Ill be genrous and when Iv enough money to have my own place Ruby can live with me and she can have her new dog with her right in her room and then when I get married and if my husband says no she cant come and live with us I'll kick him out. He can sleep on her bed even. We will all have our own rooms and you see it wont matter to me if he has flees.

My brother died and that was terrible and everyone was crying all the time. And Papa lost his job. Mama says she dont know whats to becom of us. She's is in a terrible state.

It was a terrible time. Thank God it was all long ago. Thank God it's 1970. I love everything to be modern. All mod cons. I'm Igoe

26

now – Opal Igoe. Sounds like a rhyme when you say it quick. At least it's easy to remember.

When I was a child, I lived with my family in a minuscule gate lodge in the deepest, darkest part of middle Ireland. Shudder. No running water. No sewerage. An outside toilet. Mama's knuckles always red from washing soda and friction on the washboard she used for the laundry. It was me, believe it or not, persuaded her to wear thimbles on all the fingers of her right hand to help with that washing and so she could preserve at least some kind of nails. A woman should always have good nails.

She was a stickler for cleanliness, Mama. The collars of the dresses and blouses she made for us cut rings into my neck they were so starchy. The pity of it is, she would have been stylish if she'd had the opportunity. She was beautiful and she certainly had the instincts – but, oh, God! The making-do! Thank God for money. My husband, Frank, God be good to him, inherited a lot of it. He was a good bit older than me and he was an only child. He needn't have worked a day in his life, but they had what they called a work ethic in his family, and while they were alive they worked him to the bone. He deserved everything he got, and after they'd died (car crash, both of them together, quite tidy), I insisted we put in managers for the business so he could relax and we could enjoy ourselves.

I do miss Frank. I mightn't have married him for love, but I suppose in the end I did love him.

Now that I mention it, there's no 'supposing' about it: we did love each other, certainly by the time he died. We even took to saying it to each other after he got sick, not in a mushy kind of way but in a way that said to each other we were good pals and that we cared what happened to each other. He called me his sweetheart and I called him my honey-bun. I was sincerely upset when he died.

The money helped, of course. Having the few shillings at your back can take the rough edges off bad things that happen and make good things better – and don't let anyone tell you different.

To get back to my story, my sister Pearl, who lives with me, is a writer, very little money in it, of course, but it keeps her off the streets, and so now, in our house, everything is a story! She's taller than me, and slim. And I'd have to say graceful. She doesn't seem to rush, but always gets where she's going, if you take my meaning. She has gorgeous hair – it used to be red, well, sort of red, but it's faded now to a kind of strawberry blond – but in my opinion she certainly doesn't make the most of herself. Hardly any makeup and wears that terrific thick hair of hers always up at the back of her head in a French pleat, and wears bland colours, grey or *écru*, but I suppose with her figure she could wear an onion sack and carry it off. Anyway, what I'm trying to say is that she's really beautiful but doesn't know it.

Every family has its ups and downs – isn't that what they say? When our brother was killed it seemed like the end of the world. But of course it wasn't. Nothing is the end of the world if you can keep putting one foot in front of the other.

I don't mean to make light of what happened. I did a bit of a diary when Pearl went to Dublin and it shows how upset I was. We were all upset. But, as I say, it was a long, long time ago, the dark ages, and to remember our Willie's face now, I have to look at a photo.

Pearl's asked me if it upsets me to remember the fights Willie and I used to have, but to tell you the truth, I don't remember the details of any fights. Only that he annoyed me every hour of every day.

I certainly remember the night he was killed. I was right there at the time, you know. I saw his body and it was still warm. I remember, too, how he loved horses and how Mama was never the same afterwards. I also remember a funny thing about him – well, maybe not funny (ha-ha funny) but odd. Peculiar. A peculiar thing to remember about him in the circumstances. He had these teeth. Very nice teeth. And I think what a waste it was for Willie to grow those terrific teeth that were still perfect and not a bit worn because he was only eleven. Mama was always warning us and threatening us that if we didn't take care of our teeth we'd end up like our uncle Bobby who couldn't eat meat or brown bread any more and had to take his false teeth out every night and put them in a glass beside his bed.

So Willie minded his teeth but much good it did him because now they're perfect for ever but no good for anything because they're just attached to a little skull in a graveyard. Nowadays, if there's a film or something on the telly and there's a fella in it with

28

the kind of teeth our Willie had, I get kind of choked up thinking about that little skull with those lovely, shining teeth that'll never be used.

Pearl goes on about our happy times in Kilnashone before that terrible night, but my overall memory of my early childhood is that I couldn't wait to be old enough to get out of the place and up to the bright lights of the city. Any city.

Especially out from under Lord and Lady Muck and their offspring. That's what I call them, privately, when they come into my mind, Lord and Lady Muck and the two Mucklings. They were the proprietors of Kilnashone Castle and it was their gate lodge we lived in. It wasn't that they were cruel to us or anything like that – in fact, if you asked Mama or Papa anything about them, you'd think they were canonised saints.

They were Protestants, though. I've never been clear about whether Protestants have real saints. Anyhow, I would never have let on that I thought anything bad of their highnesses, any of them. Mama and Papa would have killed me. They thought the sun shone out of the backs of those people's necks. Papa was their chauffeur, d'you see, and he had to drive them everywhere in a car that did about one mile an hour.

What was really boring about Kilnashone was the place itself. There was nothing to do. Go for walks in the woods? Please! Can you imagine that as the height of what we did for entertainment? We had no other children to play with, even the children in our class, because we were part of the Castle crowd and had to keep our distance in case we let out some secret or other.

I remember one day when I was there in the forest with Pearl – I don't know where Ruby and Willie were that day but, anyway, we were sitting there in this area beside the river, the Drynan river it was called, and as far as I can remember, we were blowing dandelion clocks. It's too long a thing to go into here but it gives you an idea of the kind of entertainment we had in Kilnashone! Next thing there was this sort of kerfuffle in the trees beside us and who comes out, like Robin Hood, but Thomas Areton, all breathless and flustered. He stops dead when he sees us. I suppose the last thing he expected to see was two girls blowing dandelion clocks.

Anyways, he goes red then and mumbles something about did we see his horse. And, actually, I could see he was wearing riding breeches. He was a big fella but growing still, I'd imagine, and those breeches were as tight as a drum. Uncomfortable, I'd say.

Pearl stands up. 'No,' she says, kind of shyly.

'Are you sure?' He looks from one to the other of us.

'Lookit,' I shot back, 'of course we're sure. Don't you think we might have noticed if a horse came through here?' I was sorry then, a bit, because I thought his face would burst with the redness. 'Sorry,' I said, more kindly. 'I didn't mean to be rude, but we didn't see any horse.'

Pearl stepped forward and put out her hand. 'I'm Pearl,' she said, 'and that's my sister, Opal. Would you like us to help you look for your horse?'

He went purple. I swear to God, he went actually purple, such a colour that his eyes looked nearly white. 'How'd you do,' says he, something like that, and they shook hands. 'Thank you very much,' he said then, 'but that won't be necessary – he'll go home of his own accord, I'm sure.' He reversed away from the two of us and went back the way he came.

'Bit of a big lump, isn't he?' I picked a large white daisy. 'Where were we? Do you want to do "He Loves Me, He Loves Me Not", Pearl?'

'All right . . .' Pearl was still looking after him, but she turned and started to walk towards the river. 'Let me wash my hands first, they're full of dandelion juice.' She bent down and rinsed them and then, even though it wasn't all that hot, splashed water on her face.

So that was an example of our entertainment, the height of excitement we had in Kilnashone for the whole year up to that. Midnight Mass at Christmas and A Muckling Loses His Horse. You can see how boring it was. At least Pearl had her books. She always had her nose stuck into some old thing, and if she wasn't reading, she was scribbling away into heaps of notebooks.

Even during the years and years she worked in Mealy's café when she came up to Dublin, she was writing away in her spare time. And then, out of the blue, wasn't Mealy's sold! That would have been about 1932 or '33, I think, though I'm not sure because I wasn't myself working there by then. So while I'd gone off into the retail trade, she went to work in the old Moira Hotel right beside where Mealy's was. She worked there until that closed, when she was well into her forties. You'd think that with her experience she'd have been able to get another job but she wasn't. She had to give up her digs because she couldn't pay the rent. So, again God be good to Frank, when I suggested she should come to live with us, he agreed straight away. This is a big house.

And then, about a week after she moved in, doesn't she announce she's going to become a professional author? 'My room is so lovely, Opal. I'm ever so grateful. And the view of the sea through that window is so peaceful. It's an ideal environment for my writing.'

Listen, the view from all the upstairs windows in this house is of Sandymount Strand and the sea. I wouldn't be big into scenery but I knew what she meant.

Her announcement made me blink, to be perfectly honest. Whatever about scribbling away in the privacy of your own place, putting it out there for everyone to have a go at you is quite another thing, isn't it? To be helpful, though, I got Frank to contact a person he knew whose sister was a real writer. The sister was kind enough and read Pearl's stories but she told Frank that Pearl would have to do a lot more work on them if she was to make them into a commercial book. The writing was too old-fashioned, apparently, and while my sister was 'a good storyteller' and her stories were 'lyrical' in parts, they were too 'slow-moving', and nowadays there was no market for 'short stories' like these.

Unfortunately, while Frank was a good man, he was about as tactful as my hat. He told Pearl the whole palaver that the sister said, and I could have killed him because I was afraid it would take away all of her confidence, but believe it or not, hearing all this only made her stubborn. 'I have to concentrate on the positive,' she said to me. 'I'm a good storyteller, I know that. And the writer said so. And I'm convinced that people like to read stories.' So, right away, she started sending the manuscripts she'd already written to every publisher under the sun. And, lo and behold, didn't one of them (a small, poor one, naturally) write back and say that, while her stories were old-fashioned, he loved the writing so much he was going to publish them, and did she have any more?

Did she what? She had lashings of them, a good twenty years' worth if she was to put out a book a year – and, remember, she's still writing away up there in her room. Then doesn't this publisher tell her she should write under a pen name. Personally, I think

31

'Pearl Somers' sounds like a great name for an author, but this chap told her it sounded kind of suspect, as if it was a pen name for something iffy – he told her there was a book or a magazine or something, *The Pearl*, or there used to be, that was a bit 'off', if you get my meaning. Anyway, now Pearl's writing name is 'Dorothy Morris'.

I've read her books, of course, because she's my sister – but although I could see what the publisher meant about the story-telling and the 'lyrical' writing, they're not my cup of tea. All about love un-something. What do you call that thing when someone loves someone and it's all one-sided? And the fields and the woods and little animals running around and trickling rivers. The good old days. (Shudder!) I'm not a reader, really – magazines are more my style – but I do like Agatha Christie. I've been trying to interest Pearl in writing books like that (after all, Agatha Christie is a woman, too) but she never takes the bait.

The truth is, in my opinion, that poor old Pearl is never going to get rich from her writing. She should go out more because she has no social life to speak of; she doesn't even go to Mass, would you believe? I did ask her why but she wouldn't tell me. Something to do with sin and not wanting to go to confession because she no longer believed in all the mumbo-jumbo that went along with it! Odd, wouldn't you think, for a spinster lady? I've never said it to her – give me some credit – but she's really wasting her life up there all alone, smoking her Sweet Aftons half the time, trying to give them up the other half, and scratching away in her notebooks with her fountain pen. She doesn't even play the radio when she's in there. I keep at her to learn how to type, but she says she likes the way the ink flows on to the page.

I ask you!

Now that I'm talking about it, Pearl did go a bit funny, just like Mama did, after the events of that dreadful night at the castle. She went very quiet – kind of like the stuffing was knocked out of her, you know? It might have been just the age she was at – she was fifteen, I think, at the time of all that stuff. Even still, when you look at her sometimes, she has this expression I can't really explain. It's sad, but kind of glassy, if you can picture that. Like she's not seeing what she's looking at, is the best way I can describe it. Now, I could be exaggerating. It might be nothing personal at all

– she could be just getting herself organised for another plot for one of her stories, but when you live with someone, I think you can guess what's what about them.

We're very different people, that's for sure. Pearl's a real lady, a gentlewoman, I think is the best way to describe her, but if you ask me, she has hidden depths. Like, you wouldn't want to push her too far – I've learned that her quiet 'no' means 'NO!' She was and is beautiful but all her life, in the boyfriend stakes, she just seemed to repel all boarders, as they say. Not that there were that many.

I did my best for her, even when it had become as obvious as the nose on my face that she was hankering after someone, because for years, first Frank and I, and then, after his death, me solo, introduced her to the nicest men, one after the other. But no dice. She was perfectly sweet and friendly to them, but there was a sort of 'exclusion zone' around her. She admitted as much to me once when, for maybe the tenth time, Frank had to make excuses for her to one of her would-be suitors and I was having a go at her about it. She got real upset, something she didn't often do, in fairness. 'I know you won't understand, Opal,' she said. 'I don't expect you to. And I don't want to talk about it – I know you must think I'm strange, as strange as Miss Harveysham' (I think I have that right, whoever she is. Didn't ask. Can't spell it) 'but I am very happy in my present condition. I have no wish to change it.'

She was right, I didn't understand – still don't, not really. She doesn't socialise, not the way I would term socialising; when she does go out it's to lectures at libraries, that sort of thing.

At least I have a few friends and a few pastimes. Did I tell you I play a bit of bridge? And although I got into the golf late in life, I enjoy it. Don't play a lot, but I like the club house and I can put up with the golf talk because I've made friends there and we do have some great laughs.

Yes, there's something about Pearl that makes you not want to pry. She's not standoffish, I don't mean that, because she's perfectly courteous to everyone and, in her own way, quite good fun when I can get her to go to the pictures or something like that, but there's a kind of a moat around her, if that makes sense.

As for me, I don't know what I am, really. Someone who just keeps going – I suppose that about sums me up. The past is the past and, yes, what happened that night was horrendous, but it's donkey's years ago and you have to live, don't you? 'Life isn't a rehearsal,' as Gay says.

I love Gay Byrne. I really do. I never miss him on *The Late Late Show* because he understands women. And you'd never know what's going to happen next on that programme, but the highlight for me so far this year wasn't the usual controversy kind of thing, bashing the Catholic Church and so forth, but something very simple – him interviewing that little schoolgirl, Dana, after she won the Eurovision. She's a dote. So shy and normal. Even Pearl, who half the time reads during *The Late Late*, got interested in Dana and, surprisingly, so did young Catherine who was visiting us that night. Like, she should love the Beatles and all the pop stars, so if her age group was thrilled, you can just imagine how the whole country went wild about Dana.

Catherine seems to enjoy our company, which, if you look at it, is a bit strange. Maybe it's because, through very complicated circumstances, she was left an orphan at a very young age and raised by our aunt and uncle, Margaret and Bobby – who are her great-grandparents so she's used to being with people a lot older than herself. For whatever reason, she's happy to sit with Pearl and me and regularly comes to watch telly with us in the evenings, if she's not studying. 'Have you nothing better to do,' I asked her once, 'than sit with two old dodderers like Pearl and myself?'

'You've a bigger telly than the one at home!' she said, as smart as a whip, but I could see it was only half an excuse. She's quite a deep one. 'Who's on next?' She pointed at the screen.

'Let's wait and see . . .' and we settled back to watch Gay break into his patter. I have to confess that I like looking at the style on *The Late Late* too – people dress up for it.

Compared to Pearl and, I suppose, Catherine too, I'm shallow.

5

PEARL

'How're ye getting on with arrangements for the big night?' It was shortly before our Easter holidays and, from her circle of companions in the school playground, a girl who didn't like us had called out to Opal and me as we passed them on the way back into class. Then, to the titters of the others: 'Enjoy yeerselves while ye can! I hear the Castle is on the Diehards' list, these days, and then we'll see who'll be wearing silk and satin dresses!'

For Opal's sake, I shrugged this off as simple bad manners: it was only, I told her, a notching up of the sneering to which we were accustomed from that type of girl and her ilk. 'Just look at them!' I put my arm around her shoulders as we entered our classroom. 'The lot of them. When last did they comb their hair or wash their faces?'

I picked up that the timing of the party was being talked about too, since we Catholics kept Lent Spartan and holy, and the party was to be on Easter Saturday night, when our family, like all the others in the village, would normally be at the Easter Vigil. But when I brought that piece of negative gossip home from school, Papa had an explanation for the choice of date. The party was being held to celebrate the seventieth birthday of Lord Areton's mother, which, by a fortunate coincidence, fell on that Saturday, 31 March when her two grandchildren, on holiday from school, would be at Kilnashone.

With provisions being delivered daily from grocers for miles around, from Kilkenny and even from Dublin, the party and speculation about it had been a major topic of conversation for weeks and was now at fever pitch. Our village was a quiet one and, notwithstanding their snide comments, our neighbours regarded

35

the preparations for this once-in-a-lifetime event as famous entertainment. One of the highlights was the arrival of a great noisy
steamroller from Maryborough. It came on a Saturday afternoon
and we heard it long before we saw it, lumbering across the bridge
at the entrance to the village towards the Castle gates. A great
throng gathered to watch as the machine, its driver and a dozen
labourers hired locally set up braziers and compacted stones under
a layer of tar to surface our avenue all the way from the gates as
far as the turning circle in front of the house. When the work was
finished, the black ribbon of road, this new-fangled 'tarmacadam',
was still warm to the touch and, after the roughness of gravel, felt
as smooth as skin underfoot.

The gossip rose to fever pitch as, in the days immediately
preceding the event, guests began to trickle in. There were rumours
that royalty would be among them and, it was said, even Henry
Ford himself was coming. (As well as Papa's car, the tractors on the
estate were Fordsons, also built in Cork.) Many of the swanks, as
they were known in the vicinity, had been installed in the guestrooms
for at least four days before the party, and on the morning of the
great day, the stables were almost full and the yard in front of
the stalls contained a short and tidily parked row of carriages and
motors, some far bigger even than Papa's. He was now so busy
collecting and delivering people from the railway station and ferrying
them about that he had told Mama to expect him only when she
saw him.

The house guests included Lord A's widowed sister and, of course,
his mother, who were rarely seen in Ireland. Very rarely. I was fifteen
years old at the time and I could recall them coming only once
before. Papa himself said jokingly that he could not remember what
they looked like and hoped he would recognise them when they
arrived in Kingstown off the mail-boat.

We still called it 'Kingstown' and had not yet got around to
calling it by its new name, 'Dun Laoghaire'. Not unexpectedly, we
took our language cues from the Castle and it was probably because
of this that we paid little attention to the bad things that were said
to be happening in other parts of Ireland. Mama and Papa rarely
discussed the outside world in our presence and they did not allow
us to read Papa's newspaper.

I, however, somewhat like Willie, as I've already described him, was inclined to be a 'little pitcher with big ears', and I did glean that the barracks in a fairly large town not all that far from Kilnashone had been set on fire because of what, mysteriously, Papa called 'The Treaty Affair'. And that even closer to home, because of their fear that something like this might happen to them, the Royal Irish Constabulary was about to withdraw from the police station in Maryborough. I had overheard this in one of the conversations between Mama and Papa, although it has to be said that Papa had vigorously pooh-poohed the idea. 'No chance of that, June. Leave Maryborough? No chance at all.'(We did not have a barracks of our own; Kilnashone was not thought big enough or, I suppose, unruly enough.)

I can recall that rather sombre conversation that day because of the contrast between it and the rather giddy mood in which we children, off school, were doing our Saturday household chores. The party was to be held exactly one week hence.

Mama was peeling potatoes in the scullery, I remember, when Papa had come in to join her. I was at the kitchen table, polishing the copper kettle and so was close enough to hear them. While I cannot remember all their exact words, I do recall Mama using the word 'mutterings'.

She had heard these 'mutterings' about the Aretons, that, amongst other things, they were planning to planning to 'clamp down' on night-time activities in Drynan Wood. 'They're saying that Lord A is going to bring in bailiffs from England. They stopped talking when I went into the shop, but not before I heard that. And then, when I was in the post office, I heard someone else say that they're considering selling most of their land, even the whole place, and going back to England for good. Have you heard any of that, Jim? What's going to happen to us?'

Papa looked over his shoulder to where I was pretending to be paying attention to my work. I lowered my head so didn't catch what he said back to Mama, but out of the corner of my eye, I did see him slowly shake his head from side to side. I did not know whether this meant he was saying, yes, he knew about this possibility, or if he was warning Mama to keep their discussions private, but when he came over to the table to take the kettle from me, he looked very serious.

There was definitely something in this, I thought, but then, what with our attendance at all the Holy Week ceremonies, plus the comings and goings as arrangements for the party built steadily to a climax, any concerns I might have had about that conversation were superseded. So, by the time the great day dawned, I had all but forgotten it.

All four of us, even little Ruby, were to help with last-minute preparations, and on the morning of the actual day, Mama dressed us in a way that she thought struck a balance between what was appropriate for physical work and the salubriousness of the surroundings. When she delivered us to the kitchen door, we three girls were wearing navy serge dresses with white collars and Willie was in 'decent' dungarees she had cut down from a pair that our father had used when he was tinkering with the engine of Lord A's vehicle. Papa was very proud of that car; he always referred to it as 'she' or 'her', as if it were a ship.

Cook herself waddled to the open door in answer to our knock and received us kindly. 'Don't worry, June,' she assured Mama. 'We'll take care of them and we won't work them too hard. I promise!'

'They're here to work,' Mama said. And to us: 'You behave now, children, and do what Cook tells you, do you hear me? Be a credit to your family.'

'They'll be grand, grand.' Cook dismissed her with a wave of a podgy arm, floured almost to the elbow. She addressed Willie: 'You, young man, go round to the yard. They could do with an extra pair of hands. You girls, follow me.' She went inside, leaving us to troop after her as she crossed to one of the pantries, hung with a row of plucked pheasants, still adorned with their beautiful tails, heads dangling. I had no time to feel sorry for them, because from one of the shelves, Cook took down three folded aprons, sewn, I think in retrospect, from bleached flour sacks. She gave one to each of us. 'Here you are, girls, put these on.'

Opal's and mine fitted us well enough, but Ruby's reached to the ground. She was just seven years old and a thin little thing: I can still see her pointed face gazing solemnly up at Cook who was issuing orders as to how a small mountain of peas should be shelled, and what should be done with the pods. 'Now, Ruby, all the waste has to go into the barrel outside that back door there, except the cooked potato skins. And there'll be a lot of them.

We'll be serving duchesse potatoes. Do you know what duchesse potatoes are, Ruby?'

'No, ma'am.' Ruby shook her curly head.

'No matter. You do understand the difference between cooked and raw potato peelings?'

Ruby glanced at me, unsure whether this might be a trick.

'She does, Cook,' I said quickly.

Opal and I were given a wider brief, to fetch and carry from the pantries and the larder, to sweep up and scrub alongside the skivvy, help her keep the ranges fuelled, and generally to make ourselves useful. Within minutes, we understood why the poor skivvy – and indeed the kitchen maid – had seemed so plum-faced and sweaty when we first saw them. Although the door and windows remained wide open, the kitchen was so hot that, within a quarter of an hour of our arrival, under the serge dress and heavy apron, the trickles between my own shoulder-blades and breasts had become a steady stream and I was continually wiping my forehead and upper lip on my sleeve.

In the early part of the morning we had other temporary help, two girls from the village, who, according to Cook's frequent laments and throwing of eyes up to heaven, were good for nothing except getting under her feet.

At around eleven, work stopped as we reacted to the sound of a crash from the scullery. Cook rushed in and visibly had to restrain herself from slapping one of those girls, who, delegated to wash the tureens, was standing, stupefied, gazing at a pile of white shards around her feet. 'Two of them!' Cook screeched. 'Those tureens have been in this family for generations. You stupid, stupid girl! Get home the hell out of here!'

Instantly the other girl removed her apron and the two of them, hips swinging, stalked off like offended cats. 'Simpletons!' Cook roared after them, through the open kitchen door. 'Good riddance to bad rubbish.' Then, whirling around, she shouted at the rest of us, 'What are ye all gawping at? Today's entertainment is over. Get back to what ye were doing. This dinner won't cook itself! You –' pointing at the skivvy '– neither will that china pick itself up. Hop to it!'

I noticed that poor Ruby's face had turned white: she was not used to being shouted at. I waited until Cook had stormed back to her range, then stuck my tongue out at her back. The ruse worked. Ruby gave a little giggle.

At one point, when there was a lull in the kitchen, Opal and I were dispatched to the laundry building to help with the table linen for the dining room. It was, if possible, even hotter in there than it had been in the kitchen; the air was full of steam from the coppers, which condensed on the stone walls and puddled on the flags. The laundry maid, a woman in her fifties, was ironing the banqueting cloths with the help of another woman at a second ironing table. Mama, when briefing us as to what would be expected of us and by whom, had warned us to be on our best, really best, behaviour with these women in particular: 'They're gossips, children. You must not say anything about us or our business, and especially not about Papa's job with Lord and Lady A. Anything you say will be around the village by nightfall.' And, indeed, the laundry maid was in full flight when we arrived, so much so that we were standing in the doorway for what seemed a long time before she saw us. 'Giving out socks to the poor son, he was.' She switched the flatiron she had been using for a new one from the hotplate of the stove nearby. 'And the mother just after arriving and she the guest of honour and that poor child being her only grandson.' She tested the heat of the sole plate by spitting on it – it sizzled. 'And this kind of thing greetin' her almost in the first hour she's in the house!

'That man,' she bashed the iron against the damask, 'royalty and all he might be, but he would want to watch his tongue, and his fists, is my opinion. Good money don't make good manners nor tells people how to behave, and that's the holy all of it. We can all dole out the odd clout or clip in the ear, but he takes things too far. Isn't that right?'

'I know, I've heard.' The other woman nodded vigorously as she shook out a tray cloth. 'It's desperate, desperate altogether, what them childer has to put up with right enough, especially that young lad. Probably just as well the grandmother came in all the same, eh? The nick of time, as they say . . .' She spread the richly embroidered cloth on her table. 'Otherwise it probably wouldn't be just a tongue-lashing that the poor lad woulda got—'

Beside me, Opal sneezed and for the first time, both women

40

noticed us. 'Oh, here's the cavalry.' The laundry maid became instantly jovial.

Our first job was to fold the starched napkins before their final pressing. We had to be absolutely precise, making sure the corners were lined up. That done, we had to help her roll what seemed like a mountain of wet bed-sheets and pillow shams through the mangle, she turning the handle, me feeding each heavy, dripping piece into the rollers while Opal pulled it out on the other side. It was very hard labour, augmented by us having to peg them to dry on the washing lines behind the building.

Back inside again, we were put in charge of the flatirons, ensuring that there was always a freshly heated one ready when needed. As she bent over her work, polishing the starched linen to a sheen, I was fascinated to see the way she made sure she didn't miss the tiniest wrinkle, even paying minute attention to every inch of the inside hem. I had thought Mama was particular, but this took the biscuit.

When we returned to the kitchen, Cook promoted us. Although we were not to lay a finger on the Waterford crystal, our next task, under the supervision of the kitchen maid, was to polish the flatware and the rest of the silver until it gleamed to the satis-faction of Mr Hamilton, the butler, who bustled in and out like a busy train official, checking everything. He held every piece up to the light and ordered a complete re-polish if he found even a speck of tarnish or dust. After one or two rejections, Opal, the maid and I were determined he would find nothing. It became a sort of game. And sure enough, from then on we garnered praise: 'Well done, girls,' he would say subsequently, having viewed the napkin rings, or the set of candlesticks ornamented with curlicues and bunches of grapes that had been truly the devil to clean.

The rest of the day passed without major incident. We chopped carrots, onions and celery for the soup and were shown how to clean asparagus, a vegetable I had never encountered before. We mashed huge quantities of the cooked potatoes with butter and cream and white pepper, beat sugar into bowlfuls of eggs and whipped what seemed to be an endless lake of cream. We peeled fruit and sieved white flour with baking powder. And although the work was physically demanding, and difficult in an atmosphere so steamy it was hard to grip anything, I have to admit that deep down I enjoyed being part of all that clanging, scurrying anticipation.

With only one brief pause for a bite of soda bread washed down with cups of tea, we worked until tea-time when Cook and Mr Hamilton called a halt for proper refreshments. 'Are you happy enough, George?' Cook's question to the butler was rhetorical and her expression brooked no dissent. It deserved none. The kitchen was in apple-pie order, food preparations complete, ovens stoked and ready for their task.

Willie and some of the yard hands joined us at the long deal table in the kitchen, as did the housekeeper, Miss O'Moore, and some of the maids, those not engaged in setting the table in the banqueting hall. We were given tea, cold ham, bread thickly buttered, and buns. When we were with our elders, we children had been taught not to speak until spoken to and so sat quietly, listening to the chat and gossip until we were kindly dismissed with a silver sixpence each for our trouble. 'You can tell your mother that you were, indeed, a credit to her today.'

Before we left, as a treat we were allowed into the Great Hall to view the fruits of our work. 'Thirty-eight!' Opal finished counting the chairs lined up like soldiers attending the banqueting table, which was decorated with posies of spring flowers set with the snowy linen, flatware and silver candelabra on which we had laboured. The table was easily accommodated in the huge room, which still showed what seemed like acres of parquet for dancing. And although yet to be lit, 'our' candelabra and flatware, along with the gold-rimmed china, sparkled and glinted under the three gasoliers hanging from the ceiling, already ignited and softly hissing.

The gallery overhanging the Hall and running along its entire length, had been draped with swags of white silk specially for the occasion, and on a dais underneath, four musicians were tuning their instruments. Just as we were about to leave, one of them tapped on his music stand with his bow, murmured a count of three and they broke into a tune. I seem to remember a waltz? Or maybe not. Memory does dim a little with the passing of years but the few minutes I spent in that room made a major impression on me. I have seen nothing since to match its splendour and, at the time, I experienced a proprietorial glow in the knowledge that I had played my part in creating it.

6

PEARL

At home, over our own tea-table, we were too excited, and too full of the Castle's ham, tea and buns to eat what was put before us. Instead we vied with each other to describe to Mama what we had seen and done. Willie's work, it turned out, had mainly involved carrying quantities of logs into the house to feed the fires in the bedrooms and main reception rooms, sweeping and tidying the yards and looseboxes, polishing the horse brasses and cleaning tack with sugar soap.

I thought this absurd. Horse brasses and tack? How likely was it that guests, presumably wearing dinner finery, would go on an inspection tour of the stables in the darkness of the night? But to repeat what Papa always said, ours was not to reason why.

Mama, who, like me, seemed to have forgotten, temporarily at least, any worries she might have had about bailiffs or the Aretons selling up, was in great form. For once she pretended not to see the titbits that Ruby was slipping to Roddy, whose little black nose was peeping out from under the tablecloth.

You see, we all knew that the pleasure of the day was not over. In fact, the best was yet to come. Our Dublin cousin, Iris, was coming by train to join us for the big occasion because Papa, being so great with Lady A, had secured permission for all of us children to view the after-dinner dancing from the silk-draped gallery. Of course, Papa emphasised, this was permitted only if we agreed to stay out of sight.

We had heard this news only the day before and were truly thrilled – not least because we had been given a special dispensation from the Easter Vigil. Instead, since it was going to be such a late night for us, Papa had told us that, for this once, we

44

could go to late Mass on Easter Sunday with all the other laggards, as he put it. He repeated his instructions as he put on his coat to fetch Iris from Attanagh railway station. 'For people such as ourselves to be present on such an occasion is the highest of privileges and must be treated as such. You must stay as still and quiet as little mice, and if anyone looks up at you, you must withdraw immediately to the back of the landing. Understood?'

'Yes, Papa,' we chorused.

'And,' he lowered his voice, 'if it looks like anyone is actually coming up the stairs towards you, as I'm sure they will from time to time, you must retreat. Mama will show you where the attic stairs are. You must be a credit to me and to Mama.'

'Yes, Papa.' Being a credit to our family was almost a full-time job in those days, but we would have accepted any stricture in order to see the gaiety and finery for ourselves. We had lived beside gentry all our lives. In a sense we had been part of their lives and they of ours. Yet, apart from watching them swish in and out through the gates either in the car or on horseback to join one of the local hunts, we had never yet seen their activities at close quarters.

Well, maybe Willie had. He was infatuated with horses and was tolerated around the stables, even allowed to help the grooms, but until today he, like we girls, had never been inside the house.

It was about seven o'clock that evening when Papa came back with Iris. The sun was setting, and although we had to wait until the Aretons and their guests had finished dinner, we were in a state of high anticipation. We girls had rags in our hair, Willie's was pomaded, and the kitchen was steamy while Mama ironed our dresses to perfection. Iris's dress, of apple-green taffeta with a white sash, didn't need ironing. She had carried it all the way down in a special little bag lined with tissue. 'It's new,' she said shyly, when we oohed and aahed over it. 'We bought it in Clery's specially for tonight.'

'You can take that off now, Iris.' Papa's tone was jovial as he indicated the brown-paper label pinned with coarse string to the sleeve of our cousin's coat.

45

Iris Madden
21 Harold's Cross Road,
Dublin
TO Attanagh Station.
To Be Collected By
Jim Somers
Kilnashone Castle

'Right, now, children,' he continued. 'I must go. Behave yourselves! Aren't the torches marvellous?' He grinned then, a rare
occurrence, and it occurred to me that he was as excited as we
were. The torches, long wooden stakes planed to smoothness and
bound at the top with linen dipped in pitch, had been placed on
both sides of the avenue from the gates all the way up to the newly
gravelled turning circle. They had been lit from early afternoon for
the edification of late-arriving guests and were indeed a wonderful
sight to behold.

Four hours later we were dressed in our Sunday best and, hair
and shoes immaculate, ready to embark on our big adventure. We
had never before been allowed to stay up past nine o'clock but we
were all too thrilled to be tired. Even Willie, who was at an age
when he wished to distance himself from girlish giggling, could
barely contain himself and was jigging like a squirrel. 'Come on,
come on – hurry up, Mama, we're missing the best bits.'

When we emerged, the torches streamed ahead of us like two
lines of fluid gold – we could hear their crack and sizzle, smell
the burning pitch. The air was so still and cold we could see our
breath, while far above our heads, like a sailboat becalmed on
a diamond-studded ocean, a half-moon hung in the midst of a
billion stars. And you have heard the phrase 'the music of the
spheres'? I had read it somewhere and it had made no sense to
me, but tonight it did. The profound silence, emphasised by the
sound of the torches, seemed to ping in my ears, as if those
faraway stars were intermittently singing. Mama put her hands
to her mouth, always a sign that she was emotional. 'Remember
this, children! You'll never see any night so beautiful in all your
lives.'

Opal, always inclined to dramatics, cast her arms wide. 'This is
exactly what I'm going to have for my wedding banquet. And to

46

eat we'll have goose with all the trimmings. And me and my groom will arrive in a white horse–drawn carriage.'

'Pooh!' As usual, Willie, who had to contradict anything Opal said, was scornful. He gave her a push. 'If it's carriages and torches you want, he'll have to be rich so you'd better think of something a bit more high-falutin' than working in a shop.'

'Mama?' Outraged, Opal appealed for support.

'Stop it, now, Willie – and as for you, Opal, it's "my groom and I", not "me and my groom". Please attend to your grammar.'

Willie held his tongue and, for once, so did my sister. Mama had not raised her voice but she had the knack of inspiring obedience.

We set off up the hill, Mama holding Ruby's hand, Willie dashing ahead. When we came to the bend, the sight of the Castle, ablaze with light, stopped us dead. In the huge open doorway, the brass buttons and epaulettes on the frock coat of the doorman glinted in the light streaming from every door, every window and from behind him in the entrance hall. We knew him as the blacksmith entrusted with the shoeing of the Castle horses but with Mr Hamilton fully engaged within the house he had been given these duties for the night because of his impressive size and comportment. It had been rumoured in the village that he had a head of such unusual circumference that Lady A had had to procure his top hat from Harrods of London.

When we arrived into the kitchen it was, as you can imagine, in a state of organised chaos, with maids and the extra hired help tripping over each other as relays of used ware were carried into the kitchen for scouring and washing. The dinner was clearly over and Cook, as red-faced and wattled as a turkey, did not notice us. Trying to make ourselves as inconspicuous as a woman and five children can, we crept into the back hall and to the back staircase, which led to the gallery and some of the bedrooms.

We were halfway up when we met Isabella Areton, who was closely followed by her brother, Thomas, the heir to Kilnashone. The staircase was narrow and we made quite a jam. 'Oh! Hello!' Isabella was surprised to see us, of course. 'What are you doing here?' She was wearing blue and her fair hair had been plaited and fastened like a crown around her head. I think she even wore a tiny tiara. But far from being regal, she looked . . . well, I don't like to say it, really, but she did look a little lumpy, much too matronly for a girl of our age. To me, our own finery, plain, round-necked dresses of cream silk, white knee-socks and black pumps, seemed nicer by far.

On our side, we waited for Mama to tell us what to do: should we turn and retreat to let them go down unimpeded? Without further ado, Isabella shoved rudely past us and, shoes clopping on the wood, descended, leaving her brother to follow or not as he pleased.

Despite the gloom of the enclosed staircase, its walls stained a sullen brown, I could see that our mother was hesitating. With Isabella having made her feelings about us so plain, I feared she might even take us home again. In the distance, I could hear a buzz of conversation underscored by the lilt of the tune we had heard being rehearsed earlier. I would die, I thought, I would just die if we had to leave now, never to see those gorgeous frocks and officers' uniforms.

Then Thomas Areton spoke: 'Please, come!' He flattened himself against the wall as best he could and waved us upwards.

'Why, thank you, Master Thomas,' Mama said. 'You're very kind.'

One by one, with me last, we squeezed past him. We had introduced ourselves about a month before the party when he was searching for his horse. He was, as I said, robust for his age and even taller than I was, although most boys in Kilnashone of my age only reached my chin. When my turn came, I could not help but brush against him, smelling soap and pomade, and the distinctive scent of clothes that have been stored with mothballs. I know Opal could not stand him or his sister – it was sort of a principle of hers – but when I stood close to him in the glade that day in Drynan Wood, I had thought he had lovely eyes and a nice manner. Anyhow, as the eldest – and the last to pass him – I thought it my duty to say again, 'Yes, thank you, Master Thomas,' and I smiled at him.

To my surprise, even in that dim light, I saw I had made him blush – it was noticeable because of his fair colouring. I looked back at him as he went downstairs and found that he was looking up at me, but he turned then and rushed down to the bottom of the stairs so quickly I feared he would fall.

His scent stayed with me until we reached the top of the stairs and – 'Stay together now' – Mama ushered us into the brightness of the gallery, the one directly above the hall. It was furnished at intervals with small, candle-lit tables and spindly chairs, all of them empty. 'Now,' she admonished us, wagging her finger, 'remember what Papa and I said about being as quiet as little mice and minding your manners. Speak only when spoken to. You too, Iris!'

So far I saw little to fulfil my expectations of glamour because below, in the meagre slice of hall visible from this angle, all I could see was a stretch of wall, against which a group of elderly people, three women and a man, stared stolidly ahead from a row of gilded chairs. Far from dancing, three of the four, separated from each other by gaps of two feet or so, apparently could not even walk unaided. The man had only one leg and two of the women were leaning on canes. The third was blowing her nose into a handkerchief held in a purple-gloved hand.

But then from directly below us rose a smattering of applause as the waltz ended with a flourish of chords. A woman's laugh tinkled above the general hubbub. 'This is no use. We have to go nearer, Mama.' I pulled at her sleeve.

Cautiously, tightly grouped, we moved across the gallery to take up a better vantage-point. Mama made an urgent up-and-down gesture with the flat of her hand, indicating that we should sit on the floor, but immediately Opal objected: 'We won't be able to see anything.' She had a point: from the floor, the silk drapes across the baluster would have been right in front of our noses. 'Why can't we sit at one of them tables?'

'"Those" tables, dear.' Mama's correction was automatic. 'I don't suppose anyone could object,' she said slowly. 'Don't forget now, if you're approached by any of the guests, you must stand up immediately to offer your seats.'

'Yes, Mama,' we chorused.

'Can you not stay with us, Mama?' Ruby was overcome with the enormity of the occasion and, when our mother turned to go, clutched a handful of her skirt.

'You're a big girl now, Ruby.' Gently Mama disengaged. 'Pearl will look after you, won't you, Pearl?'

And so, while reminding ourselves to be a credit to our family, we five, three little ladies in cream silk, a fourth in green taffeta, and a little gentleman wearing knee-length trousers and a spiffing red jacket, bagged ourselves a prime spot to watch the Kilnashone

Castle Ball. We did not know that what we were witnessing was the last grand party ever to be held in the district by our betters.

I have wondered whether at the time the Aretons themselves knew this, if they had already decided to leave Ireland because of the changing political situation and if this great occasion was, in effect, the last big show of their presence. Or was their departure so soon afterwards predicated on what happened that night?

If the former, did Papa know? Could this be why he made such efforts to cement the great event as a memory for us children? But Lady A's confidences to him were undoubtedly hedged about with their disparity in station, and so, even knowing his character as she must have, I had decided it was hardly likely he had been told about such a critical decision, one that would affect so many people in Kilnashone. Much as she might have trusted his discretion – and, as subsequent events showed, she did – he was, after all, only her servant.

7

OPAL

Looking back, I have to admit it, I suppose I did have an all-right childhood, at least until our Willie was killed. This was thanks mostly to Mama, who turned herself inside out for all of us – and thanks a little bit to Papa. He did his best, too, but he was busy all the time at the Mucks' and Mucklings' beck and call.

One night, one fateful night, the nobs on the hill threw this big party. It was just before they left Ireland for good and they invited Pearl and Ruby and my brother and me to sit and watch the dancing after dinner. Our cousin Iris was there too, I remember, wearing this green creation that was too big for her. The minute I saw it hanging off the girl I knew that her mother, our auntie Margaret, had bought it deliberately big so she would grow into it and get the wear out it.

I always thought that the reason Iris's family was so tight with money was that her mam was a pure miser. Since Uncle Bobby was a doctor, my opinion was that surely the family couldn't be short of a few bob? I liked him, anyhow, and so did my sisters, I think. I can't speak for our Willie, though.

Now, I know you shouldn't speak ill of the dead but, as I think I told you already, our Willie was just contrary. If I said I liked anything or anybody, that was enough for him to say he didn't. Pearl says there were two of us in it, and I suppose she has a point, but my attitude is, the poor boy is dead and what's the point of being sorry for something when you can't fix it? I'm the type that calls a spade a spade.

We kind of lost touch with Iris and her family for a few years. After that whole business around the time Willie died, we didn't know what we were doing, really. We did hear about her wedding

– she married a cobbler, apparently, a sickly sort by all accounts –
but that would have been years later. A very quiet wedding it was,
because our uncle Bobby didn't approve at all: felt that marrying
a tradesman was beneath Iris's station in life, him being a doctor.
Our aunt Margaret wouldn't defy her husband, but Catherine told
us that she did a little bit: unknown to Bobby, she told us, Margaret
saved up from her housekeeping money and bought Iris and her
fiancé a Foxford rug from Switzer's – and then, on the morning
of the wedding, didn't she slip out of the house when Bobby was
on house calls and get a taxi down to Clarendon Street, where the
two of them were getting married quietly in a side-chapel with a
couple of friends as witnesses? (Now you know what *that* means,
don't you? Iris was obviously up the spout. I have to say that I was
surprised. Like, I wouldn't have thought that little mousy Iris would
have had the kind of gumption to go against her father, who was
a larger-than-life character.)

Anyway, the cobbler died of TB a couple of years afterwards. At
least he gave his name – Fay – to his offspring, Catherine's poor
mother, and she in turn passed it on to Catherine, so in Catherine
Fay, something of poor Iris survives. Pearl and I were at Iris's funeral,
of course. She'd had bad asthma – when we were small we thought
it was just hay fever. She died during a particularly violent attack.

The poor woman had a tragic life, really. The child she had with
the cobbler Fay turned out to be a daughter. Bad blood. Went to
the dogs, I gather, got pregnant, had Catherine, dumped the child
on Bobby and Margaret and absconded. Hasn't been seen since.

I have to say, Bobby and Margaret did a good job rearing the
kid. Well, she's polite and, as I think I said before, seems to like
Pearl and me, so I would say that, wouldn't I? We're all very proud
of her, especially since she went to university. We have high hopes
of that girl and I just know she's not going to disappoint us.

She doesn't know it yet, of course – how could she? – but she's
going to be a lucky little thing some day: I'm pretty well off and
since there's only Pearl and me now, she gets to inherit if I die
before her – but she's the older one. So if she goes first and I'm
the last one standing, there'll probably be only Catherine. Although
I'm not all that keen on the Church, these days (I'm a just-in-case
Catholic: I still go to Mass on Sundays), and as for the cats' and
dogs' home— Well, maybe I'll give them a shout. Might be a nice

thing to do in memory of Ruby and her Roddy, the dog she adored and that she had when we were kids. Ruby would have liked that.

And I hope Mama's brothers or their descendants, if any, find out I did that. I want them to. In fact, now I think of it, I might even put in a stipulation that they're to get one pound each, with letters telling them I'd prefer to leave my estate to cats and dogs than give it to them. Apart from an hour or so at Willie's funeral, not one of those men ever came near us in our hour of need. Well, they can shove off with themselves now.

Once you're getting near sixty, you start thinking about these things, you know!

Anyway, back to the party at the Castle on that fateful night, as Pearl might call it. As we went up the avenue with Mama, we had to walk between lines of flaming torches about six feet high or maybe more. They were smelly but they made me change my mind about what my wedding should be like.

Of course, at the age of ten I was easy impressed, but my wedding was something I had been planning since I was about four. My wedding breakfast was going to be at the Gresham Hotel in Dublin. Lady A used to stay there when Papa drove her to the city and he would tell us about the beautiful carpets and easy chairs, the porters and bell boys in their lovely uniforms. But the minute I saw those torches that night I forgot breakfasts. I was now going to have a night reception in some romantic palace, with me and my rich bridegroom travelling to it in a white carriage drawn by white horses through a lane of flames.

By the way, it wasn't out of the goodness of anyone's heart that we were let in to watch the nobs dancing and stuffing their faces. Far from it. We'd earned it. We'd worked up there all day to help them get ready. Sixpence, they paid us each! Sixpence, for nearly ten hours of mullocking that even a kitchen slavey would turn her nose up at.

Yet I have to admit that when we set off to the big house that night I was seriously excited. For the first time we were actually going to see inside a nobs' do. I was going to pay attention and not miss one single second. This was the way I was going to live when I grew up: the best of food, no expense spared when entertaining.

53

And beautiful clothes. Even at that stage, I was sick of having to put up with the hand-me-downs Mama dressed us in; that night's ensembles were a dreary beige, I remember. Appallingly dull, although Pearl insisted on referring to them as 'cream'. Plain round neck, straight up and down from the neck to the knee. Not a frill or a bow – or even a belt. It was on that night I swore the oath that when I grew up I would never, ever wear anything but clothes with the smell of new off them; I'd let things fall off my back in strips, I promised myself, rather than ever again wear someone else's cast-off. And I'd have big fancy jewellery. And I'd sparkle. All promises I've kept. Grown-ups don't believe that children can make that kind of commitment. Well, I'm the living proof that they can.

So there we were, watching the dancing. Being honest with you, it wasn't all that brilliant. Half of them must have been in their eighties and most of the men were limping (a bit of an exaggeration there, but you get the drift) but what saved it for me was the style. Knock the eyes out of your sockets it would. The crisp, manly turnouts of army officers in their dress uniforms. As for the ball gowns, backless, strapless, slinky, flouncy, those women paraded in the most gorgeous, vivid colours, plus silvers and golds; one girl even had a fan of peacock's feathers with a matching headdress. And the evening bags and twinkly shoes! I would have killed for them. You'd think they were studded with diamonds – and as soon as I thought that, I reckoned that some of them probably were. I was going to have a wardrobe of outfits like these.

Lady A was flitting about most of the time, doing nothing very much that I could see, except whispering instructions into the ears of the servants who came and went with trays of refreshments, plus dancing with various people, including the boy, Thomas, who was still – would you believe? – in short trousers, under a brown tweed jacket, with a white shirt and a sort of yellowish bow-tie. At a fancy do! But the ways of the gentry were not our ways.

In fairness those trousers weren't really short, they were touching his knees, and he had knee socks on – so I suppose he looked semi all right – but I could see he was a terrible dancer, leading his mother and other women round the floor as stiffly as a toy soldier. Looking back, I suppose it was his age that made him so awkward. What fifteen-year-old boy do you know, especially one as big as he was, who's a good dancer?

54

As for the Muckling daughter's concoction – blue dress, ribbons, witchy shoes. Like something out of the Gaiety pantomime. An ugly sister, poor girl. She wasn't the best looking plum in the basket in the first place, short enough and 'big-boned', let's be charitable, but she was poured, and I mean poured, into that dress, at least on top. I think it was made of that stiff *peau de soie* fabric, which stuck out like a hula-hoop around her thick waist. And underneath she wore stockings with blue ribbons threaded through them. With those narrow-toed, pointy shoes? Who let her out dressed like that?

Anyhow, Mama had gone back to the lodge and we were just watching, enjoying it, I suppose, when Pearl turned to look over her shoulder. 'Where's Willie?' she whispered to me.

'He's probably gone home,' I said back. I knew full well that this wasn't Willie's cup of tea. Dancing? Dresses? 'Don't blame him,' I said. 'If it wasn't for the dresses I'd be gone myself.'

'Did you see him go?'

'No, I didn't.' The two of us had disobeyed orders so that we could see more of the ballroom floor. We were right up against the rails of that landing, leaning over. Pearl came off them and her eyes were all squidged up with worry – comes of being an eldest girl, I've heard: they feel responsible for everyone and everything. 'Sit down, Pearl.' I went to pull at her. 'You're attracting attention.'

'I saw him,' Ruby, who had been asleep behind us, poor tired little chicken, piped up – except, of course, what she actually said was 'I thaw him.' Ruby had a lisp.

'How long ago was this, Ruby? When did he go?' Then Pearl turned back to me, her expression entirely out of proportion to this non-problem. 'This is dreadful. Mama gave us strict instructions we were all to stay here until she came back for us.'

'Oh, sit down, Pearl,' I said again. 'What harm? You know him. He probably got bored. He's gone home.'

'He said he was going to see the horsies [horthieth].' Ruby gave a big yawn.

I was relieved. 'Well, that's all right, isn't it, Pearl? He's gone to the stables. Now sit down, or we'll all have to leave.'

Down below, the orchestra swung into a quickstep. 'That's better,' I said, settling back to watch. 'I was getting sick of them oul' slow waltzes.'

Some time later, I found myself getting sleepy – it had been a long day. 'Hey, Pearl.' I tugged at her arm. 'I've had enough – let's go home.'

'Mama said we had to wait until she comes for us.' Pearl didn't look away from the dance floor where, once again, Thomas Areton was piloting some elderly lady through a group – and not looking all that happy about it. 'Look,' I tugged harder, 'she might have fallen asleep. It's very late.'

'Just a minute. Let's wait until this dance ends, all right?' She dragged herself away long enough to look over her shoulder to where Ruby and Iris were sound asleep on the floor. 'It would be a pity to wake those two up, they look so peaceful . . .' She returned to her fascination with the dancers.

'Pearl!' I hissed. 'If you don't come, I'm going myself. I've had enough—'

Just then, the music died into silence and I leaned over the railing to try to see what had happened. One of the hired village girls was waving her arms and whispering into Lady A's ear in the middle of the floor. She had been dancing with an army officer and he, looking fierce put out, was drooping beside her, like a spare stick of celery. Next thing, Lady Areton's hand flew to her mouth and her dance partner moved in, putting an arm on her shoulder.

Loads of people crowded around to try to find out what was going on but Lady A pushed everyone off and dashed over to where her husband was sitting with a small group. The glass in his hand was slanted a little bit and, if you ask me, he looked under the weather. She spoke urgently to him, doing the same kind of hand-waving the girl had. Lord A immediately handed his glass to one of the other men and, with a face like thunder, ran towards the doorway of the ballroom. She followed him and so did Thomas, so the only one of the Aretons left was the girl, Isabella, who was standing in the middle of the floor as if someone had taken away her lollipop. 'That's it,' I said to Pearl. 'We're going. Something's after happening,' and I moved to wake up the other two.

'We stay until Mama comes to fetch us.' Pearl spoke strongly but she didn't sound all that convincing. 'Don't wake them, Opal.'

'That's rubbish. Of course we'll wake them.' I caught Ruby by the shoulder first, and then Iris: 'Wake up, Ruby. Wake up, Iris. It's time to go home.'

Pearl was getting upset. 'But—'

'We're not staying here.' I'd made up my mind. 'Look down there, Pearl. Who's dancing? There's no music. The dance is over. If you're worried about Mama, we can explain. Something has happened – and even if you're not coming, I'm going to find out what it is. Youse,' I waved my arm around the three of them, 'can come or not. I don't care.'

8

PEARL

We all followed Opal down the back stairs and into the kitchen yard. It was deserted, but we could hear a hubbub of some sort coming from the stables, access to which was across the yard and through a high archway. 'Come on!' Opal, as she always did, led the way, running ahead of us towards the stables. I was hampered a little because on each side I had the hands of Ruby and Iris, who were both sleepy. Ruby was complaining a little but even her voice was stilled at what we saw when we came through the archway into the stable yard.

The motors were mostly lined up as they had been earlier, but Lord A's, the one Papa drove, stood with the driver's door ajar and the engine throbbing halfway across the yard.

The half-doors of each stable were open, each framing a horse's head, ears pricked inquisitively at the sight of this unusual happening in the middle of the night. But one of the horses, reins and saddle dragging on the ground from a loose girth, was trotting in small circles at the far side of the yard. A few yards from its loop a clump of people surrounded something on the ground. Standing in their finery a little apart from this group, I could see Lord and Lady Areton, she clutching his arm with one hand while the other covered one of her ears, his free hand worrying his moustache.

Opal was already running towards them.

'Stay there!' I said sternly, to Ruby and Iris. 'Don't move. I'll be back in one minute.'

I did not wait to see if they had obeyed but followed Opal, running as fast as I could.

When I got there, I saw the object of the group's attention: our

Willie, lying on his back. Papa was kneeling beside him, cradling his head.

'Willie!' Opal screamed. She dropped to her knees beside Papa but was roughly pulled up by a man in full army dress, who had been running a little in advance of myself. 'Stand back, girl! Don't crowd him,' he ordered. 'I'm a doctor.'

This man then knelt beside Papa and gently tugged at his shoulder. Papa yielded, placed Willie's head tenderly on the ground and sat back on his heels. The soldier put a finger somewhere on Willie's neck, then his ear to Willie's chest. He straightened up. 'It's no use.' He turned and shook hands with Papa, who looked bewildered. 'I'm so sorry. The boy is gone.'

There was a shocked murmur from the crowd. Clippity-cloppety, clippety-cloppety went the horse. Crackle-crack-crackle went the torches, still gaily flaming. Opal burst into tears. The horse whinnied as though in reply.

I went to stand between Opal and Papa, beside poor Willie. By the light of the torches, and that of the high moon, I could see two dark trickles, just trickles, from his mouth and an ear. Papa looked bewildered. Then tears fell from his eyes. I had never seen Papa cry before. I knelt and put my arm around his waist. 'Don't cry, Papa, please. Don't cry. Willie will be all right. We'll get him to a hospital. He'll be all right.'

Someone, in memory a woman, came behind me, placed her hands under my shoulders and lifted me to my feet. 'There's nothing we can do for him now, dear. No hospital can save him. Come away. Let the men take care of him.'

But I wouldn't go. Of course I wouldn't leave my little brother lying there on the cold ground. I pulled myself from the woman's grasp and flung myself against Papa's back, bent again as, again, he cradled Willie's head in his arms. Like a monkey, Opal threw herself on to me and latched on.

Clippety-cloppety, clippety-clop went the metal hooves of the horse as it continued to circle.

9

PEARL

What happened to Thomas Areton that same night does not bear thinking about, even after all these years. Distraught as we were about our poor Willie, at least we knew it had been an accident and in time we came to accept that he himself was partly, maybe even wholly, at fault.

I can but imagine what effect the aftermath of that accident had on Lord Areton's son and heir.

I could not speak about it for many years. When Opal and I talked about Willie's death, the conversation always stopped right there. She can be insensitive at times, but I cannot believe that even she could lightly have shed the impact of what she and I saw that night just a few short minutes after we had discovered Willie – and that had been bad enough.

Ruby, at least, was spared the sight of what happened next – she and Iris had been taken away by someone. I have never learned who it was. But every time I think of our Willie, it is inextricably linked to what happened to poor Thomas.

I can talk about it now. I have even used it in one of my stories, heavily disguised, of course, because even though I have no longer any idea where the Aretons are or what happened to them in the years that followed, this is a source of sadness to me. I'm sure you find that surprising, but it is so, so true. It takes very little, perhaps just a mention of the word 'Kilnashone', for the scars on my heart to bleed again. (Oh dear! I think I'm letting my literary profession colour my day-to-day conversations and even thoughts.)

Events unfolded very quickly that night. Papa, Opal and I remained with Willie, of course, until the ambulance arrived, engine roaring, bell clanging. Papa, having exhorted us to go down to

60

Mama — 'Be gentle with her, Pearl' — went with the body (I still find it difficult to refer to our brother as 'the body'), leaving my sister and me standing at the spot where Willie had died. I had persuaded Opal to loosen her grip on me so we were standing side by side, holding on to each other so tightly I doubt if either of us knew which of us was trembling. I for one was so shocked I was almost afraid to take a step.

Seeing us standing there so upset, two of the departing ladies came over and very kindly offered to escort us home: 'You must have had a very big fright, you poor things.' The first lady was in tears. The second looked for a moment as though she were about to put her arms around me, but then thought better of it.

'No, thank you.' Through my own tears, I spoke on behalf of the two of us. 'We will make our own way. But thank you.'

The women exchanged glances. 'Well, if you're sure?' asked the first.

After they had left, we were the only two people remaining in the yard, except for Thomas Areton, who was with his horse, talking quietly to him, walking him up and down. That horse was now as docile as a lamb.

Grief-stricken though I was, I realised that Mama probably had only Ruby and Iris with her. I had no idea how much she now knew of what had happened, or indeed if she knew anything at all. She must have heard the ambulance, which always raised dread in everyone's heart. 'We must go.' I took Opal's hand but the poor girl now seemed stunned into immobility. 'Come on, dear.' I shook her gently. 'Mama needs us.' She looked at me as though she had no idea who I was. Then, obedient but shaking so hard I feared she might stumble, she walked with me towards the entrance to the yard.

We were almost at the archway when we had to jump aside: Lord Areton, his expression angrier than any I had seen on a human face before, was approaching so fast and in such a concentrated manner that he didn't see us. As he passed us I smelt whiskey, understandable in this instance: they had been having a party after all. He was carrying a shotgun.

Thomas, hearing the ringing of shoes on the cobbles, looked over and saw the gun at the same time we did. 'No, Father,' he cried. 'No!'

Lord A responded by walking even faster. 'Run, Opal.' I tried to push my sister through the archway but, too terrified to move, she clung to the stonework. I couldn't abandon her so we both huddled into the wall.

Thomas Areton's screams grew until they were unearthly. 'Please, Father, please!' he begged. 'It wasn't Doubloon's fault. He's my best friend – please, Father, don't shoot him!'

Lord A's roar was something I still hear sometimes in the still-ness of the night. 'I'm not going to shoot him,' he yelled. 'You are. You are responsible for your own horse. It was you who should have made sure he was secure and couldn't be got out of his stable by Somers's boy. I'm going to teach you once and for all to take care of Areton property. Now, do it or I'll horsewhip you!'

'I can't – I can't, Father, please don't make me – I can't do this. I love Doubloon – please, Father—' but Lord Areton caught him by the shoulder and forced him to take the gun. Thomas dropped it instantly on the ground and tried to escape, but his father was too quick for him.

'Do it!' he shouted, catching his son by the arm. 'Do it, you soft little Mama's boy!'

Thomas, who was as large as his father, although not as powerful, resisted and they struggled while Doubloon, whinnying in fright, bucked and reared against the restraint of the bridle.

Some of the other horses had by now become upset, kicking at the woodwork of their stalls and making anxious sounds.

One of the grooms, a man we knew but whose name I have forgotten – I do remember Willie had liked him very much – ran into the yard. He must have heard the shouting and the horses' disturbance. He did not see us in the shadows but, recognising his employer, stopped dead just in front of us.

Lord Areton did not notice this new arrival. His rage was escala-ting by the minute. 'DO IT!' he shrieked at the boy writhing in his grasp. 'Do it or I'll thrash you to within an inch of your pitiful life!' He caught Thomas around the neck and, with his free hand, picked up the gun and forced it into Thomas's. 'Pull the trigger, damn you. Aim and pull it!'

'I can't – I can't!' Thomas at last managed to get out of his father's grasp. With the gun pointing towards the ground, he moved to protect his horse, standing by his neck and facing Lord Areton.

'If – if you shoot him,' his voice was high and shuddering, 'you'll have to shoot me too!' Stock first, he offered the gun. A histrionic gesture, but nothing could have been as melodramatic as what was going on in reality. 'You can't make me do this, Father,' he yelled, as loudly as he could, but his voice could not sustain his courage. It cracked.

'I can and I will, you idiot, you nincompoop, you – you excuse for an Areton.' The father wrenched the shotgun from the poor boy's hands, and shoved the barrel into the horse's belly. Doubloon reacted strongly, pulling and jerking on the bridle. His eyes were rolling and his ears flat. For a few seconds, nothing happened. The stable yard was not enormous and its surfaces, being hard, reflected sound, so, soft though the words were, I could hear what he said next. 'Thomas,' he said, 'if you don't kill this animal with a shot to the head, I'll discharge into his ribs. You won't like what you'll see.'

The groom heard, too, and was galvanised. Quite bravely, with steps deliberately heavy and noisy to draw attention to himself, he walked towards father and son. 'Please, Lord Areton,' he said, 'let's all calm down.'

Thomas's father whirled and I actually thought for one horrifying moment he was going to shoot the man. 'Who the hell?' Then, recognising who it was, 'Stay out of this. That's an order. It's none of your business.'

'With due respect, your lordship,' said this courageous man, 'all the horses are my business. That's why you hired me.'

'If you've not gone from this yard by the time I count to five, you can seek other employment.'

'I'll see out my responsibilities so, sir, until I go. And Doubloon, here, is one of my responsibilities until I leave this yard. A good horse, sir.' His voice remained calm. 'You'll be proud of him. And of your youngster here. He's a good seat and they make a fine pair. And don't forget the money you paid for that horse, sir. That's a valuable animal.'

Thomas was now trembling as violently as his horse, which continued to plunge and pull, trying to get free. The boy was gazing from his father to the groom and back again.

'Damn your impertinence, man!' Lord Areton's mouth sprayed spittle. 'It's my money and I'll decide what I will or will not do with it. Now get out of my sight.' Slowly and deliberately, he turned back and again put the gun into the boy's hand, now unresisting. 'This is the last time I'll say it. I mean it, Thomas.' His tone was soft now, menacingly so. 'You put the gun to that horse's head and pull the trigger, or I'll make sure you have something worse to see.'

'Please, sir, please.' Braver still, the groom placed himself between father and son. 'Don't do this,' he begged. 'It was an accident what happened here tonight, sir. Don't blame the poor dumb animal. Don't take it out on him. I'll go – for sure I'll leave your employment. But let me take the horse with me. You need never set eyes on either of us again, sir – think of the effect on the other horses, sir. Fine animals. A gun going off so close. You can't but frighten them to death—'

Lord Areton's rage boiled over. 'How dare you, you thieving imbecile? Want to trick me into giving you a horse, eh? This is between me and my excuse for a son! Now get out. Get out of my sight and away from Kilnashone, if you know what's good for you!'

He lunged at the groom, so hard he staggered against the man and they both almost fell. Then he whirled back to face Thomas. 'Are you going to shoot that damned animal or am I going to have to do it for you?'

Poor Thomas, sobbing his heart out, hands shaking, put one arm around the horse's neck and, with his head buried in the crook of his elbow, used the other to put the gun to Doubloon's head just below the ear.

I caught Opal around the shoulders and dragged her, forced her, through the archway. We couldn't see this. Certainly I couldn't face any more of it.

Behind us, as we ran, we heard the explosion.

10

PEARL

The deaths of our brother and of Thomas Areton's horse were not the end of the happenings that night.

As you can imagine, although I closed my eyes I could not sleep; throughout what remained of darkness, the images of Willie's unmoving body and of Thomas Areton's brave but ultimately vain defence of his animal followed each other, carousel-like, in an endless circle around my horror-struck brain. I was still awake when Papa came home from the hospital, having left Willie there.

Ruby, who was too young to stay awake all night, felt me move beside her in the bed and put her little arms around me. I didn't want to wake her and so, rather than go downstairs to comfort Papa, I stayed where I was, trying without success to stem the tears flowing in sympathy with Mama's sobbing. The house was small, as I've said, and even though our bedroom door was firmly shut, I could tell that Papa, too, was very, very upset.

There seemed to be quite a lot of comings and goings outside on the avenue and at the gates. I had been given a wristwatch by my godfather, Uncle Bobby, for my twelfth birthday and, careful not to disturb my little sister, held it up this way and that until it caught some light from the window. It was just after four o'clock in the morning. Only a couple of hours more of this torture and I could get up.

For what? For the parade of misery and grief that awaited us?

For some reason, as I lay there, with Ruby spooned into my back and her breathing warm against my neck, my brain now fixated on the dark V of hair in the hollow at the base of Willie's skull. The barber had given him a very tight haircut in preparation for the

65

party but instead of shaving off that little V had carefully shaved around it. In my mind, that inverted triangle of dark, almost black hair, etched into the tide mark of pale skin below, seemed inexpressibly moving, a useless but tender fol-de-rol I would never see again unless I lifted his head from the white satin pillow in his coffin—

My body, of its own volition, curled itself into a tight comma as I tried to contain myself but Ruby woke up in any case because her little dog, Roddy, the most placid creature in Kilnashone, started to bark his head off downstairs.

We both sat up, and as I did, I realised something was awry: there was enough light now to read my watch without effort. I was puzzled. 'It shouldn't be bright at this time of the morning, Ruby. Not yet. It's only the first of April.'

'What's that noise? I have to get Roddy!' Ruby scrambled over me, opened the door and, in her hurry to get to her beloved dog, half tumbled down the staircase into the kitchen. I got out of bed and went to the window. 'Oh, my God!' Through the glass I could see the outline of the Castle's roof, black against monstrous eruptions of orange and yellow flames. Because of the hill and the bend in the avenue, I couldn't see the rest of the house.

Opal had also woken up and had come to join me. 'It's on fire,' she mumbled, but was then so shocked by her own words that she repeated them, shrieking: 'It's on fire!'

A lorry, with lights full on, was rumbling past our house towards the flames, and in front of it were many running figures.

Even before we had left for the party, Mama had made us lay out the clothes we would wear for Mass later that morning: 'You'll be late risers tomorrow, children. Do it now!'

How wrong she had been about that, I thought, as Opal and I snatched up our cardigans, put them on over our nightgowns, then dashed downstairs to find Ruby petting her dog in a futile attempt to stop his barking. Papa, who was still in his chauffeur's uniform, was struggling into his greatcoat. Leaving it unbuttoned, he pushed all three of us out of the way and wrenched open the front door. 'Christ!'

I had never, ever before heard Papa swear. 'Look after Mama,' he yelled at us. Then, 'I have to go and see what's happening to the Aretons.' Roddy, inches from his heels and still barking, followed him outside.

Almost immediately after his departure, Mama came into the kitchen. Her face was swollen and blotchy and her hair, which she always wore in a loose chignon at the base of her neck, was streeling around her ears and down her back. I also remember that she smelt very strongly like Uncle Bobby. I knew what that meant. She'd had some whiskey. 'Close that door, children,' she said, in a weak, odd voice. 'Close it out. Shut it all out. This is not our business.'

Mama never spoke to us in that childish voice. She was the one always in charge. In control. Gently, I took her hand, leading her towards the settle by the fire. 'Sit down, Mama,' I tried to sound quiet and level but I was frightened, and although I could see that Opal was too, her curiosity got the better of her. She pulled the door open wider and went outside. As she did, I heard the growl of a heavy engine approaching us from the direction of the Castle and went to the door to see what it was.

It was a lorry – bigger than the one we had already seen going up towards the house: it presented an image I have never been able to get out of my head. The open bed of the vehicle was packed with those who, only a few hours previously, had glittered by the light of gasoliers and tinkling candelabra. Shorn of finery, they were wrapped in drab blankets and shawls and were clinging to one another as the vehicle, which had seen better days, lurched and swayed down the avenue towards the gates. None of them paid any attention to us; many of the women were openly weeping.

But just behind that lorry was a motorcycle. 'Get back inside if you know what's good for you!' The man riding it slowed to speak gruffly to Opal and me. He wore a leather helmet, a Sam Browne belt over his tweed jacket and had a scarf wrapped around his mouth. Although I can't be sure of it, and probably couldn't have had time to see whether or not he carried a gun, my memory has subsequently added this detail, and given what I have learned since about events during that period, that memory could well be accurate.

We obeyed him, but after he had gone, we moved out again to see what would happen next. I cannot, of course, speak for Opal, but now that I was fully alert, every so often the reality of what had happened earlier – that our Willie was dead and that I would never see him again – rose to close off the air to my throat. But as young people frequently are, I was also caught up in the abnormality of the moment.

Within minutes of the departure of the second lorry and its motorcycle escort, two police cars came through the gate and raced up the avenue towards the fire.

'Come on.' Opal started to run. 'We have to go up there.'

I hesitated. 'We should ask Mama – or we should at least get dressed. We don't want to disgrace the family, make a show of ourselves – we can't leave Mama.'

'Come on! We won't be gone long. Mama won't notice and Ruby will be grand. 'Hey, Ruby!' Opal ran back to the open door of the house. 'We'll be back in a minute or two.'

As she came back out she had to jump into the verge, narrowly missing being struck by one of two men cycling past, each steering his machine with just one hand on the handlebars because the other was clutching a handful of reins, leading a number of horses and ponies, five or six to each man.

Even over the sound of so many hooves on the new hard surface of the avenue, the distant roaring of the fire, peppered with little explosions – I found out later they signified windows popping – and the shouting of men I could not yet see, behind me I could hear retching. 'Are you all right, Opal?' I turned to see that she was bent double. We all got sick from time to time, but of our family, Opal had the strongest stomach and it was strange that it was she who was vomiting. I put one hand on her hunched shoulder and patted her back with the other as she retched again, although I could see nothing coming out of her mouth. 'Should we go back to Mama?'

Through her coughing and spluttering, I could see her head shaking quite hard. So I waited.

At last she straightened up. 'I'm better now.' She took my hand.

'Are you sure?'

'Yes.'

We ventured to the bend in the driveway. Now we could see the entire house.

The two police vehicles were now parked at the extremity of the turning circle and we could see the officers moving purpose-fully about. A long ladder had been propped against the gable facing us, just beside the archway into the stable yard, from which we could see the glow and flicker of fire, although at that point we didn't know whether or not it was just a reflection. (It wasn't, as it turned out. The fire did a thorough job on not only the house, but the stables, laundry, dairy and all of the out offices.)

Near the top of the ladder, a man was holding a thick hose, which ran to him from the kitchen yard at the back, presumably from the well there. The blaze seemed to be burning most furiously right in the heart of the house, and while he was aiming the stream of water directly into it, its meagre flow seemed to be having little if any effect.

The policemen had organised a chain of men, who stretched from the front of the Castle down the hill and across a meadow as far as the river. They were passing up buckets. The two at the top, nearest the house, were running as close as they dared to the open front door and, while leaning away to protect their faces from the heat, were flinging the buckets' contents as hard as they could at it. Again, this did not seem to be having any impact on the flames billowing through all the doors and windows. To me, with my always overactive imagination, it seemed as though a family of dragons had taken up residence in Kilnashone Castle and were repelling all comers with their fiery breath.

The fire burned all night and for much of the following day, leaving the house and its satellite buildings in ruins. I have learned subsequently that the authorities had only the month previously established a Fire Fighting Services Committee, charged with setting up a proper system for Kilnashone and the village next to us, with shared resources and a fire tender jointly to protect us. It had been so thoroughly intimidated, though, by certain people in the area who had agendas of their own, that its members had been exceedingly slow to set anything in motion. So the saving of Kilnashone Castle, dependent on manpower, a couple of ladders, feed buckets, a standpipe fixed into a low-pressure yard well – and a shallow river – had never had a hope of success.

When I went to get milk for our breakfast later that morning, I found almost everyone in the village standing around in their doorways or in small groups outside the shops. The dairy was close enough to the gates of the Castle, yet I had to endure a wave of intense scrutiny as conversation died at my approach and people initiated what became, over the succeeding days, a wave of sympathising at the loss of my little brother.

Everyone lost something that night. We lost Willie. Papa lost his job. The whole family lost its happiness. The Aretons have to be included in this sad catalogue, since they had lost their Irish home – and also, in a sense, their son. Not in actuality – he had not died, like Willie – but as good as.

I picked this up from two women talking together in low voices inside the dairy. Thomas Areton, the first woman told the second, had gone astray in his mind. I kept my head low because, inexplicably, on hearing this, the memory of that odd, inter-mingled scent of pomade and mothballs, had invaded my nostrils as if I had again been passing close to him on the back stairs of the Castle.

Poor Ruby suffered an additional and, for her, very piercing loss. For a seven-year old child, the loss of her brother was probably too momentous to hit home all at once and could be dealt with only incrementally over many years, but the loss of her little dog – although she did not know it immediately – proved shattering. Having followed Papa to the fire, Roddy did not come home, and while I was busy looking after Papa and Mama and doing things in the house it was Opal – in fairness to her – who went with Ruby to look for him. They searched for hours.

There was a particular toy he liked: a thick twig to which Papa had attached a little whistle, and they took this with them, blowing it at intervals, hoping to see him creep out from under some hedge or other. I had tried to give hope to Ruby by telling her that all the commotion had probably upset the poor little thing and that he was just hiding somewhere until things calmed down.

He did not come out from any hidey-hole, and they eventually found him, a tattered and soaked bundle of brown fur on the bank of the river, lying half in and half out of the water at the point where the men had been taking it. His head had been stoved in.

Opal and I tried to convince our sister that his death had been an accident, caused probably by the swing of a bucket, but I could see she did not believe us. I did not believe it myself. His small head was so damaged there was hardly any curve on the skull. One side of his face was flattened too, so that his mouth was torn, his teeth exposed, his broken jaw hanging loose. All of that could not have happened with one accidental blow of a water bucket. Roddy had been battered to death. He was probably being a nuisance, playing with the men and barking, down there at the side of the river.

My two younger sisters took turns to carry him home, and although their clothes were ruined by the time they came into the house with him, no one said a word of condemnation.

We took an old potato sack and wrapped him carefully in it, putting in his toys, the twig with the whistle and a rubber ball, then buried him in the kitchen garden at the gate lodge.

Before we left him, Ruby ran into the house to fetch her dolly, the one with the silk dress. She put it on his grave so he would have company.

11

PEARL

I find it difficult to describe the atmosphere in our home during the days immediately following the catastrophic evening when Willie died. It is even harder to convey what I continued to discover was the depth of feeling in the cottages and houses throughout the village. Through many generations, I would say that at least eight out of ten of the adults living in Kilnashone were employed directly or indirectly by the Castle and its demesne. They had depended on the Aretons for the food on their tables. As, of course, had their children. This steady employment, it would seem, was literally now in ashes. Or, at the very least, hinged on the decisions to be made by the demesne owners, who were conspicuous by their absence.

Poor little Iris had been dispatched home on the midday train while Opal, Ruby and I, with not even school to distract us, hung about the house and did the best we could to deal with our individual sorrows and be of some help to Mama and Papa, who were devastated. None of us had seen sight or light of any of the Aretons. With only one working entrance to the grounds of the Castle, anyone going in had to pass our gate and it was unlikely that anyone from the family could have travelled up the avenue unnoticed. There were police and other cars now and then, but that was to be expected because, overnight and for the next few days, the constabulary guarded the smouldering house, stable yard and outhouses in order to protect them against would-be robbers and souvenir-hunters.

I thought it strange that none of the Aretons came near us, if only to extend sympathy on our Willie's death. If the situation had been reversed – if, for instance, by some freakish accident Thomas had been killed in our house or garden – we would have been beside ourselves with guilt and grief and would certainly have conveyed this in person to the Areton family.

I thought again about the rumours I had heard of Thomas, about his losing his mind. I would not have been surprised if they were true because I doubted my own mind could have remained un-affected by the ordeal inflicted on the boy by his father. Along with everything else that had happened, the sight and sound of his pitiable, unavailing stance against his brutish father on behalf of the horse continued to haunt me. Had they had to put him in an asylum? That thought was intolerable. I had never been inside one, but of course I had heard about them, who had not? They were said to be places filled with dribbling people clad only in filthy night attire.

Did they have asylums for young people? I had no one to ask.

The stream of people coming through the gate and hurrying up the newly surfaced avenue to survey the wreckage did not abate all that day and for the next few days. It was as though the villagers − and even those from far afield − had to see it for themselves before they could fully believe what had happened and, acting on a similar impulse, I went up there myself at about three o'clock that afternoon.

As soon as I rounded the bend that brought me within sight of the whole house, I stopped dead. The sun, already high in a perfectly clear blue sky, sparked off shards of stained glass littering the grav-elled turning circle to create pathways of crimson, indigo and emerald green; instead of the rose window that had, for generations, filled the space over the Castle's entrance door, there was emptiness. Although its thick walls still stood, the roofline of the great building was jagged, its joists exposed and twisted, guttering hanging like thick black vines. From deep within, wisps of smoke and steam drifted lazily upwards, and even from where I stood, I could hear an inter-mittent pop and creak as though the house was complaining that its old joints were in pain.

A rabbit to the lamp, I was drawn to go closer, but soon regretted this. When I was yards away from the back of the sizeable crowd standing outside the police cordon, someone saw me and news of my arrival spread. As it had that morning in the village, conversation died away as everyone turned to look at me. I froze. Too late. I was caught, and had to continue onwards.

This time, many in that crowd, both men and women, had tears in their eyes as they pushed in to shake my hand and tell me how sorry they were for my trouble. Faced with an onslaught of such genuine sympathy, I found it almost impossible to hold my own composure. I had to, however. As the eldest child, I had to be a credit to my family, and when the tears started into my eyes, I swallowed hard, cleared my throat and managed to keep them there.

Conversations around me were muted as people waited to talk to me, but even as I acknowledged the condolences, I heard enough to know that the cogs of the village rumour mill were fully engaged. For instance, I heard it said with heavy emphasis by one man that the Aretons were not going to repair or refurbish the ruined castle. Instead, he went on, they were definitely going to sell the entire property, including Drynan Wood, the grazing land and fishery, as quickly as possible.

Following on from that revelation, a woman who had always ignored me when I was out and about in the village clutched both my hands in hers. 'I'm sorry for your trouble, lovey. The horses, was it?'

'Yes.'

'Poor little lad. I'm real sorry.'

'Thank you.'

She lowered her head and looked me directly in the eye. 'And, by the way, just so you know, it was themselves that did this,' she said, with a jerk of her head towards the hulk of the Castle.

'I beg your pardon?' I was taken aback.

'Them. The Aretons. They're in debt up to their eyeballs but, of course, they didn't let on, with their big parties and balls and lording it. They were always going to go back to the mainland.' The words seemed to choke her. 'We've all known it was only a matter of time. This was just a handy way to do it nice and clean. Claim on the insurance so no cost to them.'

Her hands gripping mine now felt like talons. 'No protests or petitions. No begging them not to go. No having people on their consciences, like my own poor husband who looked after that bloody forest of theirs as if it was his own.' She let go and tapped an index finger against the side of her nose. 'Put-up job. Take it from me. You can bet your life on it.'

I was so stunned I could not say anything in the Aretons' defence.

74

When added to their inculcation of respect for our benefactors, the virtual moat that our parents had placed around us had insulated us children against believing this type of gossip, even in school, where for sure we were made to feel like outsiders. But I have to say that, for an instant, the thought occurred to me that the woman's theory might be bolstered by Lord and Lady A's seeming disinterest in their own disaster.

And if that were true, was the rumour also true about Thomas?

As soon as those treacherous little worms entered my mind I dismissed them out of hand. It was possible, no, *probable*, that right now, Papa's employers were too upset to appear in public. That I completely understood. So I thanked the woman for her sympathy, made general thank-you noises in the direction of those still waiting to talk to me and fled the scene, walking as fast as decorum allowed, but not so fast that people thought I was running away. And despite that mental lapse I did not believe for one moment that Lord and Lady Areton would have countenanced something so base as to burn down their own home for insurance money.

The allegation, however, so vehement, had shaken me very deeply. It was horrible that anyone could think such a thing – but I was not so cut off from reality that I did not know that while we were taught to respect the Aretons, such respect was not accorded in all quarters and if that woman thought the Aretons had set fire to their own property, so did many others.

I could not let such a preposterous idea infect my own mind: that Lord and Lady Areton had deliberately, and by arrangement with Diehards, exposed their close and extended family, including Lord A's own mother, and all their guests to mortal danger – not just to fire, but to hotheads with guns? Physically exhausted and emotionally fraught as I was, I could see that this notion was so absurd as to be risible. As I returned home, I put the episode firmly out of my mind so I would not by accident blurt it to Papa or Mama.

As you can imagine, our home that day, and for many days afterwards, was a fractured place, each of us isolated within our personal reactions to what had happened. That night proved to be the first link in a chain of events that was to destroy the unity of our family. None of us knew what lay ahead – how could we? But dread of the future, an insidious intruder, came through our door that terrible night and stayed.

What we shared immediately, of course, was grief. To add to our distress, there was a delay in bringing Willie's body home from the hospital so we could have his funeral. I never found out what caused it, but I believe it had something to do with the availability of a person to conduct an autopsy.

During those interim days our domestic routines collapsed. Mama, normally the pivot around whom we all rotated, took to her room, we girls were not at school, and when he was not with Mama, Papa, washed, shaven, fully dressed with shoes shined and tie correctly knotted, simply sat, grey-faced and silent, by the fireplace, awaiting communication from the hospital and from Lord Areton. 'His' automobile, along with others, had been burned in the fire set in the stable yard, and to conduct his business, so local story – corroborated by one of the senior policemen Papa spoke to – had it, the owner of Kilnashone Castle was now commuting between Dublin and Maryborough by train, taking rooms as required in hotels. Obviously he did not require Papa's services, certainly for the moment.

That was what we all said to Papa. 'Not for the moment, Papa.'

What we thought – at least, what I thought – was probably never again; and I am sure Papa, who was no fool, thought that too. Nevertheless, he sat and waited for something to happen. 'Lord and Lady A won't let us down,' he said, more than once, during those days of waiting, and none of us disabused him. It was dreadful to see him reduced to this: he who had been so busy and correct and who had never let us down. Or them.

By default, I became the manager of the household. With limited help from Opal, I cooked and cleaned, generally tried to keep things running and was so busy and concerned about everyone else, I had almost no time to consider my own sorrow, much less take in the enormity of the disaster. When I was not trying to be the mother of the family, I shut myself up in our bedroom and, between paroxysms of weeping, wrote reams of rubbish about Willie. I codded myself that what I was going through would be beneficial in the long run; that all experience was 'material', and the more profound the experience, the better that material would be. No writer can ever be a real writer, I tried to tell myself, unless he or she knows what it is to suffer tragedy and loss.

This was rationalisation – even self-delusion – of the highest order. What I wrote during those few days was over-emotional gibberish, as I discovered when I read it back some months afterwards. Neither Willie's death nor the violent aftermath Opal and I witnessed in the stable yard had served to stimulate my creativity or enhanced my weak skills as an author. If anything, my experience of the tragedies had had the opposite effect. After reading those papers, my instinct was to burn them as quickly as I could get to a fire grate, but I did not actually do this. Instead, I sequestered them in a shoebox under our bed, hoping that somehow – I know this was a very foolish notion, but I was just fifteen, remember – hoping that somehow, magically, they might improve with age. They did not, of course.

For those terrible days, the rooms in our little house, which normally pulsed with the affairs of the living, Mama's commmands, Papa's quietly authoritative advice, Opal and Willie's squabbling and little Ruby's singing, were as silent as the grave awaiting our brother. When we did talk to each other, it was quietly about the arrangements for Willie's wake and obsequies, uttering platitudes about it being, hopefully, a fine day for the funeral, and generalities about what I should cook . . .

What we did not talk about was the future. It was as though to broach the subject of what was to happen to us, even to ask a question about it out loud, would breach the dam that was preserving us from utter chaos. My own hope, which I knew was forlorn, was that the Aretons, having no obvious use for the gate lodge, might leave us there, at least until the sale of the estate went through. And I dared to embroider on that hope. Perhaps Papa could stay on afterwards as a sort of caretaker on behalf of whoever bought the ruin, until the plans for the place were fulfilled.

I worried about everyone in different ways – Mama's health, Papa's security and stability, Opal's seeming sang-froid. Surely that at least was superficial. Surely she was in for a fall as reality hit her.

As for Ruby – poor Ruby was literally inconsolable at the loss of her little dog. No one could comfort her. It is said that after a dog dies, the best thing to do is to get another immediately, but that was not an option in our case, for we had no idea where we were going to be living.

It might seem invidious to place a dog's death in the same context as our Willie's, but it was heartbreaking to watch and hear our little sister mourn. If she was missing from our sad house during those first chaotic days, we knew where to find her. At the end of one of the lazy beds in the kitchen garden, facing the rows of vigorous potato plants, she would be sitting on the grass in front of the additional clay hump where Roddy was buried. Sometimes we could hear her singing to him, tuneless songs she made up to comfort both the dog and the dolly, whose china limbs were now speckled with earth. Sometimes we would find her just sitting, with tears rolling silently down her face.

We had always babied Ruby because she was the youngest, but during this period, I saw for the first time how profoundly young children can suffer and, dimly, began to see that, of us all, Ruby might have been the most emotional and was certainly the deepest thinker. All I could do, during those moments I spent with her among the cabbages and potatoes, was to stroke her hair. But she did not react even to that, and since I could neither bring her dog back to life nor explain why Willie had had to die, I felt helpless. Our blithe little sister was gone. My only hope was that the absence was temporary.

Mealtimes were particularly harrowing because neither Ruby nor Mama was interested in food, and if either could be persuaded to come to the table, she sat staring at her plate. Again I hoped this was a passing phenomenon. So, on the second day after Willie died, I made soda bread, sliced it, and left it prominently on the kitchen table with butter and cuts of ham in case they should eventually get hungry.

That evening, I had to put the meat back into the safe outside the back door.

On an even more practical level, another of my worries was that we had very little food in the larder, and while our hens were still laying, we had run out of meal for them and I had no money to buy more. Mama, a great believer in freshness, had shopped every day — and, of course, we had had an additional source of supply from the Castle, now cut off. As I have told you, whenever we had a family occasion, Lady A could be relied upon to send down something apt: a cake, a cooked salmon, some buns or biscuits. In the absence of this, how were we to manage for Willie's wake? Did Papa have enough money to buy cakes? Whiskey and ale for the men, sherry and port for the women?

I shared these concerns with Opal, but she was engrossed in a periodical at the time and responded only with 'Oh, you're such a worrier, Pearl. It'll be all right. You'll see.'

Early on the third morning, knowing that he and Mama were in their room, I went upstairs to ask Papa for money so I could go into the village grocery.

He answered my knock, his face covered with white soap, his open razor in his hand. 'There's a message?'

'No, Papa. Not yet.' I explained why I was there. 'We need to lay in some supplies for the wake.'

'Yes — yes, of course. What have you in mind?' He seemed puzzled. Then, 'I'll ask your Mama. She'll know.' He glanced over his shoulder to where, through the door opening, I could see my mother's white, still face on a pillow. She was staring at the ceiling. 'Thank you, Pearl. Run along now. We'll talk when I come down. I have to get ready for wor— get ready and dressed. Thank you, Pearl. You're a good girl.' With just the trace of a smile, he closed the door.

I had been talking not to my papa but to his shadow.

When he did come down, spruce as ever in his chauffeur's uniform, he gave me the money to go shopping with an exhortation to be prudent. 'We don't know where the next wage is coming from, Pearl. But maybe there'll be a message today.'

'I'm sure there will, Papa.' Insidiously, what that woman had said about the Aretons floated to the front of my mind. Were they so lofty that they could not spare even the time it would take to send us a telegram? And then, as it had on several occasions through the mists of grief and sorrow, rose the image of Thomas Areton, as I'd passed him on the stairs, as he had propelled old women on the dance floor, as he had attempted to shield his doomed horse. Where was he?

Opal came with me to help carry the groceries, and although she said later she had not heard any gossip, I certainly had. Willie's death, the fire, and the whereabouts of the Aretons were the only topics of conversation that day in the grocer's, in the cobbler's, where I left in Papa's best shoes to be heeled, and in the dairy, where Opal and I filled three cans, two with fresh milk, one with the buttermilk we used to make soda bread. I was the centre of attention, while Opal was no help at all, moving away from me any time I was approached.

I tried to remain polite. I thanked anyone who sympathised, answered carefully, no matter what I was asked. 'Thank you. Yes, Papa is at home because the car is no longer in use.'

'Thank you. No, we don't yet know whether Lord A is getting a new car.'

'Thank you. Yes, you've heard right. Lord A is staying in hotels while dealing with the authorities.'

'Thank you, you're very kind, but no, I don't know which exact hotels.'

And since everyone was also asking when the wake and funeral were to be held, I told them truthfully that I did not know. Neither could I confirm whether or not Lady A was already in London. Nor that Isabella was in Scotland with relatives. Or – this one stabbed me but I hoped I had not let this show – that Thomas Areton had lost his mind.

As for future plans concerning the estate, and ourselves, I told everyone who asked that I simply did not know.

I retreated to the gate lodge in a state of renewed exhaustion. At least Opal helped me put the groceries away before she returned to her periodical. I let her be because, instinctively, I recognised that she was behaving in this uncaring way to protect herself from the enormity of what had happened. Nowadays, there would probably be an accurate psychological term for it but, of course, I did not have those words then.

We were each of us reeling from Willie's death, the fire and the worry of what was to happen next. In our different ways we were doing our best for each other, but suffering alone.

12

PEARL

On the fourth morning after Willie's death, another glorious day of bright sunshine and mocking birdsong, we received two messages within an hour.

The first was a telegram from the hospital saying that Willie's body was ready for release. Opal was immediately dispatched to alert the undertaker, who had supplied the coffin. She returned with the news that he had promised to be at the gate lodge within the hour to pick us up in the funeral car.

He was as good as his word and waited outside while we made final preparations to leave. We three girls were wearing our good coats – ironically cut down from Castle garments – buttoned tightly at our throats, black armbands around the sleeves on the left side. We were all ready, except Mama. I had sewn a black diamond into the sleeve of Papa's coat, which was far too heavy for the weather. He was actually sweating. 'What's keeping your mother?' he growled, and went upstairs to see what was wrong.

There was a second knock, and I opened the door to a grave-faced Joe McCurg, wearing a suit and a black tie. Joe, the Clery's salesman from the village, had heard about the fire and also about Willie's death: a good friend of Papa and our family, he had travelled all the way down from the city to offer his condolences. I was conscious of the undertaker outside, wasting his petrol on his car's idling engine, but I could not be rude. 'Come in, Joe.'

'I'm so sorry for your trouble,' he said, formally shaking my hand and closing the door behind him. Then: 'Where's your daddy?' He looked around the kitchen. 'I have a message for him.'

I called up to Papa from the bottom of the stairs, and he came down immediately. But as soon as he arrived into the kitchen and saw who was there, the most horrible thing happened. My papa, the man I admired most in the whole world, whom I had always regarded as the pillar of our family and the strongest character in the village, broke down. 'Joe!' he cried, but his voice cracked on the word as he rushed towards his friend with arms outstretched.

As the two men embraced, Ruby, woebegone, seated at the kitchen table, and who like me, had never seen our papa behave in such a way, began to wail. With tears running down my own face, I rushed to the table, threw my arms around her and hugged her tightly. Opal stayed in the middle of the room, watching Papa. Her back was to me and Ruby, and I couldn't see her expression, or if she too was weeping. Then she came to the table and sat down beside us. Her eyes were wide with fright, but dry.

After a few seconds, Papa pulled back, wiping his face with his handkerchief. 'I'm so sorry, Joe, making an exhibition of myself like this. It's just that – he – my little son – and I don't know what to do . . .' He half turned away. Joe, whose expression betrayed his consternation, patted his shoulder, as one would a favourite dog.

Still holding Ruby, who was sobbing into my neck, I managed to pull myself together sufficiently to call out: 'Joe says he has a message for you, Papa!'

In response, Papa blew his nose. 'Sorry again, Joe.' Loudly, as though choking, he cleared his throat. 'There's a message?'

'Stop apologising, Jim. There's nothing to . . .' Awkwardly, Joe trailed off. Clearly, he had not expected to face this emotional tempest. 'Of course you're upset,' he said staunchly. 'I wonder how you're even standing – but, yes,' he lowered his voice and glanced again towards the kitchen table and us three girls, 'I do have something to tell you.'

Papa blew his nose a second time. 'What is it?'

Joe, relieved that the worst of the storm seemed to be over, took a breath so deep it was audible. His expression was eager but very serious, and while he always created a story of the most trivial occurrence, I could see that this was going to be anything but a trifle. 'Well,' he began, 'when I was coming down, who do I see in the dining car of the train . . .' he paused for effect '. . . who do I see but His Nibs from the Castle. I stop by his table to say how sorry I am about what had happened. "I saw the picture in the paper of your castle at Kilnashone," I says to him. "That won't be rebuilt either today or tomorrow!"

'He invites me to join him, which I do. And, of course, as soon as I can, I bring your name in, Jim. And I ask him, tactfully, of course, what's going to happen to you and to the gate lodge. "I'm a friend of Jim Somers and his family," says I to him. "And I'd be a bit worried about their situation. There isn't a lot of work going for a mechanic, however good, in that neck of the woods and certainly none for a chauffeur. I suppose you won't be needing one?"' He paused again for emphasis, watching for Papa's reaction, and when he could not read it: 'Now, I could see that he was taking this in but he was . . .' He hesitated.

'Go on. What did he say about needing a chauffeur?' The sweat on Papa's forehead and chin glistened in a shaft of sunlight. He was so motionless he might have been carved from a mountain.

'Inscrutable, like.' Joe had found the word he had been looking for. 'You know the way he does be – and I think—' He was interrupted by a knock on the door and, being nearest, answered it. The caller was again the undertaker. 'I'm sorry, Mr Somers,' he said politely, over Joe's shoulder, 'but I have another job on at twelve o'clock and I was wondering if ye're going to be much longer?'

'I'm sorry to have kept you.' Papa still did not move. 'We will be out in two minutes.'

'Anyway . . .' Joe took the hint and, having left the door ajar, spoke faster: 'Then His Nibs says, all quiet like, "Is he going to take me to court over the death of his son?"'

'What?' Papa, scandalised, took a step backwards.

'His exact words, Jim.' Joe followed him so they were almost nose to nose. '"Is he going to take me to court over the death of his son?" Exact words. And you know . . .' Watching Papa, he hesitated again. Then, carefully, 'Mightn't be a bad idea. Even the threat of it might get you a few shillings. They can afford it, Jim. They've farms and houses all over the place.' He glanced at Opal, Ruby and me, lowered his voice and speeded up even more: 'You've a family to feed. You've given his lordship the best years of your life. He hasn't said a word to you, has he? Just left you to sink or swim. Has he said anything to you? Anything at all about poor little Willie? Has he offered restitution or to leave you here in peace?

They're not going to use this place, are they? I can't see them moving in here for their Irish holidays, can you?'

'What did you say back to him – about the – the chauffeuring and about – about the court?' Papa's face had gone really red. The sweat was pouring off him.

'He didn't answer me about the chauffeuring and I said nothing back to him about the other thing. I didn't answer him, Jim. Not really. All I said was that I hadn't been talking to you so I couldn't reassure him one way or the other. But I did say I wouldn't be surprised. I said that while you had been a loyal and faithful worker to him and his family for years now, while in that service you had lost your only son. I left him wondering, Jim.'

'You shouldn't have.' Papa covered his face with both hands, so tightly that his voice was muffled. 'Oh, Joe, I know you meant well, but you shouldn't have threatened that. Oh, God . . .'

He stopped because all of us heard the door opening upstairs and the slow descent of Mama's footsteps.

'I know you're loyal, Jim,' Joe said urgently. 'You're loyal beyond sense. But think about it. You don't have all that much time. He wants to meet you and June. That's the message. And the reason I'm worried, Jim, is that I know you. I'm afraid you'll let him walk all over you. Think about it before you talk to him. You've lost your livelihood, Jim. More importantly, you've lost your darling son.'

'When?' Papa dropped his hands. 'When does he want to see us?'

'After the funeral,' Joe said quietly. 'He'll be in Maryborough for the next week. I have the telephone number of the hotel. He says to leave word as to what day you'll be there, and what time.' He took a piece of paper from his pocket and handed it to Papa, who put it quickly inside his overcoat just as the staircase door to the kitchen opened and Mama came in.

13

OPAL

It may sound bizarre – I suppose it is bizarre – that the death of Ruby's dog, Roddy, was the main topic of conversation between us three girls in the funeral car on the way home after my brother's funeral. Pearl and I had tried to convince her that his death had been an accident – that he was hit by one of the water buckets being used in an effort to douse the fire. We all tried. Even Mama, who acted so dazed during the days and even weeks surrounding Willie's funeral, managed to add her voice to mine and Pearl's. None of us wanted Ruby to think that the world was such a bad place that someone might murder a small dog.

That whole period is a blur in my mind, thank God. As I think I've told you already, I was affected, of course I was, but not nearly as badly as the others. A neighbour at the funeral asked me if I was all right when we were milling around outside the chapel after the Mass – you know the way you do. I was standing a little ways away from everyone else, just waiting, and she came up to me. 'I'm sorry for your trouble,' she said to me, and I thanked her and then she said something along the lines of 'You look very lonely over here all by yourself.'

And I said back to her that, really, I was all right.

I really was, you know.

I was definitely sad, I remember, but not sad like the others. Maybe I'm a cold fish. Ruby had many a row with me over the years and that's what she called me frequently, and maybe she was right. Maybe I am a cold fish. But my attitude to life is, you get over things because you have only one life to live and all the rest of it, blah blah . . . move on.

I think I told you somewhere that there was no possible way

85

on earth I was ever going to stick around a one-horse town like Kilnashone, and maybe it was for that reason I was able to separate Willie's death from the fire that had destroyed the Castle. My secret hope, in the deepest part of my heart, was, when I saw the ruins, that it couldn't be repaired and that we might be moving to Dublin. I'd be going there in a couple of years anyway, but this might bring it forward. And it would be handy if we all went. I'd have company until I got on my feet.

Of all of us, Mama was the one who nearly lost her reason over Willie's death. Understandable, I guess, because they say there's nothing like a mother's love. I'm not a mother so I'll never know the truth of that. The good thing about that is that I won't have to go through that awful misery.

He was waked at home. Got a good send-off, to be fair to all concerned, and there had been a good turnout from the village. But, if you ask me, a lot of those people came not out of sympathy or respect but to have a goo at the inside of the gate lodge. People are envious, you know. Especially in a small place like Kilnashone. I'd heard a bit of spite more than once about us getting a free house when others had nothing.

Maybe that's a bit unfair because, as I say, a lot of what happened around that time is a blur, and as you get older, you sort of compress things into a set of quick snaps. I probably think that about the neighbours because, on the day of the wake, I saw one of the village women take a china ornament of a dog off the parlour mantel-piece and turn it over to look at the maker's mark on the under-side. I know now it was a Staffordshire dog – I found out when I was getting rid of Frank's parents' stuff. They'd had two pairs of the things. Some Christmas or other, Lady A had given this one to Mama, who was so charmed with it, she never trusted us to dust it, always did it herself. Don't know what happened to it afterwards. I haven't got it, for sure.

Anyhow, one of the very clear pictures I have in my mind is of an awful incident the morning after Willie came home to be waked.

We had taken turns sitting beside him all night – I suppose because he never really had a bed of his own, he was in my parents' bed, laid out in the suit and shirt and tie he had worn for his confirmation – but when daylight came, we were there all together.

The red confirmation rosette was a bit crooked on his lapel but nobody seemed to have the heart to straighten it. I stared at that a lot because I couldn't look Willie in the face. Not for long anyway. I was a bit afraid, to tell you the truth, and I wasn't afraid of much, even then. But I had never seen a dead body before Willie's.

Occasionally I did give his face a glance, and when I did, I concentrated not on his whole face but on the faint little spider web of veins on each of his eyelids. I remember wondering whether all dead people had these veins, or whether it was only Willie who had them.

Another thing I stared at to keep me from looking at Willie's face was the little row of silver flowers, like stars, that Mama had embroidered along the upper hem of the sheet that was folded halfway down our brother's chest. That sheet, a Castle cast-off, was the best in the house, made of pure linen from the mills of Northern Ireland. (That phrase is one that has been embedded in my mind: 'the mills of Northern Ireland'. Mama and Papa used it as a sort of endorsement, always nodding to emphasise how good the linen was from up there. To me it sounded like the title of a song.) Anyhow, Mama hadn't allowed that particular sheet to be used on our beds. It was too good. And she had embroidered those little flowers on it for the wedding chest.

She kept a big tin chest in the parlour and was adding to the contents all the time. Everything was white. The idea was that whichever girl in the family got married first she would have her pick of what was in it, tablecloths, lace doilies, handkerchiefs, night-dresses, most of them cast-offs, for sure, but renewed and improved by the hands of our mother – and regularly aired and refolded to keep them fresh for us. We all knew what was in that chest and I had bagsed that linen sheet for myself. But now, here it was, over my dead brother in his deathbed. Even if she washed and starched and ironed and aired it a hundred times, I didn't think I'd want it now.

Now that I think of it, did she have some premonition about Willie? There was nothing in that chest for him. But, then, maybe she would have allowed his bride to pick, if Willie had got married before any of us.

Anyways, to get back to the incident.

The bedroom window was open that morning, because there were candles lighting and the room was stuffy, so we heard the undertaker's car arriving and the men talking quietly outside as they opened the tailgate. We heard the coffin being slid out for Willie to be put into. (The usual thing was to have the open coffin by the side of the deceased's bed, but the bedroom was too small, we had nowhere else, really, to keep it overnight, and Mama refused point blank to have him put into it on the bed, which was the only other alternative.)

Papa was standing at Willie's head on one side of the bed, with me beside him, Pearl and Ruby opposite. We all looked at each other and then at Mama, who was standing at the foot of the bed and had put her hands over her ears. We had no choice but to look at her because the minute she heard the coffin being taken out of that hearse she started to cry. I can't really call it crying, though. It was more like a wolf howling – like you'd hear on one of those nature documentaries on the telly? It was really, really horrible. Awful. A sound I'll never forget.

Then Ruby joined in – and I don't blame her because she was only seven years old. But Pearl, who never had much colour in her face, went stone white and Papa seemed to be paralysed. None of us, not even Papa or Pearl, seemed to know what to do.

Somebody had to do something.

So I went to her. 'Mama,' I said, 'please don't cry like this.' I had to louden my voice, if there's such a word, so as to compete with the noise of Mama and Ruby crying, but mostly Mama. She was awful to look at, too. Because of the funeral being in public and the neighbours all being there in the chapel, she had made some kind of an effort with her hair but now a lot of it was coming loose because she was tearing at it. 'Mama, please, leave your hair alone,' I yelled, really high.

She ignored me, or didn't hear me, so I tried to think of something grown-up to say to her. Something Papa might say. 'It's no use, Mama,' I shouted. 'It won't bring Willie back. And think of the neighbours. We have to be a credit to the family.' I tried to put my arm around her waist to console her. But she threw me off so hard that I fell against the iron bars of the bed and hurt my shoulder. Really hurt it. I had a huge bruise for weeks afterwards. Then I bawled too, of course, adding to the bedlam.

Into this came the undertaker. With the commotion upstairs, none of us had heard him knocking. He had to have heard all the shouting and crying through the open window but he had come in to do his job. We never locked our front door. Nobody did, in them days.

I was nearest to him, and even though I was sobbing and holding my hurt shoulder, I could see he was a bit nervous. His eyes were kind of blinking as he took in what was happening.

As I think about it now, the scene was even funny, in a horrible dark kind of way. The dead body in the bed, Mama howling like a wolf, with Ruby as a rival in the sound stakes, me holding my shoulder, Papa like a statue, Pearl nearly fainting and this poor man standing in the middle of it all. (Of course it was not funny. I'm just talking about it in the way you do when you're relaying these kinds of scenes years and years afterwards.)

Next thing, something happened that for definite wasn't in the least amusing. When she saw the undertaker, Mama reacted like a wild thing. She went for him, her two hands like claws stretched out at him, as if she was one of those birds coming down to get a salmon or something. 'Get out! Get out!' she shrieked. 'You're too early. We don't need you yet!'

The undertaker, poor man, got quite a scare and jumped backwards through the doorway on to the landing, but she followed him and, actually, I think she was so unhinged she might have clawed him quite badly if I hadn't got to her first. Because without thinking, hurt shoulder and all, I dived on her and pulled her away from him. I was big for my age and healthy, but it was a struggle to pull her back to the room, which I did with the help of Papa, who at last managed to stir himself into action.

There was silence now. Seeing our mother like this had given Ruby such a fright she had stopped crying and even Mama herself seemed to have come to her senses, although she was a bit dazed and tears were running down her face. Standing beside Papa, who was tightly holding her arm, she was looking around at all of us as though she was trying to work out what had just happened. She looked a fright, to tell you the truth. Like a mad woman. At this stage, most of her hair was out of its bun and all over the place; even the collar of her good silk blouse was halfway up around her ear. And you know when those strings of mucus hang between your lips when you've been crying really hard with your mouth open? Well, they were part of the picture.

The undertaker was holding his ground, just outside the open door, waiting. Maybe he was used to that kind of thing.

I didn't notice what Pearl was doing or how she looked because the throbbing of my shoulder had spread to my arm and the pain was really desperate. I was also shocked. I had never, ever, ever seen that side of Mama before. And I sincerely hoped I would never see it again.

Papa broke in then, thank God, walking out to where the undertaker stood. 'I apologise,' he said quietly, then went back to stand beside Mama and put an arm around her shoulders. 'I'm very sorry,' he said again.

'That's all right, Jim.' The man adopted his soothing, undertaker's voice. 'It's completely understandable. Please don't worry about it. We'll give you a few minutes. We'll come back.'

After he had left, Mama turned her face up to Papa. 'It's too soon,' she whispered.

'It is.' Papa pushed a strand of hair off her face. He did it real tenderly. 'It is, dear.' Then: 'Clean yourself up, June. We can't let Willie down.' His voice was shaky and, almost more than anything else that happened during that terrible time, that sound, kind of broken, got to me.

14

PEARL

What can one really say about the funeral of a little brother? I am speaking as a bereaved sister and now, of course, from the distance of many years. I do not canonise Willie retrospectively. He was contrary and a scamp and a mischief-maker, and there is no doubt that he contributed in a major way to his own premature death. Although in my hearing no one had expressed anger with him about this, I had to suppress mine. There was nothing I could do about it because he had deprived me, us, of any opportunity to vent it.

Above all, though, he was my darling little brother. I had loved him – and on the day of his funeral, I discovered that love does not die with its object. On the contrary, it comes into very sharp focus and is an overwhelming component of grief.

When I think of Willie now, he is not torturing Opal or dragging his feet on the way to the woodshed, or pulling Ruby's hair. He is reaching high, from an already high branch of a chestnut tree in Drynan Wood, to knock off a choice conker or, having shinned up a beech, showering nuts on the rest of us waiting below with the skirts of our dresses held out to catch them. He is eternally young.

Each funeral of a beloved person is unique to the family. To those not intimately involved, it is a sad ritual, designed to comfort the bereaved, or so it is said. For myself, I drew little solace from the hymns thumped out on the wheezing harmonium by our teacher, who was also the organist in the chapel, or the priest's begging God to forgive Willie for his 'sins' so he could enter Paradise. What sins, at eleven years of age?

Nor could I accept the tears of our classmates when they shook my hand to offer their sympathy. They were merely reacting, as children do, to my own tears and the morbid atmosphere. I am sorry if that sounds confused, but in me, along with the mixed-up sorrow and anger, there was a wider resentment against those who still lived, who were not grieving today, who were going home to families that were still intact.

What I would not have given that morning for one more quarrel with my brother.

There had been practical tasks, which had helped keep me busy. With Papa so concerned about Mama, it was left to Opal and me, with some help from little Ruby, of course, to organise the funeral meal. We had arranged the sherry, whiskey, stout, lemonade and glasses on the sideboard in the parlour, then put plates of cold ham, bacon, buttered bread and scones, along with slices of seed and Simnel cakes, on the kitchen table. And, as protection against flies, we had covered everything neatly with a large piece of muslin – although, it being so early in the year, we didn't expect them to be much of a problem. But this was as Mama would have done, and by the time we left that morning, everything was presented as well as we could manage without her guidance. I wanted every-thing to be perfect because two of her brothers had sent word they were coming with their wives to the funeral, and I guessed she would not want to let us down in front of them.

I found out that day that when grief is personal it is physical. Mine can only be described as being akin to a knife inserted in my stomach and moved upwards, slowly slicing open my heart. Again, I apologise if this sounds sensationalist, but that is how it felt throughout that time, most particularly during that day. As though to mock us, once again the pitiless sunshine beat on our heads, shimmering on the brass plate screwed to the lid of Willie's white coffin, so that, through my tears, the lettering seemed to dance:

William James Somers
10.3.1912
1.4.1923

And when we disfigured that plate by throwing symbolic hand-fuls of clay on to it, as we were each required to do, I knew with certainty that I had seen the end of our Willie's life on earth. It was not an easy thing to do.

Mama had to be supported throughout the funeral, and not just emotionally. In the cemetery, the depth of her anguish bent her double so Papa had to hold her tightly to prevent her falling into Willie's open grave. It was just as well that, in the old-fashioned style, she had concealed her swollen face with a black mantilla. To look on such naked suffering would have been intolerable.

Soon, too soon, there was nothing more to be said or done. In the awkward silence that I now know follows the end of the prayers at all funerals, we were left standing with Aunt Margaret, Uncle Bobby and our cousin Iris, a forlorn, huddled group by the side of the grave, trying to stave off the moment when we would have to go home and leave Willie behind. The priest came and shook our hands, followed by the people from the village, who had walked solemnly behind Willie's coffin from the chapel into the graveyard behind. They murmured their condolences.

'It's a sad day, a sad day. We'll pray for you, Mr Somers . . .'

'He was a good little lad by all accounts. You'll miss him.'

'The mammy couldn't come, Mr Somers, she's bad with the rheumatism, as you know, but says to tell you she's saying a novena for the soul of the poor child.'

Despite Papa's invitations, they all declined to come back to the house. 'Ah, no, no. We won't bother you, Mr Somers . . .'

'With respect, Mr Somers, we're grateful for the invitation but, unfortunately, we can't come. But we'll be with ye in spirit. Thank you.'

In retrospect, I think that the response of one old man encapsulated the reason for all these refusals. Shooting a quick look at Mama who, limp as a rag doll, leaned against Papa's shoulder, he said: 'Thank you, Mr Somers. Thank you very much, but I won't. Ye have enough on yeer plate, God love ye all.' I also noticed that no one called Papa by his first name, and despite their obvious and sincere goodwill, I don't think I ever felt so separate from the people of Kilnashone.

Mama's two brothers and their wives, who had stood stiffly apart from us at the graveside, were the last to approach us. As a group, they had arrived just after the Mass had started and had not spoken to us until that moment. I don't think either Mama or Papa had noticed them in the chapel because they had sat way back in the pews among the general congregation, but Aunt Margaret, who had been sitting beside me, had. 'Oh, my God,' she had whispered to me. 'Look what the cat dragged in . . .'

I, of course, had never before seen any of these people but I suppose it was not too surprising that they came. To Irish people, death and funerals are sacred events when disagreements and even enmities are put aside, if only temporarily, which is why we had such a turnout from the village. I believe that the formal sympathy we received from people who would not normally give us the time of day (either because we were too big for our boots or because we were working for the oppressor) was well meant and genuine.

So, during that hiatus at the graveside, while the two women hung back a little, the men, my two uncles whose names I did not know, came up to Papa, who was still supporting Mama. 'I'm very sorry for your trouble, Jim,' one said, holding out his hand.

'Thank you.' Papa's voice was flat. 'I'm sorry I can't shake your hand.' With a movement of his head, he indicated his support for Mama. In response, the man glanced at her. 'Understandable, Jim . . . understandable in the circumstances.'

'Please accept our condolences as well, Jim.' The second man touched Papa's arm.

But sympathy went only so far. 'I'm afraid we can't go back with you to your house,' the man continued. 'Trains, you know. Time and tide wait for no man, as they say, and—'

'Don't worry about it,' Papa interrupted. I was standing beside him and felt his annoyance, which I understood perfectly. Whatever these people had against our family, they had made the gesture to come to the funeral so, for their sister's sake, they might have followed the rest of the tradition. Before I knew it, I had darted in front of my parents. 'Thank you for coming.' I repeated this as, one by one, I shook the hand of each of the four relatives. Then, to all four: 'We really appreciate your coming, and we understand the situation with the trains, but if you'll excuse us, now we need to get on.'

'You're the eldest?' One of the wives held on to my hand. 'You're Pearl?'

'Yes. My name is Pearl. These are my sisters, Opal and Ruby.' I did not know whether or not Mama was watching me, but in case she was, I used the opportunity of waving in my sisters' direction to withdraw my hand. 'Thank you again. We had better go now. The car is waiting. Come on, girls.' Gently, I took Papa's unresisting arm and, followed by my sisters, led him and Mama towards the gates of the cemetery.

I can still remember the expression on my father's face. I had always been the one in the background. I had never behaved so assertively. Not ever in my life. But now I was physically shaking, with a flash fire in my blood. I was furious, livid, raging, any adjective you care to mention. What was more, my rage was directed not only at these misguided, stupid and very rude people – why had they come in the first place if they did not want to participate fully, as family should? – but at the world. It was so unfair, unfair, unfair that at the age of only eleven years, Willie was dead . . .

The anger abated quite quickly, however, its heat far too intense to maintain and, anyhow, my parents' rigorous training in how to behave had begun again to manifest itself so that I was already regretting my impoliteness even as I became conscious of a tug at the back of my coat. I turned to find Ruby's little face gazing up at me. 'What is it, pet?'

'Is he cold down there, Pearl?'

I was undone.

Ever since, that phrase has become just one of the sights, sounds and tastes I preserve as a stuttering sequence to remind me of that day, that week, that whole month.

I cannot bear to remember but do not want to forget.

Is he cold down there?

Willie's still body in the stable yard.

The clopping of the horse's hooves on the cobbles.

The earth rattling on Willie's sunlit brass plate.

Mama's black veil fluttering on her breath.

The spaniel puppy, being walked up the Castle's avenue by one of the neighbours, that slipped his lead in front of our doorway and, his whole body wagging, dashed into our kitchen full of joy and vivid life.

The bitter taste of tea at the funeral meal afterwards, too strong because I had been generous with my spoonfuls.

The confused expression on our cousin Iris's little face, as she tried to make sense of this tidal wave of emotion that was drowning us all.

The screams of Thomas Areton in the stable yard.

Over the years I have played this visual litany again and again in my imagination. To forget these short-lived but indicative episodes would be to consign the life of my little brother to oblivion. He had lived. He did live – he would live, in my memory at least.

There is another image, which, at the time, concerned me only briefly. When we got back to the gate lodge, I had hurried inside before the others in order to remove the muslin from the food on the table. As was customary, the blinds and curtains on all the windows had been drawn and so, on this sunny afternoon, the light was excluded, rendering our house even darker than it was in reality. Yet even before I had touched it, I saw that someone had been at our table before me: while the muslin was still in place, it was not placed as neatly as we had left it and when I lifted it, I found that two slices of the bread, two of the fruitcake and some meat had been removed. Probably some tramp, I thought. Someone, anyhow, who needed the food – and since I did not want to distress Mama or Papa about it, I rearranged everything quickly before they came in so that no one would notice a thing. There was more than enough for all, thank God, especially as we had planned for far more guests than were evidently about to descend on the house.

And we did make a small sad group around our kitchen table. Having thanked everyone in a wan voice, Mama, our robust Mama, whose voice could be like vinegar but who could equally sound as soft as swansdown, again retreated to her bedroom, leaving just Papa, we three girls, Iris, Uncle Bobby, Aunt Margaret and Joe McCurg. None of us, not even big bluff Uncle Bobby, was able to lighten the gloom, and quite soon Joe, who would eat nothing and had nursed just one bottle of stout, renewed his condolences and left.

I did not blame him for not lingering. Conversation had been desultory, to say the least, and there had been none of the explosive hilarity, the release of tension, that I have encountered at many funerals since. I believe that Uncle Bobby and his family, who left not long after Joe, were quite relieved to escape.

When our own depleted family was alone again, Papa said hesitantly, 'I think I should go to her, Pearl. Can you clear up here?'

'Yes, Papa.' I regarded the still-laden table. 'You go. Here . . .'

quickly I gathered up some of the cake and poured a cup of tea '. . . take these to her. We'll be all right.'

Then, because I felt he was in such an unguarded mood that he might just answer me, I asked, 'Why did Mama's brothers and their wives not come back here to our house?'

Beside me, I could sense that Opal, who had been moving throughout the day as though floating in a personal bubble, was now paying close attention. Papa, who was about to pick up Mama's cup, instead drew a hand across his eyes. 'Now's not the time, Pearl.' He was tired, obviously, but he did not sound as decisive as he usually did and for once I persisted. 'We're not looking for a long story, just a couple of sentences.'

This was abnormally cheeky of me. I never questioned Papa and with hindsight, I think I was looking to blame someone for all my own sorrow, anger and confusion. I could safely be angry with these relatives – but not with Willie for getting himself killed.

'There's no mystery.' Papa sighed wearily. 'In a nutshell, the family took sides in the matter of your mama's marriage to me. I was only a mechanic, not good enough for her. Two sisters sided with your mama. One was your aunt Margaret, the other died years ago. It's as simple as that. It was something that was never sorted out, as it should have been with the passage of time.' Again he passed a hand over his eyes. It was so sad to see him in this condition and I wanted to hug him, but could not: he was not the hugging type. The moment passed, and it struck me that, as the eldest, it was up to me now to find a way quickly to grow up. In the days ahead, Mama would need all the support she could get, but so would my sisters and Papa. The prospect was daunting.

Right now, the gloom and stuffiness in the house were getting me down. 'Do you think Willie would mind if the girls and I went for a walk?' I asked Papa.

'Please, Papa. Please?' Ruby, who, since we had returned from the funeral, had been so subdued as to be almost invisible, joined in.

'You two go. I need to lie down. I have a headache.' Opal left and went upstairs.

'I'm sure he wouldn't mind at all.' Papa's face suffused with red and I feared he was again going to cry. I would not be able to deal with it. 'Thank you, Papa,' I cried, grabbing our coats from the hook on the kitchen door. I took Ruby by the hand and almost dragged her outside.

15

PEARL

Rather than go up the avenue, where there were bound to be people still sightseeing at the ruin, or into the village, where I had no doubt that others would again approach us with well-meant but intrusive sympathy, I decided that Ruby and I should go through the demesne to Drynan Wood. 'We haven't been there for a long time, have we, Ruby?' I assumed a jollity I did not feel. 'I'm sure the bluebells will be there still. And we could pick primroses.'

'Yes – and then we could put some on Roddy's grave and go up the cemet'ry and put some on Willie's too.'

Her sombre expression upset me all over again but I could not let her see that. 'Let's go, then.' We set off through the field at the back of the gate lodge.

To get to the wood by this route, we had to cross the meadow behind the gate lodge, then a small area of bushes and fallow land until we got to the rarely used lich-gate at the entrance to the 'old' stone-walled cemetery, where the inscriptions on its leaning and tumbled tombstones, covered with ivy, brambles and fresh new grass, were now all but illegible. It was only when Ruby was helping me to prise open the gate's rusty bolt that I wondered if, for her sake, coming this way might have been a mistake, but if she made the connection between this cemetery and the one where we had left our Willie that morning, she did not say.

Another field beyond the cemetery to cross, a quick duck under a strand of barbed wire, and we were in the aromatic coolness of the forest. 'Now, isn't this nice?' Again I took my little sister's hand and we set off down one of the paths we knew, which led to our favourite spot on the banks of the Drynan river.

The freshness and peace under the trees was balm to the heart. The place teemed with life, as all kinds of birds busied themselves, whirring and flitting through the branches, building nests or looking after their families. We stopped to watch a red squirrel scamper along a bough and then, quick as a spider, up one of the tree trunks. Safely out of reach, he sat on a stout twig, tail twitching and round eyes gazing at us. 'Isn't he lovely, Ruby?' I looked down at her. If I was going to take charge of the family until Mama was well again, I might as well start now, I thought, and ran my hand through her hair, smoothing her curls at the poll. 'Let's see what else we can find.' We moved off. We heard and saw rooks, of course, and blackbirds, the quick flash of a goldfinch, and we exclaimed simultaneously on spotting the white scut of a rabbit as it vanished into its burrow.

'Look, Pearl!' When we got to the riverbank, it was Ruby who had gone ahead a little and noticed that we were not the only ones who liked this place. Someone had built a fire right in the middle of the glade, where in the summer of the previous year we had lounged with Iris, while Willie had pegged stones and told us how he would become a racing driver.

I could not think about that. Not now. Instead I went over to examine the fire's embers, scattered and broken as though someone had doused them by stamping. This was odd. It would have been easier by far – and safer – to throw a bucket of water on them. But maybe, I decided, the poacher, or whoever had been responsible for it, had not had a vessel with him.

I sighed. The intrusion, the smell of smoke polluting that lovely fresh air, felt like a violation of 'our' place – but, of course, it was not our place at all. In any event, if the whole demesne were to be sold, how long more would we be able to come here?

Again I quashed the thought. 'Do you want to stay here, Ruby, or will we go to a different place?'

She looked around. 'Over there.' She indicated a bank on which there were not only primroses but a profusion of tiny purple violets. 'There's prob'ly bluebells on the other side.'

'You go and pick, so. I'll tidy up here.' Of all human activities, I thought, clearing a forest glade of twigs was probably the most useless. Nevertheless, I felt impelled to do it and bent to gather them up – to find that they were still warm. Whoever had been here must have heard us coming and, fearing the gamekeeper, made a quick getaway.

I glanced over to where Ruby was placing her first pickings in a neat little pile on a big stone. Seeing how careful she was that all the stems were pointing in the same direction, I smiled. It felt like I had not smiled for a month. She was such a dear little thing. 'Don't wander off, Ruby!' I called over my shoulder.

'I won't,' she carolled, as I set about my task in earnest, using the toes of my shoes as well as my hands to move the wood off the black patch it had burned into the forest floor, which, of course, would recover very quickly with the ash as fertiliser.

It took all of five minutes or so to clear the fire debris. It was two steps forward, one step back, because the embers were very brittle and kept breaking into smaller pieces. I did not mind. The chuckling of the water nearby was soothing and the air was sweet. Having finished the work to my satisfaction, I went down to the edge of the river to rinse my hands, then dried them on a tussock of clean grass.

When I straightened up to go back to Ruby, she was not in sight, but I wasn't alarmed. Her little stack of wildflowers was still on the stone. She had gone in search of some more. I called her. There was no reply.

Still not worried – what harm could she come to in five minutes? – I went across to where she had been and climbed the bank, which had formed over the roots of a huge tree that must have fallen hundreds of years previously and offered handy footholds under its soft covering of lichens, moss and scutch, many inches thick.

Ruby, a few primroses in her hand, was on the other side, sitting quietly on the ground. 'What are you doing, Ruby?'

'Sssh!' She put a finger to her lips.

I played along and whispered, 'What's going on?' As quietly as I could, I descended to where she sat. 'Why are we whispering?' I lowered myself to the ground beside her.

'Can't say!' She shook her curly dark head.

'Why not?'

'It's a secret!' But her eyes betrayed her, darting in the direction of a nearby copse.

'What's in there, Ruby? Is it a rabbit?"

She shook her head again.

'A fox?'

'No.'

'A squirrel?'

'Can't say. I promised.'

I frowned. 'Who did you promise?' We were still whispering.

'Told you. It's a secret. He made me promise.'

'Ruby!' I was upset now. Ruby had never told fibs. And although she displayed as much imagination as any seven-year old, she had grown out of the notion that animals could talk. Or that they could make you promise to keep a secret. 'Who is it, Ruby? Who made you promise not to talk? You won't get into trouble – you can tell me. I can keep a secret too.'

She hesitated, but then stubbornly clamped her lips tightly together.

I got up and walked towards the copse but before I could get there—

'It was me.' Thomas Areton stepped out into the open. 'I asked her not to tell anyone she saw me.'

I got such a fright that I was dumbstruck. It was probably as a consequence of the images instantly crowding my mind – the horse, the gun, the menace of the man, the rash bravery of the boy – that just as he had blushed on the staircase – had that been less than a week ago? – I felt my own face redden.

Little Ruby's reaction was far less complicated. 'You're bleeding!' She pointed to Thomas Areton's legs, which were indeed streaked with red. To my eyes, however, the copse from which he had come did not contain any thorn bushes. 'I'm all right.' His voice was hoarse. 'Please don't tell anyone you saw me.' He looked from one to the other of us. 'Please!'

'It's a secret, isn't it?' Ruby smiled at him.

'Yes. A secret. I'm sorry, I can't seem to remember your name?' He smiled back at her. The formality of the language, the fact that he was holding out his (filthy) hand, lent the occasion a surreal veneer: we might have been at Ascot instead of deep in Drynan Wood.

'My name is Ruby Somers,' she chanted, as she had been taught to do from earliest childhood.

'How do you do, Ruby?' Then, after he and Ruby had shaken hands, he turned to me. 'And you're Pearl, aren't you?'

'That's right. We've already met. The day you were looking for your horse?' (I did not think it appropriate to mention the encounter on the back stairs of the Castle.) 'I didn't think you'd remember my name!'

'I remember. Somers never stops talking about his family.' The veneer slipped. 'I'm so sorry for what happened to your brother. I really am.' He offered his hand to me.

It was strong and dry. I had somehow expected it to be clammy. 'Thank you. I know that.' Yet despite my training in good manners, I could not help staring. His fair hair was uncombed and wild, but what really astonished me was that, although his clothes were now in a poor state, streaked with black like those of a chimney sweep, he was still dressed as he had been on the night of the party. The bow-tie was gone, but everything else was the same. One of the sleeves of his tweed jacket was torn; the wool of his knee-length breeches was stained and had been cruelly snagged; his shoes, what one could see of them under the fallen knee-socks, were scuffed and encrusted with soot and mud.

As for the red stripes on his legs, to me they did not look like fresh wounds. 'Have you been here since the party? Have you not gone with your parents?' As soon as I had asked it, I knew it had been an absurd question, because the answer to it was standing right in front of me.

'No.'

Maybe he had got lost somehow in the confusion of the fire, and now thought he had been abandoned – but was it my place to tell him that his papa was in a hotel in Maryborough?

Even as the thought occurred to me, it was obscured by the renewed vision of the interaction between this poor boy and that brutish man in the stable yard. Once again I was tongue-tied and did not know how to proceed. Eventually I blurted, 'What I mean is, not are you still here, but have you been here – in this forest?'

'Not all the time.' Then, to my horror, while I was still trying to organise my thoughts, Thomas Areton burst into tears and raced away from us, climbed over the bank and vanished from view.

To judge by Ruby's face, she was about to break down, too, so I hurried over to her, took her in my arms and held her tightly. 'It's all right, Ruby,' I whispered, caressing her dark curls. As I held her, I suddenly remembered the larceny of the food from our kitchen. Of course. Thomas Areton, probably starving, had taken advantage of our absence – and, in his situation, who could blame him?

After a while, I do not know how long, Ruby became a bit calmer. As she did, I thought I heard Thomas Areton weeping still, but faintly, as though he was muffling the sound. 'Are you a little better now, Ruby?' I squeezed her.

'I'm sad.' She hiccuped. 'I'm sad about Willie. And I'm sad about Roddy. And I'm sad about Thomas too.' Rather than mar it, her pronunciation of his name, 'Thomath', sounded like an endearment.

'Of course you are, darling.' I tried to say the words of comfort as Mama would, but tears were threatening me, too. I would be no good to Ruby, or to anyone, if I broke down. 'I think we should go and see how Thomas is, don't you? You're right to be sorry for him, Ruby, because he's very sad too. He's lost his whole house and I believe he can't find his mama and papa. Can you imagine, Ruby? Shall we go and see him?'

She nodded solemnly.

'And maybe we can help him find his mama?'

She nodded again.

We climbed over the bank. Thomas Areton was sitting by the river facing the water. If he heard us coming, he did not react. His knees were drawn up to his chest, his arms wrapped around them, and he was rocking forwards and backwards. 'Sssh, Ruby.' I put my finger to my lips. 'You stay here for a minute. We don't want to frighten him.'

'All right,' she whispered, and sat on the ground.

As I walked towards him on the forest floor, I deliberately trod hard, allowing twigs to break under my feet so that he would not think I was sneaking up on him. He did not respond to the sound, however, so I had to touch his shoulder. 'Thomas? Are you all right?'

He sprang to his feet and made a peculiar sweeping motion with both hands from his shoulders, as if he were casting off a heavy cloak. 'What do you care, Pearl Somers?'

I was not intimidated because his beloved horse was in my eyes, and I heard his screams in my ears. 'I'm sorry for your loss too, Thomas,' I said quietly. 'I'm sure you must be very cold – and hungry.'

He coloured to the roots of his hair, confirming my suspicions about the raid on our table. 'You should not worry. I've told no one,' I said quickly, so as not to embarrass him further. 'Listen, Thomas, I saw what happened.' I had not planned to tell him this, but now that I had started, I could not seem to stop. 'My sister – not Ruby there, my other sister, Opal – she saw it too. We were there in the stable yard that night.'

He covered his face with his hands. 'I'm sorry.'

'Thomas—'

'I'm sorry. Sorry. Sorry . . .' His voice was barely audible and I did not know whether he was weeping again.

'Please, Thomas, don't.' And then I did what anyone would have done in the circumstances: I put my arms around the poor boy.

There was a split second's pause – during which I was struck with the fear that the dirt on his clothes would rub off on mine, but I was simultaneously astonished: I could feel his heartbeat, thudding like an engine against my own chest – but that sensation, too, was overcome when fiercely, I mean *fiercely*, he threw his arms around me and we hugged tightly for a second or two. At least, it seemed just that long. It might have been longer. It might have been shorter. You see, I had never hugged any boy before, except Willie, and at that moment, he did not count because my insides were melting, dripping into my hands and feet and causing the hair at the nape of my neck to lift.

Then Thomas Areton pulled my face against his and kissed me on the mouth, so that not only my stomach but the world turned upside-down.

After we came apart, we were both stunned. I know I was and, darting a quick glance at him, I could see he was too. One of us had to make some movement for we were standing in front of one another as though paralysed and I had no idea whether Ruby had been watching.

The same thought had obviously struck Thomas Areton because, in unison, we looked towards where she was still, luckily, counting her primroses and other wildflowers; at least, I think she was. I could barely see her because the blood in my palms and temples was pulsing so energetically. Thomas said something to me but I was so overcome with all these unprecedented sensations that I did not understand the words. 'I beg your pardon, Thomas?'

Keeping my eyes on my sister, who was paying assiduous attention to her task, I felt as though my feet had rooted into the floor of the glade, but I did hear him when he said, in a low voice, almost a whisper, 'I'm sorry, Pearl.'

I backed away and, not recognising the high, weird sound of my voice, said, 'That's all right, Thomas.' What I wanted to say, to shout, was 'Please kiss me again. Please. Please kiss my mouth again! Let me kiss yours . . .'

'Will you come back this evening, Pearl?' He followed me.

'The lich-gate at the old cemetery. Nine o'clock.' I had not known I was going to say that. I seemed to be in the control of some unearthly being.

'I have no way of knowing the time.' He took another step towards me.

'About an hour after dark.' I wanted desperately to touch him again but not to tempt Fate. This time, Ruby might take notice. 'I really have to go. Goodbye!' I dared to look fully at him then. When he looked back, everything else – the forest, Ruby, Ruby's flowers, my duty to my family – shrank away to insignificance and nothing now mattered except that he and I would kiss again this evening.

I turned and walked shakily back towards my sister, who was still examining the wildflowers she had gathered.

16

PEARL

I know that what I am going to tell you will sound irregular, improper, perhaps even immoral, but as Ruby and I walked home that afternoon, I could think of nothing but that I had been kissed.

My little brother, my only brother, was not yet cold in his grave. My mama was in a state of collapse. My papa was so worried I feared for his health. The future for our family, what remained of it, was bleak, and we had no idea where we were going to be living in the very near future. Yet, by arrangement, Thomas Areton and I were to meet again that evening at the lich-gate where, in all likelihood, he would kiss me again. Deliciously, it had been his suggestion to meet, mine the venue. At the prospect, my body churned, my lips prickled and my breasts seemed to swell. Sensations all new to me.

I knew I faced problems. In a household where the softest footfall was recognised by the others, I had no idea yet how I would manage to get to the rendezvous at the appointed hour. All I knew was that I would be there. No one and nothing had the power to stop me.

The first hurdle was Ruby.

We had negotiated the cemetery, had come through the lich-gate, where I almost lost my breath as I passed again under that romantic little roof and thought about what would happen to me there later. We were approaching the meadow behind the gate lodge when I took her arm. 'Ruby?'

'Yes?' ('Yeth' – never had her lisp sounded so charmingly innocent, and so dangerous.) She looked up at me from beneath her profusion of dark curls. She was the prettiest of us. Like Elizabeth Bennet in my favourite Jane Austen novel, I believed myself to be the 'second prettiest' of Mama's girls. I do not wish to be critical, but at the age of twelve, Opal was already showing a jut of chin that would in time lend character to her face at the expense of beauty. 'I have something very important to ask you, Ruby.' I took her shoulders and turned her to face me.

'Is it a secret?' Her expression was solemn.

'Yes. But a good secret. Will you promise, cross your heart, that you won't tell anyone? No one at all, not even Opal?'

'I promise.'

'Cross your heart?'

'Cross my heart, Pearl.' With both arms, she held her chest.

'Let's sit down.'

'All right.' Like a sleepy puppy, she dropped to the ground. I followed suit. 'Put down your flowers, Ruby, they'll be safe.' As soon as she obeyed, I took her hands in mine. 'Do you remember what happened back at the river, Ruby?'

'Yes.' She nodded gravely.

'What happened?'

'Thomas came out of the bushes. He was bleeding.'

'Yes. And what else?'

Her little forehead wrinkled. 'Em . . .' She made a pantomime of thinking.

'You remember, don't you?'

She nodded. 'Yes.'

'So tell me what you remember.' I was on tenterhooks. This was torture. Was it possible she had not seen the kiss? But that was a hope that did not last long, for my little sister adopted an expression that I can describe only as cunning. Then: 'You kissed him better?'

'I did.' I did not wait to analyse her expression but took the lifeline she had handed me. 'You know how Mama always kisses us better when we graze our knees?'

'Yes.'

'Well, that's what happened. But we don't want anyone to know, Ruby.'

'Why?'

'Because they mightn't understand that this is what I was doing. His poor legs . . .'

In all innocence, she stared at me. 'But, Pearl, you didn't kiss his legs.'

'No.' I was floundering. 'No, that's not what I meant, really. But – but—' Inspiration struck: 'I didn't want to get my dress dirty by kissing his legs.'

I could see she didn't believe me for a moment. In fact, she might have been stringing me along. Because even at that age, unsophisticated though she might have seemed on the surface, we all knew that Ruby was highly intelligent. She could not spell very well and was frequently slapped in school for this fault, but Mama and Papa had been told that, spelling apart, she was top of her class in every other subject and by far the best at mental arithmetic, faster and more accurate than many of the older girls. There was only one course left to me. 'Please, Ruby,' I begged. 'Please don't tell anyone about that kiss. I'd get into terrible trouble. I've always been good to you, Ruby, have I not? Will you do that for me? Will you keep it as our secret?'

She nodded solemnly. 'Yes, I will, Pearl. I'll keep your secret.'

I tried to divert her from the kiss: 'Oh, Ruby, that poor boy was so cold. And he was very hungry too. And remember I told you he couldn't find his mama?'

Ruby did not answer this. She picked up her flowers, scrambled to her feet and went ahead of me. My relief that the distraction seemed to have worked was tempered with caution, but it was the best I could hope for in the circumstances.

I needed some time to myself to think – also to put off going into our house of mourning for as long as possible. So I told Ruby I needed to visit the privy. 'Remember your promise, Ruby,' I whispered, as we parted at the back door. She shot me a look, but nodded. Then, 'May I have the lend of your necklace, please, Pearl?'

The little minx. She had always coveted the necklace in question, a small gold heart on a fine chain, another birthday present from Uncle Bobby. 'Here you are.' I unclasped it and gave it to her. 'You take care of it now, do you hear me?'

'I will,' she sang, and skipped into the house.

In the gloom of the privy, I closed my eyes and immersed myself in the sense-memory of Thomas Areton's lips, full and soft, but firm too, and questing, pushing to open mine. With one of the hens clucking around my feet, I placed my two fingers across my own lips and parsed that kiss, second by second. By my reckoning it had probably lasted just five seconds, with the last half-second being the most powerful, causing the melting sensation I've described, but a crawling too, across my shoulders, into my scalp and down my chest until it reached my tummy, phenomena that had continued even after he broke away.

I continued with the sequence, relishing each segment of each second. We had faced each other then, both breathless and tongue-tied. He had seemed as shocked as I was. 'I'm sorry, Pearl,' he had said.

And I? I had felt I was gasping for air but also exhilarated. Up to then, boys other than Willie had been strange creatures of rude habits, pushing and shoving and perspiring, insulting girls at will and breaking into high, cracked sniggers at the least witticism. Thomas Areton was different. Underneath the soot and dirt and torn clothes, I saw something extraordinary. I know this will sound fanciful, especially about a boy as sturdy as he, but to me, with that kiss, he became quicksilver.

Then I decided to amend that. The word 'quicksilver' was not evocative enough to describe the flowing, liquid feelings that had filled my normally placid belly.

I closed my eyes and hugged myself as tightly as I could while imagining again the face of my future lover, feature by feature, his skin, his hairline, the little bow of his upper lip. I tried to recall what I had done next in the sequence with him, because I wanted to lock those images for ever in my heart. I seemed to have touched his arm, or maybe his shoulder, because I could certainly re-create the feel of tweed on the tips of my fingers.

One of the young bantams Mama had been rearing squeezed under the door, cocked her head to look me in the eye and made that enquiring sound common to all hens. Erk?

'Yes,' I told her. 'It's true! Thomas Areton and Pearl Somers. Kissing.'

When I went into the house Ruby, with my necklace prominently on view outside her dress, was sitting at the kitchen table eating a sandwich made from the cold cuts left over after the funeral meal. 'Where is everyone?' I asked her.

She shrugged and continued eating.

'I'm going upstairs. Will you be all right on your own for a while?'

'Yes.' She continued to chew, but patted the necklace as though to make sure it was still there. I already regretted the decision to take her with me into Drynan Wood. If she had not been with me, who knows how many kisses Thomas and I might have shared? Each time I thought of him, I was conscious of unusual zithery feelings deep in my bones.

On the other hand, if she had not been with me, would I have found him? Would we have found each other? It was worth a gold necklace.

I really do not know how I got through the next few hours, which, naturally, were subdued and very sad for everyone – and should have been for me. I was in tumult. Of course I was sad, but I was ecstatic too.

Mama joined Papa, my sisters and me for the evening meal although she remained silent and toyed with the food on her plate. I believe none of us ate much. Neither did we talk, except in short, quiet requests for butter, salt or the jug of milk. For my own part, I was afraid to say a word, lest my tone should betray me, and I continued to watch Ruby in case she might inadvertently or other-wise let slip what had happened. The worst moment in that regard came when Opal, who had a sharp eye for what anyone was wearing, spotted the necklace around our little sister's neck. 'Where did you get that?' she demanded.

'Pearl gave me the lend.' Ruby's expression was demure.

'That's not fair.' Opal turned indignantly to me. 'I asked you a whole lot of times if I could wear that, Pearl.'

'Girls, please,' Papa's tone was weary and strained. 'With respect to the day that is in it, could we have our meal in peace?'

'Sorry, Papa.' Opal subsided. There was a silver lining to the exchange: because of that outburst, trivial though it was, I could see she had shed the unusual (for her) I-don't-care-about-anything mood with which she had cloaked herself throughout those terrible days.

Papa was the only one who did justice to the food, and it occurred to me that had Willie, who had always had a healthy appetite, been with us, he would have enjoyed the luxury of so much meat. For a few moments, sorrow overcame my exhilaration, but not for long, and I had to work hard to subdue the little geysers of excitement bubbling in the pit of my stomach. It would have been fatal to let them show through in the air of depression at that table.

111

After a while, however, I found the atmosphere oppressive. 'Papa,' I kept my tone as level as I could, 'if you like, I could go with you to Maryborough to see Lord A.' I glanced at Mama who, eyes downcast at the food on her plate, did not react. 'You will need the company and I'm sure Mama will not feel up to it just yet.'

'That would be nice, Pearl.' Papa's reply was listless. Then he seemed to come to a decision. 'Yes. We can take the hackney from the village. Perhaps tomorrow morning.'

For the rest of the meal we sank again into silence.

As Opal and I cleared away afterwards, I managed to slip a few slices of ham and some bread into Mama's shopping bag beside the dresser. But I found it very difficult to concentrate on what I was doing. I had only a few short hours to work out how I would get out of the house and to the lich-gate without being caught.

The problem might have been acute but it felt luscious.

17

PEARL

As soon as twilight descended on the kitchen and it became too dark to read, Papa announced that, since it had been such a long day, rather than elongating it by lighting the lamps, we should all retire for the night, especially since on the next day, he and I were to have an early start for our journey to Maryborough.

Using the pretext of setting the table for breakfast, then scouring the porridge pot, I let everyone else visit the privy before me. 'And don't worry about the hens, Papa. I will make sure they're secure.'

'Thank you, Pearl. You're a good girl. There's a fox about these nights.'

Opal was the last to go upstairs. Still scrubbing energetically, I told her I was not yet sleepy, and that I planned to read a little longer by the light of the Tilley lamp. It had been my habit to do this from time to time so I knew she would not suspect anything. 'You'll ruin your eyes, you know that?' She yawned. 'You'll be wearing spectacles before you're forty.' (As a matter of fact she was right there: I have been wearing spectacles since the age of twenty-two.)

'Well, that's my business,' I told her airily, too airily, for she looked closely at me. 'Go on, Opal.' Heart thumping, but forcing myself to move slowly, I put the pot down, took the lamp off the dresser and shook it to see how much paraffin it held. 'I'll try not to wake you when I come up.'

She harrumphed, but went off.

So, it had been as simple as that. I sat down to catch my breath. It was still not eight o'clock, and while I could leave now, probably with impunity, I thought it better to read as I had said I would and as everyone knew was my practice.

Opal was a very sound sleeper, but Ruby was inclined to wake and come down to the kitchen. The less time I was absent, the less chance of being caught.

Willie's settle bed remained firmly closed in its corner. 'Sorry, Willie,' I whispered as its emptiness, like a reproach, emanated from its corner. 'I don't mean to show you any lack of respect.' Of all of us, I told myself firmly, before I could go too far down that road, our Willie would have been the first to go on an adventure. 'Help me do just this one thing, Willie,' I added, as I went into the yard to make sure the henhouse was secure.

Back in the kitchen, I lit the Tilley and opened the book I had been reading for many weeks now. The print swam. Although the kitchen was peaceful, with the lamp hissing behind my shoulder and only the occasional creak from the rafters or pop from the dying logs in the range to disturb the quiet, I could not focus. So, still holding the book, I closed my eyes – which made it even more difficult to control the confusion of nervousness and excite-ment, and that prickling feeling on my skin. I was beginning to understand the saying about anticipation being the best part of any event.

The time crawled and I started every time I heard a sound from upstairs, but eventually it was a quarter to nine and time to go.

Willie did look after me, and I was able to whisper a little, 'Thank you,' towards his silent bed before I slipped out of the house.

Our run of good weather had continued, but the night air was surprisingly cold and, with just a flowered shawl over my dress, I shivered. A three-quarters moon, the same moon that at half-size had presided over the tragic night of Willie's death and the Kilnashone fire, had risen again. Tonight, however, it showed not in calm glory, but only now and then between the torn edges of wispy clouds. Its light and presence were of the type described so well by Miss Emily Brontë when she was writing about night-time moors in her novel, *Wuthering Heights*. Perhaps hindsight has lent this hue to my recollections but, luridly enhanced or not, it is how I remember the alternating dark and light as I walked across the sleeping fields towards my assignation.

He was not there.

I had built myself up to such a feverish state of expectancy that to say this was an anticlimax is an understatement. Listening hard,

I stood for a few moments in the lee of the gate's roof, but all I heard, from a distance, was the short, sharp cough of a fox.

Had I closed in the hens?

Yes, I had.

The moon was in one of its covered phases so I could not read my watch. The moment light did come through, I held it up at the best angle to read the dial. It was just a few minutes after nine.

He had no way of knowing the time. I had to give him the benefit of the doubt. With the gate timbers at my back, I settled in to wait, concealing myself as best I could in the shadows. It was so still that I could hear the fast beating of my heart and the shush-shush of blood behind my ears.

This gate was new in relation to the cemetery; it had been erected by the Aretons as a memorial to two of their menfolk, who had been killed at Ypres in 1916 during the Great War; a plaque, fixed to one of the timber uprights, said so. Although the wood was oak, at least I think so, its surface was already pitted, cracked and, despite the good weather we had had for more than a week, slimy in parts as a result of the constant Irish rain. I worried about staining my clothes.

I checked my watch again on the moon's next outing. It was seven minutes past. Still plenty of time. He might have fallen asleep.

At twenty past, I thought I heard movement in the cemetery and peered through the opening above the gate, forcing myself to stay as motionless as a stone for fear it was not Thomas but someone, or some people, with more sinister intent. Yes. There it was again, that sound. Someone was definitely there. I strained my eyes until the muscles behind them hurt, and when the moon came out again, two small glowing discs appeared near one of the tombstones.

Low. Too low. A rat. Or a cat. Even a vole or a hedgehog.

At half past nine I knew for sure he was not coming. I persisted, however. Just ten more minutes . . .

At a quarter to ten I had to face the truth. I did not know which I felt more: disappointment or humiliation.

But . . .

There was probably some good reason for his failure to come. Although his absence felt like a hole in my chest, I knew, knew, *knew* that Thomas Areton had been sincere in wanting to see me again.

I took the bread and meat from Mama's shopping bag and placed them carefully on the cross-timbers under the roof, letting a small corner of the bread show, so he would see it if he looked up.

If crows or rats got there before him they were welcome to it, but I did hope he would find it before they did.

As an afterthought, I took off the shawl, folded it as tightly as I could and wedged it into the corner at the base of the roof, opposite the food. It was still only early April. It would be cold during the night.

18

PEARL

I must admit that, for many reasons, I find the next part of my story difficult to relate. With my little brother dead, you will probably see it as controversial that for me, this short period around the party, Willie's death and my encounters with Thomas Areton represents simultaneously the happiest and saddest times of my life. In my mind, I keep intact every sequence and almost every word of those weeks, not for my writing, as I have explained, but for recollection and contemplation. I am aware, by the way, that many of the scenes and episodes in my stories have probably been informed, even triggered, by what happened to me during that short period when I was young.

I am also aware that my having placed these happenings in aspic, as it were, might be regarded as neurosis, to be compared (some-what!) to that of Dickens's poor Miss Havisham, eternally mired in the memory of having been jilted. I had not been jilted, and I am not stuck in my experiences. Nor, I hope, do I give the impression of being bitter or ruined. I do indulge these memories. I choose to do so because Thomas Areton was my choice freely made. We knew one another, in that sense, for just a couple of days, but Thomas Areton was, and is, the love of my life.

Why did I not 'grow out of it'? I did not. It is as simple as that, and if it means I am neurotic, or to be pitied by others — should they know, suspect, or guess that I entertain this secret — so be it. I do not pity myself. I have a good life. I am as happy as most people. My regret, however, is that, had I Thomas by my side, my life would be complete. Whose is?

On the morning after his non-appearance at the lich-gate, Opal woke as I was sliding out of the bed at first light, around a quarter past six. I had managed to get back into the house the previous evening without detection but had slept hardly at all.

'Where are you going?' Her voice was thick with sleep. 'What time is it?'

'It's early. Go back to sleep, Opal.'

'Well, don't bite my head off.' Huffily, she turned her back to me, pulling the blankets up around her ears.

'Sorry. I didn't mean to be sharp. It's just that I've been awake for ages. I'm going out for a walk.'

'What do I care? Bye-bye!'

I waited for her to say something more, but when she gave a tiny snore, I pulled on the clothes I had worn the previous day and, in the absence of my shawl, threw an old coat, one we used as an extra blanket, over my dress and crept out of the room.

Outside, it was that short, hushed period between the end of night and the start of dawn when the sky is light but not bright. That morning, the land was paler: the clouds that had previously persecuted the three-quarters moon, now fading and pocked like old cheese, were nowhere to be seen. There had been a hoar frost during the hours of darkness, so heavy that its crystals, hosts of tiny icicle strings, hung from tree branches and the eaves of our house. They had wrapped themselves in jagged skeins around railings and the Castle's gates, while webs of them, layered like gauze, were draped across the vegetation so that the grass on both sides of the avenue stretched towards the ruin like fields of silvery snow. Under its frigid sheet, the new tarmacadam on the avenue shimmered.

In the years we had lived here, this was a phenomenon I had never seen before – at least, not on this scale – but Papa, who was wise in the ways of weather, had mentioned it from time to time because he was accustomed to being up and about early if he had to go to Dublin or meet a train. It had, he had said, something to do with the freezing of a heavy dew.

My breath hung like mist and my shoes left imprints as I crunched through the frozen grass of the meadow yet, oddly, I did not feel cold. I was trying to convince myself that the reason for going again to the lich-gate was only to retrieve the food for fear of an infestation of vermin. It was a poor excuse, and the nearer I got to the gate, the more self-delusory it seemed and the more I felt again that jangling, zithery feeling in the pit of my stomach.

118

The bread and ham were gone, no debris or shreds on the ground under the gate or near it — which meant that, unless some adroit animal with a large mouth had been able to climb up the slippery wooden supports, or some huge bird had materialised in the middle of the night, and neither option was likely, the food had been taken by human hands.

I find it difficult to describe how mixed my feelings became. At least Thomas Areton — and I was sure it had been he — had come to the rendezvous. But if that was the case, why had he not come at the appointed time?

I did not know what to do next. The cemetery was on a low hill, and from where I was standing, I could survey the surrounding landscape. To the east, where the white fields met the sky, there was a faint but distinct smudge of pinkish light, as thin as a pencil line. The sun would rise within half an hour. I had to get back to the house.

To the west, behind me, the bulk of Drynan Wood made a hole in the lightening sky. The likelihood was that he was there, and before I knew I had made the decision, I had set out at a run towards the trees.

Just inside the first stand, I stopped to listen for any extraneous sounds, but all I could hear, besides my own harsh breathing, were a few tentative chirps from birds. They sounded as though they had not yet woken sufficiently to begin the so-called 'dawn chorus'. The hoar had not infiltrated the forest, and although it was distinctly warmer under the budding canopy, after the surreal lustre of the world outside the place felt shadowy, even menacing; who knew what went on here at night?

However, I had little time to waste in conjecture and, treading as lightly as I could, made for the glade beside the river. If he was anywhere in here, that is where he would be.

I saw him immediately. Or, rather, I spotted the distinctive multicoloured flowers that Mama had embroidered on my shawl. Thomas Areton had tucked himself into a little hollow within the over-ground roots of the willow tree and, partially blanketed in that shawl, was sound asleep.

At least, I thought he was asleep — what if he was dead, like Willie?

I fixed my gaze on one of the shawl's red poppies and, holding my breath, made a huge effort to stay still enough to see if his chest was moving. It did not seem to be.

Could he have frozen to death? I did not find it all that cold, but then I was wearing a heavy coat and I had not been out here in the depths of night. I rushed over and crouched beside him. 'Thomas?'

I was not prepared for what happened. He sprang into an upright position, banging his head on an overhead branch, then half crouched, half cowered and, eyes wide and frightened, made a guttural sound I did not understand.

I was as scared now as he. 'Please don't be afraid.' I stood up and took a few steps backwards. 'I – I just came to see if you were all right. You didn't come last night . . .'

He straightened, staring at me as though I was speaking in a foreign language, and I saw that, physical moves to the contrary, he was not fully awake. 'Thomas?' I repeated gently. 'It's me. Pearl.'

He did not immediately reply, but looked around and over my head, and I guessed he was checking to see if anyone was with me. 'I'm on my own,' I said quietly.

'Pearl?' he repeated, and then I saw him come fully awake. 'Pearl – I'm very, very sorry about last night. I—' He put his hands to his face. 'I'm – I don't know what to tell you. Just let me say . . .' he dropped his hands, picked up the shawl from where, in his leap, it had fallen '. . . I don't know how to thank you for this.' He held it out to me. 'It was very cold last night. And, of course, thank you, too, for the food.'

'I'll bring you more, Thomas. We have plenty left over—'

'It was me—'

'I know. Don't worry about it. Nobody noticed.'

Tongue-tied, we stood looking at each other. The chirping around us was getting busier as the glade, open to the sky, stepped into its morning dress. I held his gaze for as long as I could – I noticed how pale he was – but it was so intense I had to give in. When I lowered my eyes, I noticed again the reddish streaks on his bare legs. 'What happened to your legs, Thomas?' I had spoken without thinking, but when I looked up at him, I saw that tell-tale blush.

'Nothing,' he mumbled – and then, of course, I knew exactly what had happened.

120

'It's all right.' I rushed in to save him further embarrassment. 'It's none of my business, really.'

'I hate him!' The words exploded into the quiet, causing a fluttering high above our heads in the crown of the willow, which was mostly bare but with a fuzz of new leaves on its stems. Reflexively, we glanced up as a bird swooped low over the water and vanished. Again, I was confounded. How was I to react? 'I'm sure you don't hate your father, Thomas.'

'I do,' he said calmly, but the hands by his sides were balled. 'I truly wish he were dead.'

I was scandalised. 'Thomas!'

'Let's change the subject. Again, I'm terribly sorry about last night. I had to hide. I was afraid to come out.'

'But why? Why did you have to hide?'

'In case he was looking for me. There was activity here last night and the night before. It might have been him.'

'Here?'

'Not here exactly. Among the trees, although they may have come out here, of course.' He smiled faintly. 'I was actually in a big tree further into the forest.' He made a gesture encompassing almost the entire wood. 'High up. I came down only when I was sure everything was quiet.'

'But suppose it wasn't your family? Poachers? Diehards?'

'Whoever they were, I felt it safer not to show my face. It was arson, you know.'

'What was arson?' I was bewildered by the change of subject.

'After – after what you saw, Father left the yard. So did the yard man, who actually tried to comfort me. That good man even asked me to come home with him to his house if I wanted to.'

His voice shook again and he turned slightly away so I could not see his whole face. 'Do you really want to hear this? You probably want to be somewhere else.' He was suddenly shy.

I sat on 'our' stump. 'Please, Thomas. Of course I want to hear it.'

He hesitated, then sat beside me but kept his body as separate from mine as was possible, given the dimensions of the seat, and looked at his hands. 'The party was over, of course. Even if it wasn't, I had no place back in that house. So I sat, lay really, behind Doubloon. I put an arm around his poor back. His head was splattered, but from where I lay, I couldn't see that. His back was undamaged. His

121

coat was still warm – I told him I was sorry. I told him I'd done my best and apologised for not being able to stand up for him. I know he would have understood. I loved Doubloon. I think he knew that . . .' His voice broke.

I felt so sad for him – and for the horse – that I could hardly bear it. But I knew I shouldn't say or do anything: he was lost in what he was telling me.

'I know it sounds impossible in circumstances like these,' he had regained his composure, 'but I think I fell asleep.'

'I don't think it's impossible at all, Thomas—'

He went straight on as though he hadn't heard me. 'I don't know for how long I was asleep, more than half an hour, less than an hour, maybe, when the sound of the lorry and the motorcycles coming up the avenue woke me. I ran out into the archway to see what was happening. They had stopped just short of the gravel. They were wearing scarves over their mouths. I saw them jump off the bed of the lorry and unload the barrel of kerosene and two bicycles. I knew exactly what they were going to do with the kerosene but not the bicycles. Not yet. I had no way to warn anyone,' he spread his hands in a gesture of helplessness, 'I knew that. There were ten of them altogether. Four came towards the yard. As soon as I saw that I ran to the far side and through the wicket gate into the paddock. I hid behind the wall but I could see in through the gate and I knew they couldn't see me because all the light was in the yard and it was dark where I was.

'Two of them opened all the stalls and took the rest of the horses. They knew what they were doing. They were used to horses. They had no problem putting on the head collars.' He was staring straight ahead now, continuing to relive the episode. He had begun slightly to tremble. 'They took the horses out through the archway. Then the other two who had stayed behind drenched the stalls from the cans, scattered hay about the cobbles and drenched it too. Then I saw them remove two of the torches from their stands and back out towards the archway. Just before they got there, they flung those torches hard. One landed directly on Doubloon. He was in flames within seconds. His beautiful tail and mane all on fire, his beautiful coat that I had brushed only that day—' He stopped.

'How did you escape?' I hardly dared ask.

'I was in the paddock – remember? I knew my way around the

stables and everywhere to do with the horses. Those stables were my real home, the only place I felt comfortable. The horses were my only friends.' Again he stopped.

'Thomas, Thomas!' I flung my arms around him and he buried his head in my shoulder. After a few seconds, however, he jumped up, away, and turned his back on me. 'Sorry,' he muttered. 'I don't want you to see me like a cry-baby.'

'Oh, Thomas, I don't think you're a cry-baby. Honestly. Please go on.' I stood up and followed him.

He still had his back to me. 'There's one thing certain. I'm not going back to that school – I won't go.' He took a long, audible breath.

'But how long are you going to stay out here? How are you going to survive? What will you eat? And if tonight is anything like last night, it was so cold—'

'I know how to fish.' He dashed his hands against his face, then turned to face me. 'And, as you have already found out, I know how to light a fire. When I was younger, my school took us scouting. We camped. Prep school wasn't so bad . . .' He trailed off. Then he muttered, 'I thought you would be angry that I didn't come last night, Pearl. I was so looking forward . . .' He sounded shy again now and his face was streaked with dirt and tears.

'Me too.' It was my turn to blush. I smiled at him and then, in case he thought I was forward, lapsed into silence. I could not sustain this for long, though. 'If it wasn't them looking for you last night, Thomas, where's your – where's your family now, do you think?' It had been on the tip of my tongue to say, 'your papa and mama', but caught myself.

'I truly don't care.'

Because of our proximity and the increasing light, I noticed that his eyes were grey and, as though to reflect his blond lashes, the iris of the left contained a large fleck of yellow – or gold. 'That's awful, Thomas.' I really meant it. I could not have imagined hating anyone in my family so much that I did not care about his or her whereabouts and would prefer to live like a savage in a forest.

His hatred of his father notwithstanding, I thought then it was my duty to tell him about his papa being in Maryborough and I was just about to say it when he cut across the intention, kicking at a small tuft of grass. 'I know I've said it already, Pearl, but I hope you do know how sorry I am about your brother. We got on well. He was – he would have been a good horseman.' He darted a glance at me. 'So please accept the condolences of my family.'

'Thank you.'

He shot me another glance, one that landed like an arrow because I knew what it meant. At least, my body did. 'Are you in a rush, Pearl?'

I thought of Papa and Mama, of Opal and Ruby. Of Willie in his grave. I thought of the promise I had made to Papa to go into Maryborough with him to talk to this boy's father. I tried, I promise, to take everything into account. 'No,' I said. 'No rush. We're still on Easter holidays from school.'

'Shall we sit down again?' He indicated the willow stump we had recently vacated as though it were an elegantly upholstered sofa. He had manners to burn, as Mama might have said.

Heart pounding, I sat beside him. There was barely space enough for the two of us and this time he was not holding himself apart. Our shoulders were touching, and through the heavy wool of the coat I wore (I know this is far-fetched), I really thought I could feel the warmth of his skin. We were staring in opposite directions, he towards the river, and I towards the grassy bank, behind which, on the day before, Ruby had found him. He was shivering, so noticeably it was definitely not my imagination. I wanted to offer him my coat, but could not find a way to break the silence between us.

I cannot, of course, speak for him, but the longer the time ticked by, the more nervous (agitated? excited?) I became – my feelings were mixed, as if in a boiling pot, and I cannot find a precise word. It was that new and nameless disturbance, deep in my tummy. A sort of swelling, is the best way I can describe it.

The seconds lengthened. The sun had risen, illuminating the tops of the trees. The birds were tuning up. I was no expert but individually I could pick out the more common ones – blackbirds, thrushes, robins, doves, sparrows. There was a growing urgency about the situation because it would not be long before the people in my household were stirring. I hoped, I prayed to God, that Opal would be among them and would tell Papa that I had gone for a walk . . . That would probably be acceptable for a while anyhow . . .

'Pearl?'

He turned to me, and I saw that one of the nerves in his cheek was jumping. 'Yes?'

'May I—'

Time stopped. The world stopped. Nothing existed except the face of the boy, the feeling in my stomach and the banging of my heart. 'Yes.'

Gently, very gently, as though compensating for the comparative violence of yesterday's kiss, he touched my lips with his own and kept them there while his hands came under my coat to hold me under my arms, steadying me. We were at an awkward angle to one another, face to face but bodies side by side, and I had to move slightly in order to balance. In the process, his hands shifted a little until they were, intentionally or otherwise, holding my breasts.

As this second kiss of ours became deeper, I coasted on waves of sensation and answered his every move with one of my own until, by unspoken consent, we came off the willow stump to lie together on the floor of the forest.

'Please, Pearl, may I see?'

Before I could answer, which would have been in the affirmative, he had carefully opened the buttons on my bodice – luckily there were only three – and was nuzzling my chest. His lips moved to suck and bite softly on my breasts in a way that at first alarmed me, then thrilled me so deeply that I wanted him never to stop. I held his head and moved a little, first to one side and then to the other to accommodate his switch from the first breast to the second, then back again.

Reason prevailed, however, as I realised that I was, that we were, committing a grave sin. My knowledge of the precise boundaries when it came to physical contact between boys and girls was hazy to non-existent. All I knew for sure was that we girls had been warned constantly against it: that if we 'gave in' to boys, who were, it was implied, rampaging beasts, we were cheapening ourselves and disgracing our families. That way, hell beckoned.

And yet it felt so sweet. How could something like this, which was not only thrilling but felt natural, be a sin? Once the doubt was sown, however, it set roots. 'We have to stop, Thomas,' I said, holding my body rigid, when it wanted to writhe.

Instantly, he ceased. 'Whatever you say, Pearl. I wouldn't dream—'

'I want to. I love you, Thomas.' I had not known I was going to say that. I was shocked; I think we both were.

We sat up.

'And I think I love you too, Pearl.' He was the first to recover. 'No,' he said then, in a tone bordering on wonderment. 'There's no "think" about it. I do love you. You probably don't know this but every time I saw you around the house, or at the gates, or anywhere, usually at a distance, I wanted to talk to you, but I didn't know how to start. I used to think about you when I was at school. Once,' he hung his head, 'I found a little handkerchief snagged on the hedge near your house. I didn't know it was yours but I took it. It had a "P" embroidered on it, or it might have been originally an "R" because the stitching was all snagged. I chose to think it was a "P". I still have it.' He sounded almost shamed. 'I kept it high on a shelf in one of the stables, tucked into a crack in the wood. I don't know if it survived the fire – I shouldn't be telling you this, should I?'

'Oh, Thomas! I didn't know!' Mama embroidered our initials on all our handkerchiefs and this one must have been Ruby's because I had not lost any of mine. I did not tell him that.

'How could you know?' He kissed me again but differently, more soberly and quietly this time, and then, as carefully as he had unfastened them, he did up my buttons.

We talked quietly and seriously as to what would happen next. 'I have to stay hidden, at least for a while, because if I'm sent back to school in England I will run away and be caught again. I – I don't know how to say this but I want you to know the truth.' He was looking at the ground. His voice was low and intense. 'Each time I run home, I'm thrashed by my father for not being manly, and when I'm sent back again I'm immediately thrashed a second time. Pearl, if I have to go back to that school, I will kill myself. I mean that, don't think I don't.'

The vision was so horrifying that I hugged him as hard as I could. 'Don't say that, Thomas, please. You don't mean it.'

'I do. I really do!' he cried, and this time I was able to kiss him and kiss him and kiss him, and he kissed me back until we could barely breathe and had to come apart.

He stroked the back of my hand as though my skin was precious silk. 'Pearl. That's a beautiful name. Pearl. A beautiful name for a beautiful girl.'

'I'm not – I'm too tall, and my hair is all over the place.'

126

'You're beautiful and you're certainly not too tall for me.' We kissed again. Gently.

'So, you see,' he said then, when again we had stopped, 'I have to stay here until the hue and cry dies down and I can work out what to do. I have some money – my grandmother gave me two hundred pounds on the night of the party and I have all of it still here in my pocket. That should be of some use and perhaps you will help me spend it.' He looked disparagingly at his clothes. 'I certainly need a new outfit!' Then he took my face in his hands. 'Will you help me, Pearl? Will you be able to come and see me? Will it be too difficult for you? I don't mean because of the practical things. I mean would you be going against your family because of what happened to your brother?'

'Nobody blames you, Thomas – and of course I'll see you!' I cried. 'I'll think of some way – we'll think of something together. I'll bring you food and blankets in the meantime – everyone in my house is distracted and won't be paying attention. I'll look after you. We'll have each other! We'll be Robin Hood and Maid Marian . . .' But there was now some heat in the sun, and although its light had not yet reached the surface of the river, it had crept halfway down the trunks of the trees opposite. 'I really have to go.' Reluctantly I scrambled to my feet and reached down to pull him up alongside me. I put my arms around him again. 'Don't worry, Thomas,' I whispered in his ear. 'Please don't worry.' I stood back. 'I'll see you again very, very soon,' I added. 'This can be our place – this willow tree, right? I'll bring you food this evening or tonight. We'll meet here.'

'I don't want you to get into trouble, Pearl. And, as I said, there could be a lot of bad things going on at night in this wood. So don't come tonight. There may even still be some food in the larders at the Castle. I can sneak in after dark. I know my way around up there, even if there are sentries. If you can get away later today, when it's still daylight, I'll be here. Otherwise, can we meet each other early tomorrow morning like we did today?'

I gave him a final quick kiss and ran.

Like we did today – the phrase oompahed in my head until I was within sight of the house. There was smoke coming from the chimney: my household had woken. I inserted my foot into a rabbit hole deliberately to turn my ankle, just a little, so I could limp through the door and have a legitimate excuse for my tardiness and the state of my clothes. It hurt, but the pain was of no consequence when set against the exhilaration I felt now that I was in the throes of a love affair every bit as dramatic and star-crossed as that of Catherine Earnshaw and her Heathcliff.

Once in the house, I again had to make a superhuman effort to keep those feelings, wholly inappropriate in the context of my family's grief, from showing. To my surprise, Mama, who was pale and listless but, thank God, a little more like herself, was preparing breakfast when I came through the door wearing an expression as neutral as I could manage. She left what she was doing and insisted on strapping up the injured ankle, but I noticed as she wound the bandage that her hands shook, a phenomenon I had never seen before. 'Will you still be able to go to Maryborough with Papa, do you think, Pearl?'

My heart went out to her. 'Of course I will, Mama. Would you like to come with us?'

'No, dear.' She fixed the bandage in place with a large safety-pin. 'Papa can take care of that business and you will be a great help to him. I'll get Opal to bring down your good dress so you don't have to go upstairs on that ankle.' With what had just happened between me and Thomas, I felt important and very grown-up: Mama and I were discussing family affairs on an equal footing.

I was uneasy, though, about the forthcoming challenge. How was I going to face that brute? I hoped now that my role would be simply to provide moral support for Papa during the journey and if we had to wait. He would no doubt go alone to meet the man. It was not customary for fifteen-year-old girls to be party to such business.

While I was eating my porridge a few minutes later, I noticed that Ruby was staring across the table at me. 'Is something wrong, Ruby?'

'No. Was it nice out there in the forest?'

The little maggot, I thought. 'It was cold,' I said quickly, 'and dark. So I didn't stay long in there. Instead,' I stared her down, 'I walked up Turlough Hill. That was much nicer, especially when the sun started to shine. Anyway, I turned my ankle' – I showed her the bandage – 'and so I had to turn back.'

Demurely, she continued eating.

At the first opportunity, having helped with washing the ware, I made for the outdoor privy to bask untrammelled in the blissful memories of what Thomas Areton and I had done with each other until I had to change my clothes and adopt a suitable mien for the journey to Maryborough with Papa.

Looking back, it was all so youthfully overblown, impractical and, inevitably, doomed. It was April 1923 and we were fifteen years old, but for those moments in the forest on that morning of sunshine and hoar frost, I had been ecstatically happy.

I will also hope to my deathbed that, in spite of his woes and the predicament in which he found himself, for that one day at least Thomas Areton, wherever he is now, was happy too, especially with expectations, similar to mine, of more such meetings to come.

19

PEARL

I looked at my wristwatch. It was half past nine. Last Saturday morning at this time, exactly one week ago, my sisters, Willie and I were reporting for work at Kilnashone Castle. Now all was chaos. Willie was dead, the Castle was in ruins, Thomas Areton was in hiding and, as a result of my thoughts and deeds earlier that morning, I was far from being a virtuous daughter as I sat beside Papa on a horsehair sofa in the lobby of a Maryborough hotel while we waited to learn what might lie ahead for our family. In addition, and overwhelmingly, I was frantic to know what would become of the relationship between Thomas and myself.

For the moment, however, I had to concentrate on my father. 'What do you think is going to happen to us, Papa?'

'To tell you the truth, Pearl, I don't know. I think the best we can hope for is that his lordship will find another job for me with one of his friends.' Impeccably turned out in his chauffeur's uniform, my father was fidgeting with the chain of his pocket watch. It was one of his most prized possessions: it had been given to him by Lord A when the latter had inherited his own father's timepiece and had no further use for it.

'But there is no one else in Kilnashone who would require a chauffeur—'

'Please be quiet, Pearl. We will have to take what we get. Lord A has friends all over this country, I believe.' Then, realising he had snapped at me, he added, in a softer tone: 'How's the ankle? Not too sore, I hope?'

'No, Papa. It's grand.' This was only partially true. I might have been careful not to twist it too painfully, but in spite of Mama's strapping, it throbbed now. 'You're certain we'll have to move, Papa?'

I had feared this in any case, but Recent Events, as I had labelled my encounters with Thomas, had made this prospect intolerable.

'We will.' Papa tucked the watch chain neatly inside his jacket. 'We have no entitlement to stay at Kilnashone Castle now, and it doesn't matter where we move to, whether it's in the parish, up or down the country, or even to England.' He glanced sideways at me and I saw that this was what he hoped might happen. Given what I now knew about the choleric, vicious man we were about to meet, I doubted very much that he would grant Papa's wish – and hated him all the more.

I knew something awful was going to happen one way or the other. My lightly offered remark to Thomas about Robin Hood and Maid Marian had been made in the heat of the moment, but I had to face the fact that neither my lover's current living arrangements nor our own could be sustained. Yet the notion that he and I could be separated by geographical distance was too hard to contemplate.

Save for ourselves and the receptionist, who was busy writing in her ledgers, the lobby of the hotel was deserted, although a few people had passed through into the breakfast room, which was just off it and from which we could hear the discreet clink of crockery. The hall was clean and tidy: the newspapers on the mahogany table in front of us had been folded into a fan-shape; the glass on the hunting prints and the brick-coloured quarry tiles on the floor shone in the sunlight streaming through the fanlight above the entrance doors.

'When do you think he will come, Papa?' The delay irked me.

'Patience is a virtue, Pearl. His lordship has a lot of very important affairs to attend to now.' I heeded the warning tone and asked no more questions.

Ten minutes later, the man himself, accompanied by another, who was rather small, walked towards us with a hand outstretched. He was wearing a sombre expression of concern. Right now I saw no trace of the choleric, vicious man I knew him to be. That he could present himself so deceptively was intolerable and I had to try very hard not to let my indignation show as I stood up along-side Papa. 'Somers!' Lord A exclaimed, as if he were surprised to see us, although this had been an arranged meeting. He pumped Papa's hand. 'I'm terribly sorry about what happened to your boy.

Condolences.' Then, with a flick of his hand, he indicated the other man, who was carrying an attaché case. 'This chap I think you know.'

'Yes, my Lord.' Papa nodded towards the man. 'And I don't know if you've met Pearl, My Lord? She's my eldest.'

Areton gave me the barest of glances. 'Good morning.' Then: 'Shall we? The tea here is not too bad. I have a corner table. We won't be disturbed.' Beckoning his companion, he walked past us towards the breakfast room, rudely leaving Papa and me to follow. 'Should I not wait out here, Papa?' I had lost my courage and, in any event, did not think I could successfully hide my aversion. 'Who's that small man?

'He's a solicitor. From Dublin. I've met him once or twice.' Although he was whispering, he sounded anxious. 'You come with me, Pearl.'

As we arrived into the big, panelled room, the waiter, in black suit, spotless white collar and bearing a very large silver teapot, was rushing to remove a 'Reserved' sign from a table in the far corner beside a window. He pulled out one of the chairs and waited expectantly as Lord A seated himself. They conversed for a moment while the rest of us sat down, Papa and I on one side, the solicitor beside Lord A. Then the waiter gave a small bow. 'Thank you, my Lord, I understand. I'll tell them in the kitchen, and when you're ready, all you have to do is let me know. In the meantime, it's tea for four. I'll get you a fresh pot.'

'Thank you.' Lord A dismissed him with a wave, and as we settled ourselves: 'I presume that, unlike us, you've already eaten, Somers, but perhaps you would like some tea?'

'Thank you, my Lord, you are too kind. Yes, we have eaten. A cup of tea will do nicely, thank you.'

My father's obsequiousness grated. I had never before seen it at such close quarters.

'Well, there's no point in beating around the bush, Somers.' Areton held out his hand to the solicitor, who took a file out of his attaché case and gave it to him. 'We might as well get down to business while we're waiting for our tea.' He opened the file. 'As we discussed.' He nodded at the other man.

'Mr Somers – James, if I may call you that since we are already acquainted?' The solicitor had quite a deep voice for such a small man.

132

'Of course.' Papa nodded.

I could see the veins standing out on his forehead.

'I am sure you would accept, James, that in this tragic and unprecedented situation, everything has changed, and must change, in connection with Kilnashone Castle. Obviously, you will already have guessed that this has to – unfortunately – include your employment and the grace-and-favour residence enjoyed by yourself and your family, for which you pay a peppercorn rent of one shilling a year.'

'I understand.' Papa's voice shook now. Under the table, I clenched my fists to keep myself from crying. It was as we had feared. The road for us.

After a while, as the solicitor droned on, I noticed that, although the file was open on the table in front of him, Lord Areton was not reading it but had lowered his head as though listening to a sermon in church. The solicitor was his parrot. Desolation turned into rage. I wanted to claw at his face. How dare he humiliate my father to the extent that Papa, a truly honourable man, felt he had to grovel in front of a fiend like him? The worst aspect from my point of view was that I felt so helpless. Who would rate the opinions of a fifteen-year-old girl?

And yet I had to do something. 'Excuse me, sir?'

The solicitor stopped and all three men, astonished, turned to me.

'Pearl!' Papa was scandalised. 'You mustn't interrupt.'

'I'm sorry, Papa.' I had no wish to add to his troubles, but I was so angry I felt we had little to lose. 'This affects me, too, and all our family.'

Papa's face had turned bright red. 'I'm sorry about this, my Lord,' he said across the table. 'I don't know what's got into her.'

I ignored him. 'Lord Areton, may I speak directly to you?' Eye to eye, I gazed at him. He raised an eyebrow, which I took for assent. 'We have lost our son and brother,' I rushed on, 'and what I am hearing is that my father will now lose his employment and our family will lose our home.'

'Pearl!' Again Papa tried to stop me.

'Let her, Somers.' Lazily, Areton raised a hand.

But something awful happened then. I had not planned this and, having got that far, I could not think of what next to say. I could hardly, in front of Papa and this other man, accuse the beast of his crimes against his son.

'Go on,' he said, cocking his head to one side as though amused.

This was unconscionable. This was life and death for us and here he was with a smirk on his face. 'I am simply telling you the truth, Lord Areton,' I cried, with considerable passion. 'You have many houses and many staff. You are rich – you have land and farms and motor-cars and can have no idea how people like us live. We are a family who have been loyal to the death, to the death, Lord Areton' – my indignation boiled over – 'and faithful to you. You could not have – you could not have any complaints about us.'

My breath seemed to catch in my chest until I was almost panting, but I found the strength to continue. 'My brother died, my – eleven-year-old – brother – died – last Saturday, just a week ago, in your stables, and you did not even send us a letter and it is not our fault that your house burned down—' My face was flaming and I could feel the tears starting. What was far worse, those last words had sounded childish and petulant.

Deflated, I stared at the starched white napkin in front of me and memory flashed: all those napkins, dozens and dozens of them, over which Opal and I had laboured one week ago in the laundry of Kilnashone Castle.

We were the servant class. I had to get used to that.

All three men were staring at me. 'We do not deserve to be thrown out on the side of the road, sir,' I finished lamely. 'We are not disposable.'

The silence at the table lengthened, and I could feel the gaze of others on me, not only the three at the table. I did not dare raise my eyes to look at Papa. I had probably ruined whatever chance he had of further employment and, the most dreadful trans-gression of all, I had let down our family in front of Lord Areton and had shamed us in public.

To compound my chagrin, our master now applauded my speech with two lazy handclaps. 'Astonishing. She has spirit, Somers. I grant you that.' Then: 'So, miss, what in your opinion should happen next?'

Scarlet now, I shook my head.

'I am very sorry, my Lord.' I had never heard Papa's voice sound so tight. 'I shall speak to her later.'

'You do that, Somers.' Areton motioned to the solicitor to continue while smiling (not pleasantly) at me. 'It might be worth mentioning at this point,' he glanced across at the lawyer, 'that we have a proposal to make, and –' he stared hard at me, 'it might also be of interest to you, Miss, to know that you can thank my wife for it. Perhaps you should listen closely, young lady, before you treat us to another harangue. Would you agree with that?'

That was enough to rekindle my anger. I glared at him but Papa intervened: 'Answer his Lordship, Pearl!' He was very close to shouting.

'I will, my Lord,' I said flatly.

'You will what, Pearl?'

'I will listen.' Then, from somewhere, I found the strength to say, right into his face, 'I meant what I said. Papa has been a good and faithful servant, as Our Lord commanded. And it is not only him. Our whole family have been loyal too.'

There might have been yet another embarrassing silence around the table had the waiter not bustled up to us with the teapot. 'Fresh, strong and hot, my Lord, just as you like it.' With a flourish, he poured tea into all four cups. 'Will there be anything else for the moment, my Lord?'

'No.' Areton dismissed him.

'Shall I continue, Horatio?' enquired the solicitor, whose face was as smooth as new butter under hair so heavily pomaded it glistened and held together like liquorice. I was disliking him more by the minute, for no particular reason except my own bad temper and his connection to my lover's torturer – whose name now turned out to be Horatio. In our family, this had never been mentioned in my hearing; this was, should be, a hero's name. Our teacher had taught us to recite the lines:

> Then out spoke brave Horatius,
> The Captain of the Gate:
> 'To every man upon this earth
> Death cometh soon or late;
> And how can man die better
> Than facing fearful odds,
> For the ashes of his fathers,
> And the temples of his gods?'

Exactly! I thought. I would die for Thomas Areton. I would defend him to the death. Horatio, indeed. I glared anew at Thomas's father but unfortunately he did not notice because he was adding milk to the cup in front of him.

'Perhaps I should wait until we have had our tea.' The solicitor waggled the little pink fingers on his upraised little pink hand.

'No. Go ahead.' Lord A reached for the sugar basin and, fastidiously, used the tongs to select two lumps.

The solicitor cleared his throat. 'As I was saying, James, although we condole with you in your loss, we accept no liability whatsoever for the unfortunate death of your son, who entered the stable yard uninvited that night and, in fact, was clearly trespassing.

'However,' he continued, indicating the document in front of Lord A, 'we have a proposal for you. Because of your sad loss – and I emphasise once again that we have made no contribution to that – Lord Areton will offer you employment as chauffeur to him and his family on the mainland. As you know, he does have a chauffeur already in London and that will continue. Therefore, your principal place of employment will be in Scotland, but you will agree to be flexible. You will be required to be available at any time and any place convenient to his lordship, members of his family, and anyone else whom he or Lady Areton should personally choose to oblige.'

'Thank you, thank you, my Lord.'

Papa was gasping, but the solicitor held up his hand. 'Please! Do not react so quickly. Please hear the full proposal.'

'I'm sorry.'

'You will understand that this is an extremely generous offer, since his lordship for many years has managed perfectly well on the mainland with just one chauffeur. His offer is made out of compassion, and for one year only. For this year, your wife and family will be allowed to remain in the gate lodge of Kilnashone Castle on consideration of the peppercorn, and on the understanding that at the end of the year, when you return to Ireland, you and they must have found alternative accommodation.'

I glanced at Papa, whose expression, if I was interpreting it correctly, was an extraordinary combination of delight and trepidation. Looming in my own mind, selfishly, was the responsibility that would fall on my shoulders with the sundering of our family, if only for a year, especially as I was to leave school during the coming summer.

Papa, however, seemed to have few qualms. He leaned towards Lord A as though to thank him. 'That's very fair,' he began, but the solicitor broke in, warning him that there was more to come.

'There is a condition, James. Before you agree to this offer, you must sign a document confirming you accept that his lordship, his family, agents or employees had no hand, act or part in the sad death of your son. And that, in perpetuity, neither you nor any member of your family, your heirs or the executors of your estate will take any action against the Areton family, any member of it, its estate or its heirs. You must also sign a second document binding you to confidentiality. For reasons that must be obvious to you, you may not reveal the details of this arrangement to anyone,' he glanced at me, 'outside your immediate family. If asked by Lord Areton's former employees, members of your family may say that they are renting the gate lodge for the year.'

'People will ask where Papa is — we can't lie about that.' It burst out of me.

'You can say he has gone to England to look for labouring work. Many have.' He looked back at Papa, then picked up the jug and milked his tea. 'I understand you are a qualified mechanic. That could well be a good thing to say. We cannot have the whole village of Kilnashone looking to us for a similar benefit.

'So,' he added then, as though a task had been satisfactorily completed. 'Perhaps you would like a day or so to think this over, James. We will be here, Lord Areton and I, in Maryborough until next Tuesday.'

While I had not totally followed the unfamiliar phraseology, the meaning was so clear I was enraged all over again. I remembered the conversation with Joe McCurg and Papa's reaction to the mere suggestion of court action and knew that never for an instant would he have contemplated such a thing. Neither would it have occurred to him, had Joe not brought it up.

That these people would so lightly dismiss his fidelity was therefore all the more appalling. I leaned forward and was about to speak up again, no matter what the consequences, when once more we were interrupted, this time by the receptionist at the hotel. 'There is a telephone call for you, Lord Areton. It is important.'

While our host, if one could call him that, was gone, the solicitor fiddled with his teaspoon, my papa sat very still, head bowed, while I, not knowing what else to do and unable yet fully to deal with what had just happened, first milked and then sipped my tea, as though it was a most important project. The cup had to be lifted to the mouth just so; the sip had to be soundless; the swallowing had to be slow and mannerly.

Mercifully, or so I thought at first, Lord A's return was not long delayed – but when I saw the expression on his face, my stomach leaped. There was bad news to come.

It was worse than I could have imagined. The worst possible news. Paying no heed to Papa and me, he spoke tersely to the solicitor. 'He's been found – again! They were unsure what to do so one of them went to the post office in the village and telegraphed the barracks here. I told them to keep him where they found him.'

'Well, at least he's safe. You must be relieved.' The solicitor did not seem surprised. They might have been talking about a lost dog.

'He's done this kind of thing so many times. I was not worried about him, but his mother was. I shall telephone her from here.'

'Where did they find him?' The solicitor gathered up the papers and replaced them in the document file. They seemed to have forgotten Papa and me.

'In the yard. They were assessing the damage and they found him in one of the stalls, cowering in a corner. He had wrapped himself in a woman's shawl, and when he saw them, he tried to run,' his voice betrayed something close to disgust, 'but he got up too quickly and the shawl tripped him. They caught him quite easily.' Lord Areton's bushy eyebrows lowered themselves over his piggy eyes. 'I'm going to teach that pup a lesson if it's the last thing I do.'

'Shall I go with you?' The solicitor stood up.

'No,' said Horatio Areton. 'I'll deal with him myself. He'll be on the mail-boat tonight or I'll swing for him – and this time I'll put someone on the boat to watch him.' Then, as though remembering our presence, 'Have we finished our business here? Have you signed, Somers?'

'Not yet, my Lord.' Papa's voice was more strained than I'd ever heard it.

'Dammit, man! I don't have to look after you and your family.

I don't have to look after anyone in Kilnashone. The faster I get away from this damned country, the better for me and my family. Last offer. Are you going to sign that document?'

'Yes, my Lord. I am.'

'Deal with it, will you?' he said to the solicitor. 'I've to get along to the barracks.' He left us without another word.

I cannot put into words how I felt at that moment. The picture that came to my mind was one of those frontispiece illustrations in nineteenth-century novels where a heart is rent jaggedly in two. That was how I saw my own heart, bleeding not only for myself but for what had happened – and what was about to happen – to Thomas. I felt his terror and his despair. I felt it as a physical pain deep in my chest, extending into my stomach.

My shawl.

If he had not been wearing it he might have got away. If I had not been so stupid as to give it to him—

I could not show the slightest indication of what I was thinking while, as quietly as a whipped dog, my father signed the papers in the places the solicitor indicated. It was all I could do to prevent myself running, screaming, from that room.

20

PEARL

Papa had engaged the hackney car to wait for us, and the driver, whom we knew well, guessed from our demeanour that we were not in talkative mood and did not engage with us as we sat into the back seat. 'Well,' Papa said to me in a low voice, as we settled ourselves, 'a good thing is, at least we will have a whole year to sort things out.'

'Yes, Papa.' But his words did not fool me, and during the remainder of the journey home, neither of us spoke. All I could think was that my beloved Thomas was about to be removed to England and a life of bitter cruelty. Removed from my life. I managed to keep my distress from showing, at least I think so, for Papa, who had his own thoughts to contend with, did not ask me what was wrong.

By the time we got to the gate lodge, however, I could not stand the idea of facing questioning – or even to be in others' company, so I asked him if he would mind if I did not go inside straight away: I was in need of some fresh air, I said. He was paying the hackney driver at the time and simply nodded. I doubt that he had even correctly heard me.

The day had warmed and, not stopping to collect even a cardigan or a wrap, I fled across the fields, through the old graveyard and again to 'our' spot in Drynan Wood, where I sank to my knees and leaned my cheek against the stump of the willow tree, which had assumed such importance for me. I cared not at all about the rough-ness of its bark against my skin or that it might mark me or my clothes. I held on to that tree and wept aloud for Willie, for Mama's heartbreak, for our whole family, for Papa, soon to depart from our lives for a whole year. Mostly, however, I wept for Thomas. For the plight of my lost love, whose grief and terror I could feel in my own heart.

Looking back, I was being highly dramatic, but the feelings were real. They were more than real: they were as black and bleak as the world I must now enter without Thomas, without Willie, without Papa. All around me, the birds twittered sardonically and the river flowing by was indifferent to the pain in my soul. It would flow like this no matter what happened. It did not care. Nobody did but as my weeping subsided, I was drawn to watch its calm, hypnotic gush. It occurred to me that its dark surface was like the ruffled satin counterpane on a bed recently vacated and it would be so attractive, so simple, to ease myself into that bed, to let whatever happened next just happen . . .

I let go of my willow tree and went to the water's edge. I sat on the rock from which our Willie had pegged his stones and, for a few minutes, gazed into the brown depths. How would it feel just to close my eyes and slide in? To let that smooth water take me, wash away all the pain?

How cold was it?

How long before they came to look for me? Before they found me?

How would I look when they did?

As I tried to picture these things, I saw in the river's surface not my own face but Willie's, Mama's and Papa's, and those of my sisters: the grief-stricken, ravaged faces of my family as they stood at my grave, trying to deal with this additional heartbreak.

It was not in me, unfortunately, to be the cause of such suffering.

I stood up from Willie's rock, knelt on the riverbank and washed my face in the water; it was cool on my skin and some of it got into my mouth. It tasted earthy and, melodramatically, I swallowed it in order to be part of it and to have it part of me. Then I straightened and held up my face to the sun to dry it.

The warmth was soothing. But as I listened to the birds, the rushing water and the rustle of the willow, I decided this was goodbye. I would never come again to this glade, and not just because we were leaving Kilnashone in one year. 'Goodbye, Thomas,' I whispered. 'Goodbye, Willie.'

Then I turned for home, and as I crossed the pasture leading to the cemetery, my heart was so heavy I paid no attention to the

141

cowslips and dandelions that were just coming out of bud because, sternly, I was giving myself a good talking-to. It would now be up to me, I told myself, to conceal my broken heart and bury my dreams so I could properly look after Mama and my two sisters for the next year while Papa was in Scotland.

When I entered the cemetery to cross that too, I saw, out of the corner of my eye, some movement in the far corner. I hate rats but there is always a compulsion to look at them – at least, that is what I have found. Ready to run if the creature moved an inch towards me, I turned to look. Thomas was standing, half standing, with bent knees and back, supporting himself against one of the gravestones. 'Thomas!' I was so surprised that I could take only a few steps towards him as though he were a wraith and might vanish if I got too close. 'You're here – but I thought – I heard you'd been captured and that you were on your way to England . . . '

'I'm not. Pearl, I told you I'd kill myself rather than let them take me back. I said I meant it and I did . . .' All the time he was craning his neck, looking left, right and behind him. 'It's too open here. Can we go back into the woods – not to the same place?'

'But the police got you.'

'They did. But I was left in the car with just one man when the other went into the post office to make a phone call. Please, Pearl, can we get to where it's safer? We have to talk.'

I ran to him then and would have embraced him, but he took my hand and pulled me into a crouching position beside him. 'We have to be careful. I have no doubt they'll come back for me into the forest. That was why I came here instead. I knew you'd probably be looking for me and that sooner or later I'd catch you here.'

'Oh, Thomas!'

'Ssh!' Tenderly, he fastened my lips with a warning finger. Then, having cast one last look in all directions to make sure the coast was clear: 'One – two – three!' We ran, keeping low while crossing the open ground of the field until we entered the wood at the far side.

'How far will we go?' I was breathless, and not only from physical exertion.

Thomas, obviously fitter than I because of his horse-riding, showed no sign whatsoever that we had been running. 'We have to go deep.'

So we continued into a part of the forest I did not know at all. It was obviously very old, penetrated only patchily by the sunlight because the trees were huge. Perhaps because it was higher than the rest of the trees in the forest and therefore had the benefit of longer light, the canopy was already quite dense with fresh leaves. Another thing I noticed was that there was hardly any birdsong.

The floor was knee-high with undergrowth and, unlike the areas my family and I customarily frequented, it did not seem to have any previously trodden trail or pathway. 'We have to be careful from here.' Thomas stopped abruptly. 'If we walk straight through, we'll break the grass and they'll be able to follow our trail. So do what I do from now on – all right?' I nodded. Despite all that had happened and the danger I was in personally, never mind what would happen to poor Thomas if we were caught, I could not suppress a growing sense of adventure.

Obediently, I followed him in a series of what I would describe as frog or bunny hops. He would stand on the exposed root of a tree, survey his surroundings and then leap to another root away to his left or his right, depending on which was the nearer. 'Try to think of the ground as deep water,' he called, 'and that you don't want to fall in or even get your feet wet.'

We progressed in this manner, like children playing hop-scotch – and although it was almost enjoyable, my poor ankle found it rather painful. I was relieved when, after five minutes or so, he decided we had gone far enough.

He selected a particular tree, in full leaf, which offered several thick and relatively low branches on which we could sit. 'Can you get up? Will you ruin your dress?'

'Don't worry,' I replied, although I wasn't that sure. The tree was gnarled and knobbly. 'But, Thomas,' I called up to him, as I started carefully to climb towards him, 'what if they bring dogs?'

'I'll have to risk that. We'll hear them if they do. We'll be able to get a head start. Obviously I can't stay here for too long. I'm just hoping to stay ahead of them until I work out a plan. I want you to know about it, Pearl, so that we can always find each other.'

I was absurdly pleased, but then my injured ankle gave way and I almost lost my balance. His reaction was swift: he managed to grab me under my shoulder and help me to reach him. I cannot say it was comfortable, sitting up there on that branch, but it felt safe enough.

And I was with Thomas.

We held hands quietly for a few minutes, resting in the soft gloom. 'Do they hurt?' I stroked one of the weals on the leg nearest me.

'They're not as bad as they seem.'

'They look terrible. You must have been very upset.'

In response, he cleared his throat. Then did it again. A couple of times. 'As you can imagine—'

'I can imagine. I can, Thomas. I'd like to kill him too.' I told him about the morning with the solicitor.

'I'm ashamed to have that man's name,' he said quietly, when I had finished. 'I don't think of him as my father. He's a bloody tyrant – sorry, Pearl. I didn't mean to swear.'

'Please . . .' I squeezed his hands to show that I understood.

'I saw them arriving, you know – they were in a car. Official-looking people. I was watching through a gap in the stone wall beside the archway. I never found out who all of them were, but I do know that one was a policeman, a pretty high-ranking one, to judge by the decorations on his jacket. High enough to get rid of the crowd gaping at the ruins. Nobody saw me, not yet. They were probably there to survey the ruin, but they couldn't go in because there was still smoke and steam coming out of it.

'I suppose I could have escaped through the wicket gate again – I probably should have – but by the time I saw them coming towards the yard, it was too late and they would have seen me going across to it. So I ran into one of the stalls.' He was looking straight ahead and made a gesture. 'There was a lot of fire damage, of course. The doors were wooden and they were really bad, eaten away – you've probably seen them for yourself. The old stone walls were black but they were still standing. There was thick soot and rubbish everywhere. The smell inside – I'll never forget it. The straw and hay had gone up like tinder. I had to keep my hand over my mouth and nose but still I couldn't stop sneezing. I was afraid they'd hear me. But they didn't. Not immediately. I thought I'd be all right.'

'But they did find you.'

'I had crept as far as I could get into the corner of the stable I

144

was in and made myself as small as possible, with my knees up to my face, my arms around them and my head down, but the sneezing continued after they came into the yard. I tried to silence it by pressing my head into my knees really, really hard, but one of the policemen heard me and came running in. I fought him, but there were more in the yard. I did try to run—'

'But you tripped on my shawl. Oh, Thomas, I'm so sorry.'

'No. I'm the one who should apologise, Pearl. You were so good to give me that. Really. But it's spoiled now. I had to leave it where it fell. Sorry, Pearl.'

'Don't worry about it, please, Thomas – please don't worry about it.' I leaned over, careful not to lose my balance, and kissed him gently on the lips. 'It's only a shawl.'

'I'll buy you a new one.'

'Don't be silly.' But I was already thinking up excuses for when Mama would notice its loss. Disloyally, I was glad that she was in the state she was in and probably would not ask about it for a while.

Again I touched the new and livid marks on his legs. 'Did that happen when he found you?'

He hung his head. 'I knew what was coming. I could see he was in a vile mood when he came. He kept a grip on me while he talked to the men who had kept me in the yard, telling them that everything would be fine now. That they could leave. That he'd meet up with them at the gates.' He looked across at me, his expression bleak. 'Within view of your house, Pearl.' He lowered his head as if ashamed. 'They knew full well what was going to happen to me. One of them smirked. He said, "Take your time, my Lord."'

'Then, when they had safely gone, he grabbed me by one arm, dragged me into various stables until he found a riding crop. It was black and burned but fit for purpose.'

'Did you not struggle?' I cried. 'Thomas, you're so big and strong! You're even bigger than he is.'

'He's stronger. And the fight was gone out of me.' He took a deep breath and closed his eyes. 'Pearl, I wouldn't tell this to anyone – anyone except you.' He took another breath. Then: 'I wet myself.'

'Oh, Thomas!' The image was so strong. So pathetic. I felt the love for him growing so big in my chest that I thought it might

145

spill out and cover us both. Cover the whole world. Precariously balanced as we were, I was afraid to put my arms around him in case we would fall off.

When I didn't respond further to what he had said, he raised his head and looked at me. 'You're crying.' He sounded surprised.

'Of course I am – what do you expect?'

He took my hand and kissed it. Several times. Then, 'We have to make a plan. I have to get away from Kilnashone, and I will. But could we have some sort of system whereby I can write to you without anyone knowing? I don't know where I'll be.'

'I don't know where I'll be either. I'm going to Dublin to work in July and I don't know yet the address of where I'll be living.'

'Do you know where you'll be working?'

'Mealy's café.' Joe McCurg had organised it for us. 'Oh, Thomas, I don't know the address.'

'I'll find it. That's easy. Mealy's café. I'll remember that. Mealy's café. Mealy's café.' He repeated the name over and over to impress it on his memory. 'I'll find you, Pearl. You're not to worry about that.'

I knew he wanted to kiss me properly and I certainly wanted to kiss him, but where we were, it would have been very difficult, even dangerous. Like very thin glass, the prospect hung between us.

As the tension grew, I became supremely aware of the hardness of the branch underneath me, the smell of the earth below – after the long dry spell we had had, its scent was like that of a dry biscuit. I even heard the muted singing sound made by the air around me.

'Shall we get down from the tree?' It was he who broke it.

I nodded. I didn't dare speak.

'I'll go first.' He was lithe and, accustomed to tree-climbing, made it to the ground with little effort. From below, he reached up with both arms and I lowered myself until I was safely inside them. Then we lay on the soft moss and grass and kissed each other. I had a fleeting concern about the welfare of my best dress, but that could not hold a candle to the rush of physical excitement.

'It may be a long time before we can do this again,' he whispered. 'May I see you naked, Pearl?'

146

Just the words added such fuel to my excitement I did not think I could bear it – and yet I was shy. 'I – I don't – I've never—'

'I haven't either. But if you'd prefer not to, if I'm asking too much . . .'

'No – I want to, but . . .'

'Would you let me undress you? Would it be better for you if I did it?'

I swallowed, and nodded. 'All right.' My heart was thumping so hard now I felt it would choke me. We stood up to face each other. The dress I wore was one of the Castle cast-offs, but unrecognisable since Mama had reworked it. It did present a difficulty in present circumstances because it was held together at the back with a long row of tiny buttons fastened by means of loops made from the material she had cut from the skirt. Isabella was much wider in girth than I.

Gravely, Thomas turned me round so my back was to him and set to at the neck, clumsily at first, but becoming more proficient as he worked his way downwards.

Neither of us said anything but truly I felt close to suffocation. To calm down, I fixed my gaze on the tree-trunk from which we had just descended, trying to focus on the tendrils of green ivy and the yellowish lichen, which, for the first time in my life, I saw was not like a blanket but composed of tiny saucer-like caps of differing sizes. The ruse only worked partially, because through the fabric of my dress, which was silk, his fingers felt to me like a family of spiders, sparking shivers and tiny shocks all the way from the crown of my head to my toes.

With the last button undone, he turned me round again. His face, I saw, had flushed a deep crimson and he was sweating. The dress now hung from my shoulders and I was overwhelmingly aware of the air on my bare back. 'Now your shoes,' he said. He knelt in front of me, undid the straps and I stepped out of them. I held up my feet and one by one, he slid off my socks.

He stood up.

'Are you ready, Pearl?'

I knew what that meant. Shaking hard now, as I held my arms towards him, I saw that he was shaking too. But, still carefully, he slid the dress off my shoulders and down my arms exposing my bodice, which, fortunately, was laced at the side and not at the

147

back. And although God would not have been amused to be invoked in this area, I thanked Him that I was wearing the new step-ins and not old-fashioned pantaloons.

When I was standing fully unclothed in front of Thomas, I could not look him in the eye.

'You are the most beautiful living creature in the world, Pearl, more beautiful than a swan,' he said, in a throaty voice, then placed one hand, very gently, at the side of one of my breasts, the other at my waist. 'Please may we lie down together again? Is it too cold for you?'

I shook my head. To speak would have strangled me.

'Here . . .' He looked around, then led me to a spot where there was a substantial swathe of moss.

When I lay on it, it was cold and spongy, but quite soft, and within seconds had warmed enough not to be uncomfortable. Had he asked, I would have lain on a bed of nails. Gently, supporting himself on one elbow, he began to stroke me from head to toe as though memorising my body. I closed my eyes and, behind the lids, had one of those flashes one experiences occasionally, when sight seems to leave the physical eyes and sees the body from outside and above.

I saw mine, white as the swan he had mentioned, in that cocoon of intense green, with breasts, hair, mouth and mound in stark relief, like a nude in a Victorian painting. The vision lasted for just a moment because other senses took over.

Hearing: Thomas was murmuring, 'I love you, Pearl, I love you, I would never harm you, I would never let anyone harm you, I would give you my life . . .'

Touch: still very gently, he took one of my breasts in his mouth while continuing to stroke my stomach and waist.

Taste: in response, and acting entirely on instinct, I opened my eyes and raised myself to kiss his ear and let my tongue caress it.

I found the courage to ask him if he would also take his clothes off when something happened. He jumped up and, his face creased seemingly in pain, ran to the base of a nearby tree and, with his back to me, bent double and seemed to retch, his body convulsing.

'Are you all right, Thomas?' I sat up and, instinctively, picked up my dress to cover my modesty.

'I'm fine,' he said, but his voice caught in his throat and I could see he was trembling.

148

'Are you ill?' I scrambled to my feet, and, abandoning the dress, rushed over to him, bare feet skidding on the moss.

'Please, don't worry about me.' He had stopped retching but, leaning against the tree as though exhausted, he was panting. 'I'll be fine.' Fiercely, he grabbed me in both arms and crushed me to his chest. The tweed of his jacket felt rough.

Underneath it, I could feel his heart beating so fast it scared me. 'Thomas,' I said, alarmed, 'you're ill. I can feel your heart.'

'And I can feel yours, my love, my darling!' He kissed me. We kissed each other. The world seemed very far away.

It was not. We were still locked together when we heard someone or something crashing through the undergrowth. The sound was accompanied by the barking of more than one dog.

My dress was too far away to get to in time to cover my naked-ness and, instinctively, I dropped to the ground, taking Thomas with me.

I'VE GOT A SECRET.
WOULD THE REAL DOROTHY MORRIS PLEASE STAND UP?

Her latest book is about to hit the shelves. **Dawn O'Brien** talks to **Dorothy Morris**, the author of *Weeds in the Garden*, and digs deep to find out what drives this elegant writer.

She has the walk of a queen. Her real name is Pearl Somers and the first thing you notice about her is her carriage. Quietly, looking around, she enters the Tea Room of the Shelbourne Hotel, stops for a moment just inside the wide entrance and scans the room for the blonde woman who will be wearing a red scarf. Our eyes connect and, with hand outstretched, she approaches the corner table and, in one fluid movement, shakes hands and sits into her chair. She is wearing grey, a knee-length dress of fine wool, over which she has draped a devoré shawl in paler shades of the same colour. Her accessories are silver, her shoes smart but comfortable; her pale hair is sculpted in a French pleat. For someone in the public eye, she is very polite, self-deprecating and speaks quietly; she blushes if you pay her a compliment, but as you get to know her you realise there is a core of steel. She is as tall as a model, with the natural grace of a ballet dancer. She is neither: she is the successful author Dorothy Morris.

DO'B: You're taller than I expected.

DM: (laughs) I'm not sure if that's a compliment?

DO'B: It certainly is. And you have violet eyes!

DM: Oh dear.

DO'B: No, really, they're lovely. Most unusual.

DM: I think it's the light in here!

DO'B: So, let's get started. Why did you change your name? What's wrong with Pearl Somers? That's a lovely name.

DM: It's so long ago now. Something to do with there being another Pearl, I think. It was the publisher's idea.

DO'B: I've done a bit of research on you, naturally. You're from the midlands, of course. Your stories have been called bucolic and pastoral with a great sense of place – do you think your background has influenced your style of writing?

DM: That's for others to say, but yes, probably. Without sounding too precious about it, when you live in a place during your most formative years, that place is bound to seep into your bones and colour almost everything you do subsequently. Writers in particular are like sponges. They absorb in great measure.

DO'B: Tell me about your family. You live with your sister, Opal, now but you had another sister, Ruby, and I've heard that you and your sisters were called locally the Three Jewels?

DM: (laughs) That's right.

DO'B: Were you very close?

DM: Yes, we were. Opal and I still are. Unfortunately, Ruby died of cancer five years ago this month. I had a brother too – he died in childhood.

DO'B: What happened?

DM: He had a horse-riding accident.

DO'B: You're still a young woman and there has been a lot of loss in your life, Pearl – may I call you Pearl?

DM: Of course. And I'm not that young! (Laughs) I have no problem with who knows my age. I'm sixty-two.

DO'B: Well, you certainly don't look it! If I didn't know about this in advance, which I did, looking at you fresh, as it were, I'd put you down for a young fifty.

DM: Thank you.

DO'B: OK. Your brother, your sister, both gone, both younger than you – and when did your parents die? Do you think all this loss also influenced your writing?

DM: My goodness! When you compress everything together like this – all of this took place over a number of years, you know.

DO'B: I'm sorry. I don't mean to upset you.

DM: That's all right. It's just . . . (hesitates) Let's get all of this out of the way and then we can talk about my book.

DO'B: That would be great.

DM: We lived in Kilnashone, as you probably know, where my father was in service as a chauffeur to Lord Areton. With his job came the right of residency in the gate lodge of Kilnashone Castle. But the Castle burned down in April of 1923—

DO'B: What happened?'

DM: I believe it was arson. But I don't want to get into that right now – you were asking about my parents?

DO'B: Yes. Sorry. Go on.

DM: As a result of the fire, the Aretons went back to England and my father went with them for a year, while we were allowed to stay in the gate lodge, but just for that year. About six months into the year he was travelling home to visit us, but during the journey he had a heart attack and died.

DO'B: That was awful. You must have been devastated.

DM: We were. Yes.

DO'B: Sorry. Go on. What age were you at that stage, Pearl? How did your mother cope?

DM: I was fifteen and already in Dublin, working. Times were hard, and with my father now dead, my family needed as much money as I could send them so there was no question of my going home. The most urgent problem for us was to find a place to live. My father had had a great friend from Kilnashone who found Mama a tiny cottage to rent on the outskirts of the village. It had only two rooms and no water, but it had a good fireplace, a yard for our hens and was near the village pump. And it was very cheap, so really there was no alternative. My mother told Joe to make the arrangements. To eke out a living for the three of them – because, of course, I wasn't able to send them nearly enough – she took in sewing.

DO'B: I'm sorry? What does that mean, 'took in sewing'?

DM: Dressmaking or tailoring, I suppose you'd call it nowadays. Turning of overcoats, the collars and cuffs of shirts. That kind of thing.

DO'B: I beg your pardon?'

DM: This was 1923, remember. People didn't have much and an overcoat was used for decades. When it became shabby, people like my mother ripped it apart, removed the lining, then reconstructed it with a new lining and the inside of the fabric on the outside. The coat then would last many more years. She charged, I think, three shillings. She did the same for the collars and cuffs of shirts. A collar was eightpence, as far as I remember, and cuffs were fivepence each.

DO'B: I'm speechless!

DM: (laughs) You're young. This is 1970. Please God, Ireland won't see the need for turning garments ever again. That was her bread and butter in the village but she did make communion dresses and once, I remember, an entire bridal trousseau, dresses, the shirts for the groom and best man, everything. She even embroidered sheets for the wedding night! (Laughs)

DO'B: She sounds wonderful.

DM: She was.

DO'B: And when did she die?

DM: When Opal left school, she followed me up to Dublin to work while my mother and Ruby stayed in their cottage. The plan was that when Ruby, too, left school, the two of them would come up to Dublin and we would all live together again. I'm afraid it didn't work out. Just seven months before-hand, in the winter of 1930, around Christmas time, Mama got pneumonia. She went to hospital in Kilkenny and actually recovered, but then, the following July when they were packing up for the move, she slipped and fell – the cottage had a mud floor and it was a very wet day – and broke her hip. She got pneumonia again in hospital and died. I believe her lungs had been weakened by the first bout.

DO'B: Dear God! The poor thing. I'm so sorry.

DM: Thank you.

DO'B: And what happened to Ruby then?

DM: She didn't come up to Dublin right away. Our friend Joe, the man who had found the cottage for Mama— Do we have to go into all of this?

DO'B: Not if you don't want to, Pearl. Of course not.

DM: Just quickly, Ruby got a job locally in a shop and Joe found her a family to live with for a while. She came to Dublin a year later. Opal had moved on to a new job from the café where we had both worked and Ruby took her place, then went on from there to work in a clerical job for a trade union. Now, that's everyone, I think. Oh, there's also Catherine, Catherine Fay, who's nineteen and very much alive. She's a huge part of our lives. She's a dear, a cousin of ours, lives with our aunt and uncle, but she's in and out of our house like a yo-yo. And that's definitely the lot.

DO'B: Don't worry, I get the message. It's on to the writing! Just one more personal question, if you don't mind – well, two questions, and one's about writing, I promise! You live with your sister, Opal. She's a widow. You never married, Pearl? No romances in your life?

DM: What's your second question?'

DO'B: Sorry. Well, in a way it's linked to that. In anticipation of this inter-view I've read many of your stories, Pearl, and I have to say I think I've detected a theme. They have pretty settings, bucolic, pastoral, as we've already discussed, but to me, anyway, there is a definite thread going through them, not all of them, but a great number. They seem to be about loss and yearning. And, yes, I understand the losses, you've certainly had your share and, as I say, you're still a young enough woman . . . but I don't think it's necessarily family loss that you're writing about?

153

DM: That's your opinion and your privilege to hold it. They're stories, Dawn. That's all they are. I sit in a room and make them up. And some people like them and buy them to read in railway carriages and on aeroplanes or anywhere they choose. I don't mean to be rude, really. I apologise if that sounded abrupt, I didn't mean it to. But if I can turn it back on you – which authors truly know why they choose the subjects they do? I guess you'd need to be on a psychiatrist's couch to figure that out! (Laughs)

DO'B: I didn't mean to cause you upset.

DM: It's just that I'm quite a private person. I find it hard to talk about such personal things in public.

DO'B: Last question. No. Second last question. Last question will be about *Weeds in the Garden*, I promise. Are there two people sitting in front of me, Pearl? Are Dorothy Morris and Pearl Somers *ad idem*?

DM: What a question! (Laughs) I'm not evading it and I'll do my best to answer. (Hesitates) The best way to describe it, I think, and you don't have to be a psychiatrist to work this out, is to say that Dorothy Morris is the professional writer, and when she's out in public doing something like this with you, that's who you see. Mostly. But sometimes, as you've seen, Pearl comes up to bite! (Laughs) At home, certainly in my own room, they're one and the same. You could say that Dorothy is fuelled by Pearl. It's not complicated. We all have public and private faces, don't you think?

DO'B: But which is the real woman? And who was born first?

DM: Dawn! Dear God! They both are real. I have only one body and one mind. Obviously. Let's say we were born together but Dorothy was the slow learner!

DO'B: (laughs) That's really a great way to put it. I love interviewing writers. They're so deep! I guess it comes from all that thinking and mulling over.

DM: (laughs)

DO'B: Now – at last, says she! – tell me a bit about *Weeds in the Garden*.

DM: Well, at the risk of sounding pompous or self-serving, I think there are a few stories in there that people will like! I hope that readers will think I'm improving with every collection, because that's my true aim. Every book is a fresh start. The only difficulty is that if you write something substandard – by your own standards, I mean – it's going to be there for ever, hanging around accusingly on the shelves every time you go into a bookshop. And there is a full year to go before you have a chance to redeem yourself with the next book.

DO'B: I only have a proof so I don't know what the cover will look like. Covers are terribly important, don't you think?

DM: They sure are! It's the cover that prompts a potential reader in a shop to pick the book up in the first place. This one's going to be the usual surprise to me too, Dawn! I never see the cover until it's on the actual book. I believe this one has a horse on it.

DO'B: Sounds lovely. How much will it sell for?

DM: Nineteen shillings and sixpence, I believe. I suppose next year, with decimalisation, it'll be – what?

DO'B: The full pound!

DM: Yes, of course. That's inflation for you! (Laughs)

DO'B: In all good bookshops from tomorrow.

DM: In all good bookshops from tomorrow.

DO'B: Would you mind signing my proof for me? I collect them.

DM: Of course I will, Dawn. Thank you. (Signs)

DO'B: No – thank you!

We say goodbye. Her handshake is firm, her smile warm. She hands me the envelope containing the A4 head-and-shoulders publicity shot I had asked for. I thank her. Then Pearl (or is it Dorothy?) makes her way through the Shelbourne's Tea Room towards the lobby, turning one or two heads as she goes. But it is clear that this fascinating woman will continue to harbour her secrets and her real persona for some time to come yet. Will the Real Dorothy Morris Please Stand Up?

© Dawn O'Brien. June 1970

21

CATHERINE

My name is Catherine Fay.

I should start at the beginning, I suppose – with a few words about my unusual upbringing. I won't go into all the ins and outs of it just now, but the headlines are that my mam, who had me at the age of eighteen in 1951, proved incapable of looking after me. My grandparents were already dead, and the only living relatives I had in Dublin were my great-grandparents and three of my great-grandmother's nieces, cousins to me and who, at the time my mam vanished, were aged around the early-to-late-forties mark. So, when I was about three years old, I went to live with my great-grandparents, Poppa, who was a doctor, and my great-grandmother, Mandy. (Somehow 'Grandma' turned into 'Mandy' in my mouth, and stuck. Her real name was Margaret.)

As for two of the cousins, Pearl and Opal, they've been seriously important people in my life. I've spent a lot of time in their gorgeous house on Strand Road in Sandymount – one of those three-storeys-over-basement semi-mansions with small front gardens and steps to the front door. And, of course, the sisters were always part of family occasions: my First Communion and Confirmation, birthday celebrations, Christmas and so on.

The saddest day we had, when I was just fourteen, was the funeral of the third and youngest sister, Ruby. I knew her less well because she lived independently of the other two but she died of pancreatic cancer – you get that, you're a goner – and in her case it was only two months from diagnosis to deathbed. What was so sad about that funeral was that it was so small. She had only a few friends, it appeared, and, of course, hardly any relatives. As I say, I knew her less well because any time I met her it was with the other two, and when Opal is with you in full colour, everyone else fades to black and white.

The three Somers sisters had apparently been referred to within the family as the Jewels. They were very different from each other, and if I was asked to describe them in terms of dogs, I'd say Ruby was the clever poodle, Opal is the loud and gregarious Labrador, and Pearl, a.k.a. Dorothy Morris, the pen name she uses for her books, is the quiet, reserved and very well-bred Afghan hound. I don't know what kind of personalities Afghans enjoy, but if I were a writer like she is, I would probably describe her as having 'clothed herself in a mystery'. There's just something about her that intrigues me. She's holding something back, I'm sure of it.

Although almost as tall as I am, she is slender and very erect, but graceful too. She dresses usually in either dove-grey or that kind of pale *écru* colour, usually with silver accessories and plain shoes with a low heel. Her hair, a whitish strawberry blond, is beautifully thick, although she doesn't make the most of it. I have never seen it loose because she always wears it fastened into a thick French pleat at the back of her head. I tell you, if I had that hair I'd flaunt it! Mine is carroty. Well, it's not too carroty but it's definitely reddish. Genes are very powerful, aren't they? As I'm describing her, I do believe we resemble one another a little, in colouring and height anyhow, if not in elegance!

Opal's natural hair colour is a good deal darker, I think, although with all the attention it receives from her hairdresser, it's hard to tell; she moves about in a cloud of the pungent scent given off by hair lacquer and tends to like white linen blazers, red lipstick and heavy jewellery, particularly earrings. But as I think you might have gathered by now, when Opal comes into a room the air stands to attention.

Ruby was very dark and her hair was curly, although to tell you the truth, I find it difficult to remember her face. Maybe because I didn't know her as well as I know the other two and, although you couldn't call her self-effacing, when all three were in the same room together, she seemed to be eclipsed. For me anyhow.

I know very little about my mother or why she acted like she did. When I was old enough, a tight-lipped Poppa told me she had 'got into bad company' but wouldn't say any more. It was Opal who revealed that she ran off, probably to England, with 'some

157

class of a sleazy boyfriend'. She was only twenty-one. Technically, I suppose she abandoned me, but I was so young, and my great-grandparents were so good to me, I barely noticed her absence.

I certainly have no memory of crying into my pillow about her and the only snapshot I have of her, showing a thin-faced girl with saucer eyes and a halo of fuzzy curls (which I was told were red, like mine), could be that of a stranger. It is certainly no help in bringing to life any buried memories.

That 'bad company' revelation aside, neither Poppa nor Mandy ever breathed a word of condemnation about my mother, at least not in my hearing. I can't vouch for what they thought of her behaviour. They adored me, I was sure of that, so I felt very secure in their glowing little world of middle-class comfort. Our section of Harold's Cross, a settled red-brick area of Dublin's inner suburbs, was populated mostly by widows or elderly couples and since there were no other children within earshot I was the belle of the street ball. As a result I was spoiled, but on the plus side, I developed language skills well above the norm.

The neighbours immediately to the left of us were the Higginses, a childless elderly couple who regarded the opportunity to entertain me as a blessing from Heaven. They doted on me, a circumstance of which I took full advantage. To me, their house was a combination of fun palace and hotel where I could, on demand, snack on fried bread spread with golden syrup, or tinned peaches and custard, or Chivers jelly and tinned pears. When they took me out for a walk, they bought me liquorice strings, a stick of barley sugar or a packet of sweet cigarettes. Most usefully, though, they taught me to read to a level far above my age before I was even four years old.

They gave me another thing too: neither Poppa nor Mandy was physically demonstrative (but, then, in fifties and sixties Ireland, what parents, even 'real' mothers and fathers, were?) and I did wish sometimes for the type of casual physical togetherness I'd occasionally witnessed elsewhere. In the meantime, I went to the Higginses for my hugs and, all in all, took to spoiling like a duckling faced with a bright puddle.

Mr Higgins was a retired civil servant of relatively low grade: he had worked in the registry of some obscure Government department, a job that gave him lots of time to catalogue his personal collections of stamps and to read the musty books he bought for a few coppers from the barrows on the quays. He was smaller than his wife, with bright blue eyes and nicotine-stained fingers, which I happily followed on the pages of the books he bought specially for me. He was the one who, from the time he reckoned I was old enough, patiently took me through my ABCs.

Mrs Higgins, comfortably upholstered and given to thick stockings and heavy skirts under the brightly coloured cardigans she constantly produced, sat beside him to praise my progress while she knitted yet another sleeve or turned the heel of a sock.

There were disadvantages to having such elderly 'parents' and minders. When I was at that awkward age of fourteen, they were all in their mid-seventies and, in their old-fashioned way, fearful of giving me too much freedom. I suppose everyone was worried that, with my bad blood, I'd follow in my mother's footsteps. Poppa did drink a little too much at times too, but in all honesty, compared to genuine orphans, I had nothing to complain about.

I may not have missed my mother while I was growing up, but in my present circumstances, I do miss the idea of her. That sounds complicated, but it's always complicated when a mother disappears. These days, I tend to fantasise a little about how nice it would be to enjoy consoling hugs when life gets rough. Then again, how do I know she was the huggy type?

I did OK at school, not brilliantly but enough to get me into university. Poppa was so proud that on the day the Leaving Cert results came in he actually went out and bought me a car, a Morris Minor, six years old but in great shape. And with a radio too: he had been almost as delighted with his find as I was with the car. 'I had to go to a lot of garages until I found a car with a radio, Catty, although all the new ones did seem to have them all right. You young people and your music!' He had thrown his eyes to Heaven, and even though I had never been caught up in any particular music – I didn't even have a record player, preferring to spend my free time reading – I went along with his illusions that I was with the 'in' crowd. He had taught me to drive as soon as I was old enough to get a provisional licence, and two months after my seventeenth birthday I had passed the test, so from day one, I was on wheels.

I was grateful for the gift, of course, but in one large respect it represented an obligation. I had no academic ambitions, largely because I was not interested. I was longing to become independent, but could not disappoint their expectations of my university career. I knew I should be grateful for this, too, because not many girls were given this privilege, and so I bit back my objections and dutifully enrolled.

For whatever reason, maybe because I was such a reluctant student, maybe because I had been wrapped in so much cotton wool by my circle of relatives, I didn't enjoy college. Certainly not the social side of life. In fact, by the end of that first year, I was lonely.

My friend throughout my schooldays had been a girl called Frances. We had swotted the Leaving Cert together, but when the results came and I saw how much better she had done than I had, it was clear that in having her as a study companion, I had had by far the best of the bargain. Unfairly, however, her parents could not afford to send her to college so she and I had started our adult lives within very different circles. She was taken into the civil service as a junior executive officer and was bound for a stellar career there, while I – well . . . Where I was bound, nobody knew, least of all myself.

During that first year after school we met socially less and less frequently for various reasons. I had essays to finish, she had to attend a work 'do', but there was another aspect to the drift in our friendship: we began to have less and less in common. There is only so much reminiscing about schooldays, childhood and mutual hatreds you can do before the narrative begins to repeat itself. So the closeness we had shared, in which we couldn't wait to tell each other everything, began to evaporate. There were times when I felt she even resented me.

Things came to a head one Saturday afternoon at Bewley's in Grafton Street. Over coffee, I was telling her once again how I didn't fit in at college, how difficult I found it to make friends there. 'And another thing—'

'Oh, stop moaning about UCD!' Out of the blue she snapped at me and there was real venom in her voice.

'I'm not moaning!' I was taken aback.

'Yes, you are. Just shut up and be grateful for what you've got.'

'But I am grateful!'

'No, you're not. You're not taking advantage of what's been handed up to you on a plate. For God's sake, will you look beyond the people you don't like in that place and find some that you do? This is supposed to be the best time of your life. Take off the blinkers, Catherine. I'd give my right arm to be in your shoes.'

I opened my mouth to intervene but she held up a hand to cut across me again. 'Before you say anything else, such as pointing out yet again that at least I have a mother and father and you don't, would you once and for all accept the fact that, yes, you had a bad start but so have millions of people in the world. And unlike them, you were scooped up by two wonderful people and given the kind of life that most people on this planet could never aspire to. So, shut up, Catherine, and grow up!'

'I'm sorry. I didn't realise.'

'Don't be sorry. Be active. Know how lucky you are.'

We made up that day, of course – we had known each other too long not to – but although we continued to see each other from time to time it was never the same.

Meanwhile at UCD, although I did try, I just couldn't overcome my shyness. I had relied on Frances throughout school, and at home I had been cosseted by Poppa and Mandy, the Higginses, Opal and Pearl, with whom I seemed to have a particular affinity. Even the effort required to start a friendly conversation with a seat mate in a lecture hall continued to be hard for me to overcome. I was tall too, standing head and shoulders above other girls – and quite a lot of the boys.

As for 'boys': I had gone to an all-girls convent school and to me they were a different and dangerous species. I went red every time one said 'hello'.

By the end of my first year as a student, I continued to attend lectures and turn in my work on time but that was about the height of my participation on campus. While my fellow students were ragging or staying up all night discussing Sartre or falling into drunken stupors on each other's floors, I was safely asleep in my girly bedroom in Harold's Cross, with Mandy across the landing and Poppa, whose arthritic legs were no longer capable of climbing stairs, snoring away in his bed-sitter off the hallway. I tried to convince myself I was better off; that the conversations of my fellow students were superficial, that they bored me. And I consoled myself

161

that while my colleagues would be in a daze for lack of sleep, and would study only when it came time for exams, I would achieve good results by being methodical and steady.

I had opted for arts instead of what Poppa had wanted me to do, which was medicine – the length of the medicine course was too daunting and, in any event, I had no idea what career I wanted to follow. I chose to study English and classics, which would give me time to think.

I definitely wanted to 'be' something. Unlike in the dark ages, when women merely marked time in jobs until they married, now women all over the world were beginning to choose whether to work or get married and sometimes, in America for instance, to do both simultaneously. American TV showed women in their swish kitchens for sure, but also that they were making inroads into the world of work. (Poppa and I adored *The Lucy Show* and never missed it if we could help it. Lucy and her pal were actually my female heroines: two wisecracking women who were totally independent, getting into scrape after scrape yet, by the final scene, always triumphing in their own wacky way.)

To me, TV was marvellous, a cinema in our sitting room. Like everyone in Ireland who had access to a set, I was glued to *The Fugitive* and even, secretly, liked *Mister Ed* and *Green Acres* – not to be admitted, of course, in the learned halls of Earlsfort Terrace. TV for me was not just a window on the world, it gave direct access to America and the 'American way of life'.

It was with great excitement, therefore, that I learned from a beaming Poppa I was booked to fly off to the heat and humidity of summer in Chicago on the Tuesday after my last first-year exam. The joy, however, was initially complicated by guilt because I felt relieved, if you follow: Mandy was in failing health – a lifetime of smoking had damaged her lungs and she had been in and out of hospital for the previous eighteen months. Poppa himself was affected by his dreadful arthritis so he couldn't look after her by himself; he couldn't even scold her for her tobacco habit because he himself smoked and pooh-poohed the research that was trickling out with gruesome details of the harm it did. I had to help a lot with minding Mandy during the months immediately preceding my exams. He was very keen, however, that I should enjoy the 'Full University Experience', as he called it, and so, quietly, he had organised a rota

162

of live-in housekeepers and minders to look after them for the time I was to be away. 'Spread your wings, Catty. You're young, you shouldn't be hanging around with us, get out there and enjoy yourself. You've worked hard, you deserve it.'

He had arranged everything. Through a medical contact, he managed to get me a part-time job in a Chicago college library – and not only that: I was scheduled to share a three-bedroom apartment with two other girls, both students at that college. One, Dory, was the contact's daughter, who was going to work along-side me in the library for the summer; the other, Peggy, was a trainee nurse who, as part of her course, would be shadowing a real nurse in a local hospital. Even the word 'apartment' sounded exotic, far more interesting and upmarket than the Irish 'flat'. As for the address – 'Magnolia Avenue' – I was to be part of *Gone With the Wind*! And 'only for emergencies, mind, Catty,' he had organised an American Express card for me. When he revealed all of this I was so excited I could hardly speak.

Opal had insisted that I should have a 'little party' as a send-off at her house in Sandymount – but since I had few friends of my own age, I wasn't actually looking forward to it all that much. She and Pearl had been so kind and generous to me all my life, though, that I couldn't refuse.

I just could not wait until that big plane with the shamrock on its tail was rolling down the tarmac, then taking off towards the west! I would have to make two stopovers, in Shannon and Montréal – but who cared if the trip would take almost eighteen hours? I certainly didn't. I would be on my way to America!

22

OPAL

I love organising parties. It's a lost vocation for me. God, when I think of the Mickey Mouse careers I did have . . .

I came up to the city in 1926 when the trouble between the Free Staters and the Republicans had died down. While there were still a few problems in certain parts of the country, Mama reckoned I'd be safe enough in Dublin. Pearl was already there and she could look after me; she was eighteen and well established in Mealy's Café on a little street off College Green near the old Jury's. It was a hangout for Trinity types and solicitors and money people from Dame Street. Did good business.

She sent word that she'd got me a start there too. It was as a trainee waitress, or so I thought, but when I turned up on the first day I found out that I would be washing dishes. I put my foot down. I wouldn't do it. I was polite but very definite about it. I walked straight out of the kitchen and went to where Pearl was working behind the cake counter. She was boxing up six fondant slices, I remember. I waited patiently until she was finished with the customer before I approached her. She saw me immediately. 'Opal! What are you doing here? You should be in the kitchens.'

'I'm not doing it, Pearl. You'll have to tell them to find something else for me to do. I'm not washing dishes.'

She went scarlet. 'Don't be ridiculous,' she whispered. 'This isn't a game. You're in no position to make demands like that.'

'I'm not going to wash dishes,' I said firmly. 'I'm not going to have my hands turn out like Mama's.'

There was a queue of people building up in front of the counter, earwigging while they were waiting to buy their cream buns and éclairs. Pearl, who was starting to sweat, looked at her colleague, who was also enjoying the show. 'I'm sorry about this, Mary,' she said, real low, 'but I'll have to deal with it. I'll be back in a minute.'

She came out from behind the counter and brought me down to the back of the café and put me sitting at a table. 'Wait here,' she said. 'I'll never forgive you for this, Opal. You're making a show of me and our family. You should be grateful that I got you in here at all.'

'I'm not going to wash dishes,' I repeated. 'You can't make me. I'll go back home on the next train.'

'You can't do that.'

She was nearly crying and now I felt sorry for her. 'Do you want me to go with you to them? I can explain.'

'No!' She almost shouted it, but held herself in check. She was right about people looking in our direction, and it was definitely clear that we were having some kind of a row. 'You'll only make things worse,' she hissed at me. 'Stay here.' She ran off through a door marked 'Staff Only'.

She was gone a long time, and when she came back there was a stout woman with her. 'Hello, Opal,' the woman said.

I noticed that Pearl was hanging back. She'd definitely been crying. I was sorry about that but I couldn't help it. I stood up. 'Hello,' I said.

The woman looked me up and down. 'What are we going to do with you?'

'I don't know, ma'am,' I said. Then I got inspiration. 'I could sweep the floors, if you like? They could do with it. And tidy up a bit?'

The woman gave a half-smile, then wiped it off her face and looked stern. 'So it's only wet work you object to?'

'I'm sorry, ma'am.' But I made sure she knew I wasn't sorry at all. It was raining outside so the café was pretty steamy – I could feel the beads of sweat on my forehead but I wasn't going to let her see I cared.

'We-ell,' the woman said slowly, after looking me up and down again. 'Are you an honest girl, Opal?'

I shot a look at Pearl, but she was staring at the toes of her shoes. 'I am, ma'am,' I said. 'Pearl will back me up on that.'

'We're very fond of Pearl here. She's a great addition to our little family. Are you quick, Opal? Can you add and subtract and read?'

'I can, ma'am. I'll show you, if you like.'

'That won't be necessary.' She smiled again, fully this time. 'I'll take your word for it.' Then she got serious. 'As it happens, there will be a vacancy behind the counter very soon. We'll train you in. See how you are. You'll have to work very hard to prove yourself. Is that clear? And you're on a month's trial.'

'Thank you, ma'am.'

'Go with your sister. She'll show you what to do. Be a good girl now.'

'Yes, ma'am.' She went off and I sat down again. Pearl was still standing there. The black uniform with the white collar made her look older than she was. 'I should tell Mama about this,' she said quietly.

'It worked out, didn't it?' But I hated the way she looked, so thin and miserable. 'I'm sorry, Pearl,' I said. 'But I just couldn't do it. Isn't it great that we'll be working together? It'll be such fun. And you'll be a great teacher. I know you will.'

Instead of answering, she just walked away.

But Pearl was never one to hold a grudge. It turned out that the job vacancy was because the other woman she worked with behind the cake counter, Mary, was leaving to get married. She was a jolly sort, and by the end of my first day, by the time I had been taught how to use the cash register, hadn't done anything too clumsy, and my cash sums had balanced, the three of us were great pals. I may not be great at the writing, but I'm quick with sums.

Looking back, I don't know why they put up with such behaviour and demands from a green fifteen-year old just up from the country and without experience of anything at all. One reason might have been something simple, like they were just astonished. Maybe they didn't know how to react.

That was fine with me. I was going to prove myself and take the first steps into my career. A counter is a counter and customers are customers: they're buying different goods in different shops, that's all. After I'd got some experience I could move on to what I really wanted, which was to work in Arnott's or Clery's or even Switzers, after I got a bit of experience.

Although Papa was dead by the time I came up, his friend, Joe McCurg, who had arranged for Pearl to stay in his digs when she came to the city, had organised for me to stay there too. Mama was happy with the arrangement because Joe had always promised that he'd keep an eye on any of us who came up. For me, the big bonus was that he worked in Clery's and would be able to give me tips about how I should go about getting in there. 'You're too young, right now, Opal,' he said, when I pestered him for information about vacancies. 'Bide your time.'

But he did confirm to me that my instincts were right when I said that at rock bottom there wasn't all that much difference between selling a cake or a fur coat to a customer. The way to sell successfully, he said, was to let the customer believe that it was she who was making the choice. All you were doing was being helpful, pointing out quality and so forth and, where clothes were concerned, finding the right size, colour and shape. 'They have to trust you. And there's little tricks you'll learn. For instance, if she's trying on two or three things, tell her very definitely that one of them doesn't suit her. That the colour does nothing for her. Or that the cut makes her look plump. You make her believe you're on her side and not on the shop's. That way she'll believe you're an honest broker.

'When you've established that, run and get something more expensive. Rub the fabric between your hands – ask her to feel it too. "Now that's real quality, madam. What you have on you looks lovely, don't worry about that, it's lovely on you, but this one, now – this one is the cream. This one will give you a lifetime of service. Now I'm not trying to sell it to you, I just wanted to show it to you because you seem to know quality when you see it." Then you walk away, tenderly brushing little bits of dust off the garment. I guarantee, if you've handled it right, she'll call you back and want to try it on.'

He put his feet up on a pouffe and clasped both hands behind his head. 'It's like being an actor in a play,' he added dreamily, looking at the ceiling. 'You're yourself but you're not yourself, if you understand me. For the time she's with you, you're her best friend. You also behave as though you have all the time in the world and it's at her disposal. The key is to talk quietly and be calm.

'And listen, Opal, don't talk all the time either – you're a terrible chatterbox. The customer needs to believe you're listening too.'

'How do you know these things, Joe?' I was fascinated. 'You sell suits to men.'

'The technique is the same. Deep down, men are just as vain as women.' He unclasped his hands and became brisk. 'So, you use your time in Mealy's as a training course, young lady. Don't just serve your cakes, practise selling them. If you take my advice, you'll soon find that they'll be buying fruit cakes when what they thought they wanted was a scone. You're selling them a vision.'

I took quickly to living as a working young lady, looking after my clothes and my Mealy's uniform and polishing my shoes. I liked the novelty of living in digs, even if the room Pearl and I shared was very small, and to get out to the bathroom at night (indoor plumbing! Bliss!) I had to climb over her in the bed.

The house was on the North Circular Road, near the gates of the Phoenix Park. The décor wasn't great – wallpaper that had seen better days, and sagging sofas in the 'residents' parlour'. The food wasn't marvellous either – dinners of fatty bacon and big mounds of lumpy mashed potatoes that nobody had bothered to take the eyes out of (and those dinners were served on the stroke of one o'clock; if you were late they were stone cold!) – but since Pearl and I got our dinner at work, we only had to put up with them at weekends. The teas weren't all that bad, bread and butter and ham during the week, a tomato added at weekends.

Residents – five in all – us two and Joe McCurg, a lady civil servant from Cork and a travelling tea salesman who wasn't there all the time – were expected to make their beds and keep their rooms tidy so the maid could clean up every week. But at the end of every meal there I could cross my knife and fork on my clean plate and just leave it on the table for someone else to come along and deal with it.

Imagine! Pearl and me from our background and here we were with servants!

Meanwhile, I threw my heart and soul into my work and passed my trial month with flying colours. I was trusted with the cash register on my own just as much as anyone else, which made me feel very grown-up. I absolutely loved pressing those keys and seeing the drawer spring open to the sound of a bell, even though it was only a stepping-stone to what I wanted – and sooner rather than later.

Oddly enough, I loved it most when it was pelting rain outside and there were little streams of water all over the floor from umbrellas hooked on to the backs of the wooden chairs. Those stormy days, in winter especially, the café was darker than usual, and smelt more strongly of coffee, but mostly of wet overcoats. It felt peaceful and cosy, and even the waitresses, who were usually rushing around, seemed to slow down. Behind our cake counter, where my cash register was, Pearl and I and whoever else was on duty with us were never that busy on wet days, so we were able to relax and chat.

Pearl was gentle and courteous with everyone, all the staff and the customers and even me. She did her work really well, and the customers, particularly the older ones, liked her very much. But she spent most of her free time back in the digs where she was never without her nose in a book. Mealy's was closed on Sundays but all she did was go to late Mass and that was the sum total of her life. She had certainly changed since the events at Kilnashone: now she seemed to like her own company best, and even though I tried, I couldn't jog her out of it. What happened there that night had got under her skin.

I don't say it hadn't affected me too but I was the kind, d'you see, who got over things. Yes, it was terrible what had happened, with Willie dead, Papa gone and us losing our home and everything. Awful. But brooding about it wouldn't undo it, would it? Who would it help?

Pearl had gone so quiet, though, she wasn't much fun as a companion. She's still lovely, you know, despite her years on the clock. She has a capacity for love too – she should have been rewarded with a great husband and a couple of loving kids. She was built for it: had there ever been a single person in the world she had badmouthed?

Well, there had been one. That oul' Lord Areton.

In many ways, although Pearl was the eldest of the children in our immediate family, she was younger in spirit than me, far more innocent and naïve all her life, God bless her. As for looks, she never rated herself: 'Oh, Ruby's the good-looking one,' and so forth. Yes, Ruby was good-looking, or was until she lost all that hair of hers – needlessly, as it turned out, because the treatment didn't work for her and she died anyway. But I'm an expert on looks and, believe me, Pearl was the real stunner of the family.

I was three years in Dublin when I knew I had to move out of Mealy's, get a better job and digs, even a flat, of my own. Ruby would leave school the following year so her arrival with Mama – so we could all live together again – was not that far away any more. I had to get a move on.

Joe, though, was still saying that at eighteen I was still too young for Clery's and the best he could do for me was to watch out for a job in the café there. 'At least you'll have your foot in the door and get known. Once you've made an impression on the management you can watch for openings and move sideways.'

I wasn't keen. I'd done my time in cafés. That very day, on my lunch break, I went into Arnott's and asked if there were any vacancies on the shop floor. There weren't.

But then the girl scribbled something on a piece of paper. 'Mooney's on the Quays has been bought out, and I hear the new owners are looking for people. Do you know the place?' She handed me the paper with the address of the shop.

I did know it. Mooney's wasn't Arnott's or Clery's, but it was a bit of the way up that kind of ladder. It was known for being good with women's underwear, corsets and brassières and so forth. Our auntie Margaret, Iris's mother, had been a customer there. But it also sold haberdashery – and uniforms of all descriptions. There'd be opportunity there. 'Good luck,' the girl said kindly. 'I know what it's like, looking for your first job. I can remember.'

'Thanks,' I said, resisting the temptation to tell her I was a three-year veteran.

I saw immediately I walked into the interview that the fella behind the desk would be a pushover. No one could have called him a film star and by my reckoning he was at least thirty, but he had these lovely soft brown eyes and a nice shy smile. I'd dressed to the nines, of course, and after the first few minutes, I could tell I'd walked it. That turned out to be Frank. My Frank, the son of the owners of Mooney's. The manager.

I was careful not to scare him. We had a couple of 'dates' together – that is, we'd gone to the cinema and had a cup of tea afterwards, but by Christmas of that first year, I had managed to beg a couple of tickets for Clery's dress dance at the Gresham. Frank had hit the after-dinner brandies a bit too hard and got a bit tiddly so was unsteady on the old pins when I took him up for the last waltz. 'I want to dance, Frank Igoe, and if I have to carry you around the floor,' I said, making a joke of it, 'we're going to dance.'

170

'I love you,' he said, when we'd found a bit of space on the floor and I held out my arms to him. He was smiling at me with that kind of lopsided grin he had, but it was even more lopsided now because of the brandies.

Nothing like striking while the iron was hot, I thought, so I said, 'Where I come from, Mr Igoe, that's a proposal.'

'In that case, I'd like to be from there,' he said, and wobbled a bit so I had to make a grab at him to keep him upright.

Now, Frank had a degree and all from University College Dublin out in Earlsfort Terrace, but he wasn't at the races when it came to cop-on. 'Is that so?' I said, delighted with myself. 'Oh, Frank! Thank you!' and I threw my arms around his neck and, right there in the middle of the floor, kissed the mouth off of him.

'I accept your proposal,' I said to him, after I'd pulled away. 'Thank you very much indeed.' And I kissed him again. (He kissed me back this time, which was quite good, otherwise I'd have been a bit worried.) And then some young fella I didn't know from Adam who was dancing beside us gave a big 'hoo-hoo' at the top of his voice, and then didn't he run up to the bandstand and tell someone, and the next thing they'd started to play 'Here Comes The Bride'. And that's how we got engaged.

I do miss him, actually.

There was one time I asked Pearl who she missed. 'There must be someone,' I said. It was a silly question on the surface but I was born to pry, I guess.

'Our parents, of course. And Ruby,' she added, but she was going red. She has this fine, very fair skin; porcelain, they'd call it on the cosmetic counters and the slightest blush shows up instantly. This was my chance, I thought, but then again, nah! Pearl can create an exclusion zone around herself in the blink of an eye and she was doing it now. Can't describe it. You just know it's there.

I suppose that's because she's a writer. They get used to not telling nobody nothing – isn't that right? I love her lots but she drives me mad sometimes.

23

PEARL

It was the day of my luncheon appointment with my literary-editor-cum-publisher, Dan Bannon, that nice man who, from my very first submission, has taken my stories to make books out of them. We have a good working relationship; we both understand that neither of us is going to become a millionaire from the enterprise, but he genuinely likes my writing and is always gratifyingly pleased when I get a good review or when my books go into reprint – which, thank goodness, they always do. In fact, I have come to expect this now, and should it not happen with one of the collections, I think I would be very disappointed.

My books are, however, what they call *succès d'estime*, meaning that those who read them love them and the critics do not deride them, but mass readers have not yet discovered what they are missing! Sales are always steady but never spectacular and I have to admit that it is lovely to have a loyal aficionado like Dan who continues to tell me it is only a matter of time before my talent is recognised.

A Scot who has lived in Ireland for thirty years, Dan is the perennial optimist. As each publication date rolls round, he always says the same thing at our celebratory lunch: 'You never know what might come out of the woodwork, Pearl. I think there's one in particular in this lot,' brandishing the latest offering, 'that would make a handy little movie.' He has said it and meant it about at least one story in every book of mine he has published since the first, and I like him for it. It would be lovely, for his sake, if we could break through with something.

As I came down the steps towards the basement restaurant, I could see through the window that he was already at our usual table. We both liked the Country Shop on St Stephen's Green, he for the quality of its homemade soups and scones, I for that too, but also for the opportunity to buy some of the lovely artisan products, baskets, shawls, scarves, produced by the membership of the Irish Countrywomen's Association, who ran the place. For every book I published, I bought myself something as a reward; it did not have to be expensive or luxurious, simply a symbol – after all the work comes the return.

After one of these luncheons, many years previously, while we were dawdling over coffee, Dan had leaned over and taken my hand in both of his. 'Is there a chance for me, Pearl?' His meaning was clear.

I was so taken aback I dropped his hand as though it had scalded me. 'You're a married man, Dan Bannon!'

'And if I wasn't?' He held steady.

'But you are – look . . .' I had hesitated then. I really did like him and, up to that point, had had no inkling that he might have felt anything more than familiarity and friendship towards me since, to me at any rate, we had always been very relaxed in each other's company. But, of course, my antennae had been packed away for good at the end of 1923 and my soul had been fixed into Limbo. There had been but one person for me: he was gone and that was that.

Dan looked so forlorn now that I had to tread carefully along the line between encouragement and truth. Concealing my aston-ishment as best I could, I smiled in what I hoped was a neutral manner. 'I like you just the way you are. I like us the way we are. We have a long friendship ahead of us. Please, let's not complicate things.'

Immediately I saw that this had been a mistake. In my attempt to be kind I had left the door ajar. He rushed through it. 'So, you do agree that there could be something complicated, if we let it happen? That there is something special between us, I'm not imagining it?'

'Dan . . .' Again I hesitated. This was new territory for me and I did not want to be unkind – or patronising. 'I'm afraid you have been imagining things. And if I did give you the wrong impres-sion, I am truly sorry.' Gently, I took the hand that was still lying on the table where I had dropped it. 'I meant what I said. We're

173

good friends and colleagues. And that's the way I like it. I don't know what I'd do without you, Dan. I depend on you, I'd trust you with my life, and if I was ever in trouble, you would be the first person I would run to.'

'Wonderful.' Not normally evident, his Scottish accent, with its soft *d* and rolling *r*, came through. He withdrew his hand from mine and, with the index finger, traced circles on the table.

'I hope I haven't upset you,' I said quietly. 'I'm sorry, Dan.'

'I'm the one who's sorry,' he said. 'I didn't mean to embarrass you.'

'You haven't. You're a dear man. You couldn't embarrass me if you tried.' But we had run out of things to say, and it was clear we both wanted to leave now. He signalled for the bill.

Mercifully, it was raining heavily outside, giving us the perfect excuse not to linger.

'Are we all right now, Pearl?' He had to raise his voice a little against the din of the raindrops on our overlapping umbrellas.

'Of course we are.' I touched his arm.

'I wish it could be otherwise,' he said softly, and then, making a great effort to act as he usually did on these occasions, 'Cheerio now. If there's any news of interest, of course I'll telephone you.'

'Thank you. And thank you for a lovely lunch.'

He was about to say something more, but changed his mind. 'Well, 'bye now.' He turned and walked towards the Shelbourne Hotel. For the first time, he had not kissed my cheek on parting.

Some months later I met him and his wife in the foyer of the Queen's Theatre, after we had separately attended a play given by the Abbey players. I was with Opal, and we had a perfectly sociable and pleasant conversation about what we had seen. As we left the theatre and went our separate ways I was relieved the ice had been broken.

During subsequent conversations on the telephone and over the years at these lunches, neither of us had mentioned the episode. On the surface everything had returned to normal but, like the rumble of a distant storm, the memory was always there. I did not know how to dispel it, grew to ignore it and so, I think, did he. We managed. I believe no one seeing us together would have known that there was anything awry. From my perspective, however, I now felt that for meeting him I should make an effort to dress up and be extra specially cheery, even amusing, and while I favoured trouser suits for convenience, as I opened the door of the restaurant on that humid May day, I was wearing a gossamer fine silk dress over a slip, tights and high heels. I absolutely hated the feel of tights.

Summer or not, the Country Shop, with its woollens, ginghams and tartans, conveyed the ambience of a cosy winter's evening by the fire. 'Hello, Pearl.' A gentleman to the last, Dan stood up as I approached the table he had reserved in a corner. 'So nice to see you!' He shook hands with me as he always did. But something was different this time. Dan was beaming. Cheshire Cat beaming. He always smiled when I arrived but the smile this time almost reached his ears. And today there was not a trace of the awkwardness I've just mentioned, however insignificant it had become, in his demeanour.

As I sat down, he reached into the briefcase at his feet and produced the first copy of my new book. 'Hot off the presses. Bravo, Pearl!' Again, these were his annual congratulatory words. Our publishing lunches were like a well-ordered gavotte.

'It's lovely.' I ran my hand over the smooth dust-jacket, loving its feel. The sepia-tinted landscape of snow, fences and a single horse adorning the front cover of Dorothy Morris's latest opus was dignified and at the same time alluring. To me anyway. It was the type of thing I would pick up from a bookshop display. 'You've done a great job, Dan. Again. Thank you.'

'My pleasure, Pearl.' Instead of calling for someone to take our order, the next step in our formal dance, he still wore that huge smile while continuing to look across the table at me like a silly adolescent. He seemed literally to twinkle. It was most unsettling.

'Is something going on, Dan?'

He nodded vigorously and the smile, if anything, became even broader. 'Shall we order first and then I'll tell you?'

'Dan! Tell me.'

'Have you heard of Mary Lavin's collection, *Tales from Bective Bridge*?'

'Yes, of course I have.'

'Well, one of the stories in your collection here,' he tapped the book on the table between us, 'is being compared, favourably, I might add,' he dispensed a courtly little nod, 'with one of the stories in hers.'

175

'By whom? And which one?'

'Yours or hers?' He was teasing, a trait I had never seen in him before.

'Mine, of course.'

'"The Dandelion Clock".'

'Pardon?' I was taken aback. I had thought that 'The Dandelion Clock' stood out from all the other stories in the collection, all right, but for all the wrong reasons. I did not think it had worked well and had included it as the second last entry in the book simply to make up the numbers, and in the hope that, in the reader's mind, the last story, which I did like, would make up for its deficits. I had been in a strange mood while writing it and to me there are stories of much finer literary merit in the collection.

'They love it!' Dan, who had been watching my struggle to come to terms with what he had told me, was still wearing that most disconcerting grin.

'Who loves it? Dan, you're talking in riddles.'

He reached again into his bag and pulled out a sheaf of papers. 'These people. This is a contract, Pearl, from film producers and they want to buy "The Dandelion Clock" for a film. A feature film. They're serious players, Pearl. They're backed by a German TV station, the BBC is interested in putting some money into it too, they have the development finance in place and the producer is experienced. Congratulations, Pearl. Dorothy is on her way to Oz!'

'Well,' I said faintly, 'they do say that bad books make good films!'

'Pearl!'

I had not meant it. I was very pleased indeed.

At the same time I was thinking that there was no accounting for literary taste.

Dan and I had a great lunch, with, as far as I could tell, no trace of the rumblings under the surface of which I have spoken – and as well as giving me the traditional kiss on the cheek he actually hugged me.

On the way home in the bus, still not quite believing what had happened – although I had signed the contracts Dan had given me and he had explained the ins and outs of what was to happen next (it all sounded fearfully complicated) – I was trying to sort out my feelings.

I mentioned that I had been in a bad mood when I wrote that particular story. I started it just after my sixtieth birthday when all I saw ahead was a slow slide into isolation, with a withering body and a confused mind, trying to come to terms at last with the facts of my life. Reason told me that the chances of ever meeting Thomas Areton again were non-existent. And yet, in the deepest, darkest recesses of my soul, I had continued to hope that we might somehow encounter one another and – I accept this may be hard to believe – rather than diminishing, that hope had increased the nearer I got to old age.

'The Dandelion Clock' is a story about a pining, foolishly faithful woman, who spends her inheritance over two decades in a world-wide and ceaseless search for her lost lover, taking pathways as random as the dandelion clock's seeds. Her money runs out and her quest is ultimately fruitless, because it is he who finds her, years later, when she is dying, a pauper, in a hospital bed. It is a gloomy piece, outside the run of my normal work. I suppose one could call it 'bittersweet', which may be why it caught the attention of the film community. And, having thought about it, I now realise it is quite possible (authors do not always recognise their motivations) that I wrote the story as an allegory, heavily disguised, for my own situation or, rather, the desires of my imagination.

For the first few years after I left Kilnashone my hope was still bright. I was working long shifts in Mealy's café in Dublin, the name of which I had given him, and for months, years even, I had looked up with hope almost every time the bell rang when someone came through the door. As time went on, however, while I continued to hope, the fear that we would not meet began to fester in parallel. And then, when I was in my forties, Mealy's closed.

I moved to another job in the Moira Hotel, choosing it delib-erately because it was in the same street as Mealy's and, for a while, spent my breaks hanging around near the windows, or outside the door, hoping he might pass by on his way to the defunct Mealy's, but he did not. Mealy's mouldered for years and was then leased by a hairdresser who renamed it Golden Tresses, further burying the possibility of his finding me.

So even if he was still searching, I was now invisible in Dublin, living with my sister, whose entry in the telephone book was 'Igoe, Francis', even though her husband had died. 'It's safer that way, Pearl,' she had said. 'You don't put a woman's name into the directory, and using an initial is a dead giveaway. Burglars look for that, you know!'

A few times, when she was out for the afternoon, I had made attempts to find Thomas's or Isabella's telephone number in England through Directory Enquiries, but had drawn a blank. If he had a telephone number under his own name it was probably unlisted, the very helpful man told me. And as for Isabella, she too had probably married, but even if she had not, most VIPs, including the aristocracy, kept their telephone numbers secret from the *hoi-polloi*. He suggested writing to the House of Lords in London.

I did that and actually got a letter back, telling me that the Areton seat was currently unattended, and that the whereabouts of the current Lord Areton, although presumed living, were at present unknown.

I cling to 'presumed living' and entertain vivid pictures as to where he might be. The one I shed as soon as it pops into my mind is the one of him playing with his children. I disbelieve it. Our passion for each other was unique. I have to believe that. I do believe that.

The image I favour is of him wandering the world, like Yeats's Aengus, going to his hazel wood to catch his little silver trout, and finding me, no longer a glimmering girl, but my love for him burning with undiminished intensity.

24

PEARL

The 'little party' for Catherine's send-off had been set for the afternoon of 7 June and she was leaving on the ninth. 'Because it's a Sunday,' Opal had decreed, 'we'll have it start at three p.m., and people can come and go. That's always the best kind of party, don't you think? They can come for an hour or six hours. We'll have plenty of food and drink to sustain them. Let's hope it's a nice day.'

The event was no longer 'little', however. It had expanded greatly because of my own good news concerning 'The Dandelion Clock': now it was to be my party too and my sister's 'few friends coming over' included my publisher, his wife, 'And anyone else you think might like to come, Dan,' I heard her say to him on the telephone. Invitations also went to every bookseller in Dublin, with an explanatory note in her looping hand, and I even heard her on the phone to Dan a second time, asking if he could give her the addresses of 'the film people' too. In all she sent out 103 formal invitations.

On a practical note, she engaged the services of two gardeners to 'put manners on' the front and back lawns, hired a caterer, a firm that supplied marquees and canopies, in case it rained, and a professional cleaning firm to augment the efforts of her regular ladies. In addition, the rugs had to be taken up and the curtains removed for specialist dry-cleaning. As for the windows, it took a squad of three men a full day before she was satisfied. She was in her element.

'Are you sure you don't mind, Catherine?' I asked our young cousin, about a week before the big day. She had just finished her exams, poor thing, and her eyes were hollow. We were having tea in Opal's white-tiled kitchen, an extension of the original house, lit by a row of skylights. It was actually bigger than the drawing room and, in my opinion, outdid the most massive and glamorous American kitchens seen in films and on TV. Two large fridge-freezers stood side by side; there were two sinks, a huge range, cupboards and larders from floor to ceiling, and an acreage of countertop – and that was not all. In the scullery off the main room, she had had installed a third sink alongside more cupboards and a row of white goods – dishwasher, washing-machine and tumble-drier – all for two elderly women rattling around. It was a far cry from our kitchen at the gate lodge – and I think this might be what spurs Opal's passion for materialism and luxury. She and I have always had diametrically opposed memories of Kilnashone.

But she has a talent for décor, and had this kitchen, with its machines and tiles, been organised by less skilful hands, it might have appeared clinical or sterile. Instead, and hats off to her, it was a comfortable place to linger, with upholstered chairs around the huge table, from which, through a set of french windows, stretched a view of the patio, furnished for outdoor dining, and beyond, a truly lovely garden.

'Of course I don't mind that it's now your party too.' Catherine leaned across the table. 'It suits me, actually. Between ourselves, Pearl, I wasn't looking forward to hobnobbing with Opal's bridge and golfing pals. At least now there'll be Dan and Jean.' Jean is Dan's wife. 'I really like them.'

'I overheard her tell Dan to bring whoever he'd like – and I hear that some of the film people are coming too, so it won't just be Dan and Jean.'

'All the better. It will be good to have new people of our own, Pearl. No offence to Opal, of course, and don't think I don't appreciate all the trouble she's going to on my behalf, but I find there's just a bit too much "fun" –' she made rabbits' ears with the index and middle fingers of both hands to signify the quotation marks '– when Opal and her friends get together.' She smiled fondly and put a hand on my forearm. 'Now you know I don't mean to be bitchy about them, because they're gas. Really they are. But in small doses.'

I knew what she meant. Many of those in Opal's immediate circle are widows like herself, and since like attracts like, they, like her, seem determined to sip every last drop from the punch bowl of life. Quite literally sometimes, for they can certainly drink, and while they are intrinsically good, likeable people, after a few gins their communal hilarity, joke-telling and singing begins to pall.

For instance, halfway through the evening of Opal's last big get-together a couple of years ago, they formed a conga line and snaked around this kitchen, chanting, 'Live a lot, love a lot . . .' sweeping me into it in front of a most amazing creature one of them had brought along, a man who called everyone 'sweetie'. He wore a striped blazer and an eye patch, and his 'good' eye bulged in all directions from under the enormous brim of the black hat that he did not take off for the duration of the party. I am not an effusive person, and while I tried hard to go along with all their party games and singing – I escaped to my own room as early as politeness allowed. I do not think anyone noticed, actually, such was the octane level of exuberance.

So I am quite glad that Opal's parties come around only about once every couple of years – the big ones anyhow. This one, with its cast of characters from the book trade and perhaps the business side of the film world, looked set to be somewhat more sober. 'They certainly know how to party, I agree,' I said to our young cousin now, 'but what about your own friends, Catherine?'

I had worried that she seemed to have very few chums of her own age and while she had introduced one girl, Frances, to us as her 'best pal', we had not met any others. For a young girl, she seemed far too comfortable around older people; it came of being brought up among a cohort of old fogeys like us and her great-grandparents, I suppose. 'Ah – I did ask Frances,' she said airily, 'but she'd already arranged to go to Courtown with her family for June and she doesn't have a car, so it would be very awkward for her to get back here from there, and it wouldn't be worth it just for a couple of hours. I don't mind – really, Pearl. I'll be grand. Anyhow, I'll have Poppa and Mandy to look after during the party and, to tell you the truth, I'm just focused now on getting to America as quickly as possible. Can't wait!'

Alongside her squads of professionals, and with myself and Catherine as intermittent helpers, Opal worked flat out from that afternoon until, on the night before the party, there was virtually nothing left to do. She produced a terrific lasagne and, as dusk stole over the garden, impeccably tidy and colourful through the open french windows, the three of us, replete and pleasantly tired, were still sitting at the kitchen table drinking not tea but gin and tonic. Opal had been *flaithiulach* with the gin and I was feeling no pain.

Now she yawned and stretched. 'Nearly half past ten, girls. I've an early start tomorrow so I'm off to bye-byes.' She stood up and tapped Catherine lightly on the top of her head. 'See you in the morning, lovey. I still can't believe that in all the years we've known you, this is the first night you've spent under our roof.'

'I can't believe it either, Opal.' Catherine smiled up at her.

'Bobby and Margaret all right for the night?'

'They're looking forward to tomorrow. The minders are in and already well used to them. The place is running like a Swiss watch.'

'Shall we go to bed too, Catherine?' I asked, when we were alone. 'It's been a long day.'

'Let's have one more drink. Just a nightcap, eh?' She giggled.

'Surely.' She was a lovely girl and I would miss her for the next few months, not only for herself, but for the energy and gaiety she brought to our lives. Particularly to mine. 'I'd like to wish you a *bon voyage* before the madness starts tomorrow and we don't get to talk to each other at all.'

'And to wish you, Pearl,' she poured two generous measures and added the tonic, 'all the very best with your movie. To "The Dandelion Clock"!' She raised her glass.

'"The Dandelion Clock" and the United States of America!' I clinked my own against it.

'I've read it, you know . . .'

'I know. You told me.' I sipped my drink.

'No. I've really read it. I understand, Pearl.' She smiled tipsily at me. 'I've read all the stories in that collection – thanks for giving it to me, by the way. I'll treasure it – but I don't need my English tutor to tell me that "The Dandelion Clock" is the outlier in that book.'

'What do you mean?'

'You know what I mean. Pearl, I've always thought there was a bit of mystery hanging over you. That story tells me it's a man. It's far more direct, more real, than any of the others. Amn't I right?'

'Shall we turn on a light?' I was not ready to discuss Thomas

Areton with anyone and I got up and clicked the switch that operated the under-cupboard fluorescents Opal had had installed as soon as they became available. Fixed behind the lower frame of the presses, their light was subtle, reflecting on the polished granite of the counters and imparting a feeling of intimacy to the room. I stood back to admire the effect. Then, to add to the glamour, I crossed to the french windows and switched on the garden lights. 'God,' Catherine said, her tone imbued with genuine wonder. 'It's like Disneyland! It's lovely.' She had taken the hint and hopefully, there would be no more about 'The Dandelion Clock' or me. I laughed. 'Nothing but the best for the Somers Girls!

It was lovely. Like embroidery on the domes of light cast by the dozens of ground-lamps buried in the flower borders rain fell softly outside. The people who had installed the marquees, which were more like pagodas, three-sided, with conical roofs, had added their own lighting, in shades of green and blue, and they clicked on as well. 'Disneyland? You really do love all things American, don't you?'

'Oh, I do, Pearl, I love America,' she breathed, eyes shining like a little girl's.

'Don't forget to come back to us – sure you won't?' I gave her a hug.

We finished our drinks, and very soon afterwards, we went to our respective rooms. I looked in on her before I got into bed. She was asleep in the clothes she had been wearing, her overnight case still unopened. I kissed her gently on the forehead, turned out the light and tiptoed from the room.

The next day dawned a 'scorcher', as the newspapers would have it, so by the time the party started that afternoon, the marquees in the back garden, with its immaculate grass and merry colours in the borders, newly planted for the occasion, were needed more for shade than for shelter. I thought of them as jesters' tents and, actually, what with the milling crowds, the bright summer colours of the women's clothing – and even some of the men's – the scene could have been taken from a medieval pageant or joust. I doubt, however, that in the middle ages the spectators enjoyed anything as sumptuous as the running buffet manned by Opal's professional caterers and their staff.

As for the house – it was as elegant as any you would see in a glossy magazine; the sixties craze for angles and garish colour had passed Opal by, and whatever about blond wood and so on, her taste in soft furnishings harked back to a more luxurious era when opulence had reigned. Every room in the house sang with cleanliness, glowed with comfort and garnered sustained praise from her guests, almost all of whom, apparently, had accepted the invitation and had actually turned up – even some of the 'film people', would you believe?, although the most important person, the producer, was apparently off doing something tremendously urgent in Bulgaria or somewhere like that. I was introduced to those who had arrived by Opal as 'your writer', which had as much effect, I think, as introducing a flea to a dog!

Throughout, I continued to think of the party as Opal and Catherine's, an event during which my role was as usual to stay in the background and be unobtrusively helpful. Therefore I was continually surprised when someone, usually someone I did not know, came up to me with glad hands and congratulations.

I was embarrassed by all the attention and always deflected conversation about my achievement by diverting it towards Dan who, with his wife, a manager of a small bookshop in the suburbs of the city, did seem to know a huge number of the guests. 'Dan's the one who did all the work,' I said, over and over again. 'He contacted everyone in the world, practically, and someone eventually came up trumps.' And: 'Yes, it's very exciting,' I repeated. Or: 'No, I'm afraid I don't know when it will be actually in the cinemas.' And: 'Unfortunately, I will have no say in who plays any of the parts.' This was to complete strangers, two young men, one of whom sported a very large tie along which were pictured the black and white keys of a piano.

I was not rushed off my feet exactly, but people were kind, most also extolling Opal's virtues as a party organiser and praising the gods of weather.

At about six o'clock I had had enough and the party had begun to thin out, in the way parties do – one group leaves and several others, who had been hanging back from politeness, join the rush. I was standing at the open french windows in the kitchen, saying goodbye to people and thanking them for coming. Soon only the stragglers, perhaps twenty people or so, remained. They seemed to know each other and pushed several of the garden tables together to settle with their drinks in a particularly sunny part of the garden. They looked as though they were there for the long haul.

'Where are Bobby and Margaret?' I caught Catherine's arm as she whizzed by with a pen and her address book in her hand.

'In the drawing room,' she yelled over her shoulder as she crossed the lawn towards a chap who was unmistakably American because he was wearing what I believe was a cap worn by baseball players. I think he might have been one of the 'film people' to whom I had been introduced, but I had met so many strangers that afternoon, I couldn't be sure. Anyhow, she joined him and they seemed to be exchanging notes, probably addresses, I thought.

I watched them for a couple of minutes as they laughed together. He even gave her a friendly thump on the shoulder when she said something he enjoyed. And when Opal interrupted them and bore her off to meet someone else, he watched her go. I was really glad that she seemed not only to be enjoying herself but to be making connections with people her own age.

Nevertheless, impelled by the need to protect her, I went down into the garden and, casually, as if just wandering by, held out my hand. 'Oh, hello! I'm Pearl Somers – I'm sorry, I can't remember your name?'

'Hi there, Miss Somers. I'm Sam – Sam Travers! Great party, thanks for inviting us. Hey!' He looked closely at me. 'You're the writer, OK?'

'I am. Are you part of the film they'll be making?'

'Not yours. We've just wrapped one in Greece. We did a bit of post-production in London and tomorrow, unfortunately,' he glanced again over my shoulder towards Catherine, 'we go back to the US. I'm a nobody on set, Miss Somers, what they call a runner, just a summer job. You familiar with the term?'

'No.'

'Well, it's what it sounds like. I run here, run there, fetchin' and carryin' for folks who want stuff on set or in the office. It's fun, but a profession it ain't.'

'So, do you want to be in the film business?'

'No, ma'am. I'm in law school. Berkeley, California.' He was still glancing over my shoulder.

'I see you've met Catherine?'

'Oh, yeah, she's gorgeous – we said we might get together. I

185

may be in Chicago last week of vacation, we're gonna keep in touch. You know her?'

'She's my cousin.'

'Well, you got a lovely cousin, Miss Somers!'

'I know. Well, thank you for coming. And have a safe journey home.' I liked this breezy young man. Catherine would be fine with him if they did, in fact, 'get together' in Chicago.

As I went back towards the house, I felt my duty as a part-hostess had been fulfilled. It would be safe for me to go into the drawing room and join Margaret and Bobby.

Bobby, who was pink-faced and coughing, saw me come in and attempted to wave but was attacked by another spasm. 'That's bad,' I said, batting away the wreaths of cigarette smoke in which they were both enveloped. 'Why don't you give up those cigarettes, the two of you? I'm trying to – there's research that says—'

'I know all about that damned research,' he interrupted, still wheezing. 'They're gaspers for sure but I'm too old to change now. You have to have some little thing to enjoy in life, isn't that right, Mags?' He smiled at his bird-like wife, whose fingers, like his, were brown at the tips. Then he turned back to me. 'How are you, Pearl? Isn't this a great occasion?'

It was – hats off to Opal.

And when dear Catherine left to go home, I did ask her about the American boy.

'Yes, his name is Sam. He's nice – actually, he's from LA but he could easily be in Chicago for a week or so during the summer. Isn't it gas? I gave him the address of our apartment.'

I was amused to hear that she had already adapted to the American jargon. LA indeed. But I was very pleased for her.

25

CATHERINE

The apartment I shared with my two new flatmates, Dory and Peggy, stood back a little from the tree-shaded Magnolia Avenue in Rogers Park, Chicago, and was gorgeously exotic to me, with its avocado-coloured gas stove, massive washing-machine, tumble-drier and vast 'icebox'. It was perfectly situated for us, close to an L station, from which the frequent elevated trains took us down-town in twenty minutes, depositing Dory and me less than ten minutes' walk away from our campus. A further two-minute walk brought Peggy to her hospital.

Rogers Park was a northside district that announced its Jewish heritage with the presence of delicatessens on almost every corner. Up to then I had thought there were only two kinds of bread, white and brown, but it was while living on Magnolia during those few weeks that I learned to love bagels with lox and cream cheese, Reuben sandwiches, pastrami on rye and all the other staples and breads on offer.

To say that I took instantly to America is an understatement. I fell for it. Within days I was using the lingo, 'garbage' for rubbish, 'store' for shop, 'fall' for the season that was next to arrive. I drank 'sodas' instead of minerals, walked along 'sidewalks', 'called' people instead of ringing them, and used a 'purse' instead of a handbag. And, since no one else seemed all that worried, waking to the sway of my bed during a small earthquake was a source not of fear but of curiosity.

Most enjoyably of all, having taken my first ever shower, I eschewed bathing for the rest of my stay. The weather was hot and steamy but I was young and adored the novelty of standing for up to a quarter of an hour under the powerful deluge, playing with the temperature of the water.

Dory and Peggy also introduced me to new vegetables and salads – broccoli, rutabaga, zucchini, iceberg lettuce – as opposed to the limp 'salad' leaves, cauliflower and cabbage I was used to. I sprinkled exotic herbs such as oregano on my Campbell's tomato soup, I was initiated into the joys of peanut-butter-and-jelly sandwiches (and tried to get them to eat my equivalent, made with bananas and butter, which they found 'disgusting'!). I learned to use turmeric to spice up bland sauces, nutmeg to sprinkle on hot chocolate.

Monday night was girls' night in, and on Monday nights, we played music on the hi-fi, shot the breeze and dished the dirt on boys. Every day I learned more new and enjoyable slang, and to say two thirty instead of 'half past two' and 'a quarter of' rather than 'to' three. We watched television, of course – including re-runs of my beloved *Lucy Show*. We wolfed the pepperoni sausage and mushroom pizzas delivered to our door along with a six-pack of Budweiser beer, feeling bloated and guilty afterwards but happily sated nonetheless.

God, I loved it. From my L stop every morning, I was carried along in the throng of office-bound workers in their suits and whiter-than-white shirts and felt part of this real and very purposeful world. As a bonus, having been accustomed to hunching my shoulders to minimise my height, it was wonderful to feel I could stride straight-backed among all these tall people.

Overall, during that short but magical period, I almost completely shed my self-consciousness. I became an American consumer and, in that regard, it was a time of dizzying and delightful discoveries, not only 'ordering out' for food and liquor, but catalogue-shopping, through which one could expect to receive a plethora of free gifts, including quite decent watches and 'comforters' – eiderdowns – along with the goods ordered. And if you needed any household item, from a rug or a couch to a sweeping brush, the local Goodwill charity store obliged for a fraction of what I would have expected to pay. Americans threw out perfectly serviceable stuff.

There was one more thing, crucial to what was to happen to me.

Quite quickly, I discovered that, unlike the way girls in Ireland were brought up to conclude that boys were an exotic and somewhat dangerous species to be whispered about with trembling excitement, American girls and boys seemed to take each other for granted as ordinary friends, alongside the deeper girlfriend-boyfriend relationships. While Peggy had what seemed like dozens of close friends who were boys, Dory had been pinned, which meant that she wore a little gold token, called a Lavalier, around her neck, offered by her boyfriend and accepted by her to indicate a relationship. Not all that serious yet. Sort of a stepping stone.

From day one, my roommates sensed my greenness in opposite-sex matters. They took me under their wing, letting me in on the defined system of tolerance for each other's boyfriends, which included leaving a clear field in the apartment. By democratic rotation, one got to stay in while the other two went out for a couple of hours. There was no hoo-hah about it; it was just how things were.

I flowered in America. It had something to do with being away from home, with not having any history that anyone was concerned with, no responsibilities to anyone except myself. I felt as light as air, as if I could take on a new personality, if that was what I wanted. And I did want that. I found it easy in this new world of acceptance and possibility, where I had no history, where nobody cared whether I was shy or not, or an orphan, or tall, or any of it. There were no decisions to be made, no exams to face at the end of the summer; I was confident I would not have to repeat any of my UCD subjects. I had been given permission to have fun for a few months and I was ready for this challenge.

Life was to get even more exciting. In the matter of boys, the tuition of my new roommates soon bore fruit. I met Lyle McKenzie on my fifth day working in the library, which was the Monday of the second week. Although it was summer, the college, which operated a year-round four-semester rotation, was open and the library was well populated. I was at my assigned desk, still getting to grips with the complexities of the Dewey Decimal System, when I heard a polite clearing of the throat and looked up to find a beautiful boy standing there.

That is the correct adjective. He was beautiful. Scots-Hispanic, as I discovered later, his grandfather had immigrated from the Isle of Mull, his mother from Mexico City. He had blue-black curly hair, a wide, full-lipped mouth and thick eyelashes that framed eyes – I know this is going to sound like a Mills & Boon novel – the colour of aquamarines. They really were. A deep sea blue. 'Hi there, Irish,' he said. 'I'm Lyle.'

'How did you know I was Irish?' I was startled. Usually people didn't until I opened my mouth to speak.

'Well, that red hair is a dead giveaway, don't you think?'

I blushed – a response that, despite my new bravery, was proving hard to overcome. My hair is not carroty red, more a reddish blond. Strawberry. My desk was under a skylight in the library and I suppose that emphasised the colour. 'Your reputation went before you.' Lyle continued to smile. 'You're famous. We've never had real Irish in here before, only lots of second- and third-generation mutts. Welcome to Chicago.'

'Thank you.' I stood up to shake hands and found myself looking up at him. I was used, at the very least, to seeing eye to eye with men. 'And you're tall!' His smile broadened, now showing a set of what we now know as 'American teeth'.

The boy was flawless.

'I'm not that tall.'

'Tall enough to play basketball in this school! But, hey, I thought all you Irish were Little People . . .'

Well, almost flawless.

'These are my buddies.' He jerked a thumb towards three other boys behind him. They had books in their arms and were grinning. 'This is Shawn,' Lyle introduced them one by one, 'that's Irish, yeah? That's Chris over there and this jerk here is Bo.' The three came forward to shake my hand. They were all as tall and athletic as he, but in the beauty stakes none was a patch on Lyle who, having introduced them, told them to get lost. 'Scoot! I saw her first.' He waited until they'd left. Then, to me: 'Would you like to have coffee? What time do you get off?'

It was very flattering. I was very flattered.

Thus started what was the most extraordinary period of my life.

190

26

CATHERINE

For the first few days of Lyle's courtship, I could not believe that someone as popular, as intelligent, as gorgeous could be interested in me. He was a 'Greek' too, a member of a prestigious fraternity, in which membership consisted largely of college jocks – sports stars.

My boyfriend's sport was basketball. He, like many of his jock buddies, who all seemed to have single-syllable names or nicknames, were on an accelerated college programme, not taking the summer off but continuing to rack up their course credits to graduate and get out of school into the real world as quickly as possible. Along with Chris, Shawn and Bo, he introduced some of the others to me. I liked them, sort of – the 'sort of' was because they were loud, somewhat coarse, always jostling each other, always teasing. Also because, on introduction, they eyed me up and down in a way that made me feel uncomfortable. Once or twice I even felt they might be whispering about me among themselves.

Lyle was on a different plane, quieter, more respectful, definitely more mannerly, and although I frequently had to pinch myself, my confidence grew in proportion to my roommates' oft-stated envy. This Adonis could have had any girl in the college. No: make that any girl in Chicago. And he had chosen me, raw from Ireland and burdened with that particular brand of prudish, even smug, virginity that was endemic then in the 'Emerald Isle', as he insisted on calling it.

In that context, he put no sexual pressure on me. Even on nights when the girls had given over the apartment to us and we were making out on the couch, he never ventured further than the boundaries I set.

He did, of course, push those boundaries, but never aggressively, and what happened, inevitably, was that I allowed him to become gradually more intimate and even daring. After some weeks, even the most chaste of kisses between Lyle and me released a wild, agitated animal drive deep in the pit of my stomach. It was I who was now unsnapping the clasp of my brassière and offering my breasts to his mouth; I who was guiding his hands and fingers into places I had never explored myself.

At home, we had always been warned about the punishments awaiting the unwary who fell into the deadly trap of Lust – but what had never been explained was its overwhelming pleasure.

I became obsessed. During the day, as I dispensed library books and continued to wrestle with the Dewey Decimal System, my body seethed for Lyle while my brain kaleidoscoped with images of his, of which he had allowed me only small glimpses: 'No, Catherine,' zipping himself up again, 'no more. It's not fair to you.' Then, gathering me again into his arms, he would whisper tantalisingly, 'But when you're ready . . .'

Although there were no competitive games during that summer, I attended some of the knockabout sessions on the basketball court, and when I was cheering him on from the sidelines, I was watching not the run of play but the gleam on Lyle's deeply tanned thighs and shoulder muscles under the lights.

I fizzed with energy and desire, and at night I got minimal sleep – which had little to do with either the 100 per cent humidity or the rumbling of the L trains passing in close proximity to my bedroom window.

Once when I returned from work, I found a note from Peggy pinned to our notice-board: 'Sam called. He says you'll know who he is. You met him at a party.' And then his number. I hesitated. But I didn't want to complicate matters, to spend even ten seconds with anyone else. I'd just pretend I hadn't got the message, and if he called again, I'd make some excuse.

My love for Lyle was all I needed. I could think of nothing and no one else, not even poor Mandy, whose health, according to Poppa, who wrote faithfully once a week, had again deteriorated – 'but not too badly, Catty, just old age, gets us all, unfortunately! So you're not to worry about any of us, just continue to make the most of this wonderful opportunity. Wish I was young again!'

Shamefully, I buried any worries I might have entertained if I had been my normal self. I wasn't my normal self. I was a high-octane caricature of the girl who had landed at O'Hare airport such a relatively short time previously. I was consumed by expectations and visions of what was going to happen between Lyle and me. My imagination was in control of my brain. I saw myself naked on a white marble altar, offering myself for his use. I wanted to turn myself inside out so he could sample every part. I pictured it: the nibbling, the biting, the licking, some of which had already started . . .

It came to the crunch early on a hot, muggy Friday evening in mid-August, just after I got home from work. My roommates had yielded the apartment to us for a couple of hours but there was a TV special on that Dory wanted to watch at 8.00 p.m. so we had less time than usual. What was more, Lyle and his team mates were being taken to some sort of immersion sports weekend on a campus in Indiana very early the following morning, so after these couple of hours, I wouldn't see him for three whole days.

For whatever reason, that evening Lust was all-consuming and I cared little for Divine punishments or even sin. For the first time I understood what 'off my head' and 'crazy for him' meant. I wanted Lyle wholly and nothing less. I wanted him not only beside me, but above and below me. I wanted him inside me.

Even he seemed surprised by the ferocity of my drive. 'Hey, hold it, Irish!' He held me off, prising my grip from his back. 'Not so fast. It's your initiation, kid. We gotta slow down a little. We gotta make good memories. And don't worry, I brought a condom, just in case!'

He leaned down from the bed to the floor, extracted a small flat packet from the pocket of his discarded jeans, and brandished it at me. We laughed, him with amusement, me with ill-concealed fright.

That we might have needed contraception had never crossed my mind. What did cross my mind, in Capital Letters, was that we were embarked on Mortal Sin: the contraceptive debate at home, fuelled by a new and very vocal group called the Irish Women's Liberation Movement, was getting into high gear, not least in UCD. But the thought – and the fear – were momentary, because for the first time Lyle and I were playing for real and not just for teasing, and there was no going back.

Not that I wanted to. I was still clumsy in the attempt, but he was expert and drew me into his fantasy world where I was his plaything and he was mine. His kisses grew deeper and stronger, so much so that I could barely breathe, but when I responded by grabbing for him, digging my nails into his shoulders, he prised them away and pulled back: 'Hey! That hurt! Let me teach you something, Irish.' Before I knew what he was at, he had flipped me on to my stomach and was administering a quick, light but firm spanking. 'Now,' he hauled me over again to face him, 'you be a good girl, you hear? No more scratching. You do what you're told when you're with old Lyle. I'm in charge here. You get out of line again and that lovely bottom,' playfully, he reached around and caressed it, 'will really pay. Get it?' He flicked at my mouth with his tongue and then, briefly, inserted it in my ear, a sensation that inflamed all others.

I didn't 'get' anything. My head was bursting. My skin, where he had spanked it, was burning, and there was a commotion deep in my belly I had never felt before. I hardly knew what I wanted or where.

Well, I did, but I managed to restrain myself sufficiently to submit to his lead. And so, when he finally allowed us to come together, I was more than ready. I had been transported into another dimension where bodies were insubstantial and all that existed was sensation and an overpowering propulsion that led I knew not where and cared less.

Afterwards, side by side on my narrow bed, we lay on our backs, soaked and breathless. The mattress seemed as insubstantial as steam. I felt no support from any muscle, tendon or ligament; a rag doll would have enjoyed more physical tension.

Beside me, I felt Lyle stir, then felt him wiping between my legs with a towel. 'Not much blood,' he said tenderly. Staring at the light fixture above my head, which was pulsating in time with the rushing behind my eyes, I gave not a whit for modesty; whether temporary or not, all vestiges of that virtue had evaporated with my inhibitions. 'That was awesome, tiger,' my lover said, balling the towel and getting off the bed. 'You're a natural. Now, I gotta go to the washroom, clean up before your roomies come back.'

'OK.' I used my remaining strength to smile, but my eyes were closing, and as soon as he'd left the room, I moved to inhabit the full width of the bed, spread-eagling myself on the tumbled sheets to cool down.

I was drifting into a doze when I heard a sound that didn't fit. A type of whirring.

I opened my eyes to see Lyle at the foot of the bed. He was holding one of those Polaroid cameras, out of which was emerging a photograph. 'What?' I sat up and pulled up the sheet to cover myself. 'What are you doing?'

'Souvenir,' he said. 'Don't be alarmed. It's private. For us, babe! Now kick off that damned sheet and let me see you in your full glory.'

I hesitated. But this was Lyle. My boyfriend. I trusted him. I wasn't going to behave like a timid virgin because I wasn't one any more, was I? But an insistent little voice started up at the back of my brain: *Don't do this. It doesn't feel right . . .*

'Come on, Irish!' Lyle had put the photograph on the bureau beside him and was smiling behind the camera. 'Don't go all precious on me now.'

Reluctantly I let the sheet go, partially uncovering my breasts. But while he kept the eyepiece of the camera in place with one hand, he leaned down and, with the other, whipped it off so it slid to the floor and pooled.

Totally exposed, I was now really uneasy.

'Come on, babe!' he jollied me. 'You enjoyed yourself, didn't you? Let's see that you did. Give us one of those great Irish smiles!'

I forced my mouth into a stiff curve.

'Attagirl.' He clicked.

But as the second photograph emerged, I jumped off the bed, snatched up my sweatshirt from where I had so blithely discarded it on the floor and fled towards the bathroom, where I stood under the shower for much longer than necessary, my thoughts whirring like the mechanism of that odious machine.

I told myself I was being silly. Where was the harm if it was just for us to see? And hadn't he said he wanted us to make good memories for each other? Was I ashamed of what I had done?

No, I was not. I was now a grown woman. I had to behave like one. And I loved Lyle.

Still . . .

I made up my mind. I'd explain how I felt. I'd be light-hearted, tell him it was an Irish thing and he'd just have to put up with it. I'd make a joke about it, tell him we Irish were like the Red

195

Indians: we believed that photographs removed our souls. He'd understand. We'd laugh and then we would tear up the silly things. It would be one of those funny memories couples look back on when they're old and grey.

I was still mentally dithering when, over the noise of the shower, I heard him knocking on the door of the bathroom. I turned off the water. 'Be out in a second,' I carolled.

'Listen, babe, sorry, I know this is awful.' Through the door, his tone, although muffled by the wood, sounded cheery. 'I'm not running out on you or anything, but I forgot I had curfew tonight and now I'm real late. I'll get in trouble with Coach – talk Monday, yeah? You're some woman, Irish, that was great. Again, sorry, but talk soon. 'Bye!'

He hadn't told me about the curfew – the early departure for the immersion course must be the reason for it. Monday was an eternity away. 'Wait, Lyle, wait just a minute. I won't keep you!' I had to explain what I felt about those photographs. Quickly I took a towel from the rack but was still in the process of wrapping it around myself when I heard the door of the apartment slam shut.

27

CATHERINE

I fell for Lyle McKenzie as deeply as I believe any woman can fall for any man. I had foreseen my future with him. An American future, in which we would make children and live in an American house. I was ecstatically happy in his arms, and when he wasn't with me, I thought of nothing except meeting him again. I trusted him completely. And, to be honest, when I thought about it I really couldn't blame him for what happened during that Friday evening when I more or less forced him to make love to me. Personal responsibility has always been a big principle for me.

I can blame him, however, for what happened afterwards.

On the Sunday night, with Lyle still away, my roommates went to a movie, leaving me alone in the apartment. I welcomed the solitude in which to re-create for myself the feelings engendered by Lyle's lovemaking. I lay on my bed and, blow (literally!) by blow, imagined every second of our lovemaking. Only twenty-four hours to go before we were together again, and who knew what we would get up to next?

I had just switched on the TV when the phone rang. It was him! It had to be – he couldn't wait either . . .

But the weak, frightened voice at the other end belonged to Mandy. Poppa had had a heart attack. He had been carted off in an ambulance.

'But he's still alive, yes?' My heartbeat was suffocating me.

She burst into tears. 'I can't talk any more. Here's someone. They're all with me.'

There was a bit of shuffling. Then: 'I'm very sorry, love.' It was a neighbour as old as Poppa himself. 'There was really nothing we could do.'

'But he is still alive?' I gripped the phone. Very hard.

The woman hesitated. 'That's not for me to say, love. We just had a phone call from the hospital. All they said was that we had to contact all the relatives. We've booked you on tomorrow night's flight.' There was a rustling noise – she was reading something. 'It's at seven. But you have to be at O'Hare airport at four o'clock in the afternoon to collect the ticket and check in. It'll be at the ticket desk for you. Just ask for it under your name. It's paid for an' all.'

'Thank you,' I said faintly. It was too much too soon, a message too big to react to with something ordinary, like tears. I had to think about it.

'And you're not to worry about your granny,' the woman continued. 'The minder's gone with your granda in the ambulance, but we're all here, from the road. We're taking care of her. Don't worry about that.'

'Thank you,' I repeated, and hung up. Poppa was the rock. The eternal. She wouldn't tell me if he was still alive. He couldn't be dead. He wasn't dead.

Then, shamefully (I blush every time I think of this), seconds later, the predominant emotion became a frantic urge to get in touch with Lyle. He was not due home from Indiana until around six on the following evening, when he was to call me and we would go for a pizza or a hamburger. I panicked. I would be at O'Hare.

Inspiration struck. I could talk to his fraternity brothers. It was a Sunday evening so some of them would surely be in the house on campus: they'd know how to get in touch with him or, at the very least, as soon as he got back would let him know what had happened.

I scribbled Lyle a note, telling him I loved him with my heart, soul, body and mind, then explained what had happened and gave him our Dublin telephone number. I shoved it into an envelope, wrote his name on it and, in very big letters, marked it 'URGENT'. Then, grabbing my purse, I ran from the apartment to the L station.

I was lucky. A train was arriving just as I got to the platform. Less than twenty-five minutes after I'd received that phone call, I was walking towards Lyle's frat house.

There was no doorbell or knocker that I could see but the door was slightly ajar, with a light showing through the crack. Gingerly I pushed it open a few inches. I knew the house was male only. No uninvited female was ever to cross its threshold, a sacrosanct rule for all the fraternities, but this was an emergency. 'Hello?' I called. There was no response.

I pushed the door wider. From where I stood, I could see along the entire hallway, which was long, narrow and tidy enough, but showed it was definitely inhabited by boys. There was sports gear in full view on a bench seat, the light fixture hanging from the ceiling was unshaded, and the smell was a combination of floor cleaner and sweat. 'Hello?' I cried, a little louder. 'Anybody home?'

Still nothing.

I spotted a large notice-board at the back of the hall beside a door. It was one of those green baize ones with a black lattice to hold on its contents, which, from this distance, seemed to be leaflets and timetables. Could I sneak in to add Lyle's note to it? Even if I could find no one to inform about what I'd done, he'd be bound to find it there . . . But to be safe I shouted a third time. When still nobody answered, I took a deep breath and went in.

The heels of my sandals clicked far too loudly on the tiled floor and the light overhead was too bright. I was trespassing and knew it, but I kept going, telling myself this was the right, the only thing to do.

I hesitated in front of the notice-board, trying to find the most prominent position in which to tuck my envelope.

My eye was drawn to a document, columnar, roughly drawn up, boldly handwritten. Oh, God . . .

First, a vertical column of names, some I recognised as belonging to friends of Lyle: Sean, Shawn, Bo, Mack, Chris, Jeff. Beside it a parallel column of figures, familiar to anyone who has ever been to a race meeting in Ireland. A column of odds, one beside each name, 2/1, 8/1, evens and so on. Lyle's name was there. His odds, starting at 5/1, had been progressively reduced – and scratched out – until what remained was 1/10 on. Beside these odds there was a gold star.

Lyle was the winner. His reducing odds were as a result of his reported progress in seducing me. Because at the top of the sheet were pinned the two Polaroid photographs my boyfriend had taken of me.

I cannot adequately describe how I felt at that moment. I pulled down the photographs and ran. And ran. And ran. I ran until I had a stitch and could run no more. Then, panting, holding my side, I had to stop and lean against an iron gate for support.

When the stitch had subsided and I could breathe again, I looked around. I had no idea where I was. The street was residential, but deserted. There was a trash can near where I was standing. I was still holding the photographs. I tore them into little pieces – a difficult job with Polaroids, but shame and distress lent me strength. Then I stuffed the pieces as deep as my hands would go into the bowels of the bin, deep among the take-out containers, cigarette butts and old gum, some of which stuck to my fingers. I didn't care. It felt as though this was what I deserved for having been so stupid.

I saw traffic lights ahead. I made for them. Traffic lights meant a junction, meant traffic, meant cabs. I couldn't face the L, even if I could find it.

Again I was lucky. A cab, roof light illuminated, cruised by within minutes. It stopped when I hailed it. The driver, black and grizzled with age, nearly didn't take me because of the state I was in. I couldn't tell what I looked like. I know I was red-faced and damp; my hands reeked from their voyage through the trash; I was probably crying. By now the enormity of the humiliation – the degradation – had kicked in.

I held on to the door handle of the cab and wouldn't let it go. I begged. I had no pride left. The driver relented – 'I don't want no trouble, lady, hear?'

'No trouble. Thank you.' I got in.

The trip to Magnolia cost me almost every dime I had in my purse.

When my roommates got back to our apartment, they found me behaving like a dervish. I was racing around, sweeping clothes indiscriminately into my two suitcases, emptying my laundry basket into a plastic bag, rummaging through the communal medicine cabinet to extricate my stuff from among theirs. How was I going to get through the lifetime until that plane took off? I couldn't stop crying. And, of course, it came out: Poppa; Lyle; the whole deal, including the photographs.

They were taken aback, of course, and furious, and comfortingly indignant on my behalf. 'I can't speak.' Dory threw her arms around me. 'That rat! That skunk and his skunky friends . . . He'll pay for this. They all will. We'll make sure of that.'

You know the way that, when in extreme emergencies, you fasten on detail? I was frantic about that note to Lyle. To compound my shame, somewhere during my mad dash to get away from the frat house, I had lost it. The one in which I told him − actually wrote down − that I loved him with all my heart, soul, body and mind.

Oh, God!

Suppose I had dropped it on the campus and someone had retrieved and delivered it? He was a jock, a star. Everyone knew Lyle McKenzie.

Suppose − horrors! − I had dropped it on the floor of the fraternity house?

'It'll be a nine-day wonder.' While Dory continued to hug me, Peggy ran to our drinks cupboard and pulled out bottles. 'Bourbon, I think, and sweet vermouth. Don't give that note − or that jerk − another thought. We've all done something like that. Your great-granddad is what's important, not that loser or his loser buddies. Who would you prefer to be? You or him? Who's the monster here?'

'After what he's done,' Dory hugged me tighter, 'who do you think'll be able to sleep better at night?'

'I'll never sleep again.' I covered my face but couldn't blot out the image of those photographs. How many of Lyle's friends had seen them? What had they said? I could hear their laughter. 'How can you ask that, Dory?'

'She can ask it because that jerk will get no sleep by the time we're finished telling everyone on campus what he and his frat friends did to one of the nicest people we've ever met.' Peggy handed me the highball glass, clinking with ice and filled to the brim. 'Sip this. It'll make you feel calmer.'

'What is it?' I looked doubtfully at the drink, a deep, nutty brown.

'It's a Manhattan. Cures all ills. Be careful, though, it's very strong.'

201

Strong was the word: I sneezed after the first swallow, but then tipped the glass and drank the rest in one swoosh, as though it was Cidona.

'Good girl. You must have really loved your great-granddaddy.' Dory stroked my hair.

'I did.'

Neither of them was prepared for the outburst of tears and incoherence that followed. I could see them looking at one another with consternation. How were they going to manage me? Through my sobbing, I heard Dory ask Peggy, probably because of the latter's nursing experience, if she should call a doctor. 'No!' I yelled. 'No doctor! I'll be fine.' I fled to my room and slammed the door behind me. The room spun as I lay on my bed. The combination of the alcohol and the crash that usually follows a shock adrenalin rush overcame me and I fell asleep.

During that night, one or other of those lovely American roommates came in once – maybe more, given their sweet natures – to check on me. I dimly remember being covered with a blanket.

They were both gone the next morning when I staggered out into the living room, head pounding, stomach awash with nausea. They had left me a note expressing sympathy, wishing me luck with my 'sad' trip and hoping to see me again 'real soon'.

They wouldn't, because I had already vowed that I would never again set foot in America, which was a major loss to add to the catalogue. After all, what had happened was not America's fault, but I developed the (rather stupid) conviction that no matter where I went in what state, I would run into one of those fraternity members. There were Greeks on most of the big campuses throughout the US and I knew, just knew, that every one of them had seen those photographs, or had at least heard about them, and as soon as they learned my name, my shame would be revealed. I would be a legend, and not a good one.

For years my face flamed in the darkest part of night when, having woken with a sensation of dread, the lurid detail of that episode laid ambush – with the image of those spread-eagled, feet-first photos to the fore. ('We gotta make good memories,' he'd said – dear God Almighty!)

I know that, when set against the real sufferings of some people on this earth – torture, deliberate cruelty, floods, pestilence, starvation and murder – this was a minor setback and I've tried to see it in that light. At rock bottom, though, who is qualified to gauge the depth of the knife cuts in any other person?

28

CATHERINE

I've read many touching accounts of the return of Irish emigrants to the home sod, perhaps after the greater part of a life spent in the furnaces of Indiana or in service to an employer in the Bronx. For the first time, I recognised the depth of what they must feel.

After a slow descent my plane, having crossed the Atlantic during the night after a bleary-eyed stop in Montréal, crossed the west coast of County Clare at dawn, and I saw beneath me the frills of surf around the offshore islands, then cliffs. The plane banked steeply to line up for Shannon, and the patchwork of small fields, crooked walls, haystacks, cottages, straggled settlements and cows already on their feet to begin grazing became visible. There was a heavy rumble as the wheels emerged from the plane's belly, a final seesawing to straighten up for the approach, accompanied by a whining as if it was eager for land. Then a last, swooping rush before reunion with the ground of Ireland. Although I had been away for less than two months, I found it impossible to keep the tears locked behind my eyes.

Those of us bound for Dublin were required to get off the aircraft and go into the terminal building. Outside on the tarmac, the air was cool, and although it had obviously been raining until recently – there were little puddles everywhere – the sun had just risen and all round the airport the grass was spangled. An elderly couple walking alongside me couldn't get over it: 'Those brochures ["broh-shewers"] were right, Helen,' he said to her, in awed tones. 'It is as green as they say.'

'Yeah,' she agreed. 'Now I know we're not in Kansas, Toto.' They laughed together, and I really wished I could be one of them, and not me.

I hadn't slept on the plane. Every time I might have been about to nod off, like the pop-up images in a fairground shooting gallery, those photos materialised to remind me of my humiliation and what a fool I had been. Now, throat raw, I also had to come to terms with the knowledge that I would never again be able to speak to my beloved Poppa or ask his advice. I was convinced he had died. The neighbour's hesitation had told me as much.

On arrival in Dublin I was almost too tired to be emotional, or so I thought – until I emerged from the Customs hall and saw Opal and Pearl waiting at the barrier. I rushed towards them and collapsed, sobbing, into their arms.

They were wonderful, both of them. Looking back on it, they – in particular Pearl, who is far more reserved than her sister – might have been embarrassed by such behaviour in public, but they reacted with nothing but love, holding me and stroking my hair until the storm subsided.

On the way into the city, Opal outlined what had happened to Poppa. It was quite straightforward. He had been going out of the house to buy his newspaper and cigarettes as he had done every morning for years, and had collapsed on the doorstep. 'The doctors have assured us that he didn't suffer, Catherine.' By unspoken consent between Opal and herself, Pearl had sat beside me in the back seat. She was holding my hand. 'He was apparently dead before he hit the ground. There was nothing anyone could do for him. I'm so sorry.' I couldn't reply. I just held tightly to her hand.

They had brought him home to wake him, placing him in his bed in the room that had been his consulting room and, for the last few years, his bedroom too. There were connecting doors between this room and another, originally the dining room of this old house but unused for a decade. The minders had cleaned it up so that it was presentable for receiving the visitors who came in their dozens, perhaps hundreds. It certainly felt like hundreds as I sat beside Mandy to accept the condolences of the neighbours and friends who came to sit with us, bringing cakes and sandwiches and apple tarts, even saucepans full of stew. All the time I was thanking them and listening to them reminisce, I couldn't prevent my eyes straying to that still, waxy body, a head – for the first time in my memory beautifully coiffed – above a body that had been so full of bombast and laughter, of whatever

205

it is that constitutes life, so unmoving now. So dead. So uncaring. So unavailable.

I discovered that I was angry. I wanted him not to be dead. While I would never have dreamed of telling him what had happened to me in Chicago – I couldn't have humiliated myself in front of him like that – he had made me feel good about myself, no matter what, and now he had abandoned me in my hour of greatest need.

Beside me, Mandy coughed, a cough that turned into a spasm during which she found it hard to breathe. Since my return, she had barely spoken, looking out at the world through frightened, watery eyes. 'I'm fine,' she wheezed, as she regained control, but I was overcome with remorse. Whatever about my loss, she had lost her life's companion. 'Are you all right? Can I get you anything?' I tried to put my arm around her shoulders but we were interrupted yet again by the doorbell and a fresh influx of sympathisers.

By the end of that day I was exhausted, physically, mentally and emotionally. Opal and Pearl had stayed with us throughout, working quietly alongside the minder, making tea, answering the door, generally spreading an air of efficiency and calm. When they left to go home, promising to come back early the next day, I missed them. The night nurse had arrived – and I thought Mandy was relieved to see her, which added to my sense of helplessness and guilt.

I was glad to escape to my own bed, but for the second night in a row, despite extreme fatigue and jet lag, sleep eluded me for hours. It was humid and I turned from side to side, kicking off the covers and pulling them up again when I felt the draught from the open window. I could not shake off those horrific images from America. With Poppa downstairs but unreachable in his cold bed, I vacillated between anger and despair: at one minute I wanted to smash everything in the house because life was so unfair, at the next, to rip the flex off the bedside lamp and scourge myself until I bled. I'd been so gullible, such a fool, such an idiot.

My dearest wish was simply to vanish, like my mother had.

I eventually fell asleep at about half past four in the morning, but woke again an hour later from a nightmare in which, surrounded by grinning faces with red and purple smiles swirling and crowding me from all sides, I was being forced to dance and sing.

My first feeling on waking from a nightmare is always one of profound relief but within seconds, like a black tide, the reality of my situation came crashing in on me. I had toddled away from Ireland into the big world with shiny-eyed trust and, as far as I was concerned, it had turned its back on me. Poppa, on whom I might possibly have leaned, was gone. He couldn't even see my grief. To add to it, my great-grandmother, whom I loved but who wasn't Poppa, was too physically and emotionally frail, too immersed in her own sorrow to help me – in any case, it was I who should have been comforting her.

At least I wouldn't have to do it on my own, I thought. Pearl and Opal would be around, and the support systems Poppa had set up to tide him and Mandy over the summer were still in place. Then I castigated myself afresh for renewed selfishness. I jumped out of bed, fled to the bathroom and ran myself a scalding bath, as if to cleanse my weaknesses, but even that didn't help because I missed the vigorous showers I had enjoyed daily in America.

I was a self-pitying mess.

Those feelings persisted throughout my great-grandfather's obsequies. As for Mandy, she seemed to pay attention to everything that was going on, smiling at visitors to the house, not quite vacantly but in a detached manner as though she was watching a film different from what everyone else was seeing.

And so, added to my sorrow about his death and my other emotional problems, there was guilt that I couldn't seem to deal with her as a loving 'daughter' should. I vowed I would be a tower of strength later, when my energy had returned, when all the visitors had ebbed away, and she really did need me. In the meantime, I trusted the minders and her two nieces to look after her physical welfare.

Every so often, during those terrible few days after Poppa died, I would catch Pearl watching me closely, and worried that my shame might somehow be visible. I redoubled my efforts to behave appropriately.

As for the day of the funeral, I will never forget walking down that aisle after the coffin alongside Mandy's wheelchair, which was being pushed by Opal with Pearl following. We four were the chief mourners so everyone in the packed church was watching us with the peculiar, half-averted gaze people adopt in such circumstances: they don't want to appear inappropriately inquisitive but, like spectators at a car crash, cannot prevent themselves gawking. To say I was acutely uncomfortable doesn't cover the half of it. I felt as though I was held together by a single strand of very thin wire. And just as I worried that Pearl might have seen disgrace written all over me, it occurred to me that I was the focus of those semi-furtive glances for the same reason. Everyone in that packed church had been given photographic evidence of my shame.

Small images – real ones as opposed to paranoid – stand out in my memory. The clouds of bluish smoke from the swinging censer. The solemn expressions on the faces of the little altar boys, who behaved as though this was the first funeral they had ever served. Faces in the crowd – I recognised many as Poppa's old patients; my own English tutor and two of my classmates from UCD, whose names I couldn't remember but who had turned up to support me; the little knot of neighbours in the back pews – I learned at first hand how well Ireland does funerals, and in spite of my obsessive fear that everyone 'knew', I discovered how comforting the rubrics can be, both on the day and in retrospect, when the confusion calms and the images play over and over again. I was able to tell myself that my great-grandfather's life had counted.

At the time, the choir's singing of 'Nearer My God to Thee' tore at my heart as I tried to take in the reality of the engraved silver plate wavering in front of me on its mahogany bed:

Robert (Bobby) Madden,
10.1.1891–17.8.1970
R.I.P.

That inscription, so impersonal, reduced my vital, virile great-grandfather to two dates, unimportant in the wider world. It was difficult to accept that under that polished brown wood lay the remains (such a visually disturbing phrase) of the only father I had known.

Afterwards, during the lacuna that occurs after all funeral services, when the hearse is still there and people queue to murmur condolences, touch shoulders and shake hands, I was gratified that my UCD colleagues had shown up. Each hugged me in turn as though they really cared. I was also moved to see Frances, so much so that the sight of her acted like a sluice on my tears. 'Thanks a million for coming,' I sobbed into her shoulder, as she threw her arms around me. 'How did you know?'

'Oh, God.' She, too, was crying. 'You know Mam and Dad. Death notices always the first item in the paper!'

'You look great.' I took in her smart navy suit and shoes.

'I'd like to return the compliment but it's not really the right time or place, is it?'

Again I hugged her. 'Oh, Frances, I've missed you. I really have.' It was true, but even as I said it I knew that I could never talk to her about my adventures with Lyle McKenzie. For the moment, that intimacy was gone, that ball was busted, as the phrase has it, and I could see our elderly neighbours, the Higginses, who had taught it to me, in the queue behind her.

We disengaged, with promises to meet 'soon'.

Through all the confusion, Opal and Pearl acted like the Praetorian Guard to Mandy and me, watchful and close at hand to divert some of the attention if it looked as though we were being overwhelmed by the press of people. 'Will you come with us in the funeral car?' I turned to ask them at one point.

'We've my car with us.' Opal was shaking hands with a woman I recognised from the neighbourhood. 'I can't really leave it here. Pearl will go with you, won't you, Pearl?'

'Of course.' Pearl looked across to where Mandy, wearing her wavering smile, was talking to a woman who had crouched down beside the wheelchair. 'In fact we should get poor Margaret into the car right away. I think it's going to rain.'

Although I can't adequately describe it, she had this way of saying nothing but conveying volumes. Everybody that day was sympathetic, of course, but Pearl's silence, her stillness, her calm but penetrating eyes seemed to say, more than the dictionaries of words spoken by all others: *I'm here.* 'Thank you, Pearl.' I was grateful as I turned to shake the hand of yet another stranger. 'Thank you. Thank you. Yes, he was a great man, thank you very much for coming.'

'You poor girl.' Opal came over and touched my arm. 'So horrible to have to come home to this,' she swept her arm around the crowd, 'and you were so far away. You must be absolutely exhausted. But life moves on. You're young and you have everything ahead of you. You'll bounce back, you'll see.'

If only they knew, I thought, as I said goodbye and left her to help Pearl and the driver get Mandy into the funeral car.

Although dazed, I managed somehow to get through the rest of those awful hours, the long walk to the far end of Mount Jerome cemetery with its squads of old grey tombstones, hearing the clods hitting the coffin lid – and listening to my own stupid, stupid words as I continued to make the best responses I could to everyone who continued and continued and continued to sympathise.

I saw it as a great mercy that, just at the end of the burial, the heavens opened and discharged a cloudburst so severe that I could, with justification, escape from the condolence queue; even the priest fled to the safety of his car, while the minders and I man-handled Mandy's wheelchair towards and into the car, which had been allowed to follow us to the graveside. I welcomed the fact that we were drenched to the skin: it allowed me to fuss about something other than death and the image taunting me – of Lyle McKenzie accepting the congratulations of his fraternity brothers on winning the house sweepstake.

It was then that I experienced the first glimmer of anger at him. I had been so intent on blaming myself that I had forgotten what Dory had called him. Accurately.

That rat!

And he was also a jerk!

Jerk. Moron. Shite!

29

CATHERINE

Because it was such a beautiful Indian summer's day, Dun Laoghaire pier, while not swarming as it would have been on a Saturday or Sunday, was quite heavily populated with walkers, strollers and dawdlers. Those not perambulating sat with faces turned up to the sun.

It was a month after Poppa's funeral and I, too, was sitting, but not face-up. About fifty yards from the entrance to the pier, I was reading the companion stories to 'The Dandelion Clock' in Pearl's latest collection (title: *Weeds in the Garden*). I had, of course, read the one taken for the movie – before I had left for America, actually – had even questioned Pearl about it one night before the party, but out of loyalty, I wanted to read all the others too, even though I'm not actually a short-story person. I prefer a novel, the longer the better.

You see, instead of allowing Lyle McKenzie to dominate my thoughts, I had decided to fill them with books and music, college, cinema and friendship. I would go back to university the following week with my head held high: I'd done well in my exams and I had nothing to be ashamed of there, and by joining one or more of the student societies, I'd make a serious effort to integrate. I would continue to mourn Poppa, of course I would, but quietly.

And gratefully. Having seen the change in Mandy's health, I had been worrying about having to look after her fulltime, but as it turned out, Poppa had had a very good life-insurance policy and there was enough money to employ professional minders for years to come. While I would look after her as best I could and would try to be a good and loving companion to her, I could have a life of my own too. His will had ensured that also. After probate, I would have a good income, certainly enough to get me through college and into independence.

Obviously, in the weeks since the funeral I had felt and wept a great deal, but I had thought a lot too, and as a result of all that introspection, it had become clear that, having spent almost all my life with much older people, I was old before my time. Leaving the débâcle with Lyle out of it, my stay in America with two flatmates of my own age had proven, given the right circumstances, I could change that. This post-McKenzie Catherine was now determined that she was going to enjoy being nineteen years of age.

To that end, crucially, I had made a firm decision that it was time to evict Lyle, his works and pomps, from every cell of my brain and corner of my imagination, to replace every molecule of his hateful presence with something wholesome. Like reading. Or friendship. Or anything, really . . .

This decision, of course, was for daytime. Night-time was proving to be different, but I planned to deal with that night by night. Catherine Fay was going to cease behaving like a shocked rabbit.

I'd reconnect with Frances, who I knew had a wide circle of pals. If I asked her to include me in some of their get-togethers, maybe I could become part of her gang. I was going to ring her that night because every day was the first day of the rest of my life: I'd seen that saying quoted on a calendar and it had stuck. Clichés work, you know! I would rehabilitate myself by doing one thing every day that might not suit me: today I had left my sanctuaries of Harold's Cross and Sandymount and come to Dun Laoghaire to sit in public, to walk, read and simply enjoy the day. I had walked halfway down the pier and back to this seat, where I was constantly distracted by children running, dogs barking, the chimes of an ice-cream van, the tinkle of masts and sails, until I came again to 'The Dandelion Clock', the second last in the anthology.

I had read all the other stories bar the last – so I couldn't yet vouch for that – and it was again clear that, although they were up to Pearl's usual standard, 'The Dandelion Clock' stood out. My previous impression, that it was startlingly good, was now copperfastened. I liked it so much, I think, because for me it betrayed more than a hint of autobiography. Which, of course, she would deny to her back teeth. Most authors would. I had even faced her with it, but had got nowhere.

I took into account that I knew Pearl really well and that my antennae would have been twitching anyway, but I think that any alert, experienced reader would find this story more direct and truthful than any other in the book – than any in all of Pearl's books. To some student colleagues in my tutorial group, the more far-fetched and disconnected the ramblings of an author the better, but I believe that when someone is writing from the heart, there is direct communication with the reader. You can participate in the experience rather than just read about it.

'The Dandelion Clock' was about prolonged yearning for a lost lover. The protagonist's name is Lily. (Almost all of Pearl's stories are populated by characters with old-fashioned names: Violet, Arabella, Penelope, George, Albert, Ernest – and in one of this book's stories there is even an antagonist named Horatio!) Anyhow, she wanders the world seeking him, and while she doesn't manage to find him he finds her when it's too late. She's dying. As I read the last few lines of Pearl's story, my throat again constricted, despite the distractions on the pier. The reunion of the lovers was very moving.

I took a pause before I began the last story to watch the chuntering mail-boat as it came in to berth. An old couple, arm in arm, ambled past. (Well, to me they were old although they mightn't have been more than sixty – I wasn't great at judging people's ages, since to me, having been brought up almost exclusively with them, 'old' people looked normal!) These two weren't speaking, just staring ahead, but they were perfectly in step.

Whenever I gave it thought, it occurred to me what an awful pity it was that Pearl hadn't met anyone to be her life's companion. I was more convinced than ever now that I had been right about the aura of mystery she emanated. Was it possible that somewhere in her youth, she had been someone with 'prospects', as Poppa used to call someone eligible for marriage? Had she met some poor boy, maybe, who had gone off to the war and not come back? That had happened a lot in those days, hadn't it?

It was intriguing. Previously, in my role as lofty 'intellectual' student, I had thought her stories beautifully written but her heroines too passive: it was almost as though they enjoyed pining, rather than going out and getting what they wanted – i.e., a proper lover. That being said, however, recent events in my own life had taught me that what people showed on the outside was not always the full story. Maybe I had had to go through a bit of fire before I could fully appreciate the subtlety of my cousin's talent and the complexity of her characters' back stories and personalities. From that perspective, 'The Dandelion Clock' was certainly an eye-opener.

I was just a page and a half into the last story, in which Dorothy Morris seemed to revert to her standard style – or what I, with one year of UCD English under my belt, thought of as her style – when a shadow fell over me. 'Well, hello there!'

I looked up to see my erstwhile childminders, Mr and Mrs Higgins, standing in front of me. They were beaming. Mr Higgins was now on a stick, but his rotund little wife seemed as bouncy as she ever was.

I stood up to hug them.

'We didn't get to talk to you after the funeral. There were so many people and we just never got to you. He was a lovely man. We were so sorry.' Mr Higgins's eyes watered, as he stood back to look at me.

'Don't upset her, Jem,' his wife stepped in. 'How are you managing – and how's dear Margaret? We haven't seen her since.'

'We're doing as well as can be expected.' I shrugged. 'Thank God we have the professionals in.' In the weeks since Poppa's funeral, the routine in the house had run smoothly, although I thought I detected a worsening in my great-grandmother's health. Without being melodramatic, Mandy was acting mentally and emotionally as though she had had enough and her body was concurring with that decision. She was drifting.

'Will you be able to get back to America?' Mr Higgins pursed his lips. 'It's so sad you had to come home like you did. But I suppose that with your Mandy the way she is . . .'

'We'll see. I don't think so, though. Look,' I needed to change the subject, 'why don't we go to the Royal Marine for a cup of tea?' It wasn't what I might have chosen to do just then but I owed these people a lot. 'I have the car with me so I can run us all up to the door.'

The lounge of the Royal Marine was packed. There were a

few young couples, holidaymakers obviously, and one family with children, but the clientele was largely as elderly as my companions. We found a table, and as we took our seats and stowed Mr Higgins's stick safely under his chair, I knew I was in for another endurance test of sorts. They were settling in.

I loved these surrogate parents of mine, and I knew they loved me, and I don't mean to sound snooty or thankless, but since I'd grown up, I'd found our encounters a little bit difficult. They loved to go back to when I was little and wore the Fair Isle cardigans Mrs Higgins had knitted for me. Over and over again, they retraced our walks in St Stephen's Green, where we would feed a bagful of crumbs to the ducks, geese, seagulls and any other bird that happened to be in the vicinity.

The waitress came and we ordered tea for three with cream buns. 'And do you remember the chocolate, Jem?' Mrs Higgins crossed her arms under her chest while we waited.

'Do I what!' Mr Higgins chuckled, and they were off. For the walk home, they'd always bought me a bar of Cadbury's milk chocolate; if I was feeling generous I would give them each a square. 'And the Botanic Gardens!'

'Oh, I loved the Bots,' Mrs Higgins clasped her hands together. 'And the, eh – zoo? Do you remember, Catherine, how you loved to ride on the back of that elephant – what was its name, Jem?'

'Sarah!' Mr Higgins nodded owlishly.

All I had to do, God love them, was smile and say, 'That was great, wasn't it?' at suitable intervals. I kept telling myself I was an ungrateful wretch, and sitting with them in a nice bright hotel lounge for an hour or so was a small price to pay for my lengthy childhood reign as a precocious little queen over my loyal serfs.

When it came time to go, I insisted I drive them home but they tripped over each other protesting that I shouldn't.

'Ah, no.'

'You have things to do.'

'It's no trouble, Catherine, we like the bus. We meet so many nice people on the buses, don't we, Jem?'

'Sure don't we have the free travel now anyway, thanks to Charlie Haughey.'

And so on.

They were still arguing when we got to the car. I helped them in and as I pulled away, they were giggling together in the back seat at the good of meeting me on Dun Laoghaire pier, finishing each other's sentences, two peas in a pod. What would happen to the survivor when one of them died? Was it just me, or was it normal that, during a period when you'd been crying a lot, tears seemed to be on standby?

When we pulled into our avenue the first thing I saw was an ambulance, lights flashing and siren wailing, pulling away from the front of our house. A small group of neighbours stood at our gate looking after it. They spotted my car approaching and – I'll never forget this – seemed to coalesce into a tight knot, as though for protection.

Mandy.

When I pulled up, I jumped out immediately, leaving the Higginses to clamber out unaided. 'What's happened?'

'Try not to worry, love.' A woman who lived across the road detached herself from the knot. 'She just took a turn, that's all. It's desperate, isn't it, and so soon after your poor granddaddy and all? She's being brought to St Philomena's. The nurse went with her. If you hurry, you'll be there the same time as her.'

'Why is she being brought there? Why not James's or Vincent's?' I was familiar with both of these hospitals, as was Mandy. She had never before been a patient in any of the hospitals on the far side of the city, as far as I was aware. She was sure to be frightened. 'Don't know, love. Maybe they're full or something.' The woman shrugged. 'But don't worry,' she repeated, 'them ambulance men know what they're doing.'

I refused offers of accompaniment, and as soon as the Higginses were safely on the pavement, I performed a screaming three-point turn and took off.

It took me a while to find the entrance to St Philomena's casualty department, which was at the back of the hospital, not least because I was entirely unfamiliar with the north side of the city. Arnott's, Clery's, the zoo and the Botanic Gardens – and, of course, the airport – had been my lot over there.

When finally I got to the reception desk, the girl took my name and the name of the patient, then asked me to wait while she made a phone call. When she hung up, she told me to go into the waiting room and that someone would be with me shortly.

For once 'shortly' was accurate. A young nurse came out, called my name and asked me to come with her. 'One of the doctors is with her now, Catherine, but we're waiting for the consultant to have a look at her. I won't lie to you, she's very ill,' she said sympathetically, as we pushed through the curtains and into the casualty area. Although it was still only late afternoon, it was full to bursting with people in wheelchairs, on temporary beds and plastic chairs. 'Over there,' the nurse said, pointing to where one of Mandy's carers was sitting outside one of the cubicles.

She stood up immediately she saw me and came across to me. 'I'm awfully sorry, Catherine,' she said. 'I did the best I could for her but in the end I thought it best to get the ambulance. She was coughing something terrible.'

'You did the right thing. If you hang on a bit, we can talk later.' I went in to find Mandy's face half concealed by an oxygen mask. She seemed shrivelled and tiny in the bed. A wizened child. I refused to cry. I had to hold it together now.

'How is she?' I introduced myself to the white-clad medic, who was writing something into a file.

'She's stable right now but we won't know for sure, of course, for some time. The first twenty-four hours are critical.' He sounded as though he was reciting by rote as he continued to scribble. 'She could be like this for months or she might improve. She could deteriorate, it's just too early to tell, but my best guess is that she's had a stroke. She has all the signs. Her right side seems to be paralysed. She's a smoker, I gather.' He pointed with his pen at her brown fingertips.

'Yes.' Defensively, as if I was apologising for her, I picked up her unresisting hand.

'Well, that hasn't helped, but you never know – I've seen miracles happen . . .'

'Can she hear us?'

'We always operate on the basis that the patient can, yes, even though, right now, she's very deeply unconscious.' He lowered his voice and turned his back to the bed. 'I don't want to alarm you, but there's no point in giving you false hope. She's not in great shape, she's very underweight and at her age . . .' He shrugged. 'We'll just have to play a waiting game. We'll admit her as soon

217

as we have a bed. I understand she very recently suffered a bereavement.'

'Yes. My great-grandfather.'

'And she's your great-grandmother, right?'

'Yes.'

'If you don't mind my asking, how old are you, Catherine?'

His detached manner was getting on my nerves – he didn't look much older than me. But I suppose I was hyper-sensitive, wanting him to feel as badly as I did. 'I'm nineteen.'

'And you're her only living relative?'

'She has two nieces, but they're . . .' How was I to describe Opal's bustling demeanour and Pearl's elegance? 'They're middle-aged,' I said. 'Actually you'd probably say nearly elderly.'

'Was she *compos mentis* before this happened?'

'She's old, but she knows her name and recognises people.' I was getting seriously irritated. What was with all the questions? 'She managed to come to Poppa's – my great-grandfather's – funeral and she survived that.'

He sensed my displeasure. 'I'm sorry if I seem to be interrogating you, Catherine, but we like to get a rounded picture. She has carers at home, right?'

'Yes. For the foreseeable future.' I wasn't going to go into the finer details of our financial situation.

'And after what's foreseeable?'

What a question. 'I don't know.'

'Mm.' He scribbled something more. 'Look, we'll admit her as soon as we can, see what's what, and then we'll talk again. OK? Try not to worry – she's in good hands now.' He touched my shoulder and moved on to the next cubicle.

Gently I put Mandy's hand back on the thin coverlet and, careful not to disturb the mask, kissed her chilly forehead. 'I'll be back in a minute.'

'Why did he want to know my age?' I asked the minder, when I went back out into the ordered chaos of the general area. 'What does that have to do with anything?'

'I think maybe it has to do with the decisions that are going to have to be made,' she said quietly. 'Whether she will come home, or perhaps go into a nursing home.'

It was too much. The blood leached from my veins. There was

a plastic chair nearby and I sat in it. 'Are you all right, Catherine?' The woman placed her hand on the back of my neck. 'Put your head between your knees. You've gone very pale.' She pushed firmly.

After a minute or two, I felt better and sat up again. 'Thank you,' I said. 'That's never happened me before.'

'Have you eaten anything today?'

I had to think. I realised that my food intake for the past twenty-four hours had been one fairy cake at breakfast time and one cream bun in the company of the Higginses. 'Not really.'

'My advice is to go out to the shop across the road and get yourself a couple of bananas and a bottle of Lucozade. And have a proper meal tonight.' She hesitated. 'And perhaps we should talk. I'm on duty until midnight, supposedly, but now that . . .' She trailed off.

I stared at her. This was another thing I would have to attend to. In the course of a few weeks, I had been forced to travel from spoiled girl to grown-up, with grown-up responsibilities and problems. 'Would you mind staying here for a couple of hours or so until she's taken up to a ward? I need to talk to someone. I'll be back as quickly as I can. I'll come here first, and if you're not here, I'll meet you in the house. OK? Look,' I added impulsively, 'I'm sorry I wasn't there when this happened. It must have been scary for you.'

She nodded. 'You never get used to it. It's always a shock.'

'Well, thank you for doing the right thing. I really appreciate it. Again, I'm sorry I wasn't there to help. I know I'm all over the place.'

'Understandable.'

'And you know I'll want you to stay if she's coming home, but in any event, I'll try to do the right thing by you and your colleague. My grandfather would have wanted me to.'

The relief that shone in her eyes was instantaneous and I could have kicked myself for not reckoning on what Mandy's sudden turn for the worse had meant for people other than me.

'Thank you.' She smiled tentatively. 'But just while you mention it, I hope you don't mind me saying so, but we haven't been paid for the last two weeks. We didn't like to make a fuss about it, what with your granddaddy's death and all.'

'I thought the agency paid you?'

'Dr Madden made a special arrangement with us. He paid us a month in advance, like.' The woman seemed mortified.

'Please, please, don't be upset. It's me who should be upset. I'll go to the bank first thing in the morning – oh, God, I'm so sorry. I didn't think. I'll sort it out.' I was definitely feeling the weight.

'Thanks. I'll tell my colleague when I see her – she'll be delighted.'

I went back in to Mandy to say goodbye. She had not moved a muscle. Her eyes were half open, but unseeing and opaque. 'It's Catherine again, Mandy,' I whispered. 'Everything will be all right,' I picked up her hand. 'I don't know if you understand, but if you do, squeeze my hand.' It was something I'd seen in the movies.

Nothing happened.

'I'm going to take care of you.' I kissed her forehead. It was as cold as glass. Was it my imagination or had it got colder in the few minutes while I had been gone? It seemed now as cold as Poppa's just before they had closed his coffin.

I shut my eyes then and just barely moving my lips, said a 'Hail Mary', something I hadn't done since childhood. Then I whispered, 'Please, Our Lady, please don't let her die. Please? Not yet.' Then I bargained: 'If you let her live, just for another while, I'll go back to Mass. I'll even take her to Lourdes. She loved you, Our Lady.' This praying and promising was hypocrisy of a high order, but I would have promised anything and meant it. I definitely planned to fulfil it.

I kissed her again and, for a moment, stood looking down at the network of lines criss-crossing her worn face and cheeks under the garish green of the mask. One side of the elastic that held it on was twisted, cutting into an ear lobe. That might be painful, I thought, so I lifted it, placed it higher, then, very, very gently, settled her ear. I smoothed her wispy hair so it lay neatly.

Poppa had been such a dominant personality – Poppa and I together had been such a unit. Where had Margaret – not Mandy, not Poppa's wife – where had she, Margaret, lived in the equation? Who had sat with her when her sister and daughter had died, when her granddaughter had disappeared? Who even mentioned any of them any more?

I realised I hadn't actually 'seen' my great-grandmother for years.

She was always just there. With Poppa. 'I'm sorry, Mandy,' I whispered. 'I'll make it up to you. You don't need to worry about a thing now. It's all taken care of.'

Outside, almost of its own volition, the car headed not to Harold's Cross but to Sandymount.

30

CATHERINE

In the car park opposite the Sandymount house, I stared through the windscreen at the wide curve of that part of the bay, marked on one side by the promontory of Dun Laoghaire harbour and on the other by the Shelly Banks, the docks and the two new candy-striped chimneys of the Poolbeg power station. From where I sat, the progress of the incoming tide was actually visible, its satiny water only a couple of inches deep as it crept steadily across the flat sand.

It was still not five o'clock, and it has always intrigued me how, on a weekday, so many people in the city seem to have the time and freedom to walk their dogs, to amble in pairs – women imparting secrets to each other, couples holding hands – on the wide promenade.

Poppa was dead. Mandy was at death's door, yet life continued as if neither of these things had happened.

It was surprising, too, to see a jogger, a phenomenon I had seen many times in America but this was the first manifestation of that health craze I had noticed in this country. Maybe he was an American. He certainly had the tan and—

I wouldn't think about America. Before I could go too far down that self-pitying road, I hauled myself out of the car, crossed the street and knocked on the sisters' door, stiffening myself to face Opal, who was the one usually to greet visitors. She was grand, really, very kind, but in some respects, her efficiency intimidated me.

It was a relief when I saw Pearl standing there. 'Catherine!' Her pleasure was evident. 'How nice. Come on in – Opal's not here. She has an afternoon bridge session. She got her hair done this morning. Come in, darling, come in.' She opened the door wider.

'As a matter of fact I've just put on the kettle. I'm finished for the day – I've been toiling away since morning.'

I followed her into the front reception room. I'd always admired it. You'd expect, in a house like this, that it would be cluttered and old-fashioned, stuffed with antiques, but Opal had put in modern sofas and chairs, bookcases of blond wood and plain curtains of bleached linen or maybe hessian. There was a single splash of colour in the floor rug, which was cream with a wide green stripe. The only thing that jarred was the fire burning in the grate of the marble fireplace. Pearl saw me look at it. 'Oh, you know our Opal.' She smiled affectionately. 'She likes to have a fire. It finishes the room, apparently. Sit down, dear. Make yourself comfortable and I'll fetch the tea.'

'I'll come down with you.'

'Of course.'

The french windows leading from the kitchen to the garden were open and I could see Opal's gardener weeding the flowerbeds. Again Pearl saw the direction of my gaze. 'Would you like me to close the doors, Catherine? So we can be more private?'

Was I that transparent? 'Not at all.' I sat at the table. 'It's so warm today.'

'It is, isn't it?' She glanced again at me with her all-seeing eyes but for some reason, although it was why I had come here, I didn't want to launch right away into the bad news about Mandy. I think this was because talking about it to someone who cared as much as Pearl did would make it real. I wanted to postpone facing that for as long as possible.

I watched her take the caddy from the top shelf of the Welsh dresser, then spoon the tea into the pot. 'I went out to Dun Laoghaire today, and guess who I ran into? The Higginses.'

'Those lovely neighbours who minded you when you were little? I saw them at the funeral but didn't get a chance to talk to them.'

'That's them.'

'They're gorgeous people.' The kettle had boiled and she was pouring the steaming water into the teapot.

'They sure are.'

'I love Dun Laoghaire. It's so Protestant still, isn't it?' It was an odd remark, but so like Pearl to make it. With her quiet voice and

223

deft movements, she was working her magic and I felt my panic subside.

'So,' she said, when we were sitting opposite one another, teacups in hand. 'It's lovely to see you.' She sipped her tea and waited.

Outside, the gardener started up the lawnmower. Although only about two-thirds of the garden was grass, Opal always provided the best equipment for her staff. 'That's so noisy. I will close the windows, if you don't mind.' She got up and did so. Instantly, the whine was muffled behind the double glazing. 'That's better.' She sat down again. Then, quietly: 'What's on your mind, Catherine?'

'It's Mandy . . .' I poured out the story.

'How dreadful.' She was full of empathy when I had finished. 'You poor thing. And poor Margaret. I didn't think she looked well at your poppa's funeral but I had no idea . . . Would you like me to go back with you to the hospital?'

'That's — that's not why I came here,' I stammered. Then, as it sank in that I wouldn't have to face this alone, 'Would you, Pearl?'

'Of course I would. She's my aunt, after all, and even if she weren't, I couldn't let you take care of her all by yourself. What a time you've had these last few weeks. Nobody should have to face such a catalogue of disasters at your age. We'll finish our tea, though, if you don't mind, and then we'll get going. As you say, she's unconscious, so a few minutes here or there won't make any difference.'

The subdued and changing notes of the lawnmower outside were soothing as we sipped our tea and ate our biscuits. (What a diet, I thought. Obediently, I had bought the recommended bananas and Lucozade but had forgotten to touch either.)

'Not changing the subject, Catherine,' Pearl said then, doing just that, 'I was actually thinking this very day about you. You shouldn't be burdened with all of us old folk. You should be out having a wonderful time with friends. I know there's Frances, you let us meet her, but — stop me if I'm intruding — I do get the impression that you don't socialise all that much.'

'Of course I do!' The invention had been automatic. What girl wants to admit that she's weird? 'When I get back to college I'll bring a few friends over. Would that be OK?'

'It would be delightful. We might even persuade Opal to have one of her parties, eh? Just a little one!' We both laughed, I falsely. She hadn't batted an eyelid but I wasn't too sure I'd got away with the pretence. 'Actually,' she added casually, draining her cup, 'speaking of parties, I noticed you getting on very well with that American boy at the last one. You seemed to be exchanging addresses down there in the garden. Did you meet while you were in Chicago?'

She rose from the table and continued, 'You take your time, I'll just rinse the teapot and we can put the dishes in the sink. I'll leave a note for Opal.' She disposed of her cup and saucer and tore a sheet off the notebook hooked to the wall beside one of the windows. 'Remind me to put the fireguard on the grate upstairs.'

'Well, actually, we didn't,' I said to her back, a little too brightly. 'His name was Sam. He was to ring me if he did come to Chicago, but then . . .'

She turned from the sink and finished the sentence: 'You had to come home so unexpectedly.' Then, her gaze level: 'That was sad. He seemed to be a very nice young man.'

'Yes.' Despite my best efforts to control it, I felt my face go red and the air between us seemed to shimmer.

'Are you all right, Catherine?' she asked softly.

Obviously I hadn't been the only one playing detective. 'Yes, of course.' My face was on fire. 'I miss Poppa!' I blurted, but the note I had struck was phoney and she'd heard it.

'Of course you do.'

Again she waited while I searched desperately for some way out of this. At the same time, the urge to confess was growing.

'In your own time. Don't distress yourself – you can tell me, you know. I'm a good listener. You see . . .' She had been about to say more but changed her mind. 'Are you finished?' She came and took my cup and saucer. 'Shall we go?'

'Yes, we should. Don't forget the fireguard.' The moment passed.

En route to the hospital, we were caught in stop-start traffic in Pearse Street; even for that time of the day, rush-hour, it was moving unusually slowly.

It was very hot in the car, even though I had all four windows rolled down. 'Would you mind if I tried to find some music?' I indicated the car radio.

'Some music would be nice.' Throughout the journey so far, she had sat with her hands folded in her lap. I twirled the knob up and down the long-wave dial. The BBC Light Programme, was the station Poppa had loved. It was usually reliable, but today it was hissing with so much static that we could barely hear the music. 'Must be the hot weather interfering with it.' I turned it off again. I was terribly uneasy and not just about Mandy. Although Pearl was behaving as she always did, her interrogation, brief though it had been, had unsettled me and I felt she was watching me all the time.

As we reached the turn for Tara Street, I saw the reason for the choked traffic. There had been an accident involving a horse dray and a lorry at the junction with Townsend Street. The horse seemed fine – harness trailing along the ground, he was being walked up and down on the footpath by a man, presumably the driver, but the dray had overturned, spilling its cargo of kegs. Only one car at a time was able to inch past by virtue of driving with two wheels on the footpath. Behind me, an ambulance, siren wailing, was trying to get out of Tara Street fire station. Maybe the lorry driver had been injured. 'Sorry, Pearl. Looks like we're here for the duration.'

'As long as no one was seriously hurt.'

I put the car in neutral and applied the handbrake. Then: 'Pearl?'

'Yes?' She didn't look at me.

'There is something. I have to tell someone or I'll burst. Promise you won't be shocked.'

'Catherine, dear, you couldn't shock me if you tried. Are you pregnant? If you are I'll be with you every step of the way, and so will Opal.'

'Pregnant? Dear God, no!' I laughed so loudly with disbelief that a woman pushing a pram along the footpath turned to stare. 'No,' I said, more quietly. 'Sorry for reacting like that.' There had been a brief flurry of concern for the first few days after the débâcle, adding to my distress, but during Poppa's funeral I had felt the first telltale cramps and knew that this, at least, need not be added to the heap of horrors.

'But there was a boy.' It was a statement, not a question.

'Yes.'

There's something about being side by side in the confined space of a car that facilitates confidences – sort of like a confession box, where the person you're talking to is close but you don't have to look at his or her face. In spite of my decisions and intentions not to allow Lyle McKenzie have one more minute of my time or thoughts, once I had started, I couldn't stop. It all came pouring out, hesitantly at first then in a technicolour gush. Lyle, the frat house, that we had gone to bed together – the whole cinemascope production splattered at the windscreen, inches from my nose, so that I was reliving the horror yet again.

During the recital, an ambulance – its bell ear-shattering through our open windows – squeezed past and reached the scene of the accident. Because of the din, I had briefly to stop – which was a mercy, because I was arriving at the notice-board to see the photograph and I managed to stop myself mentioning it. That particular feature of the story, the crux, was too crude to share with someone as refined as Pearl. Instead, I told her the bet had been about who would bed me first – and that my name was posted in the frat house hallway, with a gold star beside his name at the head of the column. I also told her about the odds shortening as Lyle pursued his clever courtship.

I never once looked at her throughout my narrative but I could tell by her stillness that she was following every word, and when at last I glanced at her, her face was mask-like. 'What did you do?'

At least the ambulance bell had ceased its racket. The police were on site now and cars ahead were inching past the ambulance, the lorry and the horse, standing calmly on the footpath, ears pricked as though it was interested in all this activity while the gardaí, with the help of at least a dozen motorists, caught the underside of the overturned dray and heaved until it bounced on to its wheels. Others were rolling the kegs to the side of the street. 'I ran,' I said. 'I took a taxi back to the apartment and began to pack.' I lowered my head. 'I'm very sorry I unloaded all that on you, Pearl,' I said, in a small voice, looking down at my lap. 'Are you shocked?'

'If you're asking am I shocked that you've had sex, no. I haven't gone through the world for this long without knowing its ways.' She took a breath but I could hear it catch in her throat. 'I cannot find words to describe what I feel about that boy's behaviour,' she continued. 'I had guessed there was something wrong with you, something even more than the loss of your dear poppa, but,' she touched my arm, 'you poor child. You've been carrying this burden all by yourself since you came home? Oh, my dear Catherine! Why didn't you tell us?'

'How could I? I'm so ashamed. I wake up at four in the morning and it all crashes in on top of me. How could I have been so stupid?'

'What are you ashamed of? What did you do that was so wrong? Are you ashamed that you fell in love?'

Some movement beyond the windscreen caught the corner of my eye and I saw that a policeman was coming towards us, impatiently waving us on. I had been so immersed in what was happening inside the car that I had not noticed that a large gap had opened in front of us. I put the car in gear and drove carefully past the accident. It's one thing to try to convince yourself of something, another to hear and see the reaction of someone you trust completely.

Every time I had tried to shift the blame on to Lyle a hectoring voice inside my brain had shouted: *Yes, but . . .*

I had been so busy lashing myself for having been taken in by a charlatan that I had let him off the hook. Pearl was right. What exactly had I done except fall in love? Lyle was a confidence trick-ster who, having preyed on some other innocent, was probably right now preening in front of his so-called 'brothers'. I was way above his level and, as the traffic at last freed up and we crossed the Liffey, I was astonished to realise I already felt lighter. In some weird way, it was almost as though keeping the story locked inside my head had caused it to fester and that telling someone – especially someone as empethetic and non-judgmental as Pearl – had lanced the boil. Now that the air could get to it, it no longer hurt as much.

I was very grateful to her – and the next step was, if not to swap horror stories, at least to get the gist of what had happened to her. Her comeback had been anger and disgust, for sure . . . but something more. I sensed recognition. She'd had a love affair, too, that had gone wrong. A significant one.

31

PEARL

Opal was already sitting in the lobby of the hospital when Catherine and I got there – clearly she hadn't gone by Pearse Street. 'I got your note,' she said, when we expressed surprise at seeing her. 'The kettle was still warm so I knew I wouldn't be far behind and that we would meet up. Poor old Mags.' She sighed, and then stood up. 'Right. Let's do this. How bad is she?'

I left it to Catherine to explain what had happened as we climbed the stairs to the ward. Before we had left the house I had telephoned the hospital and ascertained that Margaret had been admitted. 'Poor chicken.' Opal sighed again when Catherine finished. 'It's those bloody coffin nails of hers, you know. I told her loads of times she should give them up. Knew this would happen eventually. She never ate, appetite of a bird. And Bobby a doctor! You'd think he'd have taken her in hand.'

At this point we were walking down a long corridor approaching the ward and I refrained from pointing out that Margaret's husband had smoked as heavily as she did; I was conscious that, in effect, they had been Catherine's parents.

I was still staggered by Catherine's revelations. It had been such a bizarre, callous trick for that awful boy to have played on her. Even with my writer's imagination I could not have come up with such a thing.

The Female Geriatric ward housed twelve occupants and was high-ceilinged, with large windows facing south. It should have been bright, but on the outside, the glass was caked with grime, the flowers on the bed curtains had long ago faded to a uniform brownish pink and the bedcovers, although clean enough, were very worn. The overall atmosphere was grey and smelt of strong disinfectant, bringing me back to the privy of my childhood.

What was most depressing, however, were the patients. Each old body was barely perceptible under the bedclothes. 'Nurse! Nurse!' On seeing our entrance two raised skeletal, claw-like hands, and called to us with weak, querulous voices. I have enjoyed robust health all my life and was appalled at the notion that in the not too distant future I might be one of them. These women had gossiped at the hairdresser's and badmouthed their husbands behind their backs. They had supported their friends through the ups and downs of life – had had lovers and children and jewellery, had danced in their finery at parties and balls and had thought, as I had once, that life was never-ending.

'Gosh, she looks as though she'd break if you touched her with a feather.' I could see that Catherine was shocked. In her bed, the third in her row of six, her great-grandmother was as insubstantial as the others, the veins in her hands as blue and prominent. 'How are you, Mandy?' She took one of those hands in hers and attempted to sound cheery. Of course there was no response.

'She can't hear ya, love!' With difficulty, the woman in the next bed raised her head from her pillow. 'Could ya call a nurse for me, please? I need to go.'

Catherine turned and fled the room.

'I'll be back in a second, Opal.' I followed her.

I found her outside in the corridor, on a bench seat just outside the door. I sat beside her and put both arms around her.

'Are you all right there?' We had been spotted by a nurse who, shoes squelching on the polished floor as she approached, looked only a few years older than Catherine. She came up and stood before us. 'You're Margaret's relations?' She clucked sympathetically. 'She's not suffering, I can promise you that. She's just lying there in her own little world. Here you are, sweetheart.' She took a wad of tissues from the pocket of her uniform.

'I'm sorry.' Catherine blew her nose.

'For what? Take your time. Nobody's going anywhere tonight. I'll bring you both a cup of tea, and if you stay around for a bit, I'll get the registrar to come and talk to you. Be back in a jiffy.'

'The woman beside her is looking for you.'

'Grand. I'll get yer tea first and then I'll go in to her.' She squelched off.

We watched her go. 'Why don't you stay with us again tonight, Catherine? No need to go back to that empty house. It will be very lonely for you there.'

'But I told the minder we'd have a chat.'

'We can make a telephone call. She'll be delighted to have the night off. Are you game?'

'Oh, Pearl, what would I do without you?'

'You'd be fine. You're a very competent girl. Clever and competent. Don't let what happened with the American boy knock you back because then he'll have won.'

'He's won anyway. I'll never be able to look any boy in the eye again.'

My heart went out to her more than ever. 'Of course you will.' I got to my feet. 'If you feel up to it, shall we go back inside? Opal's in there by herself. God knows what plots she's hatching!'

At least that brought a wavering smile.

As it happened, it was the great man himself, the consultant, who appeared at the bedside. 'I just happened to be in,' he said. 'There was a bit of an emergency on one of the other wards. Let's see now . . .' He took the chart from where it hung at the end of the bed and studied it.

Opal, typically, jumped in: 'Could we go somewhere more private, please? I don't think it's really appropriate to be discussing Margaret's health in the presence of so many other patients, do you?'

The man was clearly put out, but he replaced the chart. 'This way, please.'

We all crammed into a tiny office near the nurses' station on the corridor, a glass-walled cubicle rendered even more claustrophobic by the dusty manila files and untidy papers on every available horizontal surface – so many, and in such haphazard and tottering heaps, I wondered how anyone could find anything.

At first, the consultant's manner was distant but professionally soothing. Quite soon, however, he became irritated with Opal's constant interjections, giving increasingly terse replies to her queries.

Opal either did not notice or did not care, prefacing every response to his we-have-to-wait-and-see routine with 'Yes, but . . .'

In fairness to him, his patient was very new so he had some

justification for his caution. Opal, however, was having none of it. Although speaking for herself she was sweeping me and Catherine into the equation at every turn. 'Yes, but I don't think you understand what we're saying. We want her out of that ward and into a private room. That's a reasonable request. If it's a matter of money—'

'Mrs Igoe, I'm sorry but I can't conjure a private room out of thin air. It's nothing to do with money – private rooms in this hospital are at a premium.'

'Of course they are. That's why we need one. A private room is nothing less than that woman in there deserves after a lifetime of looking after her husband's patients. He died only a few weeks ago. And here she is, already on the scrapheap, thanks to you and this hospital. Look,' she softened her tone, 'that old lady has only three relatives in the world and they are all standing in front of you. She deserves the best and she's going to get it.'

The consultant frowned: '"Patients"? Was Margaret's husband a doctor?'

'Yes – why?'

'Nothing. I just wondered if I'd met her before, that's all. What was her late husband's name?'

'Madden,' said Opal, firmly. 'Dr Robert Madden. Everybody called him Bobby. Why? Does it make a difference?'

'Of course not.' But I could see that wheels were turning in his brain.

Shamefully in one respect, happily in another, Margaret was moved to a private room later that night. The nice nurse who telephoned us told Opal that it was little more than a cubicle adjoining the nurses' station and that her privacy, while not as compromised as it had been on the ward, was still limited because there was a fair bit of activity around the nurses' station and the room itself was fronted with glass. Yet she assured us that, relatively speaking, her patient was comfortable. Catherine and I, sitting at the kitchen table, could hear Opal's side of the conversation. 'Is she still hooked up to the oxygen? . . . I see . . . And still unconscious? . . . Yes . . . So is there any point in us rushing in tomorrow morning? . . . Right. Well, please telephone if there are any further developments. There is nearly always someone here.' She turned to look at me with raised eyebrows.

232

'There's been no change,' she said, when she came back to the table, 'but according to that nice girl there, that's neither a good nor a bad thing for the moment because we're still in the wait-and see phase.' She grimaced. 'I just didn't like that man, but I suppose I have to admit, grudgingly, that he did get her moved.' She filled us in on the rest of the conversation and then, yawning, 'I'm bushed. Whatever about you two, I'm off to bed.' She dropped a kiss on the crown of Catherine's head. 'Sleep well, chicken.'

Outside the French windows, the garden rested in the gloaming, that time of evening when it is neither dark nor light, not exactly twilight, for that feels almost mystical, but those few minutes when the earth seems to pause, when the sun has gone but the dusk has not yet stolen in to spread its magic.

At Opal's suggestion, the three of us had been drinking gin. We had had quite a day, and I have to say it was getting easier on my palate by the minute – I hardly noticed its bitterness.

Catherine, I saw, was feeling its effects: her eyes were over-bright, and while she was not slurring, her speech was a little slower than normal. There was no blame attached to this behaviour, which, in the circumstances, was entirely reasonable. Every time I looked at her I could not help but see her with that – that— words fail me. That boy.

When Opal had gone and we had the kitchen to ourselves, she tipped her glass and drained it. 'Will we have just one more for the road, Pearl?' Not waiting for an answer, she picked up the bottle and sloshed in some of the liquor, adding the last of the tonic. Then: 'Ooh, there's none left for you. Shall I get some more?' She was not drunk, not yet.

'No, thank you.'

Suddenly she leaned as far as she could towards me. 'What's going on with you, Pearl?'

'I beg your pardon?'

'What's your secret? I know you have one. And it's not just because I've read "The Dandelion Clock". I've really read that story, Pearl, as – as I told you before. It's brilliant. I love it. But it's the story of you, isn't it? I'm asking you what's going on not only because I've read your story, Pearl, but because you're the way you are.' She sat back and wagged her finger playfully at me. 'I know there's something. You have this – this aura, Pearl. You're sad and longing at the same time. What happened? You can tell me!' She was smiling in the foolish way of tipsy people. 'I told you mine! I told you my secret! It'll be between me and you, I promise. It'll be just the two of us.'

I cannot say I was surprised. She is a clever girl. She had trusted that American twerp with her love and her body and had been betrayed. I had trusted Thomas, in that I was certain that, sooner or later, he would come for me. He has not, so far, and this is where our stories diverge. While she should never give that person another thought, I remain to be convinced that my Thomas did not try to find me. Is not still, at some level, trying to find me. The outcome of our stories is the same – loss – but the intrinsic difference between the two losses lies in the characters of the boys we loved.

I might have been more active in seeking Thomas instead of growing into spinsterhood, like lichen on an old tree, but truly I had felt I had no choice. I considered. It might be helpful to her to know that, while the world can be unkind, there is life after loss. Maintaining secrets is tiring and I am tired of keeping mine. It might be a relief to share it.

Catherine is very young, but then, I had been even younger when I fell in love. 'If I tell you,' I said slowly, 'will you have a cup of coffee, or at least a large glass of water instead of that gin you're holding? I'm sure you'll want to go back to the hospital tomorrow. Any more and you won't be able to.'

32

CATHERINE

It was nearly eleven o'clock. It was dark outside, and only the fluorescents under the cupboards lit the kitchen. Pearl had been absent for nearly ten minutes.

Before she left, she had been relating the story of herself and Thomas Areton for the best part of half an hour, speaking calmly for the most part but having to take several breaks to steady herself.

She had just come to the part where they had been on the point of sex (which is how I had interpreted it; she hadn't been that specific). They had been in the depths of the forest, she had been 'fully unclothed' when they had heard, coming towards them, the sound of men and dogs.

Abruptly, she had broken off the narrative, saying she had to go to the bathroom. In her hurry to get out of the kitchen, she had stumbled over a chair, hurting one of her shins. She had been away long enough for me to empty Opal's coffee-maker, clean it out, put in a new filter and make a fresh pot.

I was mesmerised. Although I had been pursuing my conviction about Pearl and her love affair, I had visualised it as a sort of Victorian courtship, perhaps when she was in her twenties, with furtive, fluttering glances, pale loitering and truncated sentences where neither party came right out with anything – and certainly never went into the woods for sex.

That last phrase sounds too clunky. For by Pearl's account, she and her Thomas were true lovers. Look at the length of time that love has endured – for her. Nevertheless, I was still struck dumb at the depth of physical desire they had felt for each other. Their passion had been as full-blooded as my own blind drive for Lyle McKenzie, but when you have dealt with older people all your life,

235

you're inclined to assume that such heat is confined to your own generation. And you can't really believe that anyone could feel as passionate as you. Well, I knew differently now, didn't I?

Wouldn't it be absolutely lovely, I thought, nursing my fresh coffee between cupped hands, if I could get them together? According to her, he was probably still alive, and if he was, I should try to find him for her. I already knew how to research. It was several weeks before I had to go back to college in October, and bad as I felt about Mandy, she was in the best place for her and all I could do was to visit her often and give her as much support as I could. There would be no minding of her until she came home.

There was another thing too: if I could sort this out, it might, in a funny kind of way, balance out Lyle McKenzie's appalling behaviour. Had I not been the one to talk first, I doubted she would ever have confided in me – or anyone else for that matter: there had probably been an element in it of helping me. And the more I thought about it, the more I felt that if I could play a part in organising a happy outcome for one of us, it would actually help me enormously.

She had been right about one thing: what was I ashamed of? That I had had sex – such a strong drive in all species, not least human beings? Her description of herself and Thomas in that forest had pulverised my shame. I felt it no longer. (The jury was out, however, on my disgust with myself at having been so green. Such a patsy.)

I heard her light footsteps coming back down the hallway and descending the stairs. 'Sorry about that,' she said.

'I've made fresh coffee. Can I get you a cup?'

'No, thank you. I wouldn't sleep.' Then, with a wan smile, 'I doubt I'll sleep in any case.'

'Sit down, Pearl. You're not going to leave the story half told?'

'There isn't much else to tell.'

'You must be joking! If I don't hear the next bit I won't sleep not just this night but for the next three months. Please, Pearl.'

'Where did we leave it?' She sat down. 'But, really, Catherine—'

'It ended the night before you were going to Dublin, but you never said what happened after the two of you were discovered in the forest. You didn't actually say who was running towards you. It was the day you found out your daddy had to go to England for a year.'

236

'Scotland.'

'Sorry. Scotland.'

'It's going to sound really melodramatic.'

'Like what I told you about Lyle and me?'

'I've never talked to anyone about this, Catherine, never. It's hard. It's humiliating.'

'You don't have to tell me about humiliation,' I said, with feeling, then waited.

She closed her eyes. 'That man,' she said quietly, 'did not deserve to be called a man.'

'You mean Thomas's father?'

'He managed to control his temper at the outset,' she went on, as though I had not spoken, 'because there were others with him, two policemen, or maybe three – some of it is a blur now in my memory. He went through the charade: "Thomas! We were so worried. Where were you, son?" He actually used that word, "son", like a proper father would. Like my own dear papa.' She opened her eyes again and, in the dim light, the expression in them was difficult to see.

'What did you do?' I spoke gently.

'What do you think?' She gave a tiny, tight smile. 'I ran to put on my clothes, of course. Thomas was cornered and caught by the policemen, but Lord Areton came right up to me as I was struggling into my dress. I'd put it on back to front so that I could do up the buttons. It had what seemed like a thousand little buttons . . .'

She had told me about him undoing them, one by one, top to bottom. It had made me shiver. It did again.

'I picked up my shoes and the rest of my clothes. My instinct was to run as fast as I could, but I was unwilling to abandon poor Thomas. At first. Whatever Fate had in store for me, the outlook for him was grim. I wanted to scream and shout and rescue him, but,' her voice lowered almost to a whisper, 'these were big men and I was only a girl.' Then, with revulsion, she went on, 'And while I hesitated, that man came right up close to me. He held his face only inches from mine, so close I could smell his horrible breath. "Not so brave now, are we, miss? What would your beloved daddy say if I were to tell him what I just saw with my own eyes?"'

She almost spat the words, which, because this was ladylike Pearl, gave me quite a jolt. 'I'll never forget that moment, Catherine. I wanted to vomit. How my papa could have served that man for so long and so faithfully—' She swallowed and said, more quietly, 'Anyhow, that was what he did.'

'So what happened next? Did you hit him?'

'Catherine! The very idea!'

'Sorry. I probably would have.'

'I ran,' she said, almost inaudibly. 'I ran. I was so humiliated that that man and those policemen had seen me— I'm sorry, I shouldn't get so emotional – it was all nearly half a century ago.'

'Please, go on.'

'I have never been so ashamed of what I did. I behaved like a coward. I left Thomas to his fate. To my dying day I will not forgive myself for that. He was struggling with the policemen and shouting at his father to leave me alone, trying to protect me. And I – ran. I abandoned him.' She put her head in her hands.

'Please, Pearl. Don't be so hard on yourself. What else could you have done?'

'I could have stayed with him – it might have saved him a beating. Many beatings.'

I didn't need to ask what she meant. She had told me about the weals on Thomas Areton's legs, his terror of his father and his school. 'Pearl, you can't blame yourself. Three grown men against a boy and a girl. There was nothing you could have done.'

'I know that here,' she tapped her head, 'but not here,' indicating her heart. 'Even as he was facing a horrendous future, he was defending me, trying to get to me, shouting at his father to leave me alone – and I . . . ran . . . away.'

'So you see,' she went on, in a monotone, 'you're not the only one who wakes up at four in the morning re-creating something that will haunt you for the rest of your life.' She said this with an air of finality. As if that was the end of the story.

'Did he never come to Mealy's café like he said he would?' I asked carefully. 'Did you ever see him again?'

She shook her head. 'No.'

It was still hard to hear her. 'Sorry – if I'm upsetting you, stop me, but why didn't you look for him?'

'How could I? I had no spare money, hardly any time off.'

'But you'd like to see him again?'

'What do you think?' She rose and peered ostentatiously at her watch. 'I made some feeble efforts. I actually have a letter from Parliament in London. They say his seat in the House of Lords is unattended. Not "vacant", so that means . . .'

'Now you know the whole story,' she said briskly. 'It's time for bed. Good night, Catherine, I hope you sleep well. Better than I will, I suspect!' She smiled, or attempted to.

'Why haven't you written about this? You're an author. It's a fantastic story, Pearl.'

'It's not a "story". It's private.'

'Are you sorry you told me?'

She took a long time to reply to this. 'No,' she said at last. 'I'm not, actually. Somebody had to find out eventually – it makes it more real somehow. And in a sense . . .' She hesitated. 'I don't know how to put this . . . Maybe telling you has robbed it of some of its power.'

This so closely resembled what I had thought about revealing Mandy's illness – and the story of Lyle – to her that I got goose bumps. She didn't notice. 'I had it bouncing around in my head for so long that I was beginning to believe I'd imagined a lot of it. But I'm still ashamed—'

'Pearl, you're the one who told me not to be ashamed.'

'Mmm.' She shook herself, like a dog coming out of the sea. 'I suppose I haven't so much to be ashamed of, really.'

'Pearl! Ask yourself – no, honestly – ask yourself did you really abandon him. Physically you could do nothing to help him.'

'Mmm . . . Thank you for listening, Catherine. I'll be off, so.' Those shutters she could employ at will had come down and I knew that was all I would hear. For tonight anyhow. Impulsively I got up from the chair, threw my arms around her and hugged her as hard as I could. 'I'm sorry, Pearl. That was awful for you.'

After a few seconds, she hugged me back. 'Good night, Catherine.' She kept her head low when we disengaged. 'Those are very nice shoes. Are they new?'

'No, I've had them for ages. Listen, Pearl—'

But she was finished. 'Thank you so much.' She turned and left the kitchen.

It was probably the late-night coffee but I tossed and turned in the bed in one of the sisters' spare rooms for most of that night. I had always known that Pearl had been harbouring something huge. I dearly wanted to do something about it. I *would* do something about it.

239

In the end, the first step proved to be quite easy – and thrillingly fruitful.

Next morning, I drove straight to the National Library in Kildare Street. My student credentials held and, within minutes, I had *Debrett's Peerage & Baronetage* and the Family Index of *Burke's Peerage* under a green-shaded desk light. Lord Areton was there all right, although Areton was the family name: his title was 'The Viscount Erkina of Ballyragget' and, yes, the title had passed to his son, Thomas Christopher John. The family seat was in Oxfordshire and – oh, joy! was occupied by Thomas's sister, the Hon Isabella Anne, who was married to a businessman named Mander and had two children and three grandchildren. As the daughter of a Viscount, she was The Honourable, but when speaking to her, I should call her by her married name. It was all very complicated!

Back home in Harold's Cross, I devised what I hoped was a cunning plan. From what she and Opal, particularly Opal, had told me about the Aretons, they were not the most accommodating people where the lower classes were concerned. Nevertheless, I set to and, with the aid of helpful operators in International Directory Enquiries, got the number of the Oxfordshire pile, which had not been entered under Areton but Erkina-Ballyragget.

'There it is, love.' The operator was triumphant. 'Will I connect you?'

'Yes, please.' My heart was thumping as I heard the telephone ring at the far side. Wouldn't it be absolutely delicious to tell Pearl I'd found him?

On the other hand, maybe he was married with a squad of children and living in South Africa – why hadn't I thought of that? I was about to drop the phone back on its cradle when I heard it being picked up. 'Hello? Hello?' The voice had the cracked tone of an adolescent boy. A very posh one. ('Hellair') 'Is anybody there? Hello?'

'Hello.' I found my voice. 'I wonder could I speak to your mother, please?'

'This isn't anything to do with the fête, is it? If it is I'm to take a message. She's in the South of France. Won't be back until Tuesday.'

'No. It's nothing to do with the fête. It's a personal call from Ireland for Mrs Mander.' I spoke in what I hoped was an official tone.

'Oh. My grandmother. Would you like to speak to her, then?'

Of course. Isabella, who was of Pearl's generation, would be the grandmother. 'Thank you. That would be great.'

'Thank you for calling.' The boy, whose officiousness was quite endearing, had been well trained. In other circumstances I would have been tickled pink. I wondered what age he was. I guessed fourteen or fifteen. Dear God, around the age Pearl's Thomas had been when—

'Hello?' The voice was high, as though its owner was alarmed.

'Is this Mrs Isabella Mander?'

'George said this was a personal call from Ireland. Has something happened to Tom?'

33

CATHERINE

I could barely contain my excitement for the rest of the morning. Isabella Areton's revelation that her brother was in Ireland – somewhere – had knocked me for six. All this time! All this time wasted when they could have been together. Somehow my mission to reunite them had assuaged my own panic, heartache, distress, whatever you'd like to call it. It was something to grab on to. Something good. Or so I hoped.

After her initial shock – she had reckoned I was ringing her with news of her brother's death – she calmed down and listened to the spiel I had prepared. I hadn't wanted to reveal my self-appointed assignment straight away. Instead, I had let her believe I was a university student (true! If you're going to tell a Big Lie make use of the truth as far as possible) whose thesis was on the experiences of those who lived in the Big Houses in Ireland around the time of the civil war. I had reckoned that she would have put down the phone if I had burbled about an affair of the heart between two children who were now in their sixties.

'I promise I won't take more than an hour of your time, Mrs Mander.' I tried to sound mature yet youthfully hopeful, a difficult combination to pull off.

'But I don't know anything about the Irish civil war – except that your people burned us out. And a lot of our friends too.'

'Oh, my thesis isn't political. I'm interested in what it was like to live in those houses. How the staff behaved, how the owners were treated in the village shops. Parties. Hunt balls. It's first-hand social history I'm after. Any memories you have of Kilnashone, who your friends were, how you spent your time.'

'Who else have you spoken to?'

242

'I'm just starting on the interviews. So far I've been working purely with background research, journals of the day, contemporary periodicals and so forth.' I was proud of that. Sounded authentic.

'You mean I'm the first?'

'If that's all right?'

'Oh, very well. When do you want to come over? We're leaving for Scotland at the weekend.'

'I could come tomorrow, if that would suit?'

'Early afternoon is best. We're about an hour from Heathrow. I'll send the car. It would take you all day to get here by train and bus. Let me know what time your flight gets in. What's your name again?'

'Catherine Fay.'

'That's easy. I'll have Meadows hold up a sign. Just look out for it. When you call back with the time and flight number, if I'm not here, somebody'll take a message.' She hung up. There was obviously no messing with Isabella Areton.

The Aer Lingus reservation clerk was helpful too, took my American Express card details over the phone and I hung up with a confirmed reservation on a flight that would arrive at twelve fifty in the afternoon. I would have to pick up the ticket at the ticket desk. So far so good.

That morning, I had given both minders paid time off: 'There's really no point in your being here at the moment — I'll get on to the agency and let them know about our arrangements. That's if you want to continue with us, of course?'

They looked at each other. 'She's a little dote. Who wouldn't want to mind her?' said the first.

'So, that's settled, then. And thank you for your kindness.' I had already given them the two weeks' wages they were owed, and now handed each of them a twenty-pound note, which far exceeded what they earned for their week's work. We would meet every Friday so I could pay them for that week and each of them was to telephone the house every night to find out what the latest news about Mandy was.

I brushed off their thanks. 'Doctor Madden would have done the same. If there's any difficulty with the agency, let me know. I hope we'll be talking again very soon.'

The last phone call of that night was to the house in Sandymount.

243

Unusually, it was Pearl who answered. On hearing my voice, she grew concerned. 'No bad news from the hospital, I hope?'

'No. No news at all, and I suppose no news is good news, eh?' I couldn't prevent the leakage of my excitement and she immediately picked up on it. 'Catherine, something has happened! I can hear it.'

'Nothing has happened,' I lied. 'Really.' I had never been a good liar. 'Sorry. I may sound a little tiddly, though, because my friend, Frances, has called around and we're having a couple of drinks.'

'Oh. That nice girl from school?'

'Same one. Look, the reason I'm ringing is that she's going to stay the night and we're going shopping together in the morning and having lunch in town and then I'm going back to her place because she has a whole collection of photographs from – from our schooldays and,' I finished up in a rush, 'we're going to have a girly day together.' I should have thought this out better before I picked up the phone.

'Why are you telling me all this, Catherine?'

'Because, you see, I won't be able to go to the hospital tomorrow.'

'Of course, dear. Don't worry, Opal and I will hold the fort. Just let me get a pen and paper and you can give me Frances's telephone number in case we need to be in touch with you urgently. Just as a precaution.' She put down the phone and I could hear her tip-tapping away into the distance. Shit!

Quickly I extracted Mandy's address book from the drawer in the phone table and riffled through it until I found the Higginses' number. Now I'd have to let them in on the deal.

When she came back, I read it out quite confidently. 'That's grand, dear,' she said, 'and it's nice she lives so close to you!'

'Gosh! How – how did you know that, Pearl?' I tried to sound unconcerned.

'The first two digits of the number are the same as yours.'

34

CATHERINE

My flight landed on time and, lo and behold, there was the promised chauffeur, complete with cap, holding up a neatly hand-lettered sign: *Miss Catherine Fay*. On the way to the car, I attempted to make conversation, but his polite, monosyllabic answers warned me that this was a business arrangement, not a potential friendship.

The car, when we reached it, was impressive – a lovely grey Jag, bodywork glistening in the harsh overhead lighting of the car park. Inside, the seats were of soft cream leather. Although I would have preferred to sit in the front, he had opened the back door for me, and somehow I hadn't the nerve to ask.

'How far is it to the house?'

'Less than an hour, miss. Would you like a newspaper?'

I assumed this was another way of shutting me up. 'No, thank you, I'll just enjoy the journey.'

The car whispered out of the airport and into a maze of turns and junctions until we were on what seemed to be a huge road still partially under construction. We sailed along bits of it, then, every so often, slowed to crawl through narrow corridors indicated by bright yellow cones. 'This will be amazing when it's finished!'

'Yes, miss. They've been building the M40 for a couple of years now.' Again that closing off. I did shut up this time.

Soon we were travelling through open countryside, with pastures and croplands. What was most striking to me was the neatness, not only in the lovely villages we passed through but in the fields where even the corn seemed to be on parade. 'Chipping Norton – not far now, miss,' announced my laconic guide, drifting to a halt at a zebra crossing to give way to a young woman pushing a pram. It was the first information he had volunteered and, unexpectedly, my stomach turned over. It had been an impetuous decision to make this journey and I was more than a little unprepared to handle my interview with Thomas Areton's sister. I would have to act like the student I was – not too difficult. But how was I going to introduce her brother into the conversation without her having a blue fit at being deceived? I would have to play it by ear. I had brought my UCD library card to show her in case she doubted my credentials.

On the other hand, why would she? My plan was brilliant. I couldn't see any flaws in it, provided I didn't say something really off the wall.

The chauffeur turned the car into a small laneway, on one side of which ran an old stone wall, about six feet high, breached here and there with vegetation and, to my untutored eye, not in great condition. A quarter of a mile later, he turned in between a pair of gates that had once been painted white but now showed patches of rust and seemed permanently locked open. By my reckoning, the avenue, running between post and rail fences, which also badly needed painting, had to be at least a mile long. There were weeds and scutch in the empty pastures. Nevertheless, when the house finally came into view, it took my breath away.

At first glance it seemed to have a hundred windows along its façade, the centre of which was three storeys high, with two-storey wings on either side. I'm no expert in architecture, but you get the picture. Think of the most imposing house you have ever seen in Ireland, double the size and grandeur, and you have the image of Thomas Areton's ancestral home.

Closer in, when we crunched to a halt at the pillared front entrance, the effect was not quite so grand – it was almost sad, actually. The contrast between the lovely Jag and its owners' home was marked. There were tall skinny weeds growing through the gravel of the wide parking area, and although there were two huge fountains, each marking a boundary of the gravel, their empty ponds, cherubs and dolphins were green and yellow with algae and lichen. Along the vast length of the house, all those windows needed attention and while the enormous front door was not meant for painting, its heavy wood, black with age, was mottled and cracked in places.

'Here we are, miss.' The chauffeur held the door open for me. 'Do you need me to ring for you?' There was a rookery some-where nearby and the birds were making such a racket I could barely hear him. Anyhow, there was no need for his intervention because the front door opened and a woman came out to meet me. 'I'm Isabella. I was looking out for you. How d'you do?' She held out a hand.

On the phone she had sounded girlish and, indeed, her voice, with its cut-glass accent, was pitched high, but there any resem-blance to girlhood ended. Her grey hair was cropped midway down her ears, almost pudding-bowl style, unflattering to a tough-skinned, heavily lined face that was beyond the help of any cream or potion. She was carelessly turned out, wearing flat navy brogues and a green dress of some thick fabric, probably Viyella, that did nothing for her lumpy figure. 'Gracious, you're big!' She returned my scrutiny, giving me a quick up and down, then called to the chauffeur, 'Thank you, Meadows.' She turned to me. 'An hour, didn't you say?'

'Yes.'

'An hour, then. All right, Meadows?' With a wave, she dismissed him. 'Follow me.' She turned and went towards the house. 'I've ordered tea for the morning room.'

'Thank you.' Meekly, I followed her into a gloomy, cavernous hall decorated, if that's the word, with deer heads and antlers but also, beside the fireplace, a full-sized, snarling bear. As we passed into a corridor, she pulled a faded red rope with tassels, and some-where in the bowels of the house, I heard a bell ring. I felt I was walking through an M.J. Farrell novel.

The morning room was bright and obviously well used, with faded chintz couches and chairs and a huge sideboard on which stood a selection of bottles and decanters and an ice bucket. She saw me look towards it. 'Would you prefer a drink?'

'No, thank you. Tea would be lovely. You have a wonderful house, Mrs Mander.'

'Hmph! Come in the winter! It's the devil to heat. We live in here, the kitchen and the bedrooms. We come for the staff's sake, and for the villagers, of course. They like us to be here, but I leave most of that kind of thing now to my daughter. If it was up to me I'd sell it. Some bloody hotel chain would take it on, I'm sure

– but, then, it's not up to me. Thank God for the London house.' She plonked herself into a chair. 'Let's not wait for tea, let's get started, eh? Now you do know that I was only a girl ["gel" – I swear to God she said "gel"] when we left Kilnashone?'

'Oh, yes, I do know that. But sometimes childhood reminiscences are even more accurate than those of adults, don't you think?'

'Hmph!'

I took out my pen and the impressive-looking hard-backed notebook I had bought at the airport bookshop. 'So, Mrs Mander, could you describe your way of life at Kilnashone Castle when you were there? Did you have lots of staff, a cook, a chauffeur even? There were cars, then, weren't there?' I hadn't planned beyond this opening gambit, and if I had expected her, gasping, to launch into immediate revelations about the night Willie Somers had died and Thomas's flight, I was to be disappointed. 'Oh, yes! I remember Somers, the chauffeur, very well. Nice man.'

'Did he wear a uniform?'

'Yes.'

'Could you describe it? Do you remember?'

'Navy or black. Something like that.'

This was not going to be easy. 'Did he have a family? Would they have worked for you in some other capacity?'

'Yes. He did have a family. A couple of girls ["gels"] – I know that because my mother handed on my clothes to them. And no. They didn't work for us as far as I know. I'm not too sure about that, though. They might have.'

'And you never actually saw them?'

'No.' Then: 'Wait, perhaps I did see them. Christmas. I think we may have had them to tea. I saw them arrive on the back stairs. Think so anyway. Timid.'

'And Somers had no boys?' I was beginning to feel like Nancy Drew, Girl Detective.

'There was a boy. Bad business. He died in our yard, trespassing, you know, got trampled by one of the horses.' She frowned. 'Look here, is this about Somers or the Aretons?'

'The Aretons, of course. I'm just trying to get a general feel of what the greater household, if you could call it that, was like. In my researches I have found that when you add the context of the servants' lives it rounds out the whole picture.'

'Hmph. We were good to our servants.'

'Of course.'

The door opened (thank God!) and a woman, who had to be in her mid to late seventies, pushed a tea trolley into the room. Again this was sad: the trolley, in some sort of polished light wood with a brass rail, was antique, but the wood was scratched and the rail was dull. Its load was nothing to write home about either: just two cups with a plain Rich Tea biscuit on each saucer alongside a tarnished pewter teapot with matching jug and sugar basin.

I had flirted with the idea of coming clean with Pearl and asking her if she would like to come with me, but I couldn't find any role she could fulfil alongside me as a researcher. The only possibility would have been to backtrack on the lie and admit to Isabella why we were there. I was glad now I was on my own: she was nobody's fool and would not have appreciated the subterfuge. 'This is lovely,' I said insincerely, as the woman poured for us. I had been too jumpy to eat at Dublin airport. A combination of nerves, excitement and residual guilt at not visiting Mandy that day had given me a queasy stomach, but now, having had only corn flakes for breakfast, I was starving.

'Leave the trolley,' Lady Areton ordered, as the woman went to push it out again. 'We can pour for ourselves if we need a second cup.'

'Thank you, madam.' The woman shuffled off.

I used the hiatus to regroup my thoughts. Isabella was obviously not the chatty type and perhaps a more direct approach might work better for my purposes. 'This is lovely,' I repeated, when the woman had left the room. Then, placing my cup back on the trolley and adopting a businesslike tone: 'Perhaps, as you say, Mrs Mander, I should be concentrating on you and your family, at least initially, and then if we have time we can expand. You have a brother in Ireland?'

'Yes.' She was wary now.

I kept my head low, ostentatiously turning a page and writing swiftly in what I pretended was shorthand, a skill I do not possess. 'Right,' I said, without looking up. 'His name is Tom?'

'Thomas. Only I use "Tom".'

'Was your father's name Thomas?'

'Thomas was called after my grandfather, my father's father. There was always a Thomas at the head of our family – our father was Horatio Thomas Christopher. His father was Thomas Christopher Jocelyn. His father was Jocelyn Thomas George.'

'That's fascinating.' I finally looked up and asked, pen poised, 'Is that the usual practice in aristocratic families? That the same names are always handed down to the head of the household?'

'Probably. It's been my experience anyhow.'

'Thank you. That's really interesting. I didn't know that.' Again I lowered my head to scribble my 'shorthand'. 'I'd love to talk to Thomas too. Where is he based?'

She didn't answer. I looked up. She was frowning again. 'I'm sorry, would it be a problem if I contacted him?'

'How much do you actually know about the aristocracy, Miss Fay?'

'Not a lot,' I admitted.

'And this thesis of yours, who's supervising it?'

'I have a tutor. I can give you his name if you need to check my credentials – and here.' I rooted in my bag to pull out my student card. 'I can show you this, if you like.' I held it out to her but she didn't take it.

'All right. All right. Thomas is – well . . .' For the first time she hesitated. 'He can't be contacted.'

'Oh!' Was he a recluse?

'Look, Miss Fay – Catherine – I'd prefer it if you didn't use my brother in your thesis.'

'But I won't be using any names at all.' I was wide-eyed with sincerity. I could be sincere because it was the truth: I would be using nothing because there was no thesis. 'I'm talking to you – and hopefully to others – entirely for background information and context. I wouldn't quote you without your permission and, of course, as a matter of courtesy, I will be letting you see the finished work before I hand it in.'

She looked off into the distance. 'Well, if that's the case . . .'

'So it would be acceptable if I got in touch with him?' I tried to strike a balance between casual and matter-of-fact.

Instead of answering, she got up and went to the window, which overlooked the driveway. Then, after a few seconds, she turned back to me. 'It is my continuing sadness that my brother is not well,' she said quietly. Her demeanour had changed – even her voice was lower and softer.

I was aware that in Ireland 'not well' usually meant mental illness. Was it the same over here? I didn't want to ask.

She came and sat down again, spreading her hands on her lap. 'We had a fire,' she said. 'You probably know that.'

'Yes.'

'Kilnashone Castle was burned to the ground. My brother was never the same afterwards. He came back to school here but ran away, as he was so unhappy. I don't think any of us appreciated the effect the fire had had on him. I certainly didn't.' She looked back up at me. 'I'm of a generation that prides itself on surviving all that life can throw at us, illness, poverty . . .' she waved an arm around the room '. . . everything. We inherited strong backs and broad shoulders and are proud of that. This strain, unfortunately, seemed to have bypassed my brother.'

'Why is he in Ireland?'

She shrugged. 'I have no idea. None of the rest of us had the slightest problem leaving Kilnashone – and the insurance money was useful, of course.'

She looked off again into the distance. 'I don't know why I'm telling you this. I think, however, when I got your call last evening, as you probably guessed from my reaction, I realised that, subconsciously, I'm always on the alert for the call that will tell me he's no longer with us. The Irish police are familiar with him.'

'Is he in gaol?'

'Good heavens! No!' She regained some of her spirit. 'What made you think that?'

'The police?'

'No. He wouldn't harm a fly. That's the problem, actually.'

'I beg your pardon?'

She seemed to come to some sort of decision. 'Will any of your researches take you to other families who lived in the Irish midlands? Some of them, who weren't burned out like we were, have settled there.'

'Of course. I know there are families in Tipperary, for instance.' Desperately I trawled my memory banks. 'And, of course, the Mountcharles family in Meath, the Dunravens [Frances's cousin had had her wedding reception in the Dunraven Arms Hotel in Adare

251

and I vaguely remembered that she had mentioned there was some sort of aristocratic connection there]. And the earls of Desmond and so on. As I said, you're the first I've contacted in person. I came across an article about the fire at Kilnashone.'

'What article was that?'

'I'd need to go back over my notes. I don't have them with me, I'm afraid.'

'Mm. Look, Miss Fay, there is something I would like him to have. If I give it to you, along with ways to find him, would you hand it to him on my behalf? I'm reluctant to entrust it to the wretched postal service. I always think that registering a letter or a parcel is simply an advertisement to a rascal that there's something valuable inside.'

'Of course I will.'

'Thank you. I'll fetch it when we've finished our chat. Where were we?'

And so, mission accomplished, I went on scribbling nonsense in my hard-backed notebook and drawing on what I'd read of the aristocracy in the novels of Jane Austen. There was *Wuthering Heights* too. I thanked God I had chosen English for my degree, as I continued to ask inane questions about clothing and occasions when gloves were *de rigueur*, hunt balls and house parties, governesses, finishing schools for young ladies and how often children of the house were admitted to their parents' dinner tables.

As she spoke, she began to remember bits and bobs and warmed up a little, becoming somewhat less taciturn and more informative so that the rest of my allotted hour flew by. I almost wished I was genuinely researching the period. All the time, however, I was exultant. I was going to meet Pearl's Thomas.

'Thank you. I think that's all I had to ask.' I put away the pen and, flipping back over the pages of illegible scrawls, pretended to consult them. 'You've been so kind, Mrs Mander. I won't detain you any longer. You said you might like me to give Thomas something on your behalf?'

'Yes. Wait here if you don't mind.'

She was gone for ten minutes. When she came back she handed me a large envelope, wrapped over and over again with yards and yards of sticky tape.

'I may be stopped by Customs. Could I know what's in this, just for safety's sake?'

'Yes. It's our father's gold signet ring and the Areton family seal. I thought of Customs, as it happens, and I put in a letter explaining that they are rightfully his, d'you see? . . . Look,' she sighed, 'I owe you an explanation. Last night after we'd spoken, I began to think about Thomas. He's not getting any younger, none of us is, and he must – he must be finding things difficult.' She looked me straight in the eye. 'The reason I mentioned the Irish midlands is that you'll find him there.'

'It's a large area.' This was no longer mysterious. It was weird. 'Is there a telephone number or even an address?'

'No. That's the point. No address, no telephone number. "No fixed abode", I believe is the term. We don't like strangers knowing that this is how he lives, but your call caught me at a vulnerable moment. It unsettled me because he had been on my mind just before you rang. Quite unlike me, I couldn't sleep last night, and somehow – you know how one does at four in the morning – I began to believe that perhaps it was destiny or Fate or somesuch rubbish that you should call just at that time.'

'But how will I find him without an address of any kind?'

'The Irish police are helpful. He seems to base his wanderings in the midland counties, using the village of Kilnashone as a centre. I send him money *poste restante* from time to time to the post office there, and he always seems to get it.

'I was hoping, Miss Fay, that even the sight of the ring and seal might bring him to his senses. I was also hoping that someone outside the family, to which he seems to have taken quite a dislike, might be able, if not to persuade him, at least to suggest that he might come home.'

'When last did you speak to him?'

'He rings occasionally, very occasionally, but our conversations are stilted and I have given up nagging as there seems no point in it. He is head of this family, though, whether he likes it or not.'

'Is he, you know . . .' I found it hard to say '. . . insane?' My fantasy of an idyll for this man and my lovely Pearl was beginning to dissipate.

'His behaviour is peculiar, but there are no clinical indications of mental disorder. Not that I know of, anyway, and the police

253

don't seem to think so either. They are rather kind, you know, your police. They keep me informed each time he is arrested. It's usually the police from a place called Cullarkin who seem to telephone me. Do you know it?'

I shook my head. I was alarmed. 'Arrested? He's not dangerous or anything like that, is he?'

'Far from it.' She looked suddenly very tired. 'As I said, the opposite is the case – although, Miss Fay, you'll appreciate that I have not seen him myself for many, many years. You'll see for yourself when you meet him, as I hope you will. It's probably best if Thomas tells you his own story and why he lives the way he does. I am counting on your discretion. This thesis is not for publication?'

'No.' And if there is any question of that,' I made myself sound ultra-sincere, 'I give you my word that I shall show it to you before publication and I promise you can remove anything you might find offensive or embarrassing.' I held my breath. Had I gone too far?

She hesitated. For the first time she seemed vulnerable 'Could I have your telephone number, Miss Fay? I would like to know from your perspective, how he is.'

'Of course.' I tore a page from my notebook, scribbled my number on it and gave it to her.

'Feel free to use my name as an *entrée* to other families in your researches, with which I wish you the best of luck.'

'Thank you very much.'

'I miss him,' she said softly. 'Will you tell him that? There are only the two of us, d'you see?'

'Of course I will.'

For a split second, neither of us seemed to know what to say next. I looked down at the package. 'What will I do with this if I can't find him?'

'Oh, we'll work something out. You have my telephone number now.' Again she hesitated. 'I'm sorry to burden you with this, Miss Fay.' She cocked her head to one side. 'You're getting more than you bargained for, aren't you?'

I blushed. She might have been referring simply to my research project, or she might have seen through it and meant something else entirely, which wouldn't have surprised me. But with a quick shake of the head, as though shucking off her soft mood, she recovered her poise. 'Now, let's see if Meadows is back with the car. He's usually reliable.'

Clutching my notebook and the package for Thomas Areton, I followed her from the room. I realised that, in ordinary circumstances, I would like Isabella Areton. I felt like a heel.

35

CATHERINE

I had a map with me and it was just after half past ten the next morning when I drove into Cullarkin, which was one of those Irish towns with just one long straggling street. Near what I took to be the centre (because there was a small stone obelisk, surrounded by benches, railed off on an island in the middle of the road), there were cars everywhere, parked, double-parked, moving slowly, searching for spaces. And there were loose groups loitering outside a rather plain but elegant stone building. There were gardaí, too, leaning against squad cars, chatting quietly. Of course. The building was a courthouse and a sitting was in progress.

I found a spot further up the street, parked and walked back, approaching a pair of gardaí, one of whom was reading something aloud from the newspaper. 'Excuse me.'

'Yes?' The man holding the newspaper lowered it.

'I wonder if you could help me? I'm looking for a Thomas Areton.'

'Yeah.' The older man smiled. 'We know him all right. Who's asking?'

'I'm a friend of his sister. She asked me to contact him.'

'Is he on the list today, Jarlath?' the garda asked a colleague.

'I dunno. I'll find out.' The other man went off into the courthouse.

'You're in the right place, miss.' The first man folded his newspaper. 'Don't know what a nice girl like you is doing in a place like this,' he laughed at his own joke, 'but if you hang around long enough, you'll see him. Even if he's not on today's list he'll be on one sooner or late. But he's harmless.'

'If he's not due here, would you have any idea where I might find him today?'

'The sister sent you, eh?' He looked so keenly at me that I almost felt guilty. 'Why, I wonder, wouldn't she come over herself? How well do you know that family?'

'Well, I know they lived in Kilnashone, and I'm a relation of a family who worked there. My grandmother was a cousin of the people who lived in the gatehouse.'

'That wouldn't be the Somers family, now, would it?'

'How did you know?' I was astounded. 'It was such a long time ago.'

'Would you believe, now, that my father was distantly related there? Arrah, girl, you and me's probably cousins of some sort!'

'That's amazing.'

'I can tell you it's not. What's that they say about three degrees of separation in Ireland?' He took off his cap, rubbed his head and then put the cap back on again. 'There was a falling-out years ago.' He parked his behind on the car, crossed his feet and seemed to be settling into storytelling mode, as though we had all the time in the world. 'It's usually a will or a wake around these parts, but this was to do with a wedding. My grandfather and his brothers wouldn't go to that wedding. Any luck, Jarlath?' He'd spotted his colleague coming back.

'Not on today.' The younger man smiled at me.

'Tell you what, girl,' the first man again removed and replaced his cap, 'if I was you now, I'd go up the road a bit to the terrain around the Devil's Bit. One of the men in the barracks remarked that he saw him near there yesterday. You might have to drive around the roads a bit but you'll probably find him up that country.'

'What does he look like? Would I recognise him?'

'Hey Jarlath! Would she recognise Animal John?'

'I beg your pardon?'

'No offence. Animal John's what we call him.' They both chuckled. 'No doubt in the wide earthly world you'd know him. I don't even have to describe him to you, *alanna*. You know this young lady and me's related?' he said then to his colleague, who responded with a hearty laugh.

'Go 'way out of that! If you're to be believed you're related to half the country.' He smiled impishly at me. 'Are you staying around for a while, miss?'

The invitation was unmistakable and he was good-looking, but

I was still too freshly bruised. 'No,' I said, too curtly, and immediately apologised. 'Sorry. It's just that I have a lot on my mind. My name is Catherine. Catherine Fay.'

'Well, if you change your mind, Catherine Fay,' he was far from put out, 'there's even a dance on in Portlaoise this very night. The Royal's playing.' He swivelled his hips, miming a few steps of the Hucklebuck. 'Last outing before they leave again for Vegas. Sure you couldn't miss it.'

'Thank you – but, unfortunately, I can't.' Almost despite myself, I was flattered. The Royal Showband was top of the pops for most of us. I'd never seen them but was curious. And, pre-Lyle, I had loved dancing.

Right now, though, I didn't want to waste any more time. 'No fixed abode,' Isabella had said. If Thomas Areton had been seen in the vicinity of the Devil's Bit, which I'd heard of, he might still be there and, if not, was probably not far away. I thanked both officers again, got driving directions from them and hurried back to the car.

He was almost exactly where the guards had said he'd be. I spotted him long before I drew close to him and understood why they had been amused at my naïve question as to how I might recognise him. He was unmistakable. With unkempt beard and matted, shoulder-length hair as grey as the road, he was standing in a ditch, staring in the direction of the Devil's Bit, which, I saw immediately, was a strange hilltop valley. I knew already that there were all kinds of legends about it, one of the most fanciful being that when St Patrick arrived in Ireland, Satan fled before his advancing Christianity and, in revenge, took a bite out of the mountain peak and dropped his mouthful nearby, thereby creating the Rock of Cashel.

I didn't want to startle him so I stopped the car several yards from where he stood and, leaving the engine ticking over, got out as though I was a tourist taking in the sights. I was kicking myself I didn't have a camera with me. 'Lovely day!' I called, climbing up on the ditch to gaze in the same direction as he was. 'What an interesting sight. The Devil's Bit, yes?'

Thomas Areton's head whipped around. His black coat, green with age, was held on him by just one button at his chest, while the soles of his unlaced boots had parted company from the uppers. 'Lovely day? Not for those lambs. They're going to die today.'

'I beg your pardon?'

'I said,' he raised his voice, 'those lambs are going to die today. See that trailer there?'

He pointed towards the far side of the road where I could see an animal trailer hooked up to an ancient tractor. Its ramp had been lowered. 'I do see it, yes.'

'Well, stay here a while and you'll see those poor terrified animals being taken from their mothers, rounded up, shoved into that thing and brought off to be killed. What do you think of that now?' Fiercely, he eyeballed me.

I looked up and down the road, but it was blanketed with silence except for the distinctive hum of an Irish country summer: insects, the trundle of a faraway tractor. It occurred to me that not a single car, or even a bicycle, had passed since I had stopped.

I played for time, looking into the field in front of us where, indeed, a few dozen ewes were grazing peacefully while their lively offspring, in high spirits, jumped and played around in utter ignorance of what lay ahead. It was one of those extraordinary moments you encounter from time to time, not exactly life-changing but shedding new light into a dark corner. I had never before considered how Mandy's roast lamb got on to my Sunday dinner plate.

'Maybe they're just being moved to another field.' I glanced back at him and, to my horror, saw that, with both fists, he was punching at the tears rolling down his face.

'Only a few weeks old.' With hair and coat flapping, he jumped down from the ditch and walked quickly away from me. I stood there, my nostrils full of the pungency of the road's sun-warmed tar and my ears ringing with that exuberant but doomed infant bleating. I got down off the ditch.

This was not my business. This was the way life was.

Back in the car, I sat clutching the hot Bakelite steering-wheel. Should I drive after him? Warned by Isabella and the guards, I had already tailored my vision of Thomas Areton and hadn't been surprised by his tramp-like appearance, but his presence was far more powerful than I had expected. I dithered about what to do next. Although the guards had said he was harmless, might he turn nasty on me?

The road ahead dipped up and down, and if he was still walking, he was hidden.

I started the car and, driving slowly, watched each side of the road. But although I turned back and retraced the route to the spot where I had met him there was no sign of him. He had vanished.

I looked at my watch. Just after twelve o'clock. I had left home having eaten just a banana and was getting hungry. I decided I would do one more pass up and down this road and into a couple of byroads: on foot, he couldn't be far away. I had already made up my mind that when I did find him, as I was certain I would, I would be honest. I'd tell him straight away who I was and why I was there. But again I drew a blank and, stomach growling, headed back for Cullarkin, getting there just as people were spilling out of the courthouse after the morning session. I drove past it and parked further up the town, where there was a row of shops. Some of the shopkeepers were putting up handmade 'closed for dinner' signs on their doors but the pathways outside were full of women wearing crossover pinafores and carrying shopping bags. There could be no doubt that this was a town in rural Ireland: the flat caps and turned-down wellington boots betrayed the men as farmers.

Everyone seemed to know everyone else. Drivers of ancient cars travelling in opposite directions stopped in the middle of the street to have a chat through the open windows, while those in the vehicles waiting behind them betrayed no impatience; from one side of the street to the other, pedestrians yelled affectionate insults at acquaintances. The gossip – what I could hear of it as I passed – was friendly: 'She got called for that interview thanggod . . .'

'Good mart last Wednesday, Tommy, did you get your price?'

'It's been a long nine months, Mary, but she's in now. I've lit a candle. Say a prayer for a short labour, God love her.'

'I will, Sarah. I will. Tell her we're all praying for her. God, if men could have children, wha'? There'd be none of us here at all, wha'?' Cackling, the two women wished each other an overlapping 'God bless' and pushed off.

In the lounge of the hotel I ate over-thickened soup and a limp salad sandwich – after the experience at the Devil's Bit I couldn't face the ham or beef on offer.

It was just after two when I went back to where I had parked the car – and found it blocked in by a garda vehicle, not fully, but enough so that I would have difficulty getting past without grazing it.

Down the street, I saw people arriving at the courthouse, including a number of guards. I walked down and approached one – middle-aged, belly bulging, engaged in wiping sweat from the band inside his cap with his index finger – but was then distracted by the arrival of a squad car pulling up right beside me. Its front doors opened and two officers got out. One opened the back door on his side and reached in as though to grab someone's arm.

Blinking in the sunshine, the dishevelled man who emerged from the back seat was Thomas Areton. He seemed about to acknowledge me, but then, offering no resistance, was steered gently towards the doorway of the courthouse.

'Excuse me,' I said.

'Yes, miss?' The guard I had approached put his cap back on as though ready for official business.

'That man there who was just brought in.'

'Animal John?'

'I beg your pardon?'

'Harmless poor devil, but you can't have people going about the countryside acting like a one-man animal-liberation army.'

'What do you mean?'

'He opens gates and lets farm animals out on to the road if he thinks they're going for slaughter. You know him?'

'I do, yes.'

'Well, next time you're talking to him, will you just tell him to give us a rest? We've enough to be doing.' He chuckled.

'Is that what he's charged with today?'

'Don't know, but it's a safe bet. Must have happened only recently. He wasn't on the list this morning or I would have noticed.'

I thanked him and went inside.

It took my eyes a second or two to adjust to the brown gloom of the courtroom, which was packed and buzzing with chat in what I took to be the public benches, the day's heat drawing the smell of agriculture from well-worn serge, wool and cotton. Some were in their carefully tended Sunday best, while others, with handbags on laps and shopping baskets on the floor, were obviously there for the spectacle. Gardaí supported themselves against the side walls while men in suits and ties – obviously men of the law – sat shoulder to shoulder and perspiring in the front rows before the judge's seat. Apart from these men, the gardaí and Thomas Areton, also known as Animal John, it was impossible to say who was a lawbreaker, who a victim, who was there to ogle an offender or to support a friend they thought wrongly accused.

'All rise,' muttered a man facing us all. The chatter died down and, obediently, everyone stood as a door in the back wall opened and a small, bespectacled man bustled in and climbed into his seat.

The first cases called were obviously routine, and if I hadn't been involved, however peripherally, I would have been almost disappointed in the humdrum nature of the law. The garda on his feet before the bench was reading from a notebook in a fast monotone, and, looking at the assorted bunch of lawyers sitting there with glum faces, I couldn't have imagined any of them striding up and down and gesticulating to make their points, like Perry Mason did. I stole a glance at Thomas Areton, who was standing quietly at the back of the room, dwarfing the policeman beside him. If I were to believe what the garda outside had said, this man was sadly damaged, but his physique, even his unkemptness, lent him an almost medieval presence.

The judge, leaning his cheek on one hand while swinging his spectacles with the other, seemed impatient, bored, or both. When Thomas's case was called, he barely flicked an eye in his direction and let the prosecuting garda go through just the first page of his notes before he interrupted: 'I have a long list this afternoon, Guard. I've heard enough.' He turned to address the dock. 'I assume you're still unemployed?'

Thomas continued to stare at something only he could see in the middle distance.

'Is he still unemployed, Garda?' barked the justice.

'He is, your honour.' The garda nodded.

'Right,' the judge rattled off, 'a hundred pounds, three months to pay, seven days in default. Next case.'

The garda and the accused left the court. It was all very anti-climactic.

Outside, having to break into a trot, I caught up with Thomas as he went away down the street. 'We spoke earlier.'

'They're probably dead by now.' He didn't break stride. 'It's hopeless.'

'Thomas, please, hold on, you're walking too fast.'

'What's it to you?' But he stopped.

'Look, I don't want to talk out here in the street. I have something for you. Something from your sister, Isabella.'

That caught his attention. 'What about Isabella?'

'She gave me something for you that she wants you to have.'

'She has nothing I need or want.'

'Please, Thomas. I've driven from Dublin specially to find you – because there is something else I need to talk to you about. But not out here. It's quite private.'

'I don't know you.' He frowned. 'I don't know what you want. Are you a reporter?'

'No. I'm a student,' I said honestly. 'My name is Catherine Fay. I don't blame you for being alarmed at my arriving here out of the blue and accosting you like this – I mean you no harm. But I think you'll want to hear what I have to say.' I held my breath. My preconceived notions about people who lived rough like this were taking a knock. This man was sober, articulate and in no way a stereotype.

'Where do you want to go?' he asked slowly. I had a quick vision of the two of us sitting cosily in the lounge of the hotel where I had eaten. Perhaps not. 'You choose, Thomas. I don't know this town or even this area.'

He looked up and down the street and came to a decision. 'I know a place. Where's your car?'

Mutely, I pointed it out. We had actually passed it several strides previously. The squad car hemming it in had gone.

As we settled ourselves, with his head almost touching the fabric of the Morris Minor's roof and his knee abutting the gear lever, I wondered if this was wise, going off God knew where with a stranger who might or might not be a lunatic. A lunatic who could, by the look of him, break me in two with his bare hands, big and all as I am. But he seemed perfectly quiet now,

263

and actually, when I thought about it, and remembered that Isabella had said he wouldn't hurt a fly, his 'crimes' were the opposite of violent. Anyhow, here he was, jammed into my car. The die was cast.

36

CATHERINE

The road had petered out at the wide plateau on which we now stood. We had been climbing steadily for the last mile or so and ahead of us was a gated entrance to a pie-shaped slice of forest. But when I got out of the car, the other seven-eighths of that pie were breathtaking, a 315-degree panorama of fields, forests, hills, villages, church spires and snail trails of roads, big and small. With the movement of the clouds, sometimes one village was illuminated at the expense of another, or the windows of a car flashed as the sun struck them. 'Lovely, isn't it?' Thomas Areton was watching me.

'It's amazing. What county is this? What am I looking at?'

'Six counties, Laois, Offaly, Tipperary, Kilkenny, Carlow and Kildare.' He swept an arm from right to left as he reeled them off. 'Welcome to my world.'

'I can see the attraction.' I certainly could. On a day like this, with bees and butterflies prospecting in the wildflowers among the knee-high grass and only the chirping of birds as a soundtrack, it was paradise. 'I never would have found it.'

'Hardly anyone does. Locals never. The foresters come, of course, and a few hardy walkers, usually from Scandinavia or Germany, with their diamond-patterned socks, compasses and plastic-wrapped Ordnance Survey maps.' He laughed. 'It's not always like this, though, I have to warn you. When the mist comes in, or the clouds come down to touch the ground, or there's a storm of rain, it's a different place altogether.'

He seemed relaxed. In fact, right now he was behaving almost like a tour guide, or a proud landowner displaying his demesne. His conversation was so 'normal', it was hard to understand the eccentricity of his lifestyle. 'I wouldn't have thought the midlands were like this. I always thought of it as flat country. You know this area well, obviously . . .' Then I dared to ask the question I'd been dying to put to him. 'You let those lambs out, Thomas?'

'It made no difference. None of it does. They're dead by now.'

For some reason, I became suddenly conscious of Mandy, and my need to get back to her. 'So – is it OK to talk here, Thomas?' I made my tone brisk, like a schoolteacher's. 'I have to drive back to Dublin and time's getting on.'

'Over here.' He walked towards the verge and I thought we were going to have to sit on the ground. My skirt was white. It couldn't take grass stains and survive. So it was with relief that I saw, when I got close to it, we were approaching a long wooden bench, like the seat of a church pew, half buried in vegetation and so weathered it was camouflaged. 'So you've seen my sister.' He sat at the far end. 'How did you meet her?'

It was too early to introduce the subject of Pearl and, anyhow, I had prepared for this eventuality. 'I was researching my family history. Kilnashone Castle and your family came into it. I went over to England and met her.'

'You're connected to Kilnashone? How? Did your family live in the village?' He was looking at me from under his thick eyebrows. One of his eyes, I noticed for the first time, had a small but very obvious fleck of gold.

'No.' I took a breath. 'Not my immediate family. But my relations. My grandmother was a frequent visitor to her cousins. They lived in the gate lodge.'

I didn't need to wait for a reaction. His face, toughened by wind and sun, drained of blood so that the skin turned a vivid, yellowish grey. 'Oh, Thomas,' I blurted, 'I know Pearl would love to see you. She'd really love to.'

Instead of answering, he got up, turned his back and took a few steps away from me. But then he staggered, throwing out a hand as though to grasp at some support. Of course there was none, and he stumbled, falling to his knees. 'Thomas!' I rushed forward. 'I'm so sorry, Thomas. I didn't mean to blab like that. It just came out. I'm really sorry. I should have thought. Are you all right?' I tried to put a hand under his shoulder to help him up, but he brushed me off as easily as, with its tail, a horse flicks away a fly. The other hand was covering his eyes, and for the second time that day, I saw he was weeping. This was grief of a different ilk, though: his mouth was wide open as though he was trying to scream but could find no voice.

Helplessly, knowing I shouldn't, I watched until I could no longer stand it. Tears of empathy started to flow down my own face. 'Thomas, don't cry, please don't.' Instinctively I reached out to him, but again he pushed me away, quite violently, and there was nothing else I could do but wait until his crying, so eerily silent, weakened and passed. He took out a handkerchief (a tramp with a white handkerchief! Honestly!) and blew his nose. 'I'm sorry,' he said, almost formally, putting the handkerchief away and avoiding my gaze. 'That was dreadful. I hope I haven't embarrassed you. I – I haven't heard Pearl's name mentioned for so many years, I actually thought she might be . . .' Alarmingly it seemed as though his emotions might again get the better of him.

'No, please.' I rushed in. 'I'm the one who's sorry. I just sprang it on you. It's just that . . .' I hesitated, choosing my words now, '. . . it's just that I thought you had a right to know that she has been pining for you all these years. And before you ask, she never married.'

If I thought this might comfort him I was wrong. I might have struck him. 'Pining?' he croaked. 'She's been pining?'

I nodded.

He got to his feet, walked back to the bench and sat. 'All those years, all those years,' he whispered, but it was so still in that place I could hear him and I knew the words were not for my benefit. 'All that waste. And now it's too late.' He was no longer whispering and his voice was like a crow's.

I joined him on the seat. 'Don't say that, Thomas. It's not too late.' I grabbed his arm and held on grimly in case he tried to shove me away again. 'It's never too late. You're both alive and healthy.'

'Look at me!' he cried. 'Just look at me!' He made a gesture with both arms, sweeping his hands from head to toe, almost unseating me.

I let go of his arm and said, in what I hoped was a soothing, even motherly voice, 'Nothing that a tailor and a barber can't fix in a few hours!'

In response, he raised both hands to his face and his entire body shook. For a moment, I thought he was crying again but he was laughing his heart out. He dropped his hands, threw back his great shaggy head and roared to the sky.

'What's so funny?' I was astonished.

'Nothing.' He was still laughing so hard he was barely comprehensible. 'Nothing at all. Except me. I'm the funny one. I'm so funny I could die.' He continued to laugh, the whole bench shaking.

For something to do, I got up and retrieved Isabella's package from the boot of my car. I placed it beside him on the bench and sat down again.

'What's that?

'I mentioned it earlier. Isabella sent it.'

'Do you know what's in it?' The fit of laughter had run its course.

'Yes, I do. I had to know because of Customs.'

'So tell me.'

'No. It's none of my business.'

'It's that wretched ring of his, isn't it? She's tried over the years to give it to me.'

'There's a seal as well, apparently.'

He digested this. Then, 'I hate my family, do you know that, Catherine Fay? I want nothing to do with them.' Then he added, in a conversational tone, 'Well, I hated my father. I suppose that's more truthful. My mother was just never fully present, in a way, if that makes sense. There was never enough of her either to love or to hate – oh, I'm talking nonsense.' He looked down at the panorama below us and fell silent.

'Your sister said to tell you she misses you.'

'Isabella?' He turned to me with an incredulous expression. 'Isabella said that? She actually said that in those words?'

'Yes. She meant it, I think.'

'All these years,' he said again, gazing out over the landscape. 'All these years I've dreaded the moment when I would meet someone from the Somers family because of what happened to them at the hands of my family. At the same time I hoped that somehow, somewhere, I would be able to explain to Pearl that I did my best but I just couldn't save him. I did my best.'

He spread his big hands and studied them as though they were two pages of a map. 'I lost hope. I lost the will to be anyone. I couldn't stay in the one place but I kept going back to Kilnashone. I suppose in some dark corner I thought I'd find her there again.

'You see, Miss Fay,' he looked at me, his expression sombre, 'I wanted to explain that I did my best.' He was talking not only repetitively but in riddles.

'I'm sorry, Thomas, you've lost me. Save who? Do your best to save who? It wasn't your fault they had to leave the gate lodge. What age were you? Fifteen or something?'

'You don't really know, do you?'

'Of course I do.'

But it turned out that I didn't.

'After the fire at Kilnashone,' he began, 'I had to give in and go back to school. I had no choice.'

I knew this was going to be a narrative I shouldn't interrupt. I did interrupt: 'Did you run away again?'

He shook his head. 'No. They won. Or, at least, I let them think they did. I knuckled down, became the best student in the class, got on the rowing team and was bound for Oxford, or so they thought. I actually heard Father boasting about me at a dinner party one evening when I was home for half-term. I led them to believe I had accepted the Oxford offer but at the first opportunity, on the day I left for college, instead of travelling there, I took the ferry back to Ireland and, to all intents and purposes, vanished.'

'But how did you live? You had no money – or had you?'

'I came back.' He ignored the question. 'Not to Kilnashone, not immediately, because I knew that would be the first place anyone would look. Instead, I went north, to Northern Ireland, where I got some day labouring work on farms here and there, always moving on. That was where I learned how to survive by living off the land and in it.

'After two years or so in the north, I risked telephoning the house in London. I needed to talk to my sister. I knew I was due to come into my fund when I was twenty-one and I needed to make arrangements. I made the call person-to-person to my sister and chose a time when I was sure that Father would be in Westminster . . .' He trailed off.

'What is it, Thomas? Tell me.'

'There are things I think you don't know, Catherine, or you

269

would already have mentioned them to me. I am very ashamed that my family left this country, left dozens, maybe hundreds, of people to their own devices in a time when Ireland was in dire straits. They could have helped. The estate in Scotland was, still is, as far as I know, one of the biggest in Britain, with productive farms and lucrative shooting and fishing rights. And my father was a director of a number of big companies, as well as being in the House of Lords. So, by any standards, we were wealthy. There was even a tea plantation in India.'

'It was a different era.' I intervened because he was becoming upset and I really didn't think I could face another tidal wave, but again he went on as though I had not spoken.

'What happened to your family, your little cousin, and then his father – you probably know that after the fire, he was offered a year's work?'

I nodded.

'Well, he was based in Scotland so when Mother or Father went up there, he ferried them around, and was required to carry out personal errands for the housekeeper and the butler. One of his regular duties was to drive Isabella and me from home to school and vice versa. Father had another chauffeur and was using Somers as an aide, in a way. The other man was on permanent standby for the most trivial of journeys, but at least he was able to go home to his wife and family occasionally.

'However, in Somers's case, if Mother was in Scotland and we were at school, and my schedule and Isabella's did not coincide, which was more than common,' as he talked, his accent was changing, becoming more recognisably English, 'poor Somers was never off the road.'

'But that was what he signed up for, surely. He was a chauffeur.'

'Yes. But Father made the most ridiculous demands on him. Bringing him to London to take my mother and her friend to the opera, for instance, because he claimed that his own man had to wait to take him home after a late sitting at Westminster.'

'But couldn't he have taken a taxi? London is full of taxis.'

'Exactly. But I'm getting to that. Anyhow, Somers arrived at my school to take me home for half-term – it was around Hallowe'en – about six months after he came to England. It was a filthy evening, with one of those really dense, pea-souper fogs.' He was living the event, slipping away from where he was and right back into what he was describing. 'He was late because of the fog and, having driven all the way from Scotland, absolutely exhausted.

'I was a schoolboy, locked into my own miseries, but even I could see that Somers was in danger of total collapse. I hadn't seen him for about six weeks but in that short time he had lost half a stone or more — and he had always been thin — his cheeks were sunken and there were black circles under his eyes. I was shocked. It was only twenty-one miles to where we lived in London but I really felt he should have a rest.

'He protested — duty always came first with him — but I insisted, and went back into the school to telephone home. I would have to get a train or a bus. Anything except drag the poor man all the way down in that filthy weather.

'I had meant to talk to Mother, but she was out, and before I could say anything more, the butler had called Father to the telephone. I explained the situation but Father would have none of it. "What do I pay the man for?" that kind of thing. I tried really hard to persuade him, Catherine, I really did.'

'I know you did, Thomas.' It was clear that he was working up to something awful. His eyes were glazing as he remembered.

'Anyhow, I couldn't get Father to change his mind. And in a way, you know, Somers was just as stubborn. I was prepared for the consequences at home if I could persuade the poor man to climb into the back seat and sleep for an hour or so . . . But he wouldn't. "Lord A is expecting us, Master Thomas."

'We set off. I sat in the front seat of the Bentley, although I knew that made Somers uncomfortable — he was a great man for everyone knowing his place in the pecking order — but I felt if I kept chatting to him it might get us through. I would also be another pair of eyes.

'It was bizarre, Miss Fay. I've never experienced a fog like it since. You could smell it, for one thing, a choking, chemical smell, penetrating even that car's tight windows. And it muffled every sound. The engine was quiet in any case but you couldn't hear it at all, and as we crawled along, I had no sensation of the tyres touching the road. Somers and I could see each other, of course, but nothing else. It was as though the car was floating under the surface of a river, where the water had thickened and gelled. Every so often, shockingly, a pair of lights, red or white, would appear, but not until they were very near. Somers would brake, and we were going so slowly, it was usually all right.'

'Usually?' I knew what was coming, or thought I did . . .

'The inevitable happened. We were both panicked by one of these sudden appearances of light, a pair of red ones. Somers stamped on the brakes and unfortunately there was a lorry behind us, which rammed into us and shoved us into the car ahead.'

'He was killed?'

'No. Bentleys are very heavy cars. Nobody was really hurt because we were all going so slowly, but both our car and the car in front were written off. Father dismissed your grand-uncle.'

'But—'

'That wasn't all.' He hadn't heard me. 'He never came off the mail-boat home. His body was washed up nine days later in some bay in Dublin.'

'He committed suicide?' I was so shocked I could hardly utter the word. I know it sounds exaggerated but the sun suddenly seemed less bright.

'The inquest found that he had had a heart attack and was dead before he hit the water. So, no. It wasn't suicide. It was "natural causes", which, in my opinion, were far from natural. I blame myself.'

'Why, Thomas? For God's sake – you were fifteen years old!'

'Sixteen, nearly sixteen, at that stage.'

'Well, you were still only a boy.'

'I could have defied Father but I didn't have the courage. If I had, Somers would probably have got home to his family, to your family. He would have been in poor health but probably he would have been alive. Instead, he was abjectly apologetic about the damage to that damned car. What was even worse, he made no protest whatsoever when Father let him go. I was there. It haunts me still. "I understand, my Lord. Thank you, my Lord." I'll never forget the sight of him walking down our driveway, walking slowly. Like an old, old man. And I don't even know what age he was. That's what we were like, we aristocrats.' His face contorted with disgust. 'God knows how he got to the mail-boat. Father didn't even have the decency to hire him a taxi. And you mentioned a taxi before. Why, when Somers was in Scotland with Mother, could my father not use taxis when the first chauffeur was not available?' He took a deep breath, which cracked in his throat. 'I liked Somers. He was very kind to me – one of the few people— Miss Fay, I firmly believe my father deliberately made unreasonable demands on Somers in a calculated effort to force him to leave and go home. The car crash was the ideal excuse to dismiss him, handed to him on a plate. Somers had signed documents in which he gave up the right he or any member of your family might have had to seek redress for the death of your little cousin. So it was game, set and match to the Aretons. A free pass. And we were safely away from the village and didn't have to look at the families of people we had left to fend for themselves, some of whom may even have died of malnutrition while Father hosted his hunting parties in Scotland to slaughter birds and deer.'

'Oh, Thomas.' I went to throw my arms around him, but with a speed that defied his age, he rose to his feet. 'So you see why I can't face Pearl. Somers was her father, and after his death, her whole family broke apart. We blighted their lives. You tell me she has been pining. You have no idea how much I—' His voice broke.

He pulled himself together. 'I can't face her. Not now. Not ever. Especially the way I have lived. Someone like Pearl . . .' Then, almost formally, 'I cannot do what you ask, which I would guess is that Pearl and I should meet again. It is not in me, Miss Fay. Please try to understand that.'

There was nothing I could say.

I was so distracted throughout the journey back towards Cullarkin that, when I was still a mile or so from the town, I almost failed to see on the road in front of me something small and black and round, like a ball of tar. 'Stop! Stop!' My passenger, who had been silent throughout the journey, grabbed the steering-wheel.

I screeched to a halt just a few feet short of what proved to be a blackbird, with a little yellow beak.

We both got out, but the bird still did not move at our approach and was seemingly unafraid, although we were now hovering over it and my car, two or three feet away, was ticking over.

Slowly Thomas Areton leaned down, careful not to make any sudden or jerky movements. I was certain it would fly away but it didn't budge, continuing to look straight up at us. 'Maybe its legs are broken and it can't take off,' I whispered, but he ignored me,

273

extended both hands and closed them gently around the blackbird. Still it made no movement or sound. 'Here,' he said to me. 'Hold him. I'll look for a nest, or a safe place to leave him. He needs a perch.' While he mounted the ditch, I stood there, entranced, gazing down at the bird, which, as though mesmerised, continued to look directly into my face, its beak pointing upright. I felt my heart melt, and I know I will never forget the texture of the little body; the creature's feathers, which I would have expected to feel like velvet, were actually more like satin.

We had stopped in the middle of the road, with the doors left open. Another car arrived behind mine and tooted its horn. The blackbird stirred and, before I could prevent its escape, fluttered away into the grass. I wanted desperately to stay with it and make sure it was all right, but a second car had joined the impatient queue. So near the town, this section of road was busy and I knew we couldn't linger. 'Thomas,' I called, 'it's OK. It's gone into the grass. It's safe now.' I made a placatory gesture towards the cars behind me, got into mine and drove it up on to the verge so they could pass. I got out again when they had gone, but although I searched, I could no longer see the bird.

Until I went to tell Thomas that we had to move. I glanced down and saw a tiny heap of black feathers under the back left wheel of my car. The yellow beak was still trustingly upright.

37

CATHERINE

When we were nearing Cullarkin's outskirts, I broke the silence between us and asked him where he wanted to be dropped off.

'Right here is fine,' he said.

I pulled in alongside a small cottage, over which hung, despite the heat, a drift of blue turf smoke. He grabbed the door handle, but it was stiff with age and he had to wrestle a little with it. 'Thomas, are you sure you won't change your mind and let me talk about you to Pearl?'

'I'm sure.' He gave the handle another sharp pull and it broke off in his hand. 'I'm sorry.' He looked at it as though this were the last straw.

'It's OK. Don't worry about it. It's old – I'll get it fixed.'

'I've very little money on me now, but if you give me your address, I'll send you what it costs to replace it. I am so sorry.' Shoulders slumped, he stared ahead through the windscreen and I knew that the apology was not only for the damage to my car. 'Thomas, last chance, please reconsider. Why won't you allow me even to mention to Pearl—'

'What good would it do?' he interrupted, and again made that despairing two-handed gesture, taking in his body, his clothes, his whole being.

'You're making a mistake. What *harm* would it do? It's not often someone gets a second chance like this.' I knew I was overstepping here. 'Anyhow, what happens when you get really old?'

He shook his head. 'I'm not going to get old. You can be sure of that.' Something about the way he said this triggered alarm, but I had pried more than enough and really didn't want to explore this. So I just watched helplessly as he wound down the window and reached outside to open his door – to discover that the outside handle toggled up and down uselessly. He was trapped.

I made up my mind to stop pussyfooting. I was tired and disappointed and suddenly fed up with handling him with kid gloves. He needed a dose of reality. 'I went to a lot of trouble to find your sister and then you. At least acknowledge that much.'

I'd got his attention: he was staring at me under a frown but I ploughed on regardless: 'Your father's gone and so is your mother. All right, you don't want to see Pearl, that's fine. That's your prerogative. But you and Isabella are the last of that generation of your family so stop being so bloody self-indulgent. Get in touch with her at least. Go over and see her. She has children and grandchildren, relations you have never met.

'And listen to this, Thomas. I don't care what you think, I'm going to tell Pearl I've found you. I actually don't need your permission, you know. It's a free country. She deserves to know – she'd love to know, I'd bet my life on it. So what if you hate each other on sight? Fine. At least that way you can get over each other – but that wouldn't happen, I'm convinced of it. I can see that you're as hung up on her as she is on you. So it's your choice, but by this time tomorrow, you will both be aware of each other's existence and whereabouts.' I looked him up and down. 'Approximately.'

I was rewarded with a twitch of his lips. I ignored it. 'I've done my bit, and as soon as I tell Pearl, my job is done.'

'Self-appointed job.'

'So what?' My indignation intensified. 'You're a self-appointed tramp, a rich tramp by your own admission – you don't even seem to see the absurdity of that – with a self-appointed mission in life. You had a bad start, nobody's denying that, but it's time you got over it.' With a start, I realised I was parroting what Frances had said to me a few months previously about my own whingeing. 'You have responsibilities whether you like it or not.' I reached into the back of the car, picked up his envelope, with its wrapping of sticky tape, and more or less threw it into his lap. 'Now if you want to get out of my car, be my guest. You'll have to cross over and get out this way.' I almost took my own door handle off its moorings as I jumped from the car to let him out, and even as I did so I knew my tirade had been irrational. Right now, I no longer cared what he or anyone else thought. I had wanted Pearl to be happy. I had wanted a happy ending to this half-century saga. I had wanted me to be happy about something in my life . . .

'Are you getting out or do I have to stand here all day?'

Then something surprising happened. 'Could we talk some more, please?' He sounded subdued, even nervous.

'All right.' I got back in. My window had been half open, and as soon as I'd closed the door, I let it down fully. I needed the air. 'I've had my say. Shoot. What do you want to talk about?'

'About Pearl. What is she like now?'

My belligerence evaporated, and in the silence that followed I noticed the sweet smell of honeysuckle. I looked for the source and saw that, having wound its way vigorously through the old box hedge at the cottage wall beside which we were parked, its pale, stringy blossoms had given the greenery a rather shaggy appearance. A bit like my passenger, who was still looking at me. 'I'm sorry I was so abrupt, Thomas. That was mean and rude.'

'Truthful, I'd say.'

'Sorry.'

'Is she still beautiful?'

'She is. She's the most wonderful person, Thomas. She's gentle and intelligent and strong and very elegant. But I really think you should come and discover her for yourself. She's a writer, you know.'

'A writer? Pearl is a writer?'

'Yes. She's published, but not under her own name. She's Dorothy Morris.'

'The short-story writer?'

'You've read her books?' I was astonished.

'No. I don't read short stories, I'm afraid. But I have come across her books in libraries.'

'You go to libraries?'

'Yes. Surprising as it may seem, Miss Fay, I can read. And I am made welcome.'

'Sorry. No offence. It's just that . . .'

'I know what you meant. And you're right. You have made my case. Contrary to the cliché, appearances are not deceptive, Miss Fay. Be realistic: a cultured writer, beautiful, gentle, a lady as you say – and me?'

'Oh, Thomas, you haven't listened to a word I said. Don't let this opportunity pass. Take a few days, get yourself together. I gather from Isabella that money is not your problem. Use it, for God's sake. Come back and join . . .' I nearly said 'the human race' but at the last moment changed it '. . . the – the rest of us.'

'I am rather tired, I admit it.'

'And lonely? Where do you sleep, for instance?'

'Sleeping has never been a worry. Cold in the winter, yes. But there are still barns and sheds used by some farmers to house their stock in winter. You would be amazed, Miss Fay, how the breath of a cow can be so warming or, even better, the breathing of a row of cows. I know where to shelter when rain threatens.'

Then he told me a little about his day-to-day existence, in which no day was ever the same. 'Wind is the only element I fear.'

'Why wind particularly?' I was fascinated.

'Because in a battle between me and a cold wet wind, it always wins.'

'What happens if you get sick?'

'Somebody will look after me.' Then, after a few seconds: 'I had my appendix out. With the pain so severe, I collapsed on the side of the road. A farmer came upon me and took me in his car to the hospital. That happens in Ireland, Miss Fay. People still care for each other. It's why I stayed in this country. I really don't regret anything . . .' again he spread his hands and studied them '. . . except, of course, my lack of courage.'

'Oh, pooh!' I startled myself: I hadn't said that since I was a child. 'Sorry. Don't know where that came from.' I tried to adopt a neutral tone: 'Do I take it, then, that you have been already considering a – a – a change of, eh, lifestyle?'

'You might say that. I don't think, however, that after more than four decades of living this way I could easily integrate into so-called normal society, do you?'

I shook my head. 'But there could be a halfway house?'

'Mmm. Not sure about that.'

'But you admit you've been thinking about it?'

'Yes. I have been thinking about it. I was getting nowhere with my "self-appointed mission", in any case.'

'So why not go and work for one of the animal welfare

278

organisations? Perfect opportunity to change your whole way of life and do good at the same time, I'd say.'

'How did you get so wise? What age are you – fifty-six?'

There had been some sort of a breakthrough. I could feel it. He thought so, too: he actually grinned, showing teeth that were surprisingly good. Surprising to me, that is. I also saw that, with the sartorial adjustments I had suggested, he would be a highly attractive man. Inner beauty and personality are all very well, but show me the girl – or even woman – whose head didn't turn for a second glance at a well-turned-out attractive fella. At whatever age.

'To get back to you and Pearl, what do you have to lose?' But I knew immediately what a ridiculous question that was. He had a lot to lose. In many ways it felt better to cling to 'what if' rather than face a situation with no hope. 'Look, Thomas,' I said boldly, and took his hand. 'We're not talking about an arranged marriage here. We're talking about the reunion of two old friends who have lost each other and who have regretted that for nearly fifty years. Isn't that right? You're afraid she'll reject you, but look at it from her point of view. She'll probably be terrified that you might take one look at her and run to the hills!

He laughed then, reinforcing my conviction that, with the aid of a loofah, a barber, a tailor and a shoemaker, this man could command attention anywhere. 'Have you anyone you can talk to about this, Thomas?'

'No.' Then he seemed to make up his mind. 'All right.'

'All right what?' I hardly dared to ask.

'All right, you can tell Pearl. But be warned. I'm not going to emerge out of this . . .' once again he indicated his clothes and general condition '. . . like a butterfly from a chrysalis. I've been living this way for many, many years now. I don't know if I can change. I met you only a few hours ago, Miss Fay, although I have to say,' he grinned again, 'it does feel like a lifetime. I learned about Pearl only an hour ago. Are you always so forceful? It's been quite a day.'

'A good one, I hope?'

He didn't answer.

'I'm as sure as I know my own name,' I said, as confidently as I could, 'that this is going to work out. As you say, nothing is going to happen overnight, like in a romantic movie, but I really believe

we're doing the right thing here. And – hey! I want you to telephone Isabella. She loves you too, you know.'

After all the trauma and tears of the previous month or so, I felt
terrific, like Glinda, the Good Witch of the South.

38

PEARL

When Opal and I went in to see Margaret at visiting time on the day after her admission, we found she had come round that morning. She could not speak, however, and all the joints on her right-hand side, shoulder, arm, leg and foot, were unusable. She was going to need a great deal of therapy, but even with the best treatments Opal's money could buy, the medics did not know how far they would be able to take her. The poor little thing looked so confused and upset. I do not think she knew where she was. She certainly did not recognise either of us – she looked frightened when we approached her bed. At least, her eyes did. The rest of her face still wore that oxygen mask.

Opal, of course, went in all guns blazing. Why had we not been told she had regained consciousness? Why had the therapy not started yet? – she claimed that someone had told her, 'a very eminent person', that for stroke victims, the sooner they received their therapy the better the outcome.

I have to say that the staff were really good. They soothed her, telling her that there would be plenty of time for therapy. That even though Margaret was in her late seventies, her heart was strong, 'And, as far as we can tell so far, so are all her vital organs.' Along with the nurse on duty, the registrar had kept his patience as she stormed at him. 'Please don't fret, Mrs Igoe,' he said, when she paused to draw breath. I think he was going to pat her shoulder but, luckily for him, thought better of it, 'I promise you, she's getting very good treatment.'

'But you have to keep us informed.' Opal, somewhat mollified, was always like a terrier when she got her teeth into some issue.

281

'That's the main thing. We don't want her to think she has to go through this by herself.'

'We'll remember that, Mrs Igoe. Honestly.' And, with a smile, he was gone.

But Opal, who always takes 'no' for 'maybe', and 'we'll do our best' for 'yes', was not finished and again she prevailed. After a day-long and determined fight, Aunt Margaret was moved to Our Lady's Hospice in her own neighbourhood of Harold's Cross where we knew she would have the best and kindest care. Her heart might be strong but the outlook was not good: her lungs had betrayed her and there was some doubt about the health of her kidneys, but for the time remaining to her, she would be comfortable among her own people.

We authorised Margaret's move without reference to Catherine – or, rather, Opal did – because a bed became available and we had to make a quick decision. We had not been able to get in contact with Catherine since that phone call where she told me she and her friend were having a girly day together.

Actually, I became worried about Catherine. She has suffered a triple blow in a very short time: her beloved poppa going, Margaret incapacitated, and all on the heels of that business with the American boy. It is a wonder she is able to function at all.

One of the advantages of the hospice is that visitors are made welcome, positively encouraged. The ethos is that anything that helps the patient's sense of belonging and of feeling cared for and important is vital to his or her comfort. So I was sitting with her when, at last, Catherine came in, at about half past eight. 'Sorry I'm late.' She was breathless. 'I rang the house and Opal told me about the move. How is she?'

She sat on the other side of the bed. Having been conscious, physically at least, for most of the day, Margaret had relapsed, and although it had not been named as a coma, she was again deeply unconscious. This time, though, she looked quite relaxed and peaceful. At least, that was what I told myself.

'Sorry I've been out of touch, Pearl.' Catherine picked up Margaret's 'good' hand, as unresponsive as the bad one, and kissed it. 'How is she?'

'She's been like this for the past few hours.' I already held the hand affected by the stroke. It was curled a little so it resembled an open claw. 'I think she's in the best place now, whatever happens.'

'You don't think she's going to die, do you?'

'We're all going to die.'

'Yes, but she's not going to die now. She's going to wake up and be with us for a while?'

'Yes. I really think so.' I had been dreading going in, to tell you the truth, because local parlance had it that once you went into the Hospice for the Dying, you never came out. But this was 1970 and, as Opal had informed me when I had reacted with dismay to the news of the transfer, things were changing. 'We don't know what's going to happen. She's in God's hands now. The care in there is marvellous − she'll have the best of everything. And nowadays people do get better and recover.' Despite my assurances to Catherine, seeing Margaret now so frail and wan, I doubted this. 'Did you have a nice time with Frances?'

'Yes.' Like a small child, she leaned over Margaret's face and scrutinised it. 'Do you think she knows we're here?'

'I'm positive she does. We don't even have to say anything to her. She knows.'

So we sat on both sides of Margaret's bed, each of us holding one of her hands. The sounds from outside her room were muted, just the occasional hushed conversation, and the outside world seemed to have retreated. It felt as though time had stopped and there was no rush to do anything, not to talk, not even to think.

'It's so peaceful, isn't it? I'm glad Opal insisted that she come here.'

'Opal is a good egg.' I smiled fondly and had started to tell her about a newspaper interview I had done with a rather intrusive journalist when she cut across me.

'Pearl, I've something to tell you,' she said. Her voice was quiet, probably out of deference to Margaret, but there was something behind it. An urgency.

'Yes?'

'I wasn't with Frances yesterday or today.'

'Oh?' I cannot say I was all that surprised. Catherine was young. It was only natural that she would want some time away from all this.

'I hope what I have to tell you doesn't come as too much of a shock . . .' She hesitated, then said quickly, 'Look, could we go outside somewhere? I shouldn't be talking to you about this in here. It doesn't feel right.'

'Sure.' I was puzzled and a little alarmed. 'Is everything all right, dear?'

'Yes. But I can't keep this to myself any longer.' She was definitely agitated. 'Is there somewhere we can have a cup of tea or a drink or something?'

'Just let me get my handbag.' I stood up and buttoned my jacket, then picked the bag off the windowsill. This had something to do with that Lyle person, I was sure of it. 'I don't think we'd find a café open at this time. There's a public house up the road there but I don't know what it's like.'

'We'll try it anyway.' She almost ran to the door.

We walked to the pub in silence while I racked my brains as to how to deal with the situation. I was so angry with this Lyle that if she was going to tell me he had been in touch and was sorry but he really loved her, et cetera, et cetera, I had to be ready to react appropriately. Concerned but not didactic. That was the combination for which I would aim.

The lounge bar was dimly lit and very quiet. There were only five other patrons – a young couple and a group of three women at the counter in conversation with the young barman. 'You sit down.' Catherine stopped in front of the bar. 'What'll you have? I'd recommend a gin and tonic, or even a brandy.'

'Must be serious!' I tried to make light of it but she did not respond in kind. 'A gin and tonic would be nice. Thank you.'

I watched her as she ordered and waited for the drinks. Her body movements were tense and jerky. Whatever it was, I wasn't going to like it. I began to wonder if, after all, she was pregnant by that dreadful boy.

'I got ice and lemon for you.' She put the glass down in front of me. 'Didn't want to go to the bother of trying to convince the guy that I'm over twenty-one – too much trouble – so I just got myself a Britvic.'

'But you want me to have alcohol. What's going on here, Catherine?'

'Take a swallow there, Pearl, will you? Please.'

I searched her face. Even in the low light I saw that one of her eyelids was twitching. Instead of interrogating her, however, I did as she asked and took several mouthfuls of my drink, all the time watching her over the rim of my glass as, clenching and unclenching her fists, she tried to work up to telling me whatever it was she had to divulge. I put down the gin. 'Tell me, Catherine. Whatever it is, we'll deal with it.'

'All right. I'll tell you. But you're not to get a shock. Well,' she took a draught of her own drink, 'I suppose you will get a shock but it won't be a horrible one, I hope.'

'Catherine!'

'OK. Here it is.' Then she stopped. The seconds ticked interminably while she closed her eyes, opened them again, spread her arms wide, then folded them over her chest. 'Pearl, I have found Thomas Areton. I was with him most of today. He wants to see you.'

I shot to my feet, my body operating under its own volition. She had wanted me not to react and, for her sake, I sat down again, but so heavily that I knocked against the flimsy table, which wobbled. Both drinks spilled, the ice skidding on to the floor, the slice of lemon falling into my lap.

The barman had seen what had happened and was beside us very quickly. 'Are yiz all right, ladies?' He was so used to accidents that he did not even look at our faces. 'These things happen. I'll get yiz the same again. OK? On the house.' Within seconds, using two cloths, he had mopped up the table and removed the glasses, picked the lemon – 'Excuse me' – from my lap. I barely noticed as I stared at Catherine.

'Say something, Pearl. Are you all right? I thought you'd be pleased – I thought I was doing the right thing.'

'How did you – where . . .'

'Wait until your next drink comes and I'll tell you the whole story.'

'I'm not a baby. Just tell me!' I had snapped at her without realising it. 'I'm so sorry.' I put my hands over my face. 'I didn't mean to be aggressive. It's just . . .'

It was just what? There was no way I could put words on the feelings that were racing around my body. In quick succession I was thrilled, nauseous, terrified, dizzy, faint, but then, as the blood rushed back into my head and face, I felt overheated, very angry. 'He's in Ireland? You found him in Ireland?'

'Yes.' She had moved over to sit beside me.

The anger abated. It wasn't his fault. Or her fault. It was mine.

285

Thomas was in Ireland. He had not been looking for me all this time. If he had, he would have found me.

I had to leave here. I had to be by myself to take this in. But the barman was coming back towards us with two glasses, two bottles, one of Schweppes tonic, one of Britvic orange juice. One of the glasses clinked with ice. All of these things I noticed as though he was coming in slow motion. 'There yiz are!' He plonked the drinks on the table beside the ashtray.

'Thank you.' Then I looked up at him and asked him if he sold Sweet Afton. I could no longer call myself a smoker, having mostly succeeded in giving up the habit, but I relapsed now and then, occasionally while having some difficulty with my writing; also in times of stress, the urge was strong. 'Sure, missis. I'll bring them over to you. A ten, is it?'

I nodded, and he bustled off.

'Are you all right, Pearl?' Catherine was still very anxious. 'You see now why it wouldn't have been right to tell you in front of Margaret. I know she's the way she is, but they say that the hearing is the last to go.' It sounded like such an old-fashioned thing to say that I could smile. Dearest Catherine. She had been been trying only to help me.

I had remembered all my own rationalisations and was no longer angry. How could he have found me when I had spent most of my time in my room, living in a house belonging to a woman whose name was listed in the telephone directory as 'Igoe, Francis'?

Catherine was staring at me. 'Was it a good shock or a bad shock? He's ringing me tomorrow. That's what he'll want to know. Oh, Pearl,' she cried, 'he's lovely! You'll love him. You already do, don't you? And I know in my heart and soul that he loves you.'

The barman came back with the cigarettes and a book of matches with the name of a drinks company on it. He had already removed the cellophane from the packet. This barman would go far. 'Thank you.' I paid him and told him to keep the change. Then, fingers rather shaky as I lit the cigarette, 'You're so young, Catherine, there's been so much time . . . I've changed so much – I'm not the young girl he knew.' I took a very long drag of the tobacco.

'And he's not the young boy either. But, you know, one of the things I read somewhere is that although the body gets older, the inside of every person stays the same. You'll see him?'

'I'm afraid he'll be disappointed.'

She laughed, and her face relaxed. 'He certainly won't be disappointed, Pearl. That's the very last thing he'll be. You're quite a pair, you know. He's afraid too. He thinks you'll be disappointed in him.'

'How could I be? What's he like now? What is he doing? Where did you find him?' I had a million questions.

'I'm going to have to tell you this in bits and pieces.' Then, warily, as though she had rehearsed it: 'He hasn't had an easy life down through the years. The way he lives is a little – well—' She faltered.

'Yes?' I was now imagining all kinds of horrible things. Not an easy life . . . While trying to picture Thomas as my age, our age, my brain fizzled with further questions: had he been conscripted in that awful war? Had he been injured? Gassed? Maybe a prisoner of war in some place like Japan? 'What is he doing in Ireland?' I asked her.

'It's hard to tell you, Pearl.'

'Tell me. Please.'

'I will. First, though, when he rings me tomorrow, can I tell him you'll see him? Make the arrangements? I thought I should give you both maybe a week or ten days to get used to the idea. He'll want that time too. Maybe you should start with a telephone call, but to tell you the truth, I doubt he's any good on the telephone. I don't think he has used it much.'

'You're talking in riddles.'

'All right. Don't expect too much, Pearl.' Then, in a quick burst: 'He's been living rough for years.'

'Living rough?'

'"No fixed abode" is the official term, I believe.'

'But why? Dear God, why?' I could not comprehend this. 'Was it something to do with that dreadful father of his? Was he disinherited or something?'

'No. He chose to live this way. He's a viscount. Did you know that? And if you think you're shocked, you could barely imagine how he reacted, me turning up out of the blue with news of you.'

'What did he say? Tell me exactly, Catherine.' I took another pull from the cigarette. 'How did he react?'

'He cried as though his heart would break.'

And now the tears came from me, forty-seven years' worth, of relief, of pain, of joy – and I cared not at all that I was making a show of myself. That not only the barman but the three women at the counter had turned to look at me. That while I wasn't making any noise, I was being less than a credit to my family. 'There, there, Pearl,' Catherine was patting my shoulder. She was flummoxed but doing her valiant best.

Then, vaguely, through the deluge, I saw the barman approach her. 'Will I get yiz another drink, love?' I heard Catherine agree, heard her say apologetically, 'I'm sorry about this.'

Heard the barman's response: 'Don't worry about it, love. We're used to it. Mount Jerome on one side, hospice on the other, it's only to be expected. It's all going through life, isn't it?'

39

CATHERINE

O n the morning after I told Pearl I had found Thomas Areton, two things happened within ten minutes.

The first was that he rang, as arranged, to find out if I had told Pearl and, more significantly, how she had reacted. When I told him, truthfully, that she had reacted exactly as he had, there was a long, long pause. So long that I was reduced to going: 'Hello? Thomas? Are you there, Thomas?' but all I could hear was the crackle of the long-distance line and the sound of traffic going by. Then the pips went and he was cut off. Thank God he rang back immediately because I think I would have died of frustration if he hadn't. We made plans to meet ten days later. He said he needed that time to get ready and, as he put it, 'to get my head in order'.

The second thing that happened was that, just a few minutes after I had hung up, the letterbox rattled and the usual bills, still in Poppa's name, along with some handwritten letters addressed to Mandy, plopped on to the mat in the hall. Although the flow had eased, more than a month after his death, she was still getting what were obviously letters of sympathy, and there was a large, untidy stack of post, including bills and other unopened correspondence, to which the carers and I had added more every day, so that it now completely covered the hall table; today's batch might threaten to destabilise the pile, so it was about time I did something about it.

Even before her stroke, Mandy had been so unwell, and so sorrowful, that every time I had mentioned this heap of post she had said, in her whispery voice, that she'd get around to it 'soon'.

Other than my plan to visit the hospice later, I had nothing else on so today I should tackle it. The first thing to do was to sort the bills, some overdue, no doubt, by now, from the general pile.

I was reluctant to open the personal letters, and not just because my name wasn't on the envelopes. I was not sure I was ready yet to cope with such an avalanche of sympathy. In a way, the whole Thomas Areton thing had served as a terrific distraction from my own feelings after the loss of Poppa, the awfulness of what had happened with Lyle and the worry about Mandy but it was now time to take care of my new responsibilities.

Standing there in the hallway, it dawned on me that this would require a complete re-think about the way I not only saw my life, but conducted it. I riffled through the letters I held: one was a letter from Poppa's solicitors, also addressed to Mandy. I probably shouldn't open that, but I should ring them and ask if I should; I should ring the bank too, and what should I do about the ESB and the gas? These were things to which I had never before given a moment's thought and abruptly, it came crashing in on me that the carefree life I had lived up to the time I got that phone call about Poppa was now over.

'Right,' I said aloud, 'time to start sorting.'

The pile was too big to carry so I fetched Mandy's (my?) string bag from its hook behind the kitchen door and proceeded to sweep all the letters into it. When I had almost all of them safely enclosed and was near the bottom of the pile, a particularly thick envelope with a blue airmail sticker caught my eye. The stamp was American and there was a return address: *Magnolia Avenue, Chicago, Illinois.* The letter, to me, was from Dory. How long had it been there without my seeing it? I studied the postmark: 21 August. Four days after Poppa's death. It must have been put there by the carers.

Leaving the string bag on the hall floor, I carried the letter into the kitchen and had torn it open even before I sat at the table. The envelope contained two smaller envelopes. One, unsealed, contained a very fancy Mass card, signed by Dory and Peggy. They had put a little note inside: 'We're really sorry for your loss, Catherine. We didn't know your grandfather's name so we told the priest that he should just say the Mass for "Catherine's poppa". We hope that's OK.'

I thought this was really lovely of them: Peggy was Episcopalian and Dory was Jewish. Plus, I had not given them my address, as far as I could remember, so they must have gone to the trouble of finding it through the college administration office. I was very moved.

The other envelope was sealed. I ripped it open. In it was a letter from Dory, containing a postcard and a small, tightly folded newspaper cutting. I read the postcard first:

Hi, Catherine. Remember me? The Yank at your garden party? I'll be in Chicago just for four days, from 8/30 to 9/2. I'll give you a call at the number you gave me, if that's OK. In the meantime, maybe you'll get a couple of days' vacation and can come to the City of the Angels (Los Angeles!). Love to host you!

Here's my phone number: if I'm not there when you call, just leave a message. One of the guys will tell me.

In hope, Sam (Travers)

Dory's letter began:

Dearest Catherine,

Again I am so sorry for what you had to go through and of course for your loss. Peggy is too.

I am enclosing a postcard that came for you and an article from the local newspaper that you might find interesting. Peggy and I went to the college authorities and lodged a formal complaint about what happened to you. (We also explained how and why you had to leave your job in such a hurry and there was no problem with that.)

Unfortunately, we were told that there was little that could be done formally about Lyle McKenzie and his buddies since you had made no complaint. I do know that Lyle was called in to explain himself, but denied everything. And when the Dean went to the frat house to see if he could find the evidence, there was nothing on the wall except ordinary sports notices.

I'm very sorry.

The cousin of a friend of mine is paying off his student loans by doing some local journalism and I told him what had happened to you. He was shocked, of course, but, because of lack of evidence, said he couldn't write anything specific. I'm sending you what he did write.

In the meantime, Peggy, who as you know is still at that college, is doing her best to spread the news. Lyle McKenzie won't be so hot for a long time to come if she has anything to do with it.

I hope that jerk hasn't ruined your idea of America, Catherine. We're not all like him and there really are some nice boys here, you know!

We miss you and hope we will see you soon again. Do you think you might come back sometime? (Probably not, I guess.) But we do want you to know that, as long as we live here on Magnolia, there will always be a welcome for you and your lovely Irish brogue.

It's a quarter of three and I must finish to catch the post. But I wanted you to know as soon as possible that Lyle didn't get totally away with what he did. The administration won't be pleased with publicity like that even if it is only in a local rag and pretty vague. But I know the Dean believed us. I'd say he will be keeping an eye on that whole disgusting bunch. Their days might even be numbered in that fraternity house, and you never know, they could be dumped off campus altogether if they put even a foot wrong again.

I hope this news gives you a little bit of comfort and relief, which is why I'm telling you.

We also hope you're doing good, Catherine, and recovering as well as you can from all this.

Love and hugs from
Dory (and P) XXX

Slowly I unfolded the newspaper cutting. It was short, as Dory had said, just three paragraphs, beside a picture of the college.

Allegations of Perversion at Camellia
BY *RPH* REPORTER

Camellia College was rocked today by allegations made by two women that a member of one of the fraternities on campus, in cahoots with other members of the same fraternity, had committed a sexual perversion on another woman, not a student.

Although the allegations remain to be proven, the two women

who made the complaint to the Dean of the college on behalf of the victim, who is nineteen and who had been their roommate, last night told the *Rogers Park Herald* that she was extremely traumatised by the event. 'She was inconsolable,' said one. 'Yes,' the other agreed. 'I've never seen anyone so upset. That beast and his buddies who egged him on should be in prison. We're very worried that unless something is done about the whole bunch of them, they could do something like this again.'

It is understood that the victim has now left the US.

Carefully, leaving the postcard and Mass card on the table, I put the letter and the cutting back in their envelope. I tested my reaction, like lifting the corner of a scab to see if the wound still hurt. It did.

On the other hand, it was consoling to know that those two lovely girls had gone to all this trouble on my behalf. Dory was right. There were good people in the US.

I picked up the postcard – Sam Travers might well be one of the good guys – but put it down again. Maybe some day, but right now there was no way on earth I could trust any boy.

I went back out to the hall to collect the rest of the post and forced myself to concentrate on the question of how, in my new circumstances, I was going to organise my life.

And then a thought struck me: wouldn't it be nice to invite those two roommates of mine to visit me? I had to face facts. It didn't look as though Mandy was coming home ever again. It would be nice to put this house in order and have guests.

And, I thought ruefully, I would have friends of my own age to introduce to Pearl and Opal.

40

CATHERINE

I'm being absolutely truthful when I tell you I didn't recognise Thomas Areton at the station. When the doors of the carriages opened, I moved slowly down the platform, scanning the hundreds of businessmen, tourists and families tumbling past me in their droves but didn't spot him. It was actually he who found me, following me against the flow of humanity and catching me by the arm. 'Good morning, Miss Fay.'

I was stunned. It was amazing what ten days can do for a person, on the outside at least. Before me stood a tall, distinguished, silver-haired apparition in a dark, perfectly fitting suit, with a starched shirt, and a silvery tie knotted at his throat. He might have walked straight out of a boardroom or a medical consultant's rooms. The transformation was astonishing. The only giveaway was the 'farmer's tan': the face and hands were ruddy but there was a pale tidemark around the hairline and a glimpse of white at the neck.

'I can't believe it,' I stuttered. 'You look absolutely fantastic!' He seemed to be standing straighter, giving himself even more height. By any standards he cut quite a dash.

'Thank you, Miss Fay.'

'Oh for God's sake, "Catherine", please!' We were both shouting. The noise was phenomenal: the station had an iron roof with hard surfaces all round so, what with the sound of squealing brakes, slamming doors and the roaring of diesel engines, it was hard to converse in normal tones.

We joined the throngs queuing for the ticket barrier. 'How are you feeling about this now?' I stood on tiptoe to say it into his ear so I didn't have to yell.

'Nervous.' He leaned down. 'Terrified, but excited too. Everyone was very nice,' he said, or semi-yelled. 'The man at the bank, the man in the shop who helped me buy the right clothes. Even the girl in the jewellery shop who picked out these cufflinks —' he showed me — 'the barber, everyone. I couldn't believe how nice they were to me.'

'People are helpful when you ask them,' I yelled. 'That's been my experience anyway.'

We got through the barrier and out into the sunshine of Kingsbridge. 'Did you tell anyone what was happening?'

'No. Who would I tell?'

'Isabella, for instance — did you not ring her?'

'No. Not yet. But I will. First things first. Look, Miss Fay — sorry, Catherine — Pearl might hate me . . . I know you told me on the phone how she reacted,' we were now walking towards the Quays where I had parked my car, 'but I was so jittery when I rang you it went over the top of my head. Tell me again. What exactly did she say?'

By the time I was easing into a space in the car park opposite the sisters' house in Sandymount, he was in possession of the (less concise) version of how Pearl had reacted to the news of his discovery. I found it was quite sweet, actually, how each had feared that the other's reaction would be negative. Now, as I pulled up the handbrake, I knew the real test was about to be applied. 'Ready?'

Thomas nodded, but the bouquet in his hand rattled. At his request, we had stopped at a florist's, and although I had urged caution and suggested an all-white bouquet of asters, freesia and baby's breath, he had insisted on buying a dozen long-stemmed red roses. The florist's assistant was young and chatty. 'Anniversary, is it?' she'd chirped, while tying up the flowers. She pulled cellophane off the roll on her desk. 'Great to see ya still have the bit of romance in ya — can't beat the red roses! Isn't that right?'

Both Thomas and I had continued to gaze rigidly at the operation in progress.

'Are we still too early?' he asked now.

I looked at my watch. 'No. By about a minute. That's all.'

'And she knows everything?'

'Everything you told me, yes.'

'Tell me again how she took it.'

'With huge sympathy and indignation on your behalf.'

'Let's go, then.' Now that the moment was upon him, he seemed childlike and eager.

When the door opened, Opal, in a dress of apple-green silk jersey, looked him up and down. 'Goodness. You're very tall. I'd recognise you, though. I'm Opal, by the way – Pearl's inside. And you've brought roses, how nice. Hello, dear!' She gave me a kiss on the cheek. 'Come on in.'

We followed her and she waved us towards the drawing room. 'Make yourselves comfortable. I'll fetch Pearl. She should be here but she's probably in her room, having kittens. I don't want to guess at how many times she's changed her clothes since breakfast.' She walked off.

As Thomas and I sat side by side on one of the couches, he with his bouquet clutched tightly upright in front of his chest, neither of us saying a word, I developed the strange conviction that I'd never been in this room before – and hadn't, if you count the air in a room as contributing to its physical atmosphere. To say that we were both tense and apprehensive – in different ways – was an understatement. For some reason, I felt that I, too, had a lot riding on this meeting.

After a few minutes, we heard footsteps approaching. Women's footsteps. Two sets. Beside me, Thomas visibly flinched. 'Easy.' I reached out and touched his clenched fist. 'It's going to be all right. Really.'

Then he did a very surprising thing. Quickly he opened his hand and clutched mine very tightly. 'Whatever happens,' he said, 'whatever happens, thank you.'

I was caught off guard, but delighted, and we both stood up as, first, Opal, then Pearl entered the room.

She was wearing that dove-grey dress with silver accessories and shoes. As usual she wore no makeup but, unusually, had put on the rimless glasses she usually used only when working. (Camouflage?) Behind them, her eyes were so large they seemed luminous in the light from the windows. She was very beautiful, and if I could admire her, being as familiar with her as I was, I could only imagine what Thomas Areton, who was seeing her for the first time in forty-seven years, thought.

I looked at him. He was mesmerised. 'Hello, Pearl,' he whispered.

There was an awkward pause when none of us knew what to

do next. Opal stepped in: 'This is ridiculous. We're all behaving like children making strange at a birthday party. Look, Catherine,' she turned to me, 'if it's all right with you, I'll bring you down to the kitchen and you can help me sort out a cup of tea for us all. Or would you like a drink?' She included Pearl and Thomas in the invitation but they were still struck dumb.

'Thank you, Opal,' I said. 'Tea would be fine – and although I can't talk for Thomas, I believe he would prefer tea too.'

'Have fun, kids!' Her tone heavily ironic, Pearl's sister turned and left the room. Meekly, I followed. As I went through the door, I risked a quick glance over my shoulder. Pearl had moved a little towards Thomas with her hand outstretched to shake his. He, however, still holding his bouquet as though his life depended on it, seemed to have put down roots into the cream-coloured rug with the wide green stripe.

Down in the kitchen, Opal switched on the kettle on one of the countertops. I was wired up and couldn't relax, walking around and around the splendid kitchen. 'I love this room, Opal. Fair play to you, but it's so big it must be hard to keep clean.' My thoughts were upstairs and it was just something to say: I knew she had squads of help. Window-cleaner and gardener every week, and two women who came in on Mondays and Fridays. Mondays they cleaned, Fridays they cooked for the freezer and changed the beds. She sent out the laundry.

'Sit down and stop pacing, for God's sake,' she said cheerfully. 'You know damned well that all those machines in the scullery are just for show.' She laughed. 'Don't get me wrong, Catherine, I'm well able to work. I worked like a slave when I was young, but I swore I wouldn't wear myself out and die young like our poor mama. I believe it was hardship that killed her, make no mistake about it. And don't get me started on Papa. Those Arctons —' She stopped. 'I swore I wouldn't let them get under my skin. But I suppose that fella up there . . . he was only fifteen when it all happened so I can hardly blame him. I was there that night, you know, in the stable yard with Pearl when that brute made him shoot his horse.'

'Did you see it happen?'

'As good as. Pearl dragged me away before he pulled the trigger. I'm not like Pearl, thank God. I don't obsess about these things.

297

What's gone is gone. Here – make yourself useful and slice this.' She handed me an exquisitely decorated chocolate cake and a knife. You can put it on this.' She plonked a porcelain plate with a gold rim on one of the countertops. 'I'll make the tea.

'Doesn't say much, does he, your man up there? Strong silent type, is he? So tell me,' she poured boiling water into the teapot, 'what does he do with himself? City type, is he?'

Pearl obviously hadn't shared the information about Thomas Areton's lifestyle. I wasn't going to lie, but I wasn't ready to tell the truth. It was too early to destroy what might be happening up in that drawing room. So I answered her other questions. 'He seems that way, silent, I mean, but he's incredibly intelligent, I think. Great reader too – he knew of Pearl's books.'

'Actually read them?' Her eyebrows arched.

'No, but he was familiar with the titles. He's seen the books and knew they were short stories.'

'Well, that's a plus, I suppose.'

The kettle boiled and switched itself off. As I watched her wet the tea I decided to beard the monster. 'You know, Opal, he's very ashamed of what his father did to our family – well, your family, really.'

'He's right to be!' she snapped. But then, 'Look, as I've said, I know it wasn't his fault. I saw the way that monster treated him that night. Are you ready with the cake? Good. Now, shall we go up and see that they're not still standing there gawping at each other like china dolls? At the same time,' she looked into the middle distance, smiling affectionately, 'it's kind of endearing, though, really, isn't it? Mind you, he'd better not hurt her or he'll have me to deal with! Come on, let's go up there and burst in on them. Catch them!' She smiled mischievously, and as I followed her up with the teapot in my hand, I decided for the umpteenth time that I liked Opal very much.

They were no longer standing. He was sitting on the couch with the green cushions, she on one of the armchairs at right angles to him. I couldn't say their heads were close together, but their eyes were, if that makes sense. 'Knock knock!' Opal cried, as she came in with the tea tray. 'So, how've we been getting on up here?'

They looked up, both wearing the kind of expression I've always attributed to Bambi. 'Great.' Pearl got to her feet. 'May I help?'

Thomas sprang to his feet too, blushing, as though caught in some transgression. In his rush, he almost trampled his roses. 'Please, let me.' He took the tray from Opal. 'Where shall I put it?'

It still felt weird to see him turned out as he was and behaving like this, and I experienced a quick set of flashbacks to my wild-man image of him on the ditch at the Devil's Bit, in that dock in the Cullarkin courthouse, dwarfing the Morris Minor . . .

Opal pulled out a nest of four tables, distributed them and we all settled down with our tea and a slice of cake. 'What do you do for a living, Thomas?'

'Opal!' Pearl remonstrated.

'Well, it's important to know these things. It's not a secret, is it?'

'I'm thinking of retiring and perhaps doing a bit of study. I have independent means.'

A piece of cake went the wrong way down my throat and I had to cough. I couldn't believe what I was hearing. 'Are you all right, Catherine?' He smiled at me. He was playing every card he had. This was a peacock displaying for his intended mate. I had told Pearl about his lifestyle so I knew she had to have seen through the artifice.

He turned deliberately to her now. 'I see you have a lot of books. Are they all yours, Pearl? Congratulations on your own, by the way.'

'You know I write?' she asked.

'I'd love to read some of your work. I've come across them, of course, but had I known—' He stopped. Then: 'Would you have a spare copy of one by any chance? There's a lot to catch up on.'

While Pearl was gone from the room to fetch a book for him, the rest of us drank our tea. 'May I have the milk, please?'

Ate our cake. 'Could I have another slice of that delicious cake?'

Made conversation in the most desultory fashion: 'It's a real pet day out there, isn't it?' Even Opal had quietened.

When Pearl came back with the book, she walked straight to him, handed it over and sat beside him on his couch. 'You'll probably think it's no good, Thomas,' she said, 'but there's a story in that one that's been taken for a film. I've just signed a contract for it, as a matter of fact.'

This was something I hadn't told him and he responded sincerely. 'It's going to be made into a film? That's marvellous. I can't wait to read it – which one is it?'

'"The Dandelion Clock". Maybe you won't like it.'

He made a sound halfway between derision and mirth. 'May I take it with me?'

'Of course.'

'What's it about?'

'It's hard to say. It's a bit complicated. It's a love story, I think, but it could be taken as allegorical too. It starts in a railway station, but I've set it mostly in the countryside around Kilnashone. You'd recognise the places, I think, Thomas.' As she spoke, Pearl was becoming more animated. 'That glade in Drynan Wood—' She stopped.

They blushed like adolescents.

'What's so special about Drynan Wood?' Opal, of course, was mystified.

'You remember that glade, Opal?' Pearl tried to rescue the situation. 'Of course you do. Remember where Willie was pegging the stones that day? And the day Thomas actually came in on us when he had lost his horse?' If anything, her blush intensified, which didn't seem physically possible. She stole a glance at the even redder Thomas Areton and, finally, Opal twigged. 'Oh,' she said, trying not to smile as she glanced at me and gave a conspiratorial wink.

Faster and faster came Pearl's words about her book, to Thomas sitting beside her, and the faster they came, the more his face relaxed.

And so it continued. Opal and I might as well not have been in the room.

41

PEARL

I could scarcely believe that Thomas had been homeless for all those years.

Although he did not say this, from the way he described it his difficult way of life seemed to have been motivated by having to perform a sort of dual penance, for shooting an innocent horse and for the wrongs done to our family by his.

But for so many years? He tried hard to explain but it made little sense. On the other hand, how much of human behaviour actually makes sense? Does it make sense that I fell in love at fifteen, stayed in love for the next forty-seven years and would have gone to my grave without ever knowing whether or not that obsession was capable of realisation if it hadn't been for Catherine?

We were sitting together on one of Opal's couches with the used tea-things in front of us. Tactfully, Opal and Catherine had again left the room and were somewhere else in the house, most likely talking about us in the kitchen. They could talk about us until night fell, as far as I was concerned, because all that mattered to me now was the present.

Naturally I was very upset by what he had told Catherine about my papa's death, and he started to talk about it again now. 'I have something I want to get off my chest, Pearl. It's about your father's death.'

'Ssh!' I put my finger to his lips. How could I do anything but comfort him? 'I know what happened. Catherine told me. Nothing anyone can do will rub it out. But Papa is not suffering. He's at peace and it was a long time ago.'

Having had more than a week to get used to the idea that I would see him again, I was nevertheless still in a state of disbelief that he was real. He confessed to the same state and, for the first hour, we clutched each other intermittently as if for reassurance that we were substantial human beings and not wraiths. Taking all my courage in my hands, I finally told him that, despite Opal's best efforts, I could never bring myself to entertain any of the suitors she produced. For me, I said, not daring to look at him, there had always been only one man.

During the silence that followed this, I studied the weave of the fabric on the sofa. Every sound outside that room was magnified. I heard the clatter of the letterbox in the hall as something was pushed through, followed by the whistling of the deliverer descending the front steps. From across the road on the strand, I heard the child call out to his or her father to wait. I heard a car horn.

'Please, Pearl,' he whispered, finally, when I was approaching the end of my endurance. 'Please may I kiss you?' Without waiting for me to answer, he carefully took off my glasses and put them between us, then took my face in his hands and kissed me very gently on the mouth. His lips were trembling.

I was back in that glade, semi-naked as he undid the tiny buttons of my dress, and the feel of his fingers on my back created spiders in my blood, but those same fingers were now on my face, caressing it as his mouth kissed mine.

We came apart and held hands like the mature adults we were. We held so tightly it hurt.

I think we were both afraid to say anything.

'Where do we go from here?' he said eventually.

'I don't know,' I said. 'I'm just so happy to be here, to see you here, that I don't want to "go" anywhere. I don't want to think beyond this moment.'

I thought he might kiss me again but he did not. Instead, he got off the couch and crouched in front of me. 'I would give my life for you, Pearl,' he said. 'I want nothing more than to care for you and love you for the rest of my life, to bring you flowers, to see your hair spread out on my chest. But, you know, I'm now like a wild animal. I'm not socialised. I don't think I can live any other way than the way I have because it's been too long. I wish I could say otherwise, but it would be dishonest. And I cannot be dishonest with you.' He was getting distressed.

'Don't.' I took his face as he had taken mine and looked into his eyes, those eyes with the single golden fleck. I loved even the line of white under his hairline. Catherine had said that when she had met him first his hair was long and tumbled. I could picture it flying in the wind, as, like Yeats's Wandering Aengus, he had travelled the roads of Ireland. 'My wanderer,' I whispered, as I kissed his hair, grey now like my own, but very precious, every strand of it.

That was our language during that first rapturous hour. Excessive, emotional, but entirely our own. No one else in the world had ever spoken those words of love. No two people had kissed as closely.

Such intensity could not last, of course, and eventually we came down to earth and again sat soberly side by side on Opal's couch as we considered what on earth we were now to do. 'I don't want to let you go,' I said. 'Not ever again.'

'I don't want to let you go either.' He hesitated and then seemed to make up his mind. 'There's something else, something I have not told anyone, even Isabella. But seeing you in your honesty I have to tell you.' His expression was very serious. It worried me. Was he ill? Like my characters in 'The Dandelion Clock', had we found each other when it was too late?

It was nothing like that.

'Father died two years before my mother,' he began, holding my hand in one of his, while plucking at a loose thread on the couch with the other. He was looking at the thread. 'Before she died, she left a sealed letter with the family solicitor to be given to me unopened. In fairness to Isabella, she sent it with its seal intact. I kept it for two years without opening it because I thought that, inevitably, it had to do with my taking on the family responsibilities and so on, and I didn't want anything to do with that, or with being a viscount, like that man. Then one day I just opened it.'

'What was in it?'

'Something I wish I had known fifty years ago. I am not that man's son. That man, Areton, was Isabella's father but not mine.'

It took a moment for this to register. All that venom — 'Who was your father?' I did not recognise my own voice.

'He's dead. He died long ago. He was a groom in the family stables in Scotland. My mother had an affair with him two years after she married Areton and after she found that he was not what she wanted. Although she tried to pretend I was his, by the time

303

I was two years old I was so unlike any of that man's relatives that he hounded her into telling the truth. I think Isabella was the product of their "reconciliation". I have not told her. I don't want to make her unhappy. Her son will inherit the title in any case, if that's what he wants, as I have no child of my own. There's no point in my stirring things up at this stage.'

'How did you cope when you found out?'

'Remember where and how I lived. Coping is what society demands. I had to keep up appearances for nobody. I was furious, but again, unlike that man, I had no one on whom to vent my anger. And the more I thought about it, the more I was relieved that I did not have a drop of that man's blood in my veins. My real father, apparently, was a good man. Great with the horses. Ironic, when you think of it, eh?'

'Thomas . . .' But he either did not hear or ignored my intervention.

'For that man's type, and in his circle, outward appearance was all and a male heir was the sign of virility. So he acknowledged me as his son and bullied my mother into submission and secrecy. I think if Isabella had been a boy he might have thrown me and my mother out to fend for ourselves. I wish he had. We might have been better off. But once again, it was long, long ago. As I said, as soon as the initial effect wore off, the overriding feeling was one of sadness that I hadn't known and relief that I now did.'

'If you'd known earlier – if he had thrown you and your mother out – we might never have met.' It was trite but it worked.

'That's true.' He searched my face. 'You're not upset?'

'Why would I be upset?' I was astonished. I could see no earthly reason to be put out, except, once again, by his treatment at the hands of that awful person. 'Was this your fault? You say you don't want to take responsibility for anything. It seems to me, Thomas, that you've taken responsibility all your life for everything that other people have visited on you.'

'Maybe I have.' He was still watching me. I could not read his expression and the tension between us began again to build. 'We're behaving like adolescents,' I said faintly. 'Oh, look! I'd better put these in water.' I stood up to get his flowers, still lying on the coffee-table, but he pulled me back and I overbalanced, somehow ending up on his lap.

'Pearl,' he whispered into my neck.

I turned to him, feelings I had until this day I had thought dormant for five decades rising again to torment me. 'We can't do this.' I pulled away from him.

'Do you know what red roses mean?' he said from behind me.

'Of course I do.' With the flowers crackling in their wrapper, I stood as though frozen with my back to him. The palms of my hands were tingling.

'Turn around to me, please, Pearl.'

Slowly, as though I had no power over my own movements, I turned back to face him. He dropped to his knees directly on to the rug and, wrapping his arms around my waist, buried his head against me. 'You don't know how many times I've imagined this and longed to have you in my arms,' he whispered.

'Get up, please.' I stroked his hair. 'Someone could come in . . .' But when he obeyed, I had to drop the flowers because he embraced me fully, his grip on me so powerful that I had no choice but to surrender to the kind of kiss that seemed to reach to the soles of my feet.

'Oh dear – sorry!'

Like guilty schoolchildren we jumped away from each other to find Opal, grinning, in the doorway. 'I guess we've been getting on all right here, then? Sorry to interrupt – just coming to fetch the dirty dishes, don't mind me!'

Thomas and I could not look at each other as, still smirking, she gathered everything on to a tray. 'I'll take these too, shall I?' She picked up the roses and plonked them on top, then hurried towards the door, carolling, 'Carry on!' as she left and then, at the top of her voice while she was clattering down to the kitchen, 'Catherine! Catherine! You'll never guess—' The kitchen door slammed and we heard no more.

Thomas and I looked at one another. His smile was rueful now. 'I hope I haven't ruined your reputation!'

'I don't have one to ruin.' I smiled back at him. 'Look, we have to talk about this.' I pulled him down to sit beside me on the couch.

'Yes we do. I love you, Pearl,' he said, his expression grave.

'I know you do. And before you say it again, I do accept that we're not going to live in a little cottage on a hill with roses around the door, you smoking your pipe while I embroider samplers.'

'Do you?'

'Yes.'

'So what do we do?'

Something happened in my chest. A ballooning of something I could not identify until, with a sense of surprise, I realised that what I was feeling was happiness. I've tried to describe this sensation in my stories, doing my best to imagine and report it, but until now, I had not experienced it. I had used the words 'airiness', 'expansion', 'infusion of light', but they had come from my head. I had worked on them, trying to communicate a feeling I had only imagined. This was different. This was real and came from somewhere beneath my breastbone, spreading like a warm cloud into my face and limbs until I felt almost weightless.

Within this feeling there was no doubt and no inhibition, no worry about how another would react. 'Oh, Thomas!' I cried. 'What we do is, we do our best. We accept our love. We trust it. We live in it wherever we are, even when we're not with each other. I've lived a solitary life in many ways, my dearest darling Thomas. You have too. Until one of us dies, neither of us will ever be solitary again. It's enough that you're here now. You'll be here again. I know it's enough for you that I'll be with you wherever you are, sometimes just in your head, sometimes in person. Minute after minute, hour after hour, we'll be together.'

He took me again in his arms, gently this time, and we hugged. There was a wonderful smell of new cotton and starch from his shirt. The mind is its own master and, unaccountably, I was at one and the same time in my lover's arms and home from my job in Mealy's café one weekend when, having secured a commission for a wedding trousseau, my mama was adding lace to three bodices for the bride and her two attendants. While Opal and Ruby slept upstairs, I was helping her lay it. I felt so grown-up, one of two women with heads together in the white glow cast by the hissing Tilley, I tacking the pieces in place, her spectacles falling down her nose as she bent to the minute, intricate hand-stitching. I had been happy that night, too, despite the mud floor and the smell of poverty. 'Are you happy, Thomas?' I whispered.

'I don't know,' he whispered back. 'I don't know how to be happy, I think.'

'What do you feel?' I disengaged and looked at him, touching

306

his face with one hand, fingers memorising the roughness of the skin. He took it and kissed it, then enfolded it in both his own. 'Calm,' he said. 'Quiet. Content. Excited. Aroused. But I'm sad that I'm going to be leaving you again.'

'You'll be back.'

'Yes.'

'And I'll come to you. We'll have tea together in all the midland towns of Ireland.' .

'Will you write to me?'

'Often. And I'll teach you to be happy. And then we'll see what will happen next. Nothing to be ruled in or out.'

'Nothing at all.' We might have kissed again – the kiss hung in the air between us, but there was a rat-tat-tat on the door. 'Is it OK to come in for a moment?' Opal said from outside.

This time we did not jump apart but sat side by side, holding hands as first a beaming Opal, followed by a similarly grinning Catherine, came in to tell us that they were off to the Hospice and that we were to take our time. 'We probably won't be back for hours and hours,' Opal said.

'Hours!' agreed Catherine who, on noticing the hand-holding, now added triumph to the sweep of her grin. 'In fact,' looking at Opal, 'we were just discussing downstairs that we might go to the pictures after visiting Margaret. There's a thing on called *Butch Cassidy and the Sundance Kid*.'

'No,' Opal argued. 'I want to see *Midnight Cowboy* – I love Dustin Hoffman. He's small, but kinda cute – oh lookit, we can decide on the way into town –' she turned and dispensed an airy wave over her shoulder: ''bye now! Be good! And if you can't be good, be careful!' They both split their sides laughing, and, still arguing, left, their voices muting when the front door slammed behind them and they went down the steps and into the street.

In the silence that ensued, the pulse in the palm of the hand holding Thomas's hand felt as strong and loud as the thump-thump of a bass drum. 'What did she mean, "if you can't be good be careful"?' His voice sounded thick.

'I don't know.'

'I don't know either.'

We both knew that we both knew.

We were sitting on a sofa within the curve of one of Opal's bay windows. The sun, which had been warm on the side of my neck, had obviously gone behind a cloud because I felt its absence. 'I went back, you know,' he said. 'Often.'

I stared at the opposite side of the room, at Opal's tasteful wallpaper, pale gold with a barely perceptible self-pattern of tiny fleur-de-lys, at the framed sepia photograph hanging there: Mama and Papa on their wedding day, he in that chauffeur's uniform I remembered so well, she, hatted, wearing a toe-length dark dress with a pale trim under a high bosom. I missed them terribly. Absurdly after all these years. 'Where did you go?'

'To Drynan Wood,' Thomas said. 'I went often to Drynan Wood.'

The room had now darkened and on the window glass behind me I heard the first splatter of raindrops. 'Why did you go there?' I was still studying the photograph.

'I think that in some stupid way I thought I might find you again.' Thomas sounded as hoarse as I.

Within the room it could have been dusk now as the rain quickened. It was going to be quite a downpour. 'I went back too,' I said, 'but only once – it bore little resemblance—'

'I know.' He cut me off.

We both turned our heads to watch the streams on the window panes.

Now I could hear the first, distant roll of thunder, and although still looking out through the rain, so heavy that everything outside, cars, passers-by, the wall along the seafront, had blurred and coagulated, I felt his gaze.

'Pearl?'

'Yes, Thomas?' I raised my voice a little so he would hear me.

He pulled me round, raised me upright and as he put his arms around me and lowered his head to mine, like the hoar frost on the meadow behind Kilnashone Castle's gate lodge on that spring morning long ago, Opal's stylish drawing room dissolved, sweeping away with it the seafront across the road, Sandymount and the whole of Dublin, so that nothing physical existed except the infinitesimal spaces between Thomas's body and mine. The missing half of my heart, lost in Drynan Wood, had been restored.